Manda Scott is a veterinary surgeon, writer and climber, not necessarily in that order. Born and educated in Scotland, she trained at the Glasgow Vet School and now lives and works in Suffolk, sharing her life with a lurcher and other assorted wildlife. Her first novel, *Hen's Teeth*, hailed by Fay Weldon as 'a new voice for a new world', won widespread critical acclaim and was shortlisted for the 1997 Orange Prize.

June 16/00

Stronger
Than Death

Manda Scott

HEADLINE

'Examination at the Womb-Door' by Ted Hughes from *Crow*,
published by Faber & Faber Ltd, 1970, reproduced by permission.

First published in Great Britain 1999 by
HEADLINE BOOK PUBLISHING

First published in paperback in 2000 by
HEADLINE BOOK PUBLISHING

10 9 8 7 6 5 4 3 2 1

ISBN 0 7472 5881 3

Typeset by Letterpart Limited, Reigate, Surrey
Printed and bound in Great Britain by Clays Ltd, St Ives plc

HEADLINE BOOK PUBLISHING
A division of the Hodder Headline Group
338 Euston Road
London NW1 3BH
www.headline.co.uk
www.hodderheadline.com

For my father, with love

Acknowledgements

Thanks are due on this occasion to Chloë and Mike, both of whom read the early drafts and made invaluable comments; to Naziema, Debs, Tony and Christine for keeping me grounded; to Andy for teaching me everything I know about climbing; to George for finding details on motorbikes; and to Hester who, once again, made space in her life for a frenetic writer. Especial thanks are due to my father, the ultimate, ever-willing researcher, for the hours spent on the phone, in the library, talking to colleagues and particularly for one long summer's afternoon drive out to the Knapdale peninsula that started it all off.

The author wishes to thank the Arts Council of England for their generous financial assistance in the writing of this book.

Who owns the whole rainy, stony earth? *Death.*
Who owns all of space? *Death.*

Who is stronger than hope? *Death.*
Who is stronger than the will? *Death.*
Stronger than love? *Death.*
Stronger than life? *Death.*

But who is stronger than death?

Me, evidently.

'Examination at the Womb-Door' by Ted Hughes

Chapter One

Eric was on the ledge at the top of the fourth pitch, three-quarters of the way up the cliff. It was a good place to be: high and airy with a clear view of the sea and the gulls and the islands, an ideal spot to sit and watch the sun slide down behind the mountains of Jura, or to wait for two climbers on their way up from sea level, aiming for just that point on the ledge. We were not expecting him to be there, had made no arrangements to meet, but Eric was ever one for surprises and there's no reason, even now, to suppose it would have made the climb any faster if we'd known he was there. It certainly wouldn't have made it any easier.

No one said it would be easy. She didn't want it to be easy. All the way through the winter, reading the maps and the tide tables, hanging off abseil ropes in the pouring rain, bribing fishermen to take her closer in to the rock than any sane human being would want to go, Lee Adams was not looking for a climb that was easy. Just one step this side of impossible and no more, otherwise what's the point? And all through the winter, sitting at the top of the cliff catching the falls, driving the car to the jetty, going out to buy one more bottle of Scotch for a skipper who needed half a year drying out more than he ever needed another drink, I listened, as we all did, with half an ear to the moves and the holds and the nightmare of a chimney at the base of the crack and I knew that, when the time came for her to choose a partner to climb it with her, she would ask Eric. Of all of us, he was the only one who came close to climbing at the level she climbed. He was the only one who made sense.

But then, Lee doesn't climb to make sense. I was waiting by the car on the jetty at Tarbert on a wind-blown, rain-sodden Saturday afternoon less than a month ago when she made the last boat trip out to the cliff: one final attempt to find a way in to the base of the crack that wasn't going to get her drowned before she ever started the climb up. I remember the sight of her, soaked and scratched and decorated in odd places with algal streaks as she came up the path from the boat. I pulled a rucksack from the boot and passed her a T-shirt as she reached the car. There was no real need to ask how it went – her whole body was alive with the buzz of it, like a horse before a race, fighting the pull of the bit. She sat on the sill of the boot, staring out to sea, her focus on something a long way out of sight.

'And so?' I asked. 'Will it go?' It's good, sometimes, to get the details.

'It'll go.' She nodded, chewing her bottom lip. 'There's only one place the boat can put in with any chance of getting out

2

again in one piece and it's a real bitch of a traverse from there along to the crack. Sixty foot of blank rock with bugger all to hold on to but the seaweed.' She waited, expectant, as if I was supposed to have some kind of opinion on that.

Traverses are not really my thing. I haven't done enough of them to comment. 'I thought there was the ledge?' I said.

'Sort of.' She threw the wrecked remains of her old shirt into the boot and there was a pause as she pulled the fresh one over her head. The dry, laundered smell of it mellowed the ranker smells of rain and sea. 'It breaks up in places but it's better than nothing,' she said. 'We'll be fine as long as we time the tide right. Bearing in mind how much you hate the sea, the least I can do is see that you keep your feet dry before we get to the crack.'

There was another gap then, filled by the wind and the flapping of old newspaper on the tarmac of the jetty. I looked out to the sea and back again. She sat on the boot, her head cocked to one side, watching me.

'*My* feet?' I asked.

'Your feet,' she agreed. Her smile was indulgent; maddeningly so.

'What about Eric? I thought you were going to do it with him?'

'Only if you turn me down.' She stood up, then ducked back into the lee of the boot as a westerly gust threatened to knock us both flat. 'We'll find something with more of a challenge in it for him later. This one is for you and me. Unless you're going to tell me now you really don't want to do it?'

Maybe I should have done. I have known Lee Adams for over half my life and I know just where her limits are; a long way past mine in almost everything we do, especially on the rock. But the rain was easing and the wind was fresh and we had spent all winter planning for this one. I thought I knew where the worst bits were. Besides, in that moment, I really did want to do it.

'OK.' I pulled the car keys from my pocket and flipped them the two foot through the air to her waiting hand. 'If you're sure I can do it.'

'I'm not sure of anything. I'm not even sure I can do it. That's what we're here to find out.' She tossed the keys high up in the air and caught them again on the downswing. 'Just don't forget to trust your feet. If you can hang on to that, you'll be fine.'

You hate the sea. I don't hate it. I am terrified of it. There is a difference. Not normally, in everyday life, I'm not afraid of it then. I can walk along the shore and breathe in the salt and feel the power of it and be inspired with the rest of them. I respect it. I admire it. I wish I could paint it, or photograph it, or do something else to catch the extraordinary, restless beauty of it and take it home. I am not afraid of it. But put me on a two-inch tightrope of sea-greased rock with the water kissing the soles of my climbing shoes, with barnacles the size of walnuts knifing the palms of my hands and leathered ribbons of weed draping themselves like malign bandages over my eyes so that the rock and the sea and the rope are all flashes seen in the darkness, then I can reach a level of terror that knows no bounds. *Trust your feet.* Believe me, I'm trying. That doesn't mean I'll succeed.

'How's it going?' I felt her voice through the rope, calm and steady, a verbal life-line. If I were to take my cheek from the rock, shift my balance outwards, I could probably see her, ten feet on, just round the curve of the cliff. I would rather not do that just now.

'Don't ask.' My voice came out muffled, gagged by the rock.

'The ledge narrows down a bit just beyond your right foot. There's a finger-hold up about eye level and another one beyond the big patch of weed. You'll need them both to bridge over the gap.'

'Thanks.'

'When you land you're on the shelf. You can sit down here if you need to.'

Really? Then perhaps I am not going to die. I reached up and found the holds: smooth-shouldered dimples in the rock, just deep enough to take the crook of a finger, just safe enough to bear weight for the straddling hop across the gap to the wider platform of the shelf. I felt her hands on my waist and heard the blessed snick of the karabiner clipping safe to my belt. I leant back against the cliff and breathed in the first full breath since I stepped off the boat. Her hand stayed flat on my sternum, pressing me into the rock.

'Now how are you?'

'I don't know.' The shelf under my feet was broad and flat and here, the barnacles made foolproof friction. She relaxed the pressure on my chest and I sat down, easing the knot on the safety rope to give me the extra length. Clumps of weed slithered wetly under my legs. The sweet-salt smell of it hit the pit of my stomach and curdled the remains of breakfast. I put my palms to my eyes and breathed through my mouth. 'I'm fine.'

'Liar.' I heard the rattle of her rucksack as she pulled out her belt. 'Sit still for a while and I'll get the gear ready.' She said it as if we had all the time in the world, as if she hadn't timed this to the nearest five minutes and I hadn't already wasted all the slack dithering on the ledge. If her timing is right, the first one up should be leaving the shelf at the turning of the tide. When we got out of the boat, the mark of its highest point was thirty feet above the top of my head. We have stepped down several feet since then.

I took my hands from my eyes. 'How long have we got?'

She paused, thinking. I felt her shrug ripple down the rope. 'Not long,' she said. 'Have a look.'

At what? Looking up, all I could see was rock: a wide blank wall rearing up out of the water with the crack a dark shadow on the right. Looking down, there was only water: grey-green Atlantic water laced in lazy sworls with the foam of an ocean crossing. It slopped idly against the lip of the shelf, dark and oily and colour-coded for the depth. Shallow water sparkles with the colours of the sky and the clouds and the patternings of sand. There are places round here, off Arran, out from Oban, where you can lean over the edge of a dinghy and count the legs on the starfish three fathoms down. Water like that is friendly; it holds no menace. Here, it is deep, dark and silent and deep. It took the submarines out of Faslane to map the contours of the sea-bed round this coastline and I checked the maps before we ever came out: a thousand feet of hungry water, straight down. I heard Lee curse, a quiet, savage whisper, and saw a No. 8 nut drop from the open mouth of her rucksack and slip over the edge to the water. I reached for it, too late, and we watched as it sank, straight and fast, the krab

6

spiralling behind on its bit of a sling like a slow-motion propeller. A salutary warning, I stood up and moved in closer to the edge of the cliff.

'Lee? Give me a time scale I can believe in.'

Her watch was clipped to the gear loop on the back of her belt. She twisted round to read it. 'Lead climber needs be on the way up by seven minutes from now.'

'Right.' Just so long as I know.

I pulled my kit from the rucksack and started clipping gear into my belt: slings and krabs and nuts and hexes and the tiny 5-mm friend that I bought for a V Diff on Stanage and have never used. For eight years, it has gone with me up every route I've climbed, my talisman for when things go wrong, the one piece of protection that will save my life when everything else has fallen apart or fallen out. I clipped it into my belt, dead centre at the back where I could reach it with either hand, and then I braced myself in the harness, feet wedged firm in the angle between the shelf and the cliff, and turned round to look for Lee. She was across on the far side of the shelf, leaning back against the rock, head bent in concentration, tuning her belt in the way a player might tune an old and favoured lute. I watched her fit a set of hexes, seven of them in ascending order, around the loops on her belt, careful and neat, like her post-mortems. When she was done, she shifted a bit and stood there for a moment, one foot on the ledge, the other toeing the water: a slight, dark rock-being, making her pact with the sea. She looked up then and smiled, one of those images that outlasts the rest: the dark hair and the dark eyes and the odd, bright calm of her smile. As if she's at peace doing this and all the rest is a game to pass the time. Some of us climb for the sigh and the bit of a buzz at the top. Lee climbs because it gives her life meaning.

We stood in the silence of the ledge and I heard the tide change. The rush of it in the crack-cave to the right sounded louder suddenly and the spray began to reach higher up the rocks as the waves hit the wall with more malice. It was only then that I noticed how carefully she had picked the first stance. For thirty feet on either side, I could see waves smashing high up the foot of the cliff. Water ran off the rock, wetting the weed and the algae to a well-oiled sludge. Except where we stood. The sea beyond the shelf swirled like a pike-ridden mill-pond, but it wasn't running in over the edge. I turned round. Eight feet out, in the open sea, a rising boulder caught the shoulder of the surf, spinning it out to both sides. I looked down at my feet. For what it was worth, the rubber soles of my shoes were still dry.

I looked up and found her waiting. However calm the water it still rises with the tide. 'Shall we go?'

'I think we should.' She tossed me the free end of a rope. I tied it in a double loop and clipped it into my belt. 'Do you want to go first?'

'Absolutely not.'

'Fine.' She slid past me to the mouth of the crack, reached round and stepped in on to the knucklebone pebbles and finger-wide ridges of the walls. The rope ran out through my hands as she moved round. A red rope. Her colour, her half of the umbilical cord, an active, pro-active scarlet. My half is blue, a peaceful, dusky blue, a measure of sanity and calm.

'OK. That'll do.'

Her voice echoed and came back round a half-beat later. I

8

looked up. She stood at the far mouth of the crack, leaning slightly towards me, hovering on the edge of balance, one finger hooked in the rock behind her.

'Ready?'

'Ready.' She lifted the flat of one foot to the rock. 'OK. Let's get her done.'

It was half past three on the afternoon of the twenty-first of June on the first day of the new moon. The longest day and the lowest tide. A turning point between the worlds. The kind of day when anything is possible. I hitched the red rope tight and then let out slack as she lifted her feet off the ground and started up. Nothing was ever the same after that.

It was a bastard of a climb. Just standing at the bottom you could see that. Given dry rock, the crack would have made a good chimney. At the base, it was wide enough to take a small boat. Or a climber at full stretch, back jammed on one side and feet on the other. At the top, half a rope's length up, it narrowed to maybe the width of her shoulder, side on. The rock was reasonable: ridged and uneven with places you could push down on with heel or hand and expect one or other to stay – given dry rock. But we were not given dry rock. We were given wet, tide-worn rock that spent most of its life underwater. The kind of rock beach-pools are made of, the ones you spent your childhood splashing around in, fishing for hermit crabs and sea-anemones, where you slipped and got your feet wet because the slime spread like oil and made it impossible to walk even on a dead flat surface. This crack was made of rock like that. I stood on the shelf, paying out the line of the rope like an unravelling apron string, knowing that if a foot or a shoulder or the small of her back were to slip, she'd drop out like an egg from its shell and the best I could do would be to pull her up from the water before she drowned.

The water was lapping up round my ankles by the time she reached the first stance and tied on. I followed her up. A climb, any climb, is easier on second. Courage comes easy with a rope above you and a belay you trust. On this pitch, I can say with absolute certainty that I would never have got up it without her there to hold me. The crack was easily as bad as it looked from the floor. Every hold felt like smearing up on butter. I slipped once, about fifteen feet up, lost the traction on one foot and then a shoulder and snapped out sideways to hang, spinning, in the mouth of the crack. Getting back on the rock was harder than you'd imagine with nothing to hold on to that wasn't covered in stinking, rotten seaweed. I did the rest of it on a back-wash of bilious adrenalin and came out to stand beside her dripping with sweat and algal scum and smelling of stagnant fish.

I stepped round behind her and clipped in on the blue. 'Thanks for the lift.'

'You're welcome. Sorry you got your feet wet.'

'No problem.' We never talk sense on the first bit of a climb.

She passed me a couple of large-sized friends from her rack. 'You OK to go on up?'

'Sure.' All things are relative.

The next pitch looked better. The rock wasn't dry but it was wet only from the spray of the waves below. The barnacle-stance was long since invisible, swamped by the incoming tide.

I went up on two ropes: red to the right, blue to the left. The cliff leant out slightly which made it hard on the arms but the holds were positive and the crack took most of the protection. I reached the second stance around the time the boulder protecting the shelf finally succumbed to the water. I tied in on blue, fixed a krab for her on red and took in as she followed me up. She paused as she reached me but she didn't clip in. There was no need. I handed her the rest of the rack and then stood there paying out the twin coils of our umbilicus as she moved on the third pitch. She smiled, I think, in passing, but she was back in her own world by then; smooth and flowing, balanced between fingers and toes, a martial artist dancing with the line of the rock.

The sun moved round on to the rock as she climbed. Runnels of spray dried to white salt on the cliff-face in front of me and the rock warmed under my feet. The breeze backed round with the change in temperature and blew off the old-weed stench of the crack so that I could smell clean sea again with lines through it of bracken and spruce from the Forestry land up on top of the peninsula. Very peaceful. Even the sea, free from the echo-chamber of the crack, was at peace, turned down to a quiet background hush, like a radio not quite tuned, with the gulls and the wind and the odd sighing grunt from Lee weaving counterpoints over the top.

I leant back in the harness and looked round. Over my right shoulder, Gigha lay low in the surf. Behind me, the mountains of Islay and the Paps of Jura hauled up out of the sea, solid, enduring and steadfast. Down in the Sound, the water shifted from grey to green to aquamarine, curled into eddies by currents you couldn't begin to map. Sunlight caught on the surface, spinning mirrors of salt and water, breaking them and making them whole again with no bad luck in between. Life in reflection.

Lee finished the third pitch. A gull challenged her for ownership of the ledge at the top. I saw her talk with it for a while, the way I talk with the dog, and then she moved back and off to the right and set up a hanging belay out of range of the nest scrape. When I got there, she was still negotiating, looping the ropes over a separate sling out to one side so that they didn't impinge on territory that wasn't hers. 'He was here before us,' she said simply. And then, without changing tone: 'I think the fourth is the crux.'

Really? I very much doubt it. Nothing on earth could possibly be as bad as that traverse. But then she's not at war with the water.

I kept my eyes on the rock. 'Are you sure?'

She shrugged. 'See what you think.'

I gave myself eight more feet of rope on the belay and stood up on the ledge. The gull mewed and draped spread wings over its scrape, weaving its head in snake-patterns of threat. I shuffled a foot or two to the right and it settled back, bright-eyed and wary. I breathed deep with closed eyes and then stepped up on a pebble and reached for the obvious crack as it crossed above my head. My fingers slid over the lip into cool, solid darkness. The edges were sharp. I like climbing on sharp rock.

I stepped back on to the ledge. The gull hissed. Lee lifted one brow. I smiled and the world was at peace. 'I'll need all of the friends,' I said.

I was climbing then as well as I have ever climbed. The angled section of the crack was like walking up stairs – endless protection and good, solid holds. Disappointingly easy. You don't want anything to be too easy on a first ascent, you want it to be as difficult as possible without being fatal. That way lies fame and long life. Unless you peel off halfway up. That way lies a bed in the spinal wards and a long time wondering why.

Don't think about that.

The vertical section was less of a cruise, long and narrow and not quite the right width to hold hands or feet without them slipping. I jammed on up anyway, leaning out on clenched fists, working my feet into the back of the crack, bracing against anything that would hold. The skin shredded on the backs of both hands. Good climbers don't have scars. I have lots. I am not a good climber. This is not a good time to remember that, or to imagine what will happen if both hands slip out while a foot is jammed in the crack. Keep moving. Don't look down.

A small horizontal break, twenty feet up from the last hex, took a No. 6 nut, the kind of size I might be prepared to trust my life to. Ten feet above that, I felt a twitch in the rope and a hiss from the gull. Or maybe not the gull. I looked down. A long, long way down, the Atlantic flashed mirrors. Somewhere between me and it, a small piece of grit-worn steel spiralled down the rope like a single dandelion seed blown from a clock.

'Protection's out.' Her voice was more level than mine would have been.

'Right.'

'You could do with some more.'

'Yup.'

Later. I can't stop now. Later.

I moved on up.

The crack ran out sooner than I'd expected. Something changed in the contour of the rock and the right-hand wall stood eight inches proud of the left. You can't jam on that. I stood on a ledge no wider than the rope and I ran my fingers blindly over blind rock, searching for something to hold.

'I think it's a layback.'

No. I don't think so. I'm not laying anything back. Not on lead. Not forty feet over the last bit of decent protection. That's an eighty-foot fall. More if the friend rips out. I stood under a crag once and saw Bobby Renton fall two hundred feet down the line of a crack. Every one of his friends popped out as he fell; a long rippling crackle, like fast-opened press-studs. He landed at my feet and snapped both of his femurs. It could have been so much worse.

My right foot began to tremble – a spastic St Vitus dance of lactic acid and fear. Mostly fear. It comes when you stand too long on something too small and contemplate the frailty of flesh and the fragility of bone. For me, it comes when I start to see phantom X-rays with my name on the label and shattered fragments of bone scattered over the film: a spiralling, self-perpetuating, self-fulfilling prophecy. Every climber in the world knows that when the shaking starts, it's only a matter of time before you fall off. Unless you can find a way to go up.

I laid it back, hooked both hands over the rim of the crack, leant back on stretched arms, lifted a foot and braced it on the far wall, lifted the other to join it, then shuffled up crab-wise on arms that burned and legs that cramped and a mind that went into white-out.

14

The fourth is the crux.

How do you know?

Because I spent half of the winter hanging off an abseil rope working out the moves.

Why didn't you tell me?

I tried.

You don't want anything to be too easy . . . you want it to be as difficult as possible without being fatal . . . unless you peel off halfway up. That way lies a bed in the spinal wards and a long time wondering why.

I could peel off any moment now.

This is impossible. Madness. Insanity.

The crack ran out for real. It narrowed to the width of two fingers and then simply stopped. Somewhere, three feet below that, the gods left a break: two inches of horizontal rock where everything else followed gravity into the sea. I got a foot on it and stood up; my other foot was wedged at an angle in the depths of the crack. I jammed my right hand into the top end of the main crack, clenched hard and lost more skin to the famished rock. Fresh blood slid between skin and stone. Good lubrication. Bad friction. It'll do.

I leant in with my face flat to the rock and breathed in the fresh breath of the sea.

'You OK?'

'I'm alive.'

'You need to step up for the ledge from there.'

'Is it worth going for?'

'Like a playing field. Eric found a sheep on it last time we came down.'

'A live one?'

'Yup. There's a track from the far edge that goes up to the top. You can walk off from there if you want.'

Thanks.

I kept my cheek on the rock and turned my head up to look. The black line of the ledge stood out charcoal against the blue of the sky. Thin spikes of grass waved outwards, billowing on the rising thermals. Forget the sheep. If there's grass, then it's a good ledge. That way lies safety.

I reached up. Nowhere near. I stood on tiptoe and then on one foot on tiptoe and was still nowhere near. I spread my hands, one at a time, across featureless rock searching for holds and found none. I went back to my crack.

'How's it going?'

'Lousy.'

Some folk climb because it gives their life meaning. The rest of us climb for the buzz and the adrenalin rush at the top. We are the ones who know when to stop. This is what sets us apart from the rest. This is what keeps us alive. Whatever it was I was trying to prove, I have proved it. Or I will never prove it. I have had enough of this. There is always down.

I said it out loud, pushing my voice down the ropes. 'Lee, I can't do this. I'm coming down.'

Silence.

'Did you hear me?'

'I heard.' She sounded uncannily calm. 'Do you think you can lay back down the crack?'

Are you mad? No one does laybacks downwards. Not without a seriously well-developed deathwish. I didn't bother to look down. 'Fuck off, Adams.'

'So then can you put in some decent protection and I'll lower you off?'

More silence.

'Kellen, did you hear me?'

'I heard.'

There is no protection up here. But then she knows that.

The fourth is the crux.

Fuck it. I hate this. When we get back to safe ground, remind me that I hate this.

I found a hold, small and insecure, more like a one-finger jamming crack, a long way off to the left. With a bit of persuasion, it took my tiny half-size friend. My talisman. I didn't test it. I clipped a long sling on the end, then eased the left-hand rope up and clipped it, one-handed, to the sling.

'Clipping in on red.'

'Fine. I've got you. You OK up there?'

'Don't ask.'

I turned back to face the rock and breathed in the sea and the sweat and the earth-hard smell of stone. Cramp knifed in waves through the arch of my right foot. I eased it in the rock. It slipped.

Oh, Mother, I hate this.

'Lee, take tight . . . I'm falling.'

I fell. On to a 5-mm friend. It held. Hard rock scraped holes in the side of my T-shirt as I slid sideways across the face. The red rope ran in a single, thrumming life-line from her belt up to the sling and down to my belt. I swung out and back in a pendulum arc and slowed to a stop in the middle.

I turned into the rock and clawed back to my toe-hold. Breathing was harder than I remembered.

'Do you want me to lower you off that friend?'

'No.' It has held this long. I don't want to push it further. 'I'll find another.'

'If you like.' I could hear the shrug in her voice. The lift to the tone that said *there isn't one to find*.

I hate this. Please God never let me forget how much I hate this.

'Kellen, is there not a pebble up there on the right near where that pale patch of rock starts?'

'No.' There's nothing up there. We both know that.

I tried for it anyway. Rough rock sandpapered the ends of my fingers.

'Further up . . . and right a bit . . .'

'Shit . . . yes . . .' There was a pebble. The kind of tiny, jammed-in pebble that the weather leaves behind for desperate climbers. It was there, poking out of the rock, about the size of my thumbnail, not huge, but big enough to make the difference. Big enough to hold on to while I moved my feet up and out of that bloody crack. Big enough to push up from and reach the ledge, solid and positive and there's no way I'm going to slip off this one. I pulled up in one big, joint-wrenching pull.

Safe.

'Hey, you made it.'

So I did. 'Thank you.'

'How's the sheep?' Her voice ran up the rope, alive and buoyant.

'How the hell should I know? Just let me fix a belay and then . . .' And then any sheep that there was could have taken wings and flown and I wouldn't have noticed it. Because Eric was there, Eric Dalziel, lying in the sunlight with one arm tucked under his head, grinning his big-bear grin as if he was waiting for me and I was late. Four hundred feet off the ground on a climb no one was supposed to have done before.

'Lee . . . Lee. Eric's up here.'

'What?' Rope rippled live through the dead of my fingers. 'He can't be. This one's ours.' Her voice climbed ahead of her. Still buoyant. She could have been standing beside us. 'Hey, Eric, you bastard, what are you doing on our climb?'

No. It isn't like that. You don't understand. 'Lee. Stop pissing about. Just get up here, can you?'

We've climbed together long enough. The laughter stopped. I felt her testing the placements around her and then take them out as I fixed in the belay. She tugged on the ropes. 'Coming up.'

I sat with my legs dangling over the edge and coiled the ropes as she climbed. Red coiled on blue coiled on red. A spaghetti coil of colours. I took them in so much faster than she had paid out. You can climb anything with a rope above you.

Time moved as she climbed. The sun swung round the face of the cliff, warming the air, raising the cloud layer, shortening the shadows. There was a sheep, a small, wiry, brown-fleeced sheep with tight-spiralled horns and a pair of fire-ember eyes; hot gold with long vertical slits that narrowed to knife edges in the full face of the sun. It twitched its cleft rabbit's lip and blethered wetly at the man and the man grinned back and it was clear they'd had plenty of time to get acquainted. The sheep considered conversation with me and thought better of it. It strolled instead along the ledge to a broader spot and lay

19

down, inches from the edge, to ruminate. A sheep without vertigo. I checked the fastenings on my belt one more time and stared straight out into space.

The breeze gathered pace, carrying wisps of cloud and shadows with them so that the day became parti-coloured. The sheep belched methane spiked with the acid-sharp undercurrents of fermenting grass and the smell of it covered the other smells of the ledge. A pair of hooded crows appeared from nowhere, riding the thermals. They rose with Lee as she climbed then banked out sharply, one to either side, and vanished into the open sky as she topped out. She didn't use my pebble at all, but found other handholds in the unblemished rock and stepped up as if it was an over-graded Severe. I thought we'd found ourselves a new E3, E2 at the very least. It dropped grades with every move she made.

She saw him at much the same time I did – just in that moment when the pitch is done and you can take your mind away from the rock to whatever's around. I handed her the krab as she came up over the edge and she clipped in but she did it blindly and she didn't move. She didn't go to him. She crouched, unmoving, two inches from the edge of a four-hundred-foot drop and stared past me to the man beyond. The man who was lying at all the wrong angles against the rising wall of rock, waiting for something that was never going to happen, grinning to himself and the gods and the open sky at the immense, ridiculous irony of it.

'Eric?' She said it softly. A half-question. The way you would wake a friend in the morning, or offer a fresh mug of coffee. He gazed back as he had gazed at me for the eternal half-hour of her climb; a fixed-wide stare, seeing nothing. The breeze shifted round to the side and the smell of him flooded the fresh, barnyard smells of the sheep. He was not newly dead.

'Eric?' One more time, to wake him up. She's a pathologist, she's used to death – just not this one. She moved forward eventually and slipped her hand in his. One small, living hand lost in the bear-paw grip of the dead. She was shaking all over, a fine, vibrating tremor that rippled through her to him. His hand shuddered gently but not the rest of him. He was too big to shake much. Too solid, too long dead.

'My phone's in your pack. The flare's in mine. We can finish the route if you think it'll go. Otherwise, we'll have to follow the sheep path off and up to the top.' I have had half an hour to think about this. Thirty minutes of colour-coiled spaghetti to think the unthinkable. 'One way or another, we need to call the Rescue and get a team in here to get him off.' And we need to get him to a hospital where someone will have to do a post-mortem. She has a promise on that. I heard her make it. I never thought she'd be called on to honour it.

'I'm not on call.'

'You will do him, though, won't you?'

'Yes.' No question. 'Yes. I'll do him.' Because Eric was more than a friend.

Chapter Two

Time slowed down for a while after we found him. I sat with my legs dangling over the edge, my fingers still tight on the red rope. Lee sat there behind me, her legs crossed at the ankles, one hand in his, the other somewhere up on his arm, as if any minute now she would stand and he would stand with her and we'd walk off the ledge, a thin line of climbers and a sheep. They talked together, I think. At least, she talked and there were gaps for him to answer and the cadence of it sounded like a late-evening natter. The kind of conversation you'd have in the pub after any day's climb, chewing through the route and the holds and the protection and whether it's really safe to be lying on a ledge, even a wide one, four hundred feet up from the sea with no belt and no rope and no one there to hold the belay if you fall.

I sat out of the way and gave them time to be together and watched the sun crack open on the southernmost Pap, spilling all the light of the first half-year down into the cleavage of

23

Glen Astaile. Down below, the water of the Sound caught the overspill and spread a carpet of living fire from tide-line to shoreline and out into the open sea beyond. Somewhere in all that ardent brilliance is the moon, an invisible sliver of calm.

In time, the dark pushed forward over the top of Kintyre, shrinking the daylight. Rounded shadows flowed out over the Sound and wrapped clammy fingers across the bare skin of my legs. Even the longest day has to end eventually and the night, when it comes, is just as cold as the rest. My skin warped into goose-flesh and my fingers whitened to senseless wood. I lost the memory of my feet. Behind me the murmuring conversation petered out. When I turned to look, she had her forehead bent to his hand, the short, dark hair falling forward, moulded with sweat and salt spray into a rough-spiked halo. The dying light of the sun caught them then and cast them together, a half-cut statue moulded from living rock, the kind of image that becomes permanent if you leave it too long. It seemed a good time to call it a day.

I swivelled round on the ledge and moved in closer to the belay, pulling my feet up underneath me for warmth. If she heard me move, she didn't show it.

'Lee. We need to get off here and call the Rescue. So we can get him to Glasgow tonight.'

She could have been deaf. Or dead. For a while, I thought that, at the very least, she had fallen asleep. But she unwound her fingers from his, then stood up and stepped back to look up at the rock above his head. I watched while she weighed the height of the cliff against the depth of her conscience. It wasn't easy. If it had been anyone other than Eric, there would have been no question, we'd have picked up the gear and

taken the last two pitches to finish the route. It's nine months
since she first sat in the kitchen and spun me this climb.
Almost twice that since the first time she and Eric took the
small-boat out from West Tarbert to have a look at the height
of the coastline. She spent the winter climbing ice on Ben Lui
to stay fit for this. You wouldn't get me to climb on ice if the
world's end depended on it. And the fourth pitch was the crux.
The rest should be a walk in the park. It could be faster, in
fact, than the path. I blew hot breath on my hands and
stamped some life into my feet, just in case.

'Lee? We can go on up if you want. The light'll hold.'

It won't. We both know that. But the fourth was still the
crux.

She said nothing. Just stood there, flexing and unflexing
her fingers, her eyes moving from Eric to the rock and back
again. In time, they reached some kind of consensus, the three
of them, and she shook her head, once and sharply. Her hand
moved to her waist, fingers fighting to untie the salt-stiff rope
from her waist. Without it, she stood unprotected four hundred feet over water. There has to be something about this
ledge that inspires insanity in the otherwise sane. She waited
without comment for me to unhitch the belays and then stood
there coiling the rope as if we were safe up by the car with a
hundred yards to the edge. I watched and coiled and waited
and tried to work out if I could catch her in time if she fell.
She didn't, but when I bent to fix the blue rope to my sack, she
had stepped back and when I looked up again I saw her walk
out on the far side of the sheep as if there was no chance it
might wake and move and take the feet out from under her. I
have known this woman for nearly two decades. For most of

that time, we have climbed together. I have never in all that time seen her take risks for the sake of it.

'Lee?'

She turned back towards me. The shadows bisected her face. The half I could see was closed, inaccessible. 'No,' she said. Her voice was flat, cut from old newsprint, bereft of colour and tone. 'We can't do it now. We'll walk out and call from the top. The signal's better from the car.' She turned on her heel and started picking her way over the loose rock fall cluttering the path. I followed, more slowly, and with my shoulder pressed to the rising wall of the cliff. The sheep belched in its sleep as I passed.

She was right, the signal was better from the car. We changed clothes, turned on the heating and called the Mountain Rescue and they promised us a helicopter from the naval base at Prestwick to take him off. Not because there was any urgency – they were happy to take the word of two doctors that the casualty was gone beyond all hope of resuscitation – but because it was late and a long drive back into Glasgow and there was a team on stand-by, waiting for something more exacting than another weekend walker weather-bound on the Cobbler. And then of course it was Eric and even the lass on the phone had heard of Eric. They weren't about to send him off without a bit of a spectacle.

We met the advance team at the head of the sheep-path: a couple of the lads in regulation Rescue beards and day-glo yellow jackets who brought in a bigger flare and a radio and more climbing kit than I've ever seen outside of the shop. They shared out their ration of mint cake and we destroyed their evening for them with the news that they didn't have to climb down to bring up the body. In a while, we showed them the way in to the ledge and you could see life gradually made worth living again as they worked out the route we had taken to get up to there from the sea. They were local, both of them, and they must have known the lines of the cliff better than I know the road into the farm. New climbs are like gold dust in Scotland. Folk scour the Hebrides and live in tents on small pieces of ocean rock just to find a new route they can put their name to. To have something unclimbed within three hours' drive of Glasgow city centre is a jewel beyond price and a second ascent of any route is almost as good as the first. We didn't get around to telling them that we hadn't completed the final section.

They liked the ledge. They would, in fact, have been perfectly happy to guide the helicopter in and have them winch us all up from there but Lee had her pact with the gull and wasn't about to let them blast it clean off its scrape, so we helped them unpack their kit and put the stretcher together and carried Eric out to the flat ground beside the car. It wasn't as easy as it sounds. Rigor had long since set in and Dr Dalziel had moulded to his sharp-angled bed with all the flexibility of the rock around him. It would have taken a bone saw, by then, to get him lying flat out the way they wanted him. We stood out of the way and let them try the various permutations and it was only when there seemed a reasonable risk of losing him over the edge that Lee stepped in. She rolled him on to his side with the one broken arm folded under his head for a pillow and his one knee bent up towards his chest and they cross-tied him that way for the jog up to the car, a sleeping bear, curled up to dream.

The cavalry arrived not long after that. They could have landed, I have no doubt; the ground is flat at the top of the cliff and even with the car in the way there was room to spare. But naval exercises aren't done the easy way and so they stayed in the air and ran it all as a sea-cliff manoeuvre. We fired our small flare and the lads fired their big one and the thing homed in between the fire-flower and the mortar and hung in the air above us, blasting wind and sound on to the quiet of our crag, scattering grass and gorse and sheep-droppings and calling down Armageddon on the late-evening rabbits. Given the choice, I would have taken the car at that point but Lee was winched up ahead of me and she had the keys and so, when they lowered the rope for the third time, I let the lads with the jackets strap me in and then the pulley jerked tight and my feet left the ground and I fell the long haul up into hell.

They dropped us off at the Western. If you say it quickly enough, it sounds like a late taxi home, not a man-made monster that covered a two-and-a-half hour drive in forty minutes with a fair proportion of that spent negotiating with air-traffic control for the right to fly across their air space. By then I had thrown up everything I had ever eaten and was paralysed with the same kind of post-nausea catalepsy that comes sometimes after a migraine. I could have lived without another dangle on the winch but the Western Infirmary was built before helicopters were ever invented and there's no convenient landing pad within reach, so they hovered over the roof-top and lowered us down to the handful of white-coated clinicians who braved the screaming havoc of the blades and came forward to help. Mike Bailey was there, I remember, Lee's protégé, the failed student turned pathology technician. He stood in front of the others waving the glowing end of his cigarette like a beacon, his wild hair made wilder by the helicopter and his narcotic grin damped for once to nothing by the news of who it was. Of the others, I remember no one except Dee Fitzpatrick, the tall, crew-cut Irishwoman, on call from anaesthesia and there, she said, to see were we wrong and was Eric still within reach of a ventilator. He wasn't. He had never been, but she stayed anyway and helped us lift him across on to the new trolley and made sure that there weren't too many of the others trying to follow us down to the mortuary. For that, if nothing else, we were grateful.

He was a good climber, Eric. There are no scars on the backs of his hands. No scrapes or fresh lacerations from hanging too long on insecure jams. No bruised knees from the ungainly scramble on to the ledge. The skin on the back of his hand is a deep, weathered brown, the fingers tight curled as if he were still holding the rope of the belay. Although, of course, he had no rope, no belt, and no belay. If he hadn't been wearing his climbing shoes, you would have thought he was up there for the view and the sunset. Which maybe he was. It was worth seeing, after all.

He's softening now, I can stretch out his fingers if I try. I can mould his hand, make it less of a fist and more of a hand-shake, something to hold on to while the pathologists do what they have to do to get themselves ready. Something solid and real to keep away the freezing, bright-light hell of the autopsy room. It is so very cold in here. Even before we reached the mortuary, you could feel it: the kind of biting, psychological chill that goes with white tiled walls and fluorescent lights and the shiny precision of steel. A cold that flows into the lungs on a searing tide of preservative and disinfectant, neither of them quite strong enough to smother the smell of the dead.

The smell is less, though, now. Sitting here, this close to him, I could have imagined the smell. And if Eric is cold, he is no colder than I am, and there is still some comfort in holding his hand, in studying the neat-clipped fingernails and the roughened skin on the pads and the layering of coarse red-blond hair along the back of his fingers that turns white suddenly as the lamps above the autopsy table flick on and two hundred watts of artificial daylight flood down over the slab. And then, if you look more closely, you can see that he does, after all, bear the scars of learning, old and faint, a criss-crossed lattice of whispered lines engraved half a lifetime ago on the knuckles and tendons and then weathered in by the rock and the rain of a hundred weekend climbs. It's good to know not all the scars are new ones.

I've never been present for the post-mortem of someone I know. It makes it all so very different. Lee and her technician do this every day of their lives although I don't believe they remove the clothes with that kind of care from someone they haven't met. It was like undressing a friend before bed, fast and smooth and with a kind of modest courtesy that did no harm to what was exposed underneath. Gradually, what had been clothed was made unclothed and the breaks and the scars and the lumps that had been covered were there to be seen and to be measured and photographed and then, later, where it mattered, to be weighed. There were breaks – more than I had imagined. Not just the obvious one in his upper arm that left his elbow crooked out as if there was a new joint halfway down from his shoulder, but others in places you wouldn't necessarily expect: a fracture dislocation of the femoral neck that showed only when they rolled him over on to his side and gently lifted his leg, a shattering of the bones of one ankle that had been held together by the rising rubber of his climbing boot so that the foot flopped over, grating gently, when the boot joined the rest of his clothes in the bag. And then finally, the one that mattered, the one that only really showed up on X-ray so that we all crowded into the dark room and made fog of our breath round the dry-processor and then had to wait for the full ninety seconds until the leading edge of the film poked out between the rollers and we were able to drag it out and hold it up to the light box and see for ourselves the great glaring gap between the atlas and the axis that showed where Eric Dalziel had broken his neck.

It must have been fast, that at least is worth knowing. For every doctor I know, the worst thought in the world is a long and lingering death. We see too much of it in the wards to want it for ourselves or each other. I remember the conversation in the canteen the day Maisie Allen died in the Unit three months after any one of us would have chosen to go. Dee was more pragmatic than the rest of us, but then Dee has lived longer in a world of different values. Eric was the one who said what everyone else was thinking; that he'd rather die tomorrow in a fall from a climb – short, sharp and unknowing – than wait out the months for a slow, dragging end. So he got what he wanted, that much at least.

It still doesn't explain what the hell he was doing there in the first place.

'Kellen? Kells, he won't mend by looking at it.'

It's Lee. Lee who has changed out of her climbing things and is standing, not at all cold, in her fine cotton theatre pyjamas with the ghastly white plastic over-gown that never quite washes clean and the long, elbow-length gloves that on her come halfway up her biceps. She is standing in the doorway to the dark room and Dee is behind her and both of them are looking at me as if I'm more fragile than I think I am.

'Kellen, there's coffee next door, I think maybe we should go and sit down.' Dee Fitzpatrick spent her childhood in an Irish convent and it shows still in her voice. South of Dublin and west a little. Further south and further west as the night gets later and she gets more short on sleep. By this time of night it is utterly beguiling. I'm not in the mood to be beguiled.

'Why should I want to sit down?' My hands are curled tight in the pockets of my fleece. For the warmth. I may be tense but I am not fragile.

'I'm going to open him up. You don't need to stay.' Lee. With the extra layer to her voice that opens into the lines below the surface. She said this to me once before, the same kind of words, the same kind of tone, the same vertical groove cut deep in the space between her eyes. We were upstairs in her office then, five floors up, and it was Bridget down here on the slab. She didn't tell me not to come down then, but she gave me the option not to. I took her advice that time and stayed in her room and read old journals while she did what she had to do, so I never saw the things I didn't need to see. I didn't think about it much at the time, I just acted on instinct, but I have never regretted it since and my dreams have been the more peaceful for it these past few years, I have no doubt.

But that was a long time ago. I am different now and this is different and, most importantly, Eric may have been close but he was never a lover. Not for me. I didn't think through any of this, up there on the ledge. I was thinking of him and what he had asked for, not of her. But Eric is dead and what he wanted doesn't matter. Lee is alive and she matters a lot.

I turned and leant against the dry-processor, letting the warmth of it thaw the frost inside. My hands relaxed with the heat. I pulled Eric's last X-ray from the viewer and held it up between us so that we were both looking at it, Lee and I, so that our eyes met through the gaps in the spinal column. So that the question was there to be seen.

Dee looked at us both and nodded, once, before she left. The door swung shut behind her. The room was warm and the air smelled of developer and fixer. We could have been anywhere else in the hospital. Not all X-rays are of the dead.

'You don't have to do this,' I said, because one of us had to say something. 'We could call in someone else.'

'No. I want to do it.' She's almost a head shorter than I am but there are times when her eyes are on a level with mine. Professional eyes, inward turned, absorbed. Like they were at the start of the climb. If you didn't know her better, you might believe this was just another routine stiff to be put through the mill.

'You sure?'

'I'm sure.'

'Then I want to stay.'

'You haven't had the practice, Kells.' She isn't saying no, she's just warning. Layers on layers of warning. She may be right. But I may not be the only one who hasn't had practice enough for this. I'm not walking out now.

I reached round and slid the film back up on the viewer. It hung there, stark, simple, black and white, saying all of the things that no one was ready to say out loud. My hands felt their way back into the padded depths of my fleece, fingers wrapped tight over thumbs. For the heat.

'I'll cope.'

I followed her out of the dark room and back to the slab. Today is my day for following. On other days, it will be different.

A full post-mortem takes a lot longer than you might have been led to believe. It can take weeks before all of the lab reports come through but even the basic autopsy, the first dissection, is a long, slow and tedious process. Speed, you understand, is inversely proportional to detail and Lee has never been one for missing details. If you remember that she was a surgeon once and then imagine micro-vascular surgery performed on every organ system, every cavity, every orifice, every appendage, then you might have some idea of the process and how long it takes. The only difference is that, with the dead, there is no real need to stop the bleeding. And, of course, with the dead, all the bits end up tagged in bags on the floor.

She was right, of course, I hadn't had the practice. She, at least, had come close. She did Bridget for me and she was there for Malcolm and if neither of them were her lovers, they were close enough to be family. Dee hadn't had the practice either, but she wasn't as close to Eric as either of us so maybe she didn't have the need. Either way, she stayed for most of it, with the odd short break here and there to check on the ventilators in the ICU and a bypass in the cardiac ward that was slow in recovering. The second time she came back, she brought a plastic A4 folder stuffed with photocopies and laid it on the stool beside me.

'I was thinking, since you're staying, did you want to do something useful with the time?'

Not really. I want to sit here and watch Lee and work out how much more of this she can take before she cracks. She hasn't started on his face yet. He's still lying there with the grim rictus grin and the wide-open eyes. If she cracks for anything, it'll be for his face. About an hour or so yet, I would say. Time enough.

I opened the folder. The top paper had my name in the author list, somewhere in the middle of a string that started with Dr Deirdre Fitzpatrick and ended with Professor A. Drummond. I lifted it out and flicked through the contents. Four pages and then a half-page of references. Two weeks solid work. Last time I saw this, it was in rough-draft with a list of professional comments pinned to it that took another long weekend to sort out. I never really expected to see it in formal print. Twelve hours ago, the sight of this would have made my week.

'Happy?' There was concern in the music of her voice, as if it mattered that I be happy. I'm not used to that with Dee.

'Yes. Thank you. I didn't know you'd got it back—'

The sudden scream of a power saw knifed through us both. Mike, in gloves and goggles, cut down the sternum into the thorax. Lee reached in and lifted out a heart that, three days ago, was beating less than two yards from mine. It lay still in her hands, a red-brown egg of a thing, as cold and lifeless as the air around it. Her face was set in stone. Mike's was haggard beyond anything I've ever seen, old long before his time, his beak of a nose turning blue with the cold and the rest of it red with the things he was seeing and not saying.

Of the four of us, he's the only one showing any reasonable range of emotion. We can't all keep it up for long.

I slipped the papers back into the folder and handed it to Dee.

'Not now.'

'Grand.' She slid the folder on to the floor and sat down beside me. 'So long as you've read it by Monday.'

'Monday . . .?'

One eyebrow arced upwards towards the razor-cut edge of her hair. 'Monday,' she repeated. 'The day after tomorrow. You and me are defending this to the gathered sceptics of the West of Scotland Medical Association at two o'clock in the afternoon.' Her eyes flickered from grey to green and back again. Hard eyes, like her hair, so much harder than her voice. Not comfortable to be with. She leant forward and laid the paper once more on my lap. 'You hadn't forgotten?'

Oddly enough, I had.

Lee tested the lungs for buoyancy and found that there was air present in the alveoli at the time of death. So he didn't drown, but then we knew that. My fingers, holding the paper, were damp. In spite of the cold, they were damp.

The paper was glossy. A reprint of August's *Journal*. One of the sharp-edged, expensive copies they send to the senior author ahead of publication. I turned to the third page and looked at the diagrams. It took me close to three working days fighting with Photoshop to get those diagrams right.

There was warmth in the air behind me and Dee was there, looking over my shoulder. 'They've come out well,' she said.

'They have.' And there I was thinking I was wasting my time. 'I really didn't believe they'd accept it.'

'You'll learn faith in the end, if we work on it long enough — Oh, fuck it.' Her pager hummed. She lifted it from her belt and watched a message scroll in green across the screen. 'Would you believe it? Boy Wonder's found an appendix. Now doesn't that just make the night perfect . . .' She pulled a theatre hat from her pocket and jammed it on her head, softening, briefly, the effect of her crop, and smiled a surgeon-eating snarl. 'See you in the morning.'

'It's only just gone eleven, Dee.' Even the SHO can cut an appendix in less than forty minutes.

'I know. The child thinks he's on a roll. Wish me luck.'

'Luck.'

She left. What peace there had been in the room went with her.

I don't think of Dee Fitzpatrick as peaceful. She brings peace, unquestionably, to her patients, but then for Dee, the patients are the people and the medics are the idiots and that, largely, is what sets her apart from the rest of us. It's not a problem, but it makes for a different mind-set and it took me a while, after we started working together, to accommodate. Dee's not your usual medic. She's one of those women who found her vocation late in life and the extra ten years spent living in the real world has made all the difference. Even as a student she was different: the single adult in a class of post-adolescent children, all revelling in the discovery of sex, drugs and crossed fingers as a way of life. Some of them have never grown out of it. Dee, as far as I can tell, never grew into it – although, being Dee, if she had, I wouldn't necessarily know. She's deeply, obsessively private and she guards the details of her personal life with a dedicated passion. We have shared an office for the past two years, she and I, and I still couldn't tell you the names of her parents or her lovers or any of her homes before the flat she lives in now. I know the details of her professional career because they're printed in the register. I know bits of her running career because she took time off last year to run in the Three Peaks and came back to work with the news she'd come second. I know what she likes to eat, I know how she takes her coffee and I know, in explicit detail, what she thinks of her professional colleagues, me included, but beyond that, I know nothing. I used to think that as a therapist I could reach to the core of a person within the first few hours of meeting. With Dee Fitzpatrick I am discovering that this is not the case.

All that aside, she is the perfect clinician for a palliative care unit: a fully qualified anaesthetist with a sub-speciality of pain control in the chronically ill. There are not many of those about and even fewer prepared to learn the ropes of terminal care. For a profession that spends so much of its time with the dying, we know very little about what we can do to make the closing stages of life bearable rather than unbearable, to make death an experience to be embraced, rather than one to be denied even after the event. We are learning, but slowly, and with decades of wilful ignorance to be cleared before we can start from a decent baseline. For me, I am growing out of an early scepticism to see the Unit as something deeply worth while. For Dee, this is the vocation she has been looking for and where I might be prepared simply to sit at the bedside and hold a hand and talk and help to build the images that will manage the pain, Dee has the need for the wider world to know and to listen and to be made to understand. So we've spent the last eighteen months finding ways to measure the unmeasured, to quantify the unquantifiable and on Monday, we will present our first paper outlining preliminary work on the use of guided imagery to reduce the dose of analgesics in the terminal cancer patient. Some members of the audience will listen. A few may understand. If we're lucky, the rest won't take it apart. And it will all go more smoothly, no doubt, if I have some memory of what we are supposed to say.

So I did my best. I turned over the pages. I studied the diagrams. I tried to remember the patients by name because, that, in the end, is what matters: people and their pain. Or their relative lack of it. In the meantime, Lee finished the thorax. She went through the abdomen and found nothing. Starting on the skeleton, she measured the breaks and the angles of impact and the bruising on the limbs. The next time I looked up from the whirling diagrams, she was standing at the top of the slab with his head in her hands. The line between her eyes was a chiselled gorge. Her hair had matted again to her forehead and this time it had nothing to do with the salt spray of the sea. Still, she didn't weep.

39

Dee came back, kicking the door shut behind her. It was just gone one o'clock. She looked about as good as you'd expect after an extra hour in theatre. She looked at me and she looked at Lee and she said nothing. She pulled off her theatre cap and carefully, silently, she tied it in a knot and threw it into the clinical waste bin. The soft noise of its landing rang round the room. A very vocal gesture. Very little rattles Dee but the Boy Wonder probably comes closer than most. I leant over towards her. She may not have needed to talk but the silence needed words.

'How was it?' I asked.

'Slow.' She tore off her mask and it joined her cap in the bin. '"A good surgeon deserves a good anaesthetist. A bad surgeon needs one." *British Journal of Anaesthesia* editorial, nineteen hundred and something small.' She smiled, a dry, wry, self-deprecating smile. 'I don't think I've got what it takes to compensate for the Wünderkind throwing a late-night technical tantrum.'

'That bad?'

'Worse. The child thought he'd practise doing the whole thing through an incision you could barely get one finger through. Read it somewhere in an American journal. I expect they used a 'scope to go with it and forgot to mention it in the text. Or he didn't read that far.'

'He only looks at the pictures.' That from Lee, who can, apparently, draw a scalpel along a scalp line and still join in hospital gossip without losing the place. Mike, I think, held his breath.

Dee looked at her and nodded slowly. 'That figures,' she said. 'It doubles the surgery time at any rate. And he had to

40

open up to the normal length in the end anyway. I thought I might just mask him down with isoflurane and do the surgery myself next time.' Her voice carried more humour than her eyes.

'You just bring him to us. We'll do everything he needs.' That from Mike, who will do whatever it takes to keep the silence at bay now, because he, of all of us, knows just how much Lee can take.

Dee tilted her stool back and hooked her heels up on the edge of the slab. 'I think you'd find the theatre nurses killing each other in the crush to get down here and take over your job,' she said. The air moved in places where it had stopped before. Mike grinned for the first time since he'd wheeled the trolley off the roof. 'No problem,' he said. 'We've plenty room. We'll cut him into wee bits and they can have a slab each to play on for as long as they want . . .'

And so the atmosphere warmed, slowly. The air stayed frigid but the chill of it bit less deep in the lungs and the line between Lee's eyes softened with it. It's the standard medical response to death, and we do it consciously. If everything is reduced to impersonal nouns and the ritual dismemberment of the boy wonders in theatre, then the unbearable becomes that much more bearable. And tomorrow, which would otherwise be impossible, leans at least, towards the probable.

Chapter Three

Tomorrow is Monday and by then I will feel different. Today, it is Sunday. It was Sunday when I went to bed, it was Sunday still each time I woke up.

Early on, I heard Sandy drive into the yard. He called the colt across the paddock behind the pond and tethered him at the gate. Feed buckets rattled and the tap sang and the door to the tack room swung in the breeze as he fed and watered and polished his child. Some men polish their cars on a Sunday morning. Sandy Logan, horseman and yard manager, polishes his colt. It never lasts. By this evening, the lad will have run and rolled and kicked grass. The burnished copper will be matt with dust, the white socks streaked with green. If this is a good week, the star on his forehead might stay white beyond Wednesday. I sleep and dream of copper horses lined up along a cliff edge. They kick something off. I fall into endless water.

A car door closes down in the yard. Wee Jon calls the rest

of the ponies in from the paddocks. Eight of them: the full string for a Sunday. More cars. More people. A clattering of mounts and mounting. A babel of voices: German, Australian, English, a slurring of east-coast Scots. Wee Jon trying to make himself understood. He calls a command to move that the ponies know if no one else does. Horse feet crunch in tandem on the gravel. They head off into the sunrise for a half-day trek up round the loch. In the dream, the sun cracks open on the back edge of the ben. Eric steps out, Eric the clinician all done up in his white coat and his stethoscope. He calls me into a hospital ward where Nina is lying in a bed and explains to me that she is dying and that he has done all he can. He switches off the ventilator. My world ends.

The back door opens. Someone puts the kettle on the Rayburn. The dog takes the stairs in three strides and lands on the bed with the fourth. I roll over to give her room. Keep rolling. There's more space in the bed than there was. I hadn't realised I was alone. Nina has gone. She was never here. The world has ended.

I can't handle this. God, let me go now and never come back.

Air stirs around the bed. The room smells faintly of horse, of surgical scrub and disinfectant, of lemongrass and ginger. I am not alone.

'Kellen?'

She hasn't gone. She's there now, sitting at the end of the bed, caught in the small triangle of sunlight which is all that's left of the morning. She has wood-shavings in her hair: two or three fragments caught up in the wild chestnut tangles, another hooked on the short sleeve of her shirt. The wind lifts

the edge of the open curtain and the smell of surgical scrub is
stronger than the smell of horse or of her.

'Kells? Are you OK?'

I sat up in the bed.

'You've been in to work?'

An unnecessary question. One day she will manage to stay
away from that place for a full twenty-four hours. Just not yet.

She smiled and scooped the cat on to the bed, a wilful and
effective distraction. I moved over to give him space, ran my
fingers down the ratchet of his spine, scratched along the
old-cat fuzz of his coat. He rasped and dug his claws in the
pillow and pushed his head at the back of my hand. We played
games, old-cat games, the three of us. In time, I asked it again.

'So? Did you go to work?'

'Only for a wee while,' she said. 'Mo's away and Steff's got a
mare in the ward with a bad sinus. I gave her a hand to flush it
out.'

'I thought that's what the students were for.' A token
protest, out of habit.

'It's exams next week. They're all locked in the library.'

'No stamina.'

'No.'

There was a gap, a comfortable, comforting silence. Outside, a car engine cut off in the lane. I never noticed it arrive.
The silence settled closer like an old duvet. The dog slid off the
bed; her nails clattered loud on the wood of the stairs. The cat
followed, more slowly. Outside in the yard, two dogs and a
man joined in a frenzy of greeting. In the bedroom, still, there
was peace.

She doesn't push, Nina. She gives me the space to sort myself out when I need it. If I didn't love her for anything else, I would love her for that.

I stretched and rubbed the dreams from my eyes. I found all the muscles the climb had stretched, the bruises on both knees from the scramble for the ledge, and the hardening scabs on the backs of both hands. *He was a good climber, Eric. There are no scars on the backs of his hands.*

Nina sat on the edge of the bed, watching, appraising, waiting. Her eyes are walnut, a shade or two darker than her hair. Once, they were the only gateway to the hell inside. Now, they stay peaceful unless she's angry. There's no anger now, just a simple concern and the warmth of the morning.

I slid across the bed, reached for her hand, lifted it and kissed the palm. I ran my fingers, by habit, up the snake-line of the scar on her forearm. There was a time when she would never have let me touch that scar. A time, later than that, when I would have left the room to keep the scar, or the arm that bore it, safely remote. Other times and other places. Now, this close, the warm smell of her outweighs the rest: the smell of horse and of lemongrass, of home and of peace. I wrapped my fingers round the curve of her elbow and tugged her close – a reflex born of the night. Nina smiled her half-smile and her hand slid on past mine, smoothing across the arc of my ribs, moving round to knead the muscles of my spine, brushing across a graze I didn't know was there.

'Sorry.' The hand moved on. 'Did that hurt?'

'Mmm.' It did. It does. Did.

'Let me look.'

She pushed on one shoulder, turning me sideways. My legs

46

hung loose over the edge of the bed as they had over the cliff. I watched the shrinking triangle of sunlight play shadow patterns on the old wood of the floor beneath my feet and felt her fingers explore grazes and bruises and the places in between. Fingers of warm, drifting laughter moved forward round the lines of my ribs and on and up to places where there were no bruises. I tilted my head back and she slid in behind me. Her knees held me close, bony and angular, with a small crescent on the left one, just under my fingers, where a foaling mare kicked out and caught her with the edge of a shod hoof. She's all scars, this woman.

The breath of her voice fell on my shoulder, erratic and damp. 'You OK?'

'Kind of.' As close as I can get.

I felt the silk of her shirt brush across my shoulders as she opened it and then the skin-warmth of her mould to my back. My head rested in the crook of her neck. Her arms crossed around me, pulling me tighter. One hand reached down and lay flat across a bruise on my thigh. Damaged purple tissue splayed out beneath her fingers. We looked down at it together. 'You're pushing too hard, Kells.'

Good climbers don't have bruises.

I am not a good climber.

But I am still alive.

Eric grinned at me from the shadows on the floor. I shut my eyes and he grinned still. In the white cold of the autopsy room, Lee lifted his hair and peeled back the scalp line. I pressed my palms to my eyes and held them there. In the darkness and the flaring lights, there was no forgetting. The dregs of the night returned, together. I took a hard breath in.

The arms that held me relaxed and let me go.

I took my hands from my eyes. 'Is Lee still here?' I asked.

Nina slid back on the bed. My back felt cold with her gone. 'She's outside with the colt,' she said, and her voice was almost even. 'She took the dog for a walk earlier on. They came back about an hour ago.' She spun me back to face her. Need and concern gathered in her eyes, in her voice, in her hand, lying quiet in mine. Her other hand refastened the buttons on her shirt. I don't think she knew that she did it. For a while she said nothing, just watched. Then, eventually: 'It was bad, wasn't it?'

'It wasn't good. Has Lee not told you?'

'No. She said to ask you.'

And so you say nothing and hold me and wait until I'm ready. I do love you so very much.

I folded her hand in mine. Looped my fingers round hers and curled them up. There is no good way to do this.

'We made it most of the way up,' I said. 'There was a ledge two pitches down from the top. Eric was there.'

'Eric?' She smiled then, a smile to match the sunlight on the floor. She likes Eric. She owes him her life. It counts for a lot. 'What was he there for?'

'I don't know.' I shrugged. 'We weren't expecting him.'

If I don't say it aloud, I can go on pretending it's not real. You don't know and so for you, Eric is still alive. This time yesterday, we didn't know. He was dead, but we didn't know and so for us he was alive. We could stay like this for ever.

It will never last.

I took her hands again and held them, both of them, as in prayer. 'He was dead, Nina. He *is* dead. Eric is dead.' The man

48

who kept you living when otherwise you would have died, is dead. And then move on, because the magic of the morning has died and the walnut eyes have flashed to a black I had thought was gone for good. 'He fell. He must have fallen. God knows why he was even on the rock but he broke his neck when he hit the ledge. Lee and Mike did the autopsy last night. Mike will have faxed it all through to the police by now. There'll be an inquest. We'll have to go.'

Her body didn't move but her hands lay where I held them. Long, surgeon's fingers curled tight round mine, holding on as if I were the last hand-hold over a thousand-foot drop to nowhere. 'Why?' Her voice came from far away, thin and taut with the effort.

'Because it was us who found him.'

'No, Kellen. Why Eric? Why is he dead?'

'I don't know.' We have questions. We have no answers. 'He just is.'

We have questions.

I dressed and they didn't change.

Downstairs, the kitchen smelled of new-baked bread. A loaf lay warm by the Rayburn. Wee Jon's mother was the village baker. She retired years ago but it hasn't stopped her rising every morning with the dawn to heat the ovens. When she stops making bread it will be because she has joined Eric and the world will be the poorer for it. The world is poorer already.

I cut bread and slid an apple from the fruit bowl into one pocket, then another, for the colt. Next door in the study, Nina switched on the computer. I heard her drag the chair to the desk and pull a file from the shelf. More than most of us, she takes refuge in her work. She didn't weep. She hasn't wept. I have the breath of her still warm on my palms, but no tears. Later, when the work is over, there will be time for that, for both of us.

Through the window I could see the colt standing in the shade of the hawthorns at the gate to the pond field. Lee sat on the wall at the edge of the sunlight. Her jeans were rolled halfway to her calves, her spare T-shirt carried the folds of a day and a night in the rucksack; she hadn't bothered with shoes. Sometime, not long ago, she finished sorting her climbing rack, a completion ritual for a climb that is not yet complete. A neat array of ropes and slings and krabs lay on the stones beside her. Bright, electric colours overlaid the muted grey-green of the wall, too bright for the day. She sat still, curled in on herself like a leaf in autumn, knees pulled up to her chest, chin balanced on knees, eyes locked on a horizon that may yet yield answers. Seen in profile, even from this distance, her skin was too pale from lack of sleep, her eyes too dark, her soul too still, too much like the blank silence of the autopsy room. For all of my adult life, Lee Adams has been my touchstone for vitality. She is the fire that drives the rest of living. Last night in the mortuary, she withdrew to a place I couldn't reach. Blank rock took the place of laughter, of anger, of the sharing of pain. From here, it doesn't look as if the night has changed anything. I would like that not to last. More even than Eric, I would mourn the loss of Lee. I cut more bread and went out to join her.

The day was still, gathering heat. The air around the duck pond smelled wet and green. The pond was busy with insects.

Water boatmen skimmed the surface from patch to patch of algae. A new-hatched dragonfly unfurled on the dead stump by the wall, launching a bright, electric body into a world already cluttered with bright metallic paint. A spider spun on a single thread high above the water, a climber with no fear of falling. One flick of a finger and the rope would be gone. But there would still have been a rope. Even a spider doesn't climb without one. I walked round to the far side and pulled myself up on the wall. The colt stretched his neck out and snuffed shallow, exploratory huffs, rolling his eyes as if I might, just this once, be a phantom. I held out my fist, fingers up and let him tease them apart to find the squashed mess of bread hidden inside. The sharp ends of his whiskers tickled my palm as he ate. The air filled with his breath. I shared the rest of the slice with Lee and we ate in silence. I didn't come to talk. Normally, we don't have to. Just now, it would be good to have some words in the stillness.

She leant forward and fed the arc of her crust to the colt. 'How's Nina?' she asked.

'Alive. We'll talk about it more when she's had time to let it settle.' I broke the apple and shared it out. 'Good walk?'

'Ish. Your dog wants to hunt.'

'Nothing new. She'll get rabbits enough when they're not feeding young.'

'I know. I told her. She didn't believe me.' She held out the core of the apple for the colt. He teased her fingers open as he had teased mine, gently and with care for the damage he could do. Sandy may have spoiled him as a foal, but he put manners on him while he did it.

'Is the dog not around?' I asked.

'With MacDonald,' said Lee. She nodded out past the colt. I followed the line of her gaze. At the far end of it a flash of pale hair showed a dog lying flat in the grass. In time it rose and divided and became two: mother and daughter, a tan-in-white collie and her half-breed lurcher offspring, the original and the almost-clone. Between them a figure in shirt sleeves leant on a long-handled crook. Like that, grey-haired and bent, he looked every bit his age, a man not far off retirement. Then he stood up straight and whistled and swung the stick out sideways and both dogs dropped flat to the ground, a blatant display for the audience and impressive at that. He held them steady for a minute or so and then turned towards us. The dogs fell into step behind him and the three of them walked back up along the line of the wall. Now, you wouldn't put him much the far side of forty. He sheds years when he comes here simply because he lets go of his work as he drives in through the gate. This is his refuge, his escape from the world of law and order. Except on the two occasions when it has directly concerned me, I have never discussed police matters with Stewart MacDonald. It's not my business what he does with his nine to five, or his eight to twelve or twelve to six or whatever shift it is that he's working. But that doesn't mean that any one of us forgets what he is and what he does for a living.

'Did you speak to him?' I asked Lee.

'A little.'

'Has he seen the report?'

'I e-mailed him a copy home last night. He got it before he left this morning.'

'And?'

'And he's on duty again this afternoon. He'll come round with one of the lads and take statements when he's in a position to do it in an official capacity.'

That's a start. 'Did he say when?'

'He's due in at one. He'll be round just after that.'

'That doesn't leave much time to pick up your car.' We left the Saab at the top of the cliff when the helicopter came. Mike gave us a lift back to the farm. I can think of several good reasons to go back to that cliff, her car is simply the most obvious.

'Forget it. It's a Sunday morning. Loch Lomondside will be nose-to-tail caravans. Anything that's there will wait till tomorrow. There are things we need to look at here before we go back to the rock.' Lee picked a green krab from the wall beside her and tossed it high over our heads. It tumbled in the still air, spinning colour to the sky and back. She reached out and caught it as it fell towards the colt. A second joined it and then a third. They juddered in the morning air, not smoothly caught. She bit her lip, concentrating.

She is not as I thought she was. The new day has changed some things. There's a containment in the stillness now. Questions burn behind the stone of the walls. It's better than nothing. The krabs spun faster, more smoothly, a metal rainbow arcing over the water of the pond. I moved back along the wall to give her space.

'How did he get there, Kellen?' Her eyes were on the juggling. Her mind was on Eric. 'Did you see his bike at the cliff?'

'No.' She knows that. I didn't see it when we arrived, I didn't see it in the half-hour we spent waiting for the Rescue. Equally, I wasn't really looking. 'Did you?'

'No. But I didn't think of it till I woke up this morning.'

'Just because we didn't see it, doesn't mean it isn't there. He doesn't leave it out in the open any more than you do. We can look for it when we pick up your car.' Another good reason to go sooner rather than later.

'Maybe.' A fourth krab joined the others: the big pear-shaped loop that holds the belay. Two thousand kilos breaking strain. She chewed on her lip, narrowing her eyes against the morning sun. The rainbow faltered. She lost two of the smaller krabs. The pear-shape danced a brief, erratic dance with a pale gold partner and then the two of them thudded down on to the turf in a staccato duet. 'I think I should go back home first,' she said. 'His bike might be there. And his gear. We need to see if he took his gear. If he didn't, then we'll know he wasn't meaning to climb.'

I looked at her carefully. She reached out and tugged a stray hair from the colt's mane. She has never been any good at asking for help.

I slid down from the wall, feeling in my pocket for the keys to my car. 'You'll need a lift,' I said. 'I'll tell Nina.'

She caught my arm. 'You don't have to come. I could get a taxi.'

Right. That's not even worth the effort of an answer. 'What about the statements to MacDonald?' I asked. 'Are we going to be back here by one?'

'No need. They'll meet us at the flat. Unless I tell him now that we're not going.'

MacDonald was less than half a field away. I waved and he raised the stick in greeting.

'No. We'll go.'

54

The colt set off down the field to meet the dogs, head down, neck snaking, a parody of the stallion at war. I threw the half-core of my apple into the shade of the hawthorn where he could find it later. The krabs lay in the grass at my feet: pink, green, gold, all dull in the shadow of the wall. I scooped them up and dropped them back on top of the ropes. 'Come on, let's go. It won't get any easier with waiting.'

Lee's home is a ground floor flat on Park Terrace with panoramic views of Kelvingrove Park and the Art Gallery, tastefully furnished throughout in modern Scandinavian style. I know all of this because I read the estate agent's description before she ever moved in. Flats on Park Terrace don't come cheap even without the panoramic views and the sanded wood floors. The agency percentage on the sale was more than my annual salary and you could feel the saliva dribbling through the prose. They didn't, naturally, mention that the flat was on the market because the owner's wife had finally given up the battle to persuade him that women made better bed-mates than men, or specifically, that she made a better bed-mate than a twenty-eight-year-old bio-engineering post-grad working in the orthopaedics department at the Western. Anna Dalziel divorced her husband for adultery which was risible given her own track record but they had to have something for the paperwork and she didn't cite Andy in the correspondence which was, I gather, part of the deal. It was a remarkably peaceful separation under the circumstances, except for the flat. They'd have gouged each other's eyes out over the flat. Anna wanted her pound of flesh, or at the very least, the six figures she'd put into buying her half and then turning it into

Little Sweden in the middle of Glasgow. Eric wasn't that bothered about living in a Scandinavian transplant but he liked the view and he was quite attached to the fact that he could run through the grove to work without breathing in too much carbon monoxide on the way. He'd been there long enough to feel at home and he wasn't in a hurry to move out.

I remember sitting at the table on a Saturday afternoon in the November after Bridget died. Lee sat on one of the limed ash counters teasing the flat-faced blue and cream cat, Anna's last attempt to integrate into the British way of life. I was absorbed in the third page of the estate agent's drivel.

'Hey, people, is the master bedroom really seventeen by twenty-three feet?'

'It is.'

'Plus the walk-in wardrobe.'

'God. And underfloor heating?'

'Absolutely. She put it in last winter.'

'Essential in Sweden.'

'Allegedly.'

'Probably true. It's forty below in Sweden in the winter.'

'What does it get to here?'

'I think it clocked up minus five one day last February . . . Oh shit, here we go, children. Make way for the ravening hordes.'

The doorbell rang. Lee slid off the counter. The cat hissed and made for the cat flap in the basement. I moved the mugs to the sink and stuffed the papers in my back pocket.

'Bye, guys.' We followed the cat, all three of us sprinting down the stairs into the basement and out into the garden at the back. The cat vanished into the depths of a small, spreading acer. Lee led the way down the path to the gate. The combination on the padlock opened for the date of Eric's graduation and let us out into the higher parkland of the grove. We ran down the slope, across the bridge and back up towards the Art Gallery, slowing as we reached the path. The air was sharp and cold. The leaves on the path crunched like blown glass. We were both still drunk, I think, with the novelty of being alive. It felt good. Lee spun on her heels, out of breath, laughing. 'The Man?' she asked.

'Where else?'

Byres Road heaved with shoppers charging out their fifth shopping weekend before Christmas. Students fenced dope. Ex-students fenced copies of the *Big Issue*. The ones without degrees sat in the entrance to the Hillhead Underground and drank El Dorado from unconcealed bottles. A lad with fading scarlet hair and a complacent whippet spun a diablo for a crowd of kids, practising for the summer and the Edinburgh tourists. Lee chucked two bits of silver into his cap. They sparkled, angle-edged amongst the coppers.

'Why'd you do that?'

'Dog needs a feed.'

Ever the sucker for a complacent whippet.

The Man in the Moon sits round the back, out of the tourist gaze. We commandeered a table on the balcony and ordered water. I was still on water by orders of every doctor I knew except me. Lee has never been on anything else. The estate agency papers dug into my back as I sat down. I threw them on the table between us.

'Do you think she'll buy it?' I asked.

'Ms Advocate?' She shrugged. 'I doubt it. She was driving a Porsche.'

'Which means she won't buy it?'

'Which means she's got the money but not the taste, so, no, she probably won't buy it.'

The water arrived. I buy this for something to do, not because I enjoy the experience. I toyed with the ice cubes and turned back to the page I'd been reading. 'It has three bedrooms,' I said.

'I know.'

'Where's the third?'

'Downstairs. In the basement. Second on the left after the shower room.'

The second shower room. 'So why's it got an *en suite* shower?'

'All bedrooms in Sweden have facilities *en suite*. Allegedly.'

'Has anyone ever actually checked this?'

'No. But it was Anna's money. She's entitled to her own fantasy.'

Clearly. Up to and including marrying Eric. A triumph of hope over all the available evidence.

We sat in peace for a while. Lee watched the crowd, out of habit. I read through the details of Eric's home, matching the hyperbole to the reality of what I had seen. They had missed the bits that really mattered, the things that set it apart from the Little Sweden of the superstores and catalogues, all blond wood and chrome and everything still Hampstead underneath. It's the small things that make the difference. Things like the taps that take you ten minutes to figure out how they work but are so much more effective than anything I've got at home; like a shower room with a shower head fitted beside the loo to function as a self-operated bidet and a floor that slopes in two planes so that water spilled anywhere in the room runs down to a spiralling drain in the corner. And the duvet covers. Remarkable things, Scandinavian duvet covers. I helped her make a bed up once and found the duvet covers had hand holes in the blind end so you could reach through and pull the quilt straight in. Sheer genius. Very un-British. Sadly, they went straight back to Uppsala when she moved back home.

I turned the last page over and back to the beginning and sat staring at the interior picture of the living room, Anna's show-piece in white wood and hessian with an incredible, intricate bronze-in-cream Danish rug laid exactly one third of the distance from the fireplace to the far wall. It's the kind of room where all the cushions are set at symmetrical angles and the magazines are bought for their front covers alone. That room apart, it's not a bad place to live. If I had to live in the city again, I'd give quite a lot to live there.

'You can see why he doesn't want to move,' I said.

'Mmm.' She was staring over the balcony, flexing her fingers, one at a time. She did that a lot, that winter.

'Why doesn't Andy buy her out?'

'C'mon, Kells, the lad's a post-grad. He's on eight grand a year. That wouldn't pay the estate agents, never mind the bank.'

True enough. 'How about you?'

'Not unless I won the lottery.'

'Or if you sold Otago Street.' She bought half the building we had lived in as students just after I moved out. I never asked where she got the money although I would put a bet on Mad Mhaire Culloch as the likely source. It didn't cost that much. The house price balloon hadn't taken off in those days.

By the time Eric was selling up, prices were heading for escape velocity and Otago Street was somewhere up there in stationary orbit.

'Have you had it valued recently?' I asked.

'I haven't, no.' She looked at me, her head on one side, considering. 'Maybe I should.'

'Would you cope sharing with Eric?'

'If anybody.'

'Eric *and* Andy?'

'It's a big place.' She smiled, flexed all her fingers in one go. 'I expect we'd manage.'

It took four days to find a buyer for the tenement in Otago Street and another three to sort the contracts with Anna. Two weeks after that, Lee moved in and Andy was invited to follow. He dithered and delayed, moved half of his stuff into the basement bedroom and then didn't quite follow through. Lee and Eric stacked his books on the bed out of the way and fixed some bolt-on climbing holds on to the wall, next to the *en suite* shower. Andy finished his Ph.D. and moved, books and all, to a new job at MIT in time for Easter. Lee and Eric took out the shower and set up an angled bend-crete wall in the corner with a simulated jamming crack and a thirty degree overhang near the top. Not long after that, they took out Anna's oatmeal carpet and put in wall-to-wall crash mats instead. At Hogmanay the next year, they made a joint resolution that no lover on either side should stay for more than three consecutive nights. They both keep their resolutions.

We let ourselves in the front door. The air in the hallway hung warm and still, mid-day, mid-summer heavy. Lee hit a switch on the wall and the air conditioning kicked in: a soft flutter of electric fans in the background. A pile of medical junk mail littered the floor. His and hers, two matching sets. Lee pulled an airmail envelope from the heap and ripped it open with her index finger. I sorted the rest, checking the dates on the postmarks as I went. 'When did you leave on Friday morning?'

'Hmm?' She didn't look up. 'Normal time. Six. Thereabouts.'

'Before the post arrived?'

'Yup.'

'So if anything came in for you while Eric was here, where would he put it?'

'On the table in the kitchen.'

'I'll take a look.'

'If you like . . .' She was miles away. Nepal, I would say, at a guess. She folded the letter across and across and shoved it into a back pocket. 'Kells . . . do you want to check downstairs? I ought to feed the cat. I'll follow you down in a minute or two.'

'You sure?' Ten minutes ago, nothing mattered but finding his bike.

'I'm sure.' The line was back between her eyes, short and deep, as it was last night in the morgue. A singular index of stress.

The stairs to the basement go down from one corner of the kitchen. It's dark down there, an optical contrast to the wide windows and well-placed lights of the rest. I made my way down into the gloom, felt my way into the corridor, shoved open the sliding door on my right and hit a switch. The workshop flared into life. This place, of all the rooms in the house, was never Anna's. Eric set it up the year they first moved in and Lee joined him later, by invitation. You can count the Christmases they've been here by the tool sets ranged around the bench. A set of chisels glimmered on the far wall; a lathe stood underneath them, bolted on to the four-inch oak of the bench; a butane cylinder sat in the corner with a rack of nozzles off to one side. An arc-welder huddled squat in the shadows, complete with gloves and mask. Eric's plumbing kit cluttered the doorway, thrown in after an emergency change of washers. Just beyond it, a motorbike sat shrouded under a dust sheet. I stepped over the tool kit and lifted the edge to look. It was a Ducati, glossy and black and six inches shorter than any bike Eric ever rode. Lee Adams is five foot one. Her bike is suitably small. She came up behind me. I lifted the sheet higher.

'Yours?'

'Mine.'

A second dust sheet hung draped over a vice on the bench. There was no second bike. 'Would he leave it anywhere else? Out in the back garden, maybe?'

'It would invalidate the insurance if he did.'

'We ought to look, all the same.'

'If you like.' She was already in the corridor. I took a quick look into the shower and followed her into the climbing room, the place that was once Anna's third bedroom and is now a verrucose cave. Artificial climbing holds in grey-green plastic stud every flat surface like malformed stalactites. Long, thin, flat ones mimic cliff edges. Smaller, rounder ones with cut-away centres act as limestone finger-holds. The smallest and most rounded function as pebbles although they're never as hard to pull up on as the real thing. All of them come off and go on again with a twist or two of an allen key. The pattern of the routes changes with the months and the seasons but at any point in time and from any point on the perimeter, Lee and Eric can climb up the wall, across the ceiling and down the other side without ever touching the floor. At my best, when I'm feeling fit, I can go all the way round the walls. On the day I can climb to the top of the bend-crete overhang without falling off, I will take off my boots and retire.

Lee stopped just inside the door and started sorting through the ropes and the racks, the crampons and the ice-axes and the spare kit bags that hung from pegs along the wall. I sat down on a mat in one corner and watched her. A long, smooth hold pushed into the small of my back. A fan flickered on the opposite wall, chopping daylight into bite-sized portions. A haze of climbing chalk filtered upwards, pulled on visible currents of air, swirling in a soup of ancient sweat and perishing rubber. With my eyes closed, I can imagine this place on a Thursday evening in the winter: a place to escape to after work, away from the dreich December rain. Eric bolting a new route on the wall beside the door. Lee falling from the overhang because her fingers still can't quite take the weight of a one-handed pull-up. Dee, the learner, sliding off a simple rounded hold and lying splayed out on the crash mats, cursing and laughing in a string of breathless Irish oaths. Sarah pushing all the limits to get across the roof in one go. Sarah who is now in Nepal and who writes letters to Lee that bring back the line between her eyes. I will hear about that. Later, when the line is gone.

'He's taken his kit.' Her voice came round twice with the echo of the room, hard and hollow.

'Has he? What's gone?'

'Two of the 9-mm ropes. His belt. His rack. All of the spare friends.'

I picked at a scab on the back of my hand. That's pretty much what we had. 'Could he fit that lot on the bike?'

'Easily.'

'So we better find where it is then, hadn't we?'

And then we can find out if he was carrying it with him. And after that we can try to work out why the hell he wasn't using any of it when he fell.

MacDonald arrived with his sergeant just after one. We were still in the climbing room, kneeling on the mats, making an ordered list of what was missing, trying to remember exactly how much of it was in Lee's car and how much could have gone with Eric. They waited in the kitchen while we finished the inventory and then they split us into separate rooms for the statements: Lee and the sergeant – a brittle, nicotine-stained red-head in his late thirties – stayed in the kitchen. I followed MacDonald through to Anna's pristine hell of a living room.

'This is a full list of what's missing, aye?' He folded the sheet of paper into the back page of his notes.

'Pretty much.' I sat on the floor with my back to the armchair. He perched uncomfortably on the edge of the cream leather sofa. I found an old copy of the *BMJ* on the floor beside the chair and slid it across the floor for a coffee mat. Even now, you wouldn't want to risk a coffee ring on the polished wood of the table.

I leant back against the chair, hugging my mug to my chest. It's a long time since I've had a formal conversation with this man, longer still since he took notes of what we said. I looked down at the floor and drew patterns on the carpet with my finger. 'If I was you,' I said, 'I'd concentrate on finding his bike first. It's a silver-green BMW. Lee will have the model and the registration number. If it's anywhere, it'll be in the woods at the top of Ardpatrick Point. At least then we'll know if he was alive when he got there.'

'Fair enough.' I heard the pen scrawl across the book. 'You think he might have been dead before he ever reached the cliff?'

'I don't know. It has to be a possibility. Just because you find a body at the bottom of a wall, doesn't necessarily mean it was pushed from the top. It's more likely than him climbing up and falling off on his own.'

'Uhuh?' He wrote that down, too, or an approximation of it. 'Dr Adams has estimated you'd need a height of fall of around seventy-five feet to sustain the injuries she found at autopsy. Any more and the impact injuries would have been greater, any less and he might not have died.' He flipped back a page in his notebook. 'According to the Rescue, the height of the cliff above the point where the body was found is one hundred and twenty-five feet.' He looked up, caught my eye and held it. 'If it makes you feel any better, I think we can say that he definitely wasn't pushed from the top.'

I'm not sure if that makes me feel better at all. I looked across at the notebook balanced on his knee. There was a lot more written where that came from. I nodded, once. 'Go on.'

'If you say so.' He shrugged, short and heavy. 'I'm sorry, you're not going to like this. There is no evidence whatsoever of him having been moved after he died. That kind of thing shows up at post-mortem. It's very difficult to disguise.'

'So then he died where he fell.'

'He did. And he fell roughly half the height of the cliff at that point.' He moved the coffee out of the way and leant forward, his hands clasped together in front of his knees. The hands were red, raw and over-scrubbed from a morning's work in the fields. His voice was soft, unsettlingly so. 'Kellen, did Eric know you and Lee were going to climb that cliff yesterday?'

'Of course. Everyone knew.'

'And how did he feel about it? I mean' – he straightened up – 'was he sore that it was you going with Lee and not him? They normally climbed together did they not?'

'Mostly, yes. She didn't think it was enough of a challenge for him.' I feel nervous now, just because of the way he's speaking. 'What are you trying to say?'

'I don't know. I'm just wondering if maybe he had something to prove.' The notebook flipped shut and he dropped it in a pocket. 'We have a time of death of twenty-four hours before you found him, give or take three either way, so we'll say he fell sometime on Friday afternoon or early evening. That's twelve hours before you two got there to start your climb up from the sea.' He chewed the corner of his thumb and wasn't keen to meet my eye. 'It seems an awful coincidence, that's all. You have a lump of rock no one's ever been on before and suddenly there's him climbing the top part less than a day before you two make a stab at the bottom. I'm wondering if perhaps he was making a point?'

' "Anything you can do I can do better?" '

'More or less, yes.'

'You never met Eric, did you?'

'Not socially. Should I have done?'

'Probably. If you had, you wouldn't be saying that.'

'He wasn't the kind to fall off a rock?'

'He wasn't the kind to climb up a rock of any kind without someone else standing at the bottom with a good grip on the ropes. If you said it of Lee, I might believe you. She might give it a go if she felt she had something to prove – to herself if not the rest of the world. But not Eric. He didn't take risks.'

'He's still dead, Kellen.'

'Clearly.' I stood up and led the way out of the room. 'And we need to find out how it happened and why. But mindless stupidity isn't the answer.'

'They think he was climbing alone and fell off.' I was back in the kitchen, sitting on a counter nursing a fresh cup of coffee and the beginnings of a headache.

'I know.' Lee shrugged and opened the windows. Fresh air filtered in, clearing the stale tobacco. The cat came out of hiding and sat on the table, purring his flat-faced purr. 'They have no reason to think otherwise.' She filled a jug and began watering the plants along the window ledge. She's never been into plants, particularly. I suppose this is as good a time as any to change that. 'With the best will in the world, they can only run on the evidence. MacDonald's no fool. He'll keep looking till he finds something. Then he'll listen.'

'You think there's something to find?'

'I'm an optimist.' She flexed the fingers of her spare hand. 'There has to be something.'

'Right.' I would like to think I could believe that. He

deserves answers, Eric. He would do no less for either of us.

I finished the coffee. It did nothing to fill in the hollow space growing under my ribs. I was exhausted, sucked dry by the outflowing tides of adrenalin. I don't think I was alone.

We were quiet for a while. I searched through the cupboard at my back and found some Ponstan. Lee filled her jug again and knelt by the great clay pot holding Eric's avocado plant. *Her* avocado plant. Hers, along with the flat and everything in it. That will take some getting used to.

She slid her hand in her back pocket and brought it out again, empty.

'I had a letter from Sarah,' she said.

'Uhuh?' She had her back to me but if I had to bet, I'd say the line was back between her eyes. 'Is she OK?'

'No. She's got dysentery. She ran out of iodine tablets and now she's on a drip in the central hospital in Kathmandu.'

'Oh. Shit.'

'Don't, Kells. I'm not in the mood for it.'

'I wasn't . . . I'm sorry.' I am a medic. She is a medic. Sarah is a medic. All three of us know the benefits of intravenous fluids. We also know the risks of infected needles. I might trust the Western not to contaminate my bloodstream. I would have to be very, very desperate to trust a hospital in Kathmandu. 'Is there anything we can do?'

'No.' The avocado had more water than it needed for a month. She emptied the rest down the sink and turned the jug upside down on the rack, then dried her hands on a tea-towel and threw it on to the back of a chair. The cat looked up at her face and left. Lee sat down on the floor with her back to the wall and pulled her knees up to her chest. It's how she sits when she's hassled. She looked up at me. The line was there.

'When did she write it?' I asked. There's a logic, always, to the way she thinks.

'It's dated the twenty-eighth of May. Postmarked on the thirtieth.'

Three weeks. 'So by now she's better or she's . . .'

'. . . past ever getting better. I know.'

'She'll call when she can.'

'I know.'

'You're sure she hasn't tried already?'

'I'm sure.'

'So give it time, huh?'

'What else can I do?'

She didn't call. Not that afternoon nor that evening. There was no real reason why she should have called when she hadn't the day before or the one before that but we waited and we watched the phone because now we knew and before we didn't. In theory, we could have put in the six-hour round-trip to Knapdale and gone looking for Eric's bike but the momentum had gone out of that one. We didn't talk about it, just neither of us brought it up. Lee fired up her computer and spent the afternoon sending e-mails to the people she thought needed to know about Eric. I sat in the kitchen reading Dee's folder of papers and data and trying hard to remember the names and the pain scores and the treatments that, a week ago, were somewhere up there on the list of priorities. Standing on a platform addressing two hundred sceptical colleagues is a fair way to bring on the adrenalin rush, it's just hard to get wound up about it when there's been a death in the family.

At eight, I gave up and put in an hour on the climbing wall. Every muscle I've ever climbed with screamed for the first thirty minutes and then relaxed and eased into work. At nine, I wandered into Lee's room with a fresh mug of tea and found her asleep across the keyboard. At ten, with her safely in bed, I called Nina and told her I was on the way home and found that Dee had been round with a pile of last-minute data and a promise to come back to pick me up at seven o'clock the next morning so we could go over the presentation one last time before the real thing. On the way home, I stopped at the top of the lane and watched the fine silver of the new moon setting in the wake of the sun. I think the pre-talk adrenalin might have kicked in somewhere around then but I was too tired to take any notice.

Chapter Four

෨

I picked a stone from the beach. Round and flat, just big enough for the curve of finger and thumb. The trick to chuckie stones is the flick of the wrist. I remember my grandfather showing me, on another beach on the opposite shore of this loch. I flicked and the stone spun, bouncing as it hit the ruffled surface of the water. Three of us stood and counted until it sank.

'Five. Not bad.' Dee Fitzpatrick had her own stone and her own theories of skimming. She knelt down beside the child. 'Your turn now,' she said.

He was four, if that. Just old enough to understand the theory of competition, not yet old enough to compete. He wrapped his small child fingers around the pebble she had picked for him and threw it, overarm, at the water. It hit the surface three feet away and sank. 'One,' said Dee gravely. 'That's not bad either.' The child stared at the spot where the stone had been. Small spumes of white foam crested the wavelets for a moment and then vanished. His lips quivered. I was six when my stone did that. My grandfather told me parables of physics and falling. A diversion into Newton's universe, full of apples and inevitability. I don't remember if I cried. The child was close. He pushed a small, fat hand through damp straggles of mouse-blond hair. His chin wobbled. 'Pick another stone,' offered Dee. 'I didn't pick a good one. It needs to be round. And very flat.' Children change so fast. The pout dissolved. All he needed was a reason not to have lost. The game changed to a search for the ultimate chuckie stone.

I sat on the rock and listened to the loch turning over the pebbles on the beach. Behind me, the whitewashed bulk of the Ben Lomond Lodge hotel sat quiet. Somewhere inside, two hundred delegates of the West of Scotland Medical Association voted new members on to their committees. The few who had sent their apologies ordered short drinks in the bar and kept their conversation quiet. A moorhen muttered low noises, hussling a string of dark-fluffed chicks along the side of the loch. Out across the water, near the far shore, small boats raced for a buoy, a string of white kites tacking into the wind. A container lorry winding silently along the A82 vanished behind the trees and reappeared again as the road snaked up the line of the loch. When I was a child, the journey up Loch Lomondside was a nightmare, something we did only in the wee small hours of the morning when the traffic was low and the queues for the passing places could be expected to be short. Now you can cruise up to Inverarnan for lunch at the Stagger Inn and be back in time for tea.

The child found a driftwood log and sat on his haunches

right at the water's edge, floating it out into the water, waiting for the wind to blow it back. Dee settled back on the pebbles above the water-line and let him play. She looked up and caught me looking back.

'OK?' she asked.

'Not bad. It went better than I thought. They didn't eat us.'

'Sure, and some of them listened well enough to ask intelligent questions.' She was relaxed and very Irish. 'And we had better slides than the rest.'

'Thank you.' Amazing what you can do with an afternoon on Powerpoint. 'Did you think Sean McLaren's lot were on beta blockers?'

She laughed and tossed a new pebble to the child. He caught it with both hands and a body block. 'I know Joey Duncan was, I wrote him the prescription. The rest were just stoned.'

'You wrote them the prescription for that too?'

'Hardly . . . I met round the back of the —' Feet scuffed on the pebbles. A shadow slid across the rock. Dee turned, shading her eyes and then stood up, holding out her hand. 'Professor . . . the wee lad's fine. Except I think he might have got his feet wet.'

The child had inched into the shallows, still crouched on his haunches, absorbed with his boat. His feet were quite definitely wet.

'If that's all he gets wet, his mother will be delighted.' Professor Randolph Duncan, FRCS, dropped his tweed jacket on the pebbles beside the rock and lowered himself down on to it with the care of arthritic age. He looked up at me. 'May I?'

'Be my guest.'

He leant his back against the rock and looped his long surgeon's fingers behind his head. 'Sorry about that,' he said, 'One of those things one discusses with the patients as a consequence of ageing. Tedious beyond belief to find it happening to oneself. Difficult to explain to the lad. I'm most grateful for the impromptu childcare.'

'You're welcome.' I feel slightly surreal. 'It was Dee did the caring.'

He grunted a non-committal grunt, the verbal equivalent of a shrug, and turned slightly to look at me. His eyes were a watered brown, the whites yellowing with age. There was the beginning of something that looked like a cataract clouding his left lens. His hair was close to white. 'You should be at the meeting,' he said. If you heard him right, you could think it was a question.

'I'm not into politics.'

He grunted again, a different tone. I have heard that grunt too often in my past. It makes the hair stand on the back of my neck. 'You should,' he said, and it wasn't a question. 'They need more people like you.'

He doesn't know who I am. Not a clue. Dee stuck a twig upright in the log, a mast for a non-existent sail. Today is a day for fantasy. 'Why?' I asked.

'The profession's changing. Needs new perspectives. You've been away and you've chosen to come back. Gives you a chance to look at things from both sides of the fence. You should be sharing what you see.'

So he does know who I am. 'Maybe next year,' I said.

'Ever the one for procrastination.' He closed his eyes and

sank back against the rock, settling again. The quiet returned. I sat and watched the moorhen bob beneath the surface for weed. The water rippled where she used to be. Her chicks huddled at the edge, peeping. Across the loch, the lead dinghy passed through the paired buoys marking the winning line. The old man let the sun warm the age-marked paper of his skin. He has mellowed with age. And I have been alive long enough not to crumble at implicit criticism. Twenty years ago, both of these were different.

Twenty years ago, Randolph Duncan was a consultant surgeon and the Dean of the medical faculty when I was a medical student. His ward rounds were one of the most uniquely unpleasant experiences of my student career. The only good thing that could be said about them was that they didn't happen often. He taught abdominal surgery by the Inquisition technique long after the time when the educational psychologists proved that negative reinforcement is a spectacularly bad way to learn. In our year, there were folk who would pay a week's rent to bribe their way off his theatre list. Lee took most of the offers, if not the money, but then Lee would have walked through hell and back if that's what it took to get her surgery boards. You'll have noticed that she's not a surgeon now. Randolph Duncan is part of the reason for that. Quite a large part. It was fortunate, in many ways, that she chose not to come to the conference.

The child became aware, suddenly, of his new audience. He dragged the log up the beach, passing Dee on the way and demanded help with the relaunch. His grandfather stood up much more slowly than he had sat down. He scuffed pebbles as he walked across the beach and he stooped as he stood at the water's edge watching over the child and the log. If he found more than frustration in the infirmity of age, he bore it well. It occurred to me then that perhaps he was not the man we all thought. The child had no fear of him, certainly. Between them, they sent the log on an epic voyage.

Dee stepped out of their way and came to sit beside me on the rock. We watched the captain rescue his ship from certain disaster on the shoals. He flashed a grin at Dee. She waved encouragement.

'You're good with him,' I said. 'I wouldn't have thought it of you.'

'You wouldn't, would you?' She laughed and picked another pebble from the beach. 'I ran a playgroup for a while. In my previous life.'

'You had kids?' There is so much about this woman's past I don't know.

'No. We were going to. I thought I maybe should get the experience, just in case I didn't like it.'

'And did it put you off for life?'

'Not at all, I loved it. We were all set to go ahead when Beth died. Single motherhood didn't have quite the same appeal.' The stone was flat and slightly oval. She spun it, left-handed, across the surface of the water, well away from the child and his grandfather. It bounced six times before it sank. 'I took up medicine instead,' she said. 'It's all much the same in the end.' It came out easily and lightly. She was looking at the water. I was looking for a new chuckie stone. I pay so little attention to the things that are really important.

I never found my new stone. We had barely finished talking when all hell broke loose behind us. Inside the main conference room of the Ben Lomond Lodge, the AGM passed its final resolution of the day and two hundred medical professionals, all used to giving orders and having them obeyed, tried simultaneously to establish precedence at the bar. The afternoon melted into chaos. The noise was unreal. The child looked up at the sound of it, then looked again, beaming. We turned, Dee and I, to see Jessica Duncan fight her way through the scrum that had gathered in the hotel doorway and run across the lawn towards us as fast as dress heels and an infant on one hip would allow.

She arrived out of breath and kissed her father-in-law lightly on one cheek. 'Dad . . . Dee . . . Kellen . . . I'm sorry . . . hadn't expected the sodding thing . . . to go on this long.' She stood for a moment with her free hand to her chest, breathing heavily. No one expects to be fit seven months after childbirth. Not many of them expect to be back at the cutting edge of their career, either. She's an impressive woman, Jessica Duncan. Her paper on paediatric analgesia was one of the better ones of the morning and she presented it, clearly, without the benefit of drugs. I didn't find out until later that she had two children in the crèche on top of the other, older, who was waiting at home. Anyone who can hold the attention of an entire medical audience for half an hour in between nappy changes has my unqualified respect.

She pulled herself together and turned round, scanning the bar. 'Has anyone seen . . .? Oh, Daniel, *no* . . .'

The boat had caught a small current and was off on a new adventure. The child was in water up to his knees and wading further. He looked over his shoulder and grinned his father's grin. The shoreline gives way very fast on the east side of Loch Lomond. Dee was first to the water's edge, mother and grandfather not far behind.

The child grabbed his boat, turned and sat down. The water came up to his chest. 'Daddy,' he said. It had the tone of a demand.

You'll be lucky, kiddo. Joey Duncan was not one of those who sent his apologies to the meeting but he was a long way past sober none the less. It would have been surprising, frankly, not to have found Joey Duncan at least half-cut at an official occasion, but on that day, of all days, he had at least a reason for topping up. When we all signed our names in the register at nine o'clock this morning, our senior surgeon was plain old Mr J. Duncan, orthopaedic consultant to the masses. Then, at lunchtime, a small bird flitted past from the top table with news of the interview results and Joey became, in the space between courses, Professor J. Duncan, the consummate heir to his father's throne. He started celebrating round about then, a steady consumption of alcohol on top of whatever beta blockers he'd taken to help the morning's presentation flow smoothly. The chances of levering him out of the bar before dinner were close to nil and falling.

'No, Daniel, Daddy's got to . . .' This is motherhood, explaining the duties of professional care to a child. Daddy's got to what? Sober up? Give the after-dinner speech? Present the prize for the best paper of the meeting? All of the above. Does any of that matter to a child in water?

'No he hasn't. Never fear. Daddy's here.' And he was. The new President of the Association, fresh from claiming his chain of office, was there. With his jacket slung over one shoulder and his shirt sleeves rolled up and his Royal College of Surgeons tie leaking loosely from one pocket and a full glass in his free hand, Joey Duncan was there. Big, broad Joey with his thinning mouse-blond hair and the big boy's grin that keeps his patients from noticing the alcohol. And they don't. I really believe they don't. They trust him with their bodies, which is what surgery is all about, and they wouldn't do that if they had the slightest idea how much damage his liver took between Friday night and Monday morning, or, indeed, any average evening of the week. But they love him, his patients, every one. As do his residents, his nurses, his students. In that respect at least, Joey Duncan is almost entirely unlike his father; the first universally popular Professor the surgery department's had for years.

At least he was.

It didn't last for long.

It was eight o'clock when the department's new appointee rolled up his trouser legs and waded in to fish his son and heir from the water of the loch. Somewhere after ten, he stood up, toasted the monarch, the coming Republic and the Association in terms that would have had him struck off the register for life if they'd ever made it to print. He presented his wife, in the face of some serious heckling, with the prize for the best paper of the conference and then he launched into the kind of skin-stripping, eye-watering character assassinations for which he has been famous since he organised our first-year student revue. By eleven, those of us with weak livers left to go to our rooms and watch the ceilings revolve. Joey Duncan stayed on in the bar, moved up a gear and kept the

Chronic Cirrhosis Club entertained for the rest of the evening and on into the early hours of the following morning. It was light enough to read the labels on the bottle by the time he pocketed the remains of the Lagavulin and headed up for his room. At six, one of the maids spotted him lying in an alcove overlooking the loch, reclining with his head on one of the Ben Lomond's thick pile cushions, mouth open, eyes shut, the faint smell of vomit clogging the air. The lass says she thinks the doctor was breathing when she passed but she didn't check for a pulse. Chambermaids don't do pulses. It was Jessica Duncan, called eventually from her room to minister to her comatose husband, who felt for the pulse and then called, still un-panicked, for a stethoscope. The news of what she found filtered down, grey and quiet, through the hang-overs of the morning to the dining room where Dee was eating breakfast and I was taking water to rinse down the analgesics. Short snatches of it passed unnoticed through the throbbing heat of my skull.

'. . . Daft bugger . . .'

'. . . thought he knew how to hold his drink . . .?'

'. . . forget to roll over. First rule of good drinking, always roll over . . .'

'. . . fast though, very fast . . .'

And then finally, in the way of medics who have never quite learned how to pass on the fact of bereavement, Frazer Buchanan, consultant nephrologist, leant over our table, waved his poached eggs and bacon dangerously close to my nose and said, 'Looks like the Association's going to have to elect a new president, people. Joey Duncan's just tied his last knot.'

★ ★ ★

'Bad head?'

'Don't ask.'

'We've got some Ponstan in the cupboard.'

'I've had as much as my ulcers can stand.'

'I/v drip?'

'Fuck off, Adams. I don't need your sanctimonious pre-scribing.'

'Sorry.' She grinned, a brief spark in the chill of the room, and held out a gloved hand. 'Pass the suction, can you?'

I passed the suction. She moved round to the head and tilted back the chin. 'But was the dinner good?' she asked.

'As much of it as I remember. The salmon was reasonable.'

'Difficult to mess with salmon.'

'True.' Difficult to mess with brandy either but I don't particularly want to think about that at the moment. 'Joey was good.'

'He always is. It goes in direct proportion to his blood alcohol level. I'll be able to tell you exactly how good in about twenty minutes. Less if Mike gets his act together.'

'Isn't it a tad academic?'

'Maybe – can you hit the switch – but we'll need it for the report.'

I hit the switch over the suction pipe on the wall. Lee pulled up her face mask against the splash-back and angled the tip of the suction catheter into Joey Duncan's open mouth. The mortuary filled with a soft slurping gurgle as of soup through a straw and the stomach-turning stink of stale vomit surged up from the slab and hit the back of my throat. I sat down, suddenly. Lucky I've nothing left to throw up, really. Maybe

81

it's fate. I will always empty my guts before I enter a mortuary, it saves the risk of despoiling their sinks.

Lee leant over and directed the tip of the suction catheter down the back of the throat, almost the same kind of movement Dee makes when she's sucking saliva out of her patients after anaesthesia so they don't drown in their own juices when she pulls out the tube. For Joey, it came eight hours too late. He lay cold on the slab in the same way Eric lay cold on the slab except that where Eric was climbing fit, Joey spent his life hunting down brilliant, inspired after-dinner speeches in the bottom of the brandy bottle and his body is a testament to his success: not obese, but bigger all round than it should have been. His liver will sit in a jar in anatomy, preserved for posterity as a warning to other rising stars of the staff–student revue.

Pieces of part-digested salmon clogged the catheter. Lee nodded and I flipped the switch off and back on again. The sucker cleared and sucked and sucked again in rhythmic, pulsing waves until there was nothing more to suck. I switched it off. Lee sealed the jar and wrote the time and date on the label. The smell subsided, or possibly I simply became less sensitive. The Ponstan finally working, perhaps. I thought of tablets and remembered something of the time before the brandy.

'He was on propanolol,' I said, 'did you know?'

'No. Who told you that?'

'Dee. She wrote him the prescription.'

'Oops.' Lee turned and stashed the suction jar on the bench behind her, lining it up neatly with the bags that held Joey's clothes, his watch and his rings. 'Shouldn't be any problem,' she said, turning back. 'The only interaction's an additive effect on impotence. From incapable to totally incapable. It's hardly lethal.'

'Lucky Jessica.'

'He wasn't drinking any less when she married him.'

'True.'

She changed gloves, picked up a camera and took three photographs of his face. Not ones for the family album. Few people look good in death. I sat on the stool at the side and tried to work out if I was well enough to spend the rest of the morning in the office meeting deadlines on the paperwork. The doors swung shut behind me, which was odd because I hadn't heard anyone walk down the corridor. There's only one person I know who can walk as quietly as that.

'Bad head?' It was a low, resonant voice, rounded and smooth like Dee's but deeper and with a different lilt. Totally distinctive.

'Inspector MacDonald.' I caught the back edge of Lee's smile. 'What in heaven's name are you doing here?'

'So glad to meet you too, Dr Stewart. I could ask you the same thing.'

'I work here.'

'There, and I thought you were across the way in the shiny new building with the folk who're still breathing. Amazing how fast you get out of date if you don't keep your ear to the ground . . .' He wandered past me and took a long look in Joey's mouth. A lot closer than I would have gone. The man with the cast-iron stomach. He looked up, his eyebrows arching. 'Professor Murdoch's left her new job, has she? And you're taking over instead?'

'In my dreams.' Lee had her back to us both, writing something necessary in the day-book. MacDonald looked at me and one eyebrow rose another notch.

'The day Professor Murdoch leaves,' I said, 'Dr Adams will break her lifelong stretch on the wagon and drown herself in champagne. And I will not be going for the job.' The ache in my brain narrowed to a fine point. A power drill pushed in somewhere just behind my temporal lobes. I pushed my thumbs into the soft space at my temples. 'I'm here to pay my last respects to a friend and colleague,' I said, carefully. 'What's your excuse?'

'I don't need an excuse. I'm entitled to be here to observe duty pathologist in the discharge of her duty in any case of sudden death.' He watched with interest as Lee laid out her dissection kit. 'I heard he drowned in his own vomit. Would that be right?'

'Looks like it. I'll tell you for sure when I get a look at the lungs. It's that or plain straightforward alcohol poisoning, but with Joey, I'd be surprised. From the sound of things, he wasn't anywhere near his personal limit.'

'No. That's what I'd heard.' He watched her fit a blade to the scalpel handle and remembered, suddenly, why he'd really come. 'The local lads at Knapdale have found your friend's motorbike,' he said. 'They're bringing it back into town now, so—'

'His kit? Did they find his climbing kit?' Lee, the optimist, who believed there was something to find.

'The keys were with it but we haven't opened the panniers yet. It weights in at a kilo or two overweight. The lads are expecting something big inside. I'll need someone who can identify the contents.'

★ ★ ★

So I didn't, after all, spend the morning filling in forms. I spent it instead in the passenger seat of Stewart MacDonald's car, hanging on to the dashboard and trying not to remember that plate of poached eggs and bacon. I think, on the whole, I would have been better staying in the mortuary. On a day like this, it's the only place in the Department that's reasonably cool. Outside in the real world it was hell; hot, muggy Glaswegian hell. Not the best thing for a migraine.

'Can I ask you a question?' he asked. 'On the record.' We turned left out of the Ambulance exit and headed down Byres Road. The power drill bit deep into my optic chiasma.

'If you like. I'm not making any promises about the quality of the answers.'

He pulled out to overtake a taxi. I held on to the arm rest. 'Yes or no will do fine.' We stopped for the lights at the Old Dumbarton Road. He chewed on a thumbnail and watched two of the cars ahead of us jump the amber. The taxi cut past us to jump the red. He chose not to look. The pedestrian lights came on. A lass with three kids tried to persuade them all to cross at once. There are worse things in life than a headache. MacDonald slid his car into neutral and wound down the window. He laid his elbow on the sill and propped his chin on his fist.

'Why was it Dr Adams did the autopsy on your friend?' he asked.

'Because he was a friend,' I said. My fault. I had a head-ache. Not a good time to be smart.

We got a green. He slid into gear. I think he sighed. 'Sharpen up, Kellen. That's not going to wash with the Fiscal.'

'I'm sorry?'

'She wasn't on call. The man was a friend. You two found the body. If it's an accident, you might get away with that. But you're saying it wasn't.'

A blow torch joined the power drill and together they set about removing my eyes from my skull. There wasn't much room in my head left for thinking. 'I'm sorry. I still don't understand.'

MacDonald put his foot down and we cruised out towards Whiteinch. 'In any case of sudden death,' he said carefully, 'it is usual for someone to find the body. It is usual for someone else to perform the post-mortem and for someone else again to inherit the totality of the estate. It is very, very unusual for the same person to accomplish all three in the same case.' We pulled left, cut across some traffic and turned into an unmarked gateway. Ahead of us, a grim, grimed, semi-derelict warehouse sat amongst other very much more derelict warehouses. On either side, the hulking ruins of the Clydeside shipyards blocked any view we might have had through to the river beyond. This is the kind of place where it's dangerous simply to walk along the street. I put my elbow to the door and nudged the button. The noise of the central locking hammered another nail into the soft parts of my brain. MacDonald turned in his seat. 'Kellen, listen to me. In a fatal accident inquiry, no one gives a toss who's named in the will. In a murder inquiry, it matters a lot. Folk are paid to notice that kind of thing. Folk with a lot less patience than me.' He stopped. His eyes were grey, like the buildings around us. Outside in the car park the sky flashed white and a gull stooped to collect something unspeakable from the concrete. I closed my eyes. It didn't alter the pain. 'Why didn't you tell me she stood to inherit the flat?' he asked.

'You didn't ask.'

There was a pause. I heard his thumbs drumming on the steering wheel. His voice came flat and hard. 'Kellen . . .'

'Look, they lived together, they worked together, they climbed together. When you climb at that level, there's always a risk one of you's going to hit the deck and not get up again. Neither of them has any dependants. Each of them knew how much the place mattered to the other. Who else do you think they would leave it to? I didn't tell you because I thought it was staringly obvious.'

'So then why, in heaven's name, did she not hand the autopsy over to Professor Murdoch?'

'Because it was Professor Murdoch.'

He stopped drumming his thumbs. 'Go on.'

'It was a promise. She made a promise. We were all at the flat the day Murdoch was appointed Head of Pathology. Eric said he'd rather die than have his post-mortem done by Medusa.'

I opened one eye to look at him. He watched a car passing along the road.

'It was a joke,' I said.

'Yes, I could tell.' He chewed the edge of his thumb. 'I take it they didn't get on? Him and Professor Murdoch.'

'He hated her guts.'

'Would you be able to tell me why?'

A white Transit van drew up beyond the gateway. This time MacDonald reached for a pad and noted down the number. The gull lurched and took off, circling slowly as if one of its engines wasn't firing on all cylinders. The van sat still with the engine ticking over. No one got out.

'They worked together on a clinical research programme a year or two after we all qualified,' I said. 'Four of them: Eric and Lee, Joey Duncan and Hillary Murdoch. Eric was in medicine, Lee and Joey were in surgery working under Joey's Dad. Murdoch was in pathology, finishing off her Ph.D. One of the trials they were working on went wrong and the patients died. As far as Eric was concerned, Murdoch was responsible and should have resigned. She didn't. He's done his best not to speak to her since.'

'And Lee? Is she the same?'

'You could say. Lee was three weeks away from her part two surgery exams when the shit hit the fan. Twenty-one days from being a fully qualified consultant surgeon. There aren't many female surgeons now. There were even fewer then. I can't begin to tell you how hard she'd worked to get there.'

'I can imagine.' He stared straight forward out of the windscreen. Odd how the crow's feet twist when he's not smiling. 'She's not a surgeon now, Kellen. What went wrong?'

'Everything.' I found the lever to tilt back the seat. The roof of his car was dark and matt and easy on the eye. Memories, dusty and long hidden, hovered just out of reach. It's not a time I would wish to remember, given the choice. 'Lee was off clinics, revising for the exams. We shared a flat in Otago Street and I didn't see her from one weekend to the next. She was in the library before I got out of bed and she came home after I'd gone to sleep. She wasn't keeping tabs on the wards at all. Then she did a weekend's ward duty for Joey and one of her own patients came in on the Saturday

morning with everything possible going wrong. I don't know
the details but even for surgery it was rough. The lass died on
the Sunday night. Probably she would have gone sooner but
I don't think Lee was ready to give up. She hadn't seen the
others, she had no idea what had been going on. It took her
apart.' And Lee is not Eric. She didn't blame Hillary Murdoch. She blamed herself. Whatever else has happened in the
life of Lee Adams, she measures herself against the actions of
that weekend.

The Transit cut its engine. A lad in jeans and a faded Celtic
football shirt wandered down the street, going nowhere, just
passing the van. MacDonald half closed his eyes.

'Did she resign?' he asked, softly.

'Hardly. She went to the Senate as soon as she came off
duty on the Monday morning and asked them to bring a
malpractice suit against Professor Duncan and the rest of the
surgery department.'

'Christ.' He winced. 'And they didn't like that?'

'Not much. If it was now, they'd call an enquiry and she'd
be a media hero. But we're talking fifteen years ago. Life was
very different then.'

'She lost her job?'

'She'd lost it before she ever walked in the door. They had
the letter typed and waiting.'

'And what's it all got to do with our shiny new Head of
Department?'

'Hillary Murdoch was the one who designed the trial.'

'Ah.'

We sat in the stillness of the car and said nothing. A wasp
cannoned into the windscreen and danced along the length of

the wipers, whining and angry and painful on the ear. MacDonald twitched the controls. The wiper blades sang in a single dry arc. The wasp whined away into the heat of the day. The van coughed twice in starting and pulled away from the kerb. The lad in the green striped shirt had vanished from sight.

I unhitched my seatbelt and flicked open the door. Damp Glaswegian heat flowed in like a tide. Somewhere under all the smog, you could smell the river: brown and slow and dirty. Difficult to believe that St Mungo ever pulled out a live salmon. I got out of the car and leant on the bonnet. MacDonald stood up and swung on his door and said nothing. The silence hung still and filthy, like the smell.

'Murdoch went to the States as soon as she got her Ph.D.,' I said. 'Lee took the job in pathology. Everybody got on with their lives and tried to forget. Then Prof. Gemmell died and they needed a new Head of Department. Lee should have been next in line but she's spent her life doing clinical work, not writing papers, which wasn't necessarily the best career move. It's the lines on the CV that count when it comes to rising up the ranks. Murdoch's got them, Lee hasn't. They let Lee take over as Acting Head for three years while they came up with a package that would lure Murdoch over from Boston and then that was it. End of story. Thank you, Dr Adams, it's been a pleasure, please step aside.'

'How long's she been back?'

'Murdoch? Just under three months. Long enough to put her mark on the Department. Research is in, real, live, hands-on clinical pathology is out. If you can't turn it into a paper, it's not worth doing. Medical totalitarianism at its most efficient. Which is why, if you look, you'll see Dr Adams looking less than happy in her work.'

'She could resign.'

'She could, but it's not her style. Anyway, she had Eric. They were a good team. Hospital's a madhouse at the best of times. They worked well together. They kept each other sane.'

'Until now.'

'Quite.' And that's the thing I have been trying to avoid since I saw Eric lying on the rock in the sunlight. There is no one, now, to take the pressure off her days.

The heat picked up water from the river and let it out in soft, soaking patches under my arms and around my waist. Old memories crowded on new ones and I had no real wish to pay attention to any of them. There is only so much to be gained from churning over the past. I left the car and walked over to the warehouse. 'Suppose we take a look at this bike? I'm on clinics this afternoon. I need to be back at the Unit by two.'

'No problem.' He pulled out a bunch of keys from his pocket, carefully so they didn't make too much noise. 'It's inside,' he said, and he kicked open the door.

Inside: a dark, foul, filthy mass of urban detritus where the air was saturated with a nose-clogging mix of dust and desiccated bird shit, where the only light came through three barred and broken windows at the back so that all you could see was a huddle of shrouded shapes gathered in the middle of a vast wasted space. MacDonald switched on a light. A scattering of small birds erupted from the rafters, screaming shock at the sudden intrusion. The ceiling rained bird shit. I put my hand to my head, thought better of it and pushed it deep in one pocket.

The birds whirled and vanished. MacDonald stepped forward and lifted one of the cleaner sheets. Even in this light, the bike underneath shone with the opalescent silvered green of a fish in water.

'The make and registration matches the one we were given. It's his, yes?'

'I think so. It looks the same. Can we see what's inside?'

He pulled a set of keys from a chain on his waist and fitted them in the lock. Nothing vital fell out of the panniers – no clues, no last-minute notes, no pleas for help – just a selection of standard climbing gear: two ropes, the slings, the friends. MacDonald spread the sheet on the floor, clean side uppermost, and then pulled on a pair of gloves so he could lay it all out for me to check.

I stood back, watching, trying not to breathe in too much bird lime. 'Do you normally take prints from the property of an accident victim?'

'If I think it might be useful.'

'Fine.' I crouched down and counted everything. Thought back and counted again. *Two of the 8-mm ropes. His belt. His rack. All of the spare friends.* All of the spare friends. I had him lay them out in order of size, retentively neat, like Lee. Five of them. Two ones, a two, a three and a four. Nothing as small as 5 mm.

'One of these is missing. The smallest.'

'Are you sure?'

'Yes, I gave it to him last Christmas.' I remember the card – clichéd, to match the season: *For Eric; a friend for a friend.* A friend for a friend. He may not have used it but it's not the kind of present you break the day after Boxing Day.

MacDonald searched through the panniers, but found nothing more. He came back to crouch at the side of the sheet. 'Are you sure he had it with him?'

'No, I'm not sure of anything any more. I'll ask Lee.'

'Yes. He always took it with him.'

'You're sure it's not at home?'

'I'm sure. I've looked everywhere. It's not in the flat and it's not on my belt. If it's not on yours then it was on his rack when he packed.'

'Or he's lost it.'

'The only way you lose a friend, Kellen, is if you leave it behind in the rock. I would know if he'd done that anytime before Friday.'

'Fair enough.' A pause. I sat on my stool in the morgue with my back to the white tiles of the wall. It was cool in there, gloriously cool. The only place in Glasgow where the temperature wasn't out to get me. Someone, probably Mike, had brought in a bunch of sun-yellow chrysanthemums and left them in a measuring cylinder on the bench. The colour changed the temperature of the air in the room. It helped me think. 'You wouldn't know if it was stuck somewhere further on up from the sheep ledge. We didn't get that far.'

'I know.' She moved along the bench, laying out kits for the kids. 'And you don't use a rope if there's no one holding the other end.' She turned round, stripping the surgical gloves from her hands. 'If the friend's in the rock, then he was climbing and he wasn't alone. So all we have to do is find it. After that, it's up to MacDonald.' She looked up at the clock. 'When are you free?'

"I could get out this afternoon if I had to. Officially, I'm not off till Friday afternoon.' I should be at the farm but they can live without me once in a while. 'You?'

There was a noise from the corridor. Half a dozen fourth-year students on vacation experience gathered in a huddle outside the door. They were more ordered than usual, notice-ably subdued. At times like this, the hospital grapevine works faster than the speed of sound. All of them knew Joey Duncan was dead and that his body was in the mortuary. It's unnerving if you're not used to it.

Lee found a clean set of gloves in her pocket. 'I've got a practical class with this lot all afternoon so I can't go today. I could probably do Friday. I'm supposed to be on call but I can work on Murdoch and see if I can get her to cover for me. Otherwise we'll have to make it Saturday.'

'See what you can do. I'll be in the Unit for the rest of the week.'

'OK. I'll let you know.'

Chapter Five

'It's early in the morning, maybe around six, half six. That space between the birds waking and the sun rising. The sky's clear and cold. You can see the clouds banking up on the horizon but they've not pulled across yet. It's the best part of the day. Always. The birds are making a hell of a racket, mind. You know the noise. You hate it when it wakes you up and you love it once you're out and walking. You don't hear it in here. Too many buildings. Not enough trees... Anyway, we're out for the morning and the dogs are working the field. Guinness – that's the Labrador, cracking little dog – she's out quartering the plough. It's autumn. We ploughed yesterday. We'll be putting the winter wheat in any day now. So, she's there, working across and across without me ever telling her where to go. If there's a pheasant there, she'll find it. It's October now so she's legal at least. Rastus is away on his own doing terrier things: hammering into the hedges, diving down rabbit holes. Scruffy little tyke. We bred him for Sally and

95

then she went off to college, so he comes out with me all the time now. Wouldn't be without him. God knows what he'll do when—'

'What can you smell? Tell me what you can smell, Jack.'

'Smell? That's difficult. If I'm honest . . . you want me to be honest? I can smell the incense the lass lit when she came in. And the wound, I can smell the bloody wound. Smells like something the dogs have rolled in. Too long dead. And melted . . . I don't want to melt, Kellen.'

'I know. I know.' Who would want to melt? 'We can leave this if you want. Just go with more morphine and let it be at that.'

'No. No. This is better. Bit of a daydream never hurt anyone. Not now, anyhow . . . Take me back in.'

'You're in the fields, early morning in October. With the dogs. I'd guess it would be frosty but you'd still smell the plough underneath. And you might catch your arm on a bramble on the way past . . .'

'What? Oh, aye . . . a bramble . . . There and I was thinking it was a needle . . . Frosty? Aye, it's frosty. A grand, rare frosty morning. Beautiful, you know? White, like crystal all over the plough. And cold: that lovely sharp, clear cold that makes you feel warm as you're walking. And I can smell it. You're right. You can always smell the plough . . . There's nothing in the world smells like the earth, just turned over . . .'

We waited for the half-dose of morphine to take, me and a nurse called Jo McCauley. In another world, Jack Souter took his dogs for a walk across the fields and through the woods, past hawthorns in late berry and oak trees that shed leaves down in front of him as he walked. He turned down a side path and nearly walked into a marsh but the terrier grabbed his arm, in the way terriers do, and worried at it to get him to turn round. In the world of the ward, Jo began to unwrap his bandage. The dog bit deeper into his arm. He made it a game, pulling and cursing, swinging the dog up in the air, growling at it as it was growling at him. His arm lay still on the bed. Jo teased the last layer of melolin from the great, melting ulcer that ate into the tissues of his forearm. A wash of decay and putrefaction flowed out, more than you could drag out with the air conditioning or cover with incense. With care, Jo washed the puckered edges of the lesion and eventually the dog let go. She started the first layer of the dressing and out in the wood, Jack Souter peeled back the sleeve of his shirt to find that the dog had broken the skin. Nothing serious. 'Just a flesh wound . . .

'. . . and then we're on the way home. I have my scarf wrapped round my arm where the dog got it. Daft bloody thing. She didn't mean to, mind. Just playing. And I can walk up the stairs now, wooden ones at the bottom and then they're covered in lino and the room's all done in yellow, pale yellow, like old beeswax, and I can smell the incense and the grass outside and . . . heather, I can smell heather. The smell of the bandage isn't as bad as it was . . . Are you done?'

'We're done.' Jo backed out through the door, the foul mess of the old dressing sealed in a clinical waste bag, on its way to the incinerator.

The man opened his eyes. The nurse turned at the door and smiled. Red-blonde hair and freckles and wide grey-green eyes. He smiled back and gave her a nod. His gaze wandered the room, searching the walls, the drip stands, the rack of tablets, the bedside table. Anywhere but on the bed.

'I was right. It is heather.' He reached out to touch it. 'Was that you brought that?'

'Yes. You said you liked it.' I lifted it up for him to smell. He's not old. Early fifties maybe. Old enough to have lived a full life. Still too young to die. Almost everyone in here is too young to die. They still do it all the same. He looked down at last. Layers of white gauze wrapped fresh round his arm. A turn or two of micropore held it all in place. Neat and clean and innocent. Could be covering a dog bite. 'Is it bad underneath?'

His eyes are back, holding mine. What can you say? 'It's not good.'

He closed his eyes. Now he looks old. His skin is the parched yellow of terminal hepatic failure; dry and crinkled like the oak leaves he was walking through. Two weeks ago, when we first walked the dogs, it was spring in his fields. Soon it will be winter. The mind follows these patterns.

'How much longer?' He still had his eyes shut. The blue veins stood out round his temples.

'I don't know. I can order an X-ray if you like. Or we can get some more blood tests. But we're guessing at best. You know that.'

'Aye. Never mind. I'll go in my own good time.' His breath came harder than it used to. 'Not long now.'

'No.' His hand was firm in mine. There was nothing wrong with his mind. It's just his body that was riddled through with the secondary spread from the melanoma on his arm. If he's lucky, his liver will give out before anything else. It's the most peaceful way.

'How did your talk go?' His voice was quiet. I leant over to hear.

'Not bad.' I'd almost forgotten about that. 'They listened and they didn't laugh and one or two of them asked intelligent questions. It was better than I expected.'

'So they're not about to turn the whole place into a Palliative Care Unit?' He was laughing, but only with his mouth.

'Not this year, Jack. I need to get more facts before they take us seriously.'

'Does this morning count?'

'It will if you don't mind us filling in the questionnaire. You had half the dose of morphine you were having on the ward. Do you think it hurt twice as much?'

'Don't be daft.' He reached for the pen and the printed sheet that I gave him. 'It's nothing to do with the morphine, woman. You know that. It's to do with the lass holding my hand like I was a real human being and you remembering about the heather and both of you knowing my name so I'm not just "the aberrant melanoma with multiple metastases in bed three" with a bunch of white coats standing round discussing sizes and growth rates like I was a steer at the sales.'

'I know. But this is the age of science, Jack, you can't write statistics about knowing someone's name.'

'Bollocks to that.' He cleared his throat and peered down at the sheet. 'You know, I never thought I'd end up a statistic.'

'I know.' No one ever does. 'I'm sorry.'

'Just make it count, all right?'

'I'm doing my best.'

Dee was waiting for me in the office. She was white, shaken in ways I've never seen her shaken before.

'What's up?'

'Room five. Can you give me a hand?'

'Sure.'

Room five is back down on the first floor at the far end of the corridor from the one that Jack is in. I followed Dee up the stairs, reading the case notes as I went. Claire Hendon, twenty-three. Stage four cervical adenocarcinoma, picked up too late because no one expects cervical cancer in a lass of twenty-three. Rapid local and distant spread. Minimal response to radio- or chemotherapy. Urinary and faecal dysfunction. Permanent cystotomy placed two weeks ago to bypass urethral obstruction. Colostomy offered and refused. Referred to the Unit by her oncologist, the one who asked the intelligent questions after the talk on Monday. So maybe you can make changes without statistics. We reached room five. Dee was grey, the colour of wood-ash. 'Do you know her?' I asked.

'No.' She pushed both hands to her eyes. Her voice came out muffled past her wrists. 'I was supposed to talk her in. I can't do it.' Her hands came away. Her eyes looked just like Jack Souter's: without hope. 'Have you the time?'

'Sure. Will you be around afterwards?'

'I guess.'

'We'll have lunch, huh?'

'Sure.'

Room five has an east-facing window that looks out towards the Art Gallery. If you stand at the right angle, you can see the sky reflecting off the surface of the Kelvin. The walls are green, spring green, to pick up the colour of the grass and draw it in. Someone had lit a candle. The flame flickered as I walked inside. Claire Hendon lay on the bed: a white half-ghost with the quarter-inch crew-cut of radiotherapy and the wasting translucency of chemo. With her hair longer and some colour to her face, she would have been stunning. Instead, her cheekbones poked out sharply beneath the dark pits of her eyes and she looked like the dead, newly risen from the grave. A syringe driver fixed to a stand by the bed fed morphine into the drip in her arm. A button by her hand gave her control of the flow. Patient-controlled analgesia, one step better than handing out a bottle of aspirin and leaving them to get on with it. She saw me standing in the doorway and reached out, her thumb twitching on the button. The driver whirred and then stopped. Already on maximum dose.

'Hi, Claire. I'm Kellen Stewart. I've come to welcome you to the Unit.'

'You're a doctor?'

'Kind of. A therapist, mostly.'

A short, derisive snort with more energy in it than I would have imagined. 'So you're going to therapise me out of here?'

'No, I don't think it works like that.'

'Nothing fucking works.' She threw the button from the bed. Plastic cracked on glass. A nurse hovered by the door, caught my eye and left. 'All you need to do is get that fucking thing to work and I'll be gone. *Finito*. Out of your hair. No more problem.' Morphine overdose. It's reasonable. It's what I would do, given the choice. We are not often given the choice.

'I'm sorry.' I shook my head. 'I can't do that.'

101

She turned away to face the window. A kite swooped in the air above the gallery: a multi-coloured delta, carving the wind like a knife.

'Does your head hurt?'

'It always hurts.' She has mets in her right hemisphere. The scan results came through this morning. That's why they sent her up here.

'Do you want me to help with that? There are things we can do, things that go beyond morphine.'

'No.' She closed her eyes. 'I've had it with doctors. Get lost.'

'OK.' I sat down by the bed. Her free hand, the one without the drips, lay palm up on the bed. I laid mine beside it. Not touching, just close enough that she would know it was there. Time hung like the kite. Neither of us spoke. In a while, a long while, I felt her move. Her thumb lay across mine, curled round it, tightly. Her hand shifted sideways and hard-bitten nails dug deep into the skin of my palm. Somewhere in the quiet of the room her breathing changed and it was clear that she was weeping and that she was speaking and when the words came more clearly they were no different to Jack Souter's, just said with less tact. 'It's not fair. It's not fucking fair.' I have no answer for that.

I stayed for a while. The syringe driver clicked round on the hour and released another dose of morphine. Her finger crushed the button, drained the machinery dry and, slowly, the desperate grip on my hand began to relax. She was asleep, I think, when I left.

Dee Fitzpatrick sat in one of the staff room's armchairs, a great emerald cocoon of a chair placed with its back to the door and its face to the big bay windows that give out on to the lawns. It was a good place to hide. I stood behind it. From there, all I could see was the top of her head – the flat white-blonde hair cut level, like a lawn. She sat very still.

'Hungry?'

'No.'

I pushed a sandwich round the side into her line of view. Salmon and cream cheese on sun-dried tomato bread. The canteen's finest. She reached out and took it. 'Thanks.'

'No problem. How are you?'

'Crap. If I was on fags, I'd be on the second packet by now.'

'Don't start.'

'I don't intend to.'

I put my coffee on the window ledge and sat down slowly on the parquet flooring with my back to her chair. 'What's up?'

She peeled the plastic from the sandwich. 'Everything. I've lost the plot, Kellen. I've just completely, totally lost it. I don't think I'm cut out for this any more.'

A week ago, we were planning the next six months' protocols and a submission to *Pain*. For all her wilful opacity, I wouldn't have said Dee Fitzpatrick was one for sudden changes of heart.

All you can do is go with what you know. 'Claire Hendon.' I said the name with care. 'Do you want to talk about her?'

Silence.

Outside on the lawn, a lass in her early twenties walked a black Labrador and a scruffed tyke of a terrier from the car park to the fire exit by room three. Behind us, the staff room filled with nurses, with orderlies, with the day's rota of volunteers. Without the volunteers, we'd be dead. That is to say, the Unit would have closed before we ever got it off the ground.

Dee put her sandwich back on the window ledge. 'She's Beth,' she said. Her gaze roved back and forth across the upper branches of the sycamore at the far side of the lawn.

'I'm sorry?'

'Claire Hendon, she's Beth. It's been fifteen years and she's come back. She looks like Beth. She sounds like Beth. She's dying the same way Beth died. I can't handle it.'

Oh. Christ.

I reached for her hand. 'I'm sorry, Dee.'

'So am I. You'd think that after fifteen years, we wouldn't still be fucking up the same old things.'

'What have we fucked up?'

'Claire. Her life. What it was, what it is now, what it could have been. Fucked up by a bunch of useless bloody medics who couldn't make a diagnosis if it stood up and wrote its name on a board. Would they have blown it this badly if she was their daughter, their partner, their mother? I don't think so.'

Maybe not. But you'd burn out in a month if you treated everyone who came through a standard medical ward as if they were a close blood relative. And, just at this moment, it is not Claire who matters most. Her arm lay tense on the arm of the chair. My hand lay on hers. 'Was it like this for Beth?' I asked.

'More or less.' She watched the dogs play chase-a-ball across the lawn. They were out of sight behind the rhododendrons before she decided what else to say. It takes courage, sometimes, simply to remember. She looked down at my coffee and nodded as I handed her the mug. 'It wasn't the secondaries that got her. She didn't have any secondaries. It was the things rotting inside that they couldn't keep together. She had the colostomy first. It didn't work but it gave us hope, for a while. It's amazing how you can get used to the idea of living with an external bag when the alternative is not living at all. Then her bladder broke down and they took her in for cystotomy and we still believed them when they said that she was going to get better.' She stopped, biting her lip, and then shook her head as if that way she could clear it of images. 'I spent six weeks nursing a woman with no lower bowel and another with only half a bladder.' She stole a long drink from my coffee, smiled a strung-out, hard-edged, self-mocking smile. 'We were four days from the last surgery when she died. Iatrogenic death. Real bad for the statistics. The consultant was furious.'

Christ.

I made hand signals to Jo and she brought me two more coffees, one white, no sugar, one black with two. Dee folded her hands round the warmth of the mug and stared out at the empty garden. Her face and her voice were balanced, almost bland. Her eyes burned. 'We trusted them, you know? For weeks, we hung on every word they said. They were the doctors and so, of course, they knew what they were doing.'

'You weren't at med school when it happened?' It doesn't take long inside the system for the trust to wear off.

'Nowhere close,' She shook her head. 'Beth was the one with the brains and the degrees. I had my "O" grade biology but that was about it. I was running a nursery school during the day and doing an art degree at college in the evenings. I was going to be a world-famous potter. And kids.' Her teeth gripped hard at her lower lip. 'We went for the smears because we were going to have kids.'

How often have I heard this? How often has she?

I found a clean tissue in my pocket and laid it on her knee. She wasn't weeping. She wouldn't weep, I don't think, in front of me. But fifteen years is a long time to bury the pain. 'So why are you not out there throwing pots for the great and the good of Glasgow, Dr Fitzpatrick?'

She shrugged and blew across the top of her mug. 'I made a promise. The kind of thing you do when you're sitting by a bed holding the hand of the person you were going to spend your life with, watching her die in front of your eyes. We thought, in our naivety, that the white coats would listen to one of their own, that someone on the inside, if they had enough guts, could work on the people, on the system, that they could really make a difference. So I promised her that I'd do it, that I'd go back to college and get my own white coat, that I'd become one of them without ever becoming one of *them*. That I'd stop it and not be a part of it . . .' Her lips compressed to a thin, hard line. 'She was dead within forty-eight hours. I started at college that October, and got a place in med school three years after that. It was twelve years ago this year.' The tissue crumpled under her hand. She flicked her wrist and it bounced off the edge of the bin in the corner. 'Twelve years and I've made not the slightest fucking difference. I'm as much one of *them* as anyone else and I've stopped nothing. It's all just exactly the same . . .' Her fingers, wrapped round the mug, were white to the bone. She might have thrown it, I think, the same way as the tissue, but I was there. She sat instead with one knuckle gripped tight between her teeth. Her eyes were dry.

I took the mug from her hand and put it down on the floor. 'You're a good anaesthetist, Dee. That makes a difference.'

'No, I'm not. I anaesthetised her.'

'Who?'

'Claire. She had a cystotomy. Two weeks ago. I did the anaesthetic.'

'So she had an anaesthetist who understood. Better you than anyone else. At least you care.'

'I don't think so. I pretend, but underneath, I am just another white coat, no different to all the rest. I saw her and I knew who she was and what she was going through and I still sent her under and brought her out again.'

'That's what you're there for. What else could you do?'

'I could have let her die on the table, Kellen. It's what Beth always wanted. To go out under anaesthetic. Quick, peaceful, not knowing . . .' She looped her fingers together and locked them over one knee. 'I knew that and still I couldn't do it. Twelve years and I was more worried about my career and the protocol and not having a twenty-three-year-old patient die on the table for no good reason.'

'You'd be in front of an inquiry now if you'd let her go.'

'I know. So I am afraid of the men in suits and Claire Hendon has to live through three weeks of unbridled hell.' Her eyes closed and reopened. The world outside the window didn't change. 'Two weeks ago, I thought there were still things I could do that would make a difference. Now,' she shrugged, short and loose – 'what's the point?'

'The Unit? Is that not the point?'

'No, not any more. It's not enough.' She turned to look at me. Her face was a study in exhaustion, close to defeat. 'I don't want to go on, Kells. Just at this moment, I really, really don't want to go on.'

And how often in this place have I heard those words said with that tone? But never before from a member of the staff. Never before from a friend.

Outside, Sally Souter led her father's dogs back towards the car park. A sprig of heather stuck out from the collar of each. Tomorrow, as we change the dressing, we will walk them in winter. In the meantime, there is nothing I need to do in the Unit that won't wait.

'Dee . . . if I offered to take you home, would you come?'

'What? No. I'll run. I need the exercise. Thanks.'

'I didn't mean to your home. I meant home to the farm. I don't think you need to be on your own just now.' I collected the empty mugs and stacked them on the trolley by the bin. 'We could go for a ride up to the loch and back. You don't have to stay after that if you don't want to.'

She thought about it, staring out at the sycamores. Something changed in the hard planes of her face. She looked up at me. 'Would you mind?'

'Let me get my bag.'

'How's the hangover?'

'Getting better.' It was better after I went walking with Jack Souter. Letting go of reality does that sometimes.

'I didn't know you drank that much.'

'I don't. Not normally. I needed to sleep.'

'Did it work?'

'More or less. After I finished throwing up. I'm sorry if I kept you awake.'

'You didn't.'

'Thank you. Do you feel any better?'

'Don't ask.'

Fair enough. I lay back on the towel and looked at the sky. Pure blue, not a single cloud. And still. It's not often still up by the loch. When we rode up, I could feel the breath of a breeze. Now, it might simply have been the breath of our moving. Behind me, the dog lay panting, too lazy to roll into the shade of a rock. The horses moved slowly, cropping harsh mouthfuls of grass. Horse flies whined. A hoodie crow cackled in passing. Jack Souter would love it here.

Dee lay beside me face down on her towel, soaking in the sun. Small beads of sweat gathered at the nape of her neck and in the dips of her spine. All the way down the back of her head, the short cropped hair gathered the light and held it close in a halo of liquid fire. I reached out to touch it and found an unexpected softness.

She lay very still. 'What are you doing?'

'Seeing if reality matches the image.'

'Does it ever?'

'Sometimes.' But not now. In so many ways this woman is not what she seems. I let my hand fall away. 'Did you cut it for Beth?' I asked.

'Kind of. There were a lot of women on her ward with no hair. It was a symbol, I think, of what medicine can do in the name of healing.' She propped her chin on her hand and stared out across the still surface of the loch. 'But I think if I'm honest, I did it more for me. I needed a break, something to make the difference from who I was then to who I am now.'

'Did it work?'

'It did to begin with. I probably don't need it now, I'm not going back.' She rolled on one side, shading her eyes with the crook of her elbow. 'Should I grow it, do you think?'

I tried to imagine a Dee with longer hair but my mind is not that agile. 'No.' I shook my head. 'It wouldn't fit.'

'Good.' She smiled, as dry as ever, her eyes odd-coloured in the light. 'That was the right answer.'

We lay quiet for a while after that. I turned over to lie on my stomach and watched the reflection of a solitary cloud drift out across the surface of the water. My mind drifted with it, teasing out the threads of courage and despair, matching them side by side with my own, and finding mine shorter, weaker, thinner, altogether less well-formed. I am a product of my parents, my school, my peers. For all my early life I was going to be a doctor. I was five years qualified before it ever occurred to me that I could do anything different and even then the parting was half-hearted and short-lived and I am back now because I have nothing else that I can do. It is not an honourable thought.

'Kellen?' I felt her finger, cool on my shoulder and turned to look. She stretched on her side and sat up. Her smile was warm. Wherever she had been, it was a more friendly place than mine. 'Can we swim in there?' she asked.

'Feel free.'

'Not on my own.' A hand reached down to my arm. 'Swimming's never any fun on your own.'

The water was cold. Shockingly, breathlessly cold. It burned, hotter than the sun, making wax of muscles that should have been swimming so that I felt like a rag doll, weighed down by the water. I swam in small circles near the edge and then turned back and stepped out on to the grass and the dry warmth of the towel. Dee is immune to the cold. She reached the rock of the far shore, turned and pushed off and swam back towards me in a strong, rhythmic crawl, stroke after stroke making white waves in the green ice of the water. The blonde halo of hair sleeked down on her scalp like a swimming cap, growing thinner with every stroke. By the time she reached the bank beside me for the second time, it was invisible. I thought she might come out then but she flipped on her back and reached out again and swam, more lazily now, to the place at the head of the loch where the river drops down from the heights of the ben. She found a rock with a flat top, pulled herself up on to it and dived off, neat and clean, to race back to the shore. Her breath was coming hard when she stopped, the way it does when she runs. She stood up in the shallows, the water streaming down from her shoulders, eyes and teeth bright against darker, sun-drunk skin. I'd say that her smile, this once, was real. She swivelled round on one heel to face me.

'That was good. Thank you. I'm glad I came.'

'Good.' I threw her a towel and she came to sit on the grass beside me, rubbing away the jitters and the goose bumps and the wrinkling skin. 'There are apples in the saddle pack.'

'You're just desperate to get me to eat something, aren't you?'

'No. I'm just desperate to eat. You don't have to join in.'

An apple lobbed on to the turf by my cheek. 'Has the headache gone yet?'

'Totally. Yours?'

'I didn't have a headache.'

'But has it gone?'

No answer. Just a hard, crunching bite, white teeth into acid skin. Then: 'Roll over, my towel's wet.'

I rolled over, one arm angled up to shade my eyes from the sun. She lay down on her stomach beside me, elbows propped on the grass, working her way through the apple. I felt the cool of the water and the warm of her skin beneath it, the soft shift of her breathing. We lay in silence for a while and then, in time, I heard her voice, quiet and musing. 'There was someone else, wasn't there, before Nina?'

I wasn't expecting that. Not at all. I haven't thought that far back for a long, long time. I'm not sure I want to, particularly. I closed my eyes to the sun. 'Her name was Bridget.'

'Were you together long?'

'Eight years. And then another four when we should have been but I was too pig-headed to go home and apologise for being a total shit.'

'And then she found someone else?'

'No. Then she died.'

'Oh.' A soft sound in the silence. 'I'm sorry.'

'Thanks.'

The apple cores lay on the grass by my hand. I picked them up and took them to the horses; tossed one over to Balder out at the place where the grass meets the heather. Maddie came in for hers, blowing warm breath on my shoulder, so much more gentle than the colt. I ran my hand across the brown and white patches of her skin as she ate. I always wanted a skewbald. It took years to persuade Sandy that she wasn't going to taint his precious breeding plans and even now he isn't sure. Colour prejudice is alive and well and living in central Scotland. I hadn't thought, until now, of what Bridget might have said about that.

The mare finished her share and pushed her nose to my chest, turning me back where I came from. Dee lay quiet on the towel, her hands clasped, chin looped on the hammock of her fingers, staring out across the loch. The breeze was up, cutting small ruffles on the surface. The dog closed her eyes and stretched out in the shade of the saddles. Nothing else moved. I walked over and sat, cross legged, on the towel.

'Does it not feel like a betrayal?' she asked. Her eyes were still on the loch. Her voice was soft and rounded and smooth, like a rock from the river. Questing but not intruding.

'Does what not feel like a betrayal?'

'Being with Nina.'

Difficult. I had to think about that one, too. Then, eventually: 'No.'

'Why not?'

'It's different. I'm different. She's different.'

'Even at the start?'

The start was hard for all kinds of reasons. Bridget, oddly, wasn't one of them. 'No. Never. Mostly, I wanted to be able to tell her what was happening.'

A curlew flew over, silently. I was glad. I didn't need, just then, that kind of keening.

'Do you think she knows?'

'About Nina? I don't know.'

'But it would be good to think so?'

'Maybe.' But if she doesn't, it's because it doesn't matter. Another space. Her face was quite still. I am learning, I think, to see beneath that. I picked a stalk of grass and chewed on the end. It's fifteen years since she went into medicine. It's a long, long time to be single. 'Dee, has there been anyone for you since Beth?'

'No.'

'Because it would feel like a betrayal?'

'I think so.' She rolled over, on to her side, facing me. She reached out a hand. It slid into mine, hand in glove. 'And I haven't wanted it. Yet.'

They are grey-green, her eyes, and quite still, with tiny pin-point pupils narrowed down by the sun. Her hand is cool and still damp from the swim. Beads of water gather along her collar bone. A moment ago, they rocked with the rhythm of her breathing. Now, they are still.

In another time and another place, this could be so different.

'Dee . . .'

Her hand changed. It didn't move, but it changed. Her eyes stayed on mine. 'You're married. I know.' She smiled; a real smile, no masks. 'It's OK. You can relax . . . Life is complicated enough. I wasn't going to do anything. Just that . . . we needed to know. *I* needed to know.'

'Thank you.'

'You're too good a friend.'

'Thank you.'

She moved away half an inch. Her hand stayed in mine. I squeezed it. 'Thank you.'

114

She squeezed back. The smile teased, gently and without rancour. 'Say something different?'

'I can't. There's nothing left. You said it all.'

'No.' She pulled herself up and sat facing me, knee to knee. 'Not all of it. There's "life's too short" as well.'

'Maybe. That one doesn't fit so well with all the others.'

'I know. That's why I didn't say it. And then again' – she swivelled her hand and we sat, palm to palm, fingers splayed – 'there's more to life than sex.'

'There is.' I reached out my free hand, ran my fingers a second time through the damp lawn of her hair. 'You need to ask Lee about that.' I changed the palm press, slid my hand back into hers. 'I'm sorry. Do you mind?'

'Of course.' Her fingers looped through mine and locked. Her smile was distant, gently mocking. 'But I'd mind more if you said anything else.' She stood up, pulling the towel with her as she went. 'You're one of the few constant things in my life, Kellen Stewart. I couldn't handle it just now if you changed.' She reached down a hand and lifted me up to my feet. 'It's getting late. If we don't go soon, they'll send out search parties. Shall we go down and see if we can find something in the freezer to surprise them for dinner?'

The fire glows low in the grate. The windows hang open, the doors with them. The updraught of the flames draws air into the room more than if the fire was not lit. If I need an excuse for a fire, that is it. And the cat likes it, there is that as well.

A bottle of wine stands on the hearth, close to empty, the dregs in the bottom too warm now to be worth finishing. Dee is in bed in the spare room, chaste in a borrowed T-shirt with the promise of spare clothes for the morning. She's Nina's size more than mine. Not quite so angular, perhaps, but not far off. We'll find something.

I lie back on the rug in front of the fire. The cat stretches out beside me, purring his ancient-cat purr. He was Bridget's before he was ever mine, the last of the links to a past that feels so long ago, it could be another life. Except there are memories and things learned, which make a difference to the way we live now. It is not good to make the same mistakes too often.

'Drink?'

'If there's something cold.'

'There's apple juice in the fridge.' Bare feet scuff across the floor. A glass arrives on the hearth. Firelight makes it amber, turning the juice to liquid gold. The sharp, bright taste of it clears the mellow memory of the wine. Nina sits on the floor, legs crossed at the ankles, leaning back against the weight of the fireside chair. I roll over and look up into deep, walnut eyes. They ask a question. She reaches out to touch the cat. He is our point of common contact. 'Do we have something to discuss?'

I sit up with my back to the other chair. That she feels free to ask says something. I stand my glass, with care, on the hearth, and shake my head. 'No.'

'Not yet? Or not at all?'

'Not at all. Not now, not ever.'

'Why not?'

I have to think about that one. It is important for both of us to know, for now and for later. There are words, and there is the truth. Only one of these matters. The last of the flames flickers down, leaving a bank of peat glowing like lava in the grate. Her eyes hold mine, mellow in the reddening light, still searching. In time I find the answer. I stretch out a foot, push it up against hers. We don't need the cat as intermediary. 'She isn't you.'

A hand reaches down. Cool fingers wrap around my ankle. She smiles, a half-lit quirk of a smile. 'Thank you.'

It was Wednesday night. For a space, the world was at peace.

Chapter Six

You could smell the mortuary from halfway up the corridor: the ugly, sweet, clinging stench of week-old meat left out in the sun. Melting and fly blown, like Jack Souter's arm distilled and condensed and sprayed out through the air conditioning. The room was busy with folk ostentatiously not in uniform. I stood at the back looking at a semi-circle of tall, faceless officers of the law. I don't carry a handkerchief but it comes as a necessary accessory, it seems, for a man not-in-uniform. Handkerchiefs: cotton, white, six inches by six inches square, noses for the holding of. Lee caught my eye through the crowd. She shook her head. I left. Clearly she didn't get Friday afternoon off.

The gods send these things, sometimes, for a reason. In theory, I could still have taken the rest of the afternoon off and gone back to the farm. If it wasn't for the heat, I probably would have done. But it was too hot to work, too hot to ride, too hot seriously to contemplate anything more active than sitting still in the shade with the cat. I would have done that, probably, but for a mounting pile of unfiled case records on my desk and a bad conscience over a backlog of reading, planned but never done. I worked for an hour or so in the Library until the heat and the clattering air conditioning drove me out and back to the Unit to catch up on the paperwork. And then, without any clear intention and certainly without being part of the rota, I was on the ground floor, walking along the primrose-yellow corridor towards Jack Souter's room.

It's winter. In the heat of summer, this room is in winter. A sudden snap of cold when I thought we might get through another week of mild weather. But now there's snow, lying two feet deep on the ground. And all the dogs have come back. A lifetime's collection. The black Labrador bitch and the tangled mess of a terrier. Behind them, an aged Welsh springer with arthritic hips and a tumour deforming her muzzle. Beyond them again, a scattering of other spaniels and Labradors, the gun dogs and companions of decades past. There was a cat somewhere, fat and orange-striped, lying close to death on a blanket.

'It's yourself.' He turned his head on the bed. His skin was yellow, the colour of old corn. His voice was rustled paper. 'I thought you'd come.'

'I'm here.' I took his hand. 'Where's Sally?'

'She's on her way. The lass called her a while ago. And Joan. They'll be here, no worries. I'll not go before they get here. Will you let them bring in the dogs?'

'Of course.' I sat on a chair by the side of the bed. Jo McCauley sat opposite. The bandage on his arm was half a day old. The last in this lifetime. I took his hand and wished I'd brought in more heather. 'Who are the others?'

'You were listening, aye? No problem. The spaniel was Bramble. First dog I ever had. Died when I was twenty-one.' He smiled. His eyes were at peace. 'The year I met Joan.'

'And the cat?'

'Sally's cat. Came as a youngster the day she was born. Just turned up at the back gate. Stayed with us ever since, like a shadow. Pined for a week when she went to school. He died last year. Before we knew about this.' His arm lifted a fraction from the bed and fell back again. You could barely hear the soft noise of it over the air conditioning.

'They're all walking with you?'

'No, no. We're not walking now. No need. Thought we'd sit in by the fire. Watch the snow out of the window. Listen to it falling off the roof. Bring all the animals into the house with the family for the big meal.'

'Is it Christmas?'

'The day after.'

'Christmas is for families, Jack, do you want me to go?'

'No, no. You're part of the family, now. Maybe when they get here. Stay here and talk to the dogs with me, meanwhile. You can bring yours in too. And the pup. Plenty room at the fire. We can . . .' A heaving, rattling, shuddering cough, tore at his lungs. It racked through him for minutes and there was nothing any of us could do. Jo sat by with the oxygen mask and held it up to his face for him to breathe when he could. I thought we might lose him then.

He lay back on the pillows when it was over, the mask on his face, breathing fast and shallow, his skin grey over the yellow, as if the frost had layered the corn. His eyes sunk back in his head, raisins pushed in on a melting snowman. I sat and held his hand and told him stories of the old cat who spends his nights by my bed, how he is fading away like the Cheshire cat until all that is left is his purr.

'You'll not make him go on too long?' His hand tightened on mine. His voice was hollow, a husk. 'Promise me you won't make him go on past his time.'

I picked up his other hand, brought them together and kissed them. I tasted salt and realised it was mine. My vision blurred until all the yellow of him melded with the yellow of the walls and I couldn't tell one from the other. 'I won't, Jack.'

'We can give them that, at least. A decent ending.'

'I know.' It makes so much difference. I squeezed his hands, hard. 'The day he stops eating, we'll know that it's time and we'll let him go. I promise.'

'Good lass.'

He didn't speak after that. I sat holding his hand in the cool of the room, staring at the melting heat beyond the window and made stories for him of Christmas and dogs playing in snow, of cats catching mice in the winter barns, of pups seeing ice for the first time, finding what it is to walk on water and then what it is for the ground to break underfoot as it breaks in the melt. His eyes flickered from shut to open and back again and his mind came and went with it. The door to the room brushed open and shut and his wife and his daughter came to stand by the bed, the two dogs there in the flesh, calm with the instinct that doesn't need to be told it's a time to be quiet. I would have let go of his hands and gone then but they said no with their eyes and the lass came to stand by my shoulder, her hands on his arm. He opened his eyes once after they got there and smiled and his wife took over the story, pulling in the colour I didn't know, from the places that had been home and his daughter leaned over and whispered in his ear that she loved him and that she'd take care of the dogs and he died as they spoke to him, the two of him, with only the smallest struggle marking the ending.

The mortuary was cold, that evening, and smelled of disinfectant. The slab had been scrubbed clean. The air conditioning was on full, drawing good, sulphurous, Byres Road air down into the room. The chrysanthemums were still in the measuring cylinder at the side, splashing colour into the cold sterility. I topped up their water from the hose that dribbled lightly over the stains on the floor and went looking for Lee. She was in the lab at the back of the mortuary. It was a small room, just as white as the rest but slightly less cold and smelling of formalin-based embalming fluid more than anything else. She was perched on a stool, her eyes fixed to the binocular lenses of a microscope, both hands manipulating a pair of long, fine probes that led under the primary optic. I stood in the doorway and watched her.

'Are you done?'

'More or less. Come on in.' She looked up. 'Bad day?'

'Fairly. Jack Souter's dead.'

'I'm sorry.' She put out an arm, squeezed a hug round my waist. I put my hands on her shoulder and kissed the top of her head. It passed the barriers we'd normally keep to at work but there are times when a friend matters more than propriety.

'It was good. If you have to go somehow, it wasn't bad.'

123

'Liver failure?'

'Mostly. Lungs as well. I think everything just shut down all together.' I pulled up a stool at the side of her microscope and cast around for a smooth change of subject. 'Where's the Gorgon? I thought you were going to get her to cover for you today?'

'So did I.' She shrugged, a loose, preoccupied shrug. 'You win some, you lose some. Doesn't matter. I'm nearly done.' She bent over to the eye pieces again, picked up the long rod from the bench and angled it back under the optics.

'Can I look?'

'Sure.' Her voice came out muffled. 'Try not to jog the rig, will you?'

'I'll do my best.'

Her microscope has a teaching attachment – an expensive add-on that gives the students a preview of the magnified world of their elders and betters. I peered in through the lenses. The world, today, looked like white blotting paper would look from the viewpoint of a monocular bluebottle; a coarse weave of bleached thread with long wisps of finer cotton sparking off at odd angles. A lump of chalk sat in the centre, white, rough edged and granular. Except, of course, it wasn't chalk.

'What's that?'

'I think it might be soda lime. Watch this.'

A glass pipe the size of an elephant's trunk loomed in from the left and deposited a football of liquid on to the rock. The whole mass of it turned a sudden, lurid purple, leaching out into the wide weave of the filter paper.

'Eureka.' She sat up and pushed her stool away from the

124

bench. 'We test positive for soda lime. Now we can go home.'

'Picturesque, anyway.' I took my eyes from the lenses, blinked and refocused on the far side of the room. A name and a picture were pinned to the wall. Our Association's ex-president smiled for the camera, resplendent in full cere-monial regalia. It must have been taken a few hours before he died. 'How are you getting on with Joey?' I asked.

'I don't know.' She spun round in the chair. 'Would you come and have a look?'

'Sure.'

Joey Duncan was still identifiable. His body slid, head first, from the cold-store. The winding sheet came up to his chin, covering the more obvious signs of post mortem investigation.

'What am I looking at?'

'Look at his face. What do you see?'

I'm not a pathologist. Like any art, the ability to see what's there comes with practice. 'I see Joey. He's white. His face is puffed up. His eyes look bruised.' As if someone pressed very hard to get his eyelids to close. In the old days, they used pennies and doubled them up as payment for the ferryman. Now, we use a good long push on to pads of wet cotton wool and leave the dead to pay their own way. This is the price of progress. I looked up. 'What am I supposed to be seeing?'

'You tell me. Look round his mouth. An inch or so either side of his lips and then again on the bridge of his nose.'

I don't have the eyes for this. Or the stomach. I searched his face and tried not to remember too much of what it was like when he was alive. 'He looks dead, Lee. I can't go any further than that.'

'Try this . . .' She pulled an anglepoise lamp down from its resting place on the wall and shone the beam horizontally across the planes of his mouth. His lips threw puckered shadows across to the far wall. His nose shaded half of his face. 'Here.' She traced a finger around two patches of skin on either side of his mouth and another further up on his nose. 'It's bruising. Can you really not see it?'

'Maybe.' I crouched down with my cheek to his shoulder and looked along the line of the beam. With the eye of faith and a deal of imagination, you could see them: three ghosted shadows, greasy fingerprints on the bone china of his skin. I stood up, stretching out the crick in my back. 'If you tell me they're there, I'll believe you,' I said. 'I wouldn't like to say I'd have found them on my own.'

'Fair enough.' She pushed the lamp back up against the wall. 'That's you and Mike both. Maybe I'm hallucinating. Nothing would surprise me.'

'I'm sorry, I can't—'

'Don't be. There's every chance I'm seeing things. It would make more sense if I was. But then we still have to explain the rest.' She turned round and pulled a colour Polaroid print from a file, 'Here, have a look at this.'

It's easier to look at anything pathological at one remove. Or maybe I'm just more used to looking at photographs. A wide expanse of pale pink filled the frame. In the centre, a crescent of red flared like a new moon done in blood. 'What's this?'

'The back of his throat.'

I don't want to think about how she gets wide-angle photographs of the back of a dead man's throat. I looked at it, imagining the original. The crescent resolved into something more mundane. 'Is that a nail mark? A fingernail? Did he stick his finger down his throat to make himself sick, maybe?'

'That's what I thought.' She slid the photograph back into the file. 'So I checked both index fingers. Then I checked all of the others, thumbs included. If he'd made a mark like this, there'd be something to find.'

'So?'

'I don't know.' She shrugged. 'He did a lot of things with his hands that night. He picked his nose. He scratched his back. He made up something banana flavoured for the kid and he mixed it with the index finger on his left hand. As far as I can tell, he ate a fair bit of his own meal without bothering with the cutlery. What he didn't do was stick any one of his fingers down the back of his throat. Not enough to make this kind of mark. And his hands weren't anywhere close to his face when he was sick.'

'That's not altogether surprising, Lee. The man was out cold.'

'He was. Which was odd because his blood alcohol level wasn't all that high. Not for Joey, at any rate.' She tucked the file under her arm. 'Wait here.'

She was back in a moment, a black rubber mask in her hand, a twin to the one Jo McCauley used to give oxygen to Jack Souter as he died. The anglepoise lamp came back down to the horizontal. The fingerprints, a second time, were more obvious, as if, having seen them once, the eye was drawn back to them again. Laid very carefully on Joey Duncan's face, the edges of the mask matched exactly with the bruising. I held my breath and peered very close. When Lee switched hands to hold it right-handed, the heaviest of the marks matched her

127

fingers. We looked at each other across the body.

'Someone tried to give him oxygen?'

'No. I've spoken to Jessica and the paramedics. He was long past oxygen when she found him. And anyway' – the lamp swung back up to its bracket on the wall. The room mellowed without it – 'these are not post-mortem marks. You'll have to take my word for that. If I'm right, and I'm not falling into some bizarre forensic hallucinations, then someone held a mask to Joey Duncan's face while he was still alive and I don't think that they were trying to revive him.'

'Why?'

'I don't know.' She pulled the winding sheet into place and slid Joey Duncan back into his frozen limbo. 'And up to a point, that's not my problem. I've faxed a full report through to MacDonald telling him what I think I can see. If it's still in the realms of imagination by Monday, I'll get Colin Storey-Pugh over from Edinburgh for a second opinion. If he agrees, then it's over to the police from here on in. In the meantime' – she slid the prints back into their file and stored it in a folder on the wall – 'there are a couple of things I need to pick up from the office and then we get the hell out of here while there's still some of the day left.'

Her office is the smallest of all the rooms in the mortuary suite. She had the windows wide open, letting in the heat of the evening, letting out the smell. There were flowers here, too; a mixed bunch, hand-picked from the grove, throwing out a haphazard patchwork of colour and scent. The vase was a rough-thrown pottery thing that I found at the shop in Broadford in April when the three of us – me, her and Eric –

went up to Skye and took a long, hard look at the Cuillin ridge and then decided we'd save it for another year. She keeps the vase as a reminder, a small token of chaos marooned in the sea of order that is her desk. It is so much more organised than mine, her desk. Half a dozen photographs lay in a two by three grid in the space beside the flowers. Mug shots. Blue and bloated and long, long dead. Stomach turning, even without the smell. All the same, I turned round the top one for a closer look. 'Was this the stiff from this morning?'

'Mm?' She looked up. 'Him? Stiff wasn't in it. You could have poured him through a sieve by the time we got him.'

'Thanks.'

'Sorry.' She shook her head and grinned, a weary, half-fired grin. 'I've spent too long staring at bodies today. I'm losing perspective.'

'This one?'

'And Joey. And another look at Eric.' She leant over the desk and turned the top row of prints round, one at a time. 'It's Martin Coutts,' she said. 'Murdoch's pet statistician. Do you remember him?'

'No.' Nor, at this moment, do I wish to.

'Take a look. The bruising on this one's—'

No thank you. 'Lee.' I took her gently by the arm, lifted her bag from her chair and hooked it over one shoulder, then spun her round to face the door. 'It's Friday night. The lad's dead. He's not going to get any deader. It's time to switch off your brain and come home.'

'Kellen . . .'

'You're not staying here.'

'I know. I don't want to.' She turned round. 'What about

129

Knapdale? We were going to go up and collect the car.'

'We were. And we were going to look for a 5-mm friend on the top two pitches of your killer climb. But then you were going to have the afternoon off and I hadn't planned to spend two hours with a dying man. The only way we'd make it there and back in decent time would be on the bike and I'm not sitting behind you on a two-wheeled coffin-filler with us both in this frame of mind. If you still want to go, you can come back and stay at the farm tonight and we'll go up tomorrow. In the car.'

'The weather will have broken by tomorrow.'

'Then we won't die of heat stroke on the rock.'

She leant back against the door-frame, her head on one side, watching me. 'Did I ever tell you you're a control freak, Kellen Stewart?'

'Daily. So we can go to the flat instead, if you like. Or down to the Man for a drink. Or anywhere else that doesn't leave you feeling badgered. Just not three hours up to Knapdale and back. I can't handle it.' I stacked the photographs in a nice, neat, careful pile and laid them upside down on her desk. 'Shall we go?'

The Man is closest and at six o'clock on a Friday night, there's still a fractional chance of finding a seat, especially if you know Bruce and Bruce happens to be running the upstairs bar. We got a half of bitter and a bottle of water and two chicken salads and a seat at the back of the balcony where the air flow is 360 degrees and the smoke's gone out through the ventilation system before it's had time to insult your eyes. Not bad at all for a Friday night in the west end.

Lee drew streaks in the ring from her glass. She only does that when she's tired. 'How's Dee?' she asked.

'Quiet. Introverted. Cranky.'

'Back to normal.'

'More or less. She went home last night.' The salad was warm. Everything that night was warm and sticky and hard on the lungs. 'So you won't have to share the spare room.'

A small spectre of a smile. 'Thank you.'

'I expect it could be arranged if you wanted.'

'Kellen?'

'Yes?'

'Fuck off.'

'You're welcome.' Even the bitter was warm. There was cold condensation down the sides when young Bruce splashed it down on the table. It didn't last for long. 'You haven't heard from Sarah?'

'No.' She shook her head. 'I'd tell you if I had.'

'Sure.'

Peaceful. Close to the bone, but peaceful. And there was no line between the eyes. Yet.

Bruce floated past. If we stay long enough he's going to ask about Eric. I don't really want to get into that. I don't want Lee to have to get into that. Better if we're seen to be talking. 'You were going to tell me something about the pictures on your desk?'

'Mmm.' She smiled sleepily and leant back in her chair. 'I'm not sure you're going to want to know.'

'Try me.'

'OK. The lad in the prints was Martin Coutts. Forty-two years old. Divorced. Lived alone. If you think back to Otago

131

Street, you'll have met him in the Department sometime around then. He's a medical statistician. He worked with Murdoch and the Duncans way back in the days when I was still in surgery. He was one of the few who was happy to see her back. Apparently he liked the way her mind worked.' You would have to know Lee very well to appreciate the irony of that one. You wouldn't have heard it in her voice. I watched her take a long drink straight from the bottle, swallow and smile. The lines around her eyes were no deeper than they should have been. She finished the bottle and spun it carefully in the centre of the table. 'He went to work last Friday morning to another exciting day as a post-doc statistician up on the hill, soft money, no tenure. Got bored of that and went home at lunchtime complaining of a migraine. Nobody saw him again until Ms Friendly Neighbour came round to rescue her cat from his greenhouse about ten this morning and noticed his curtains drawn and a "bad smell" coming from the bedroom. She called in the police who, with their usual tact and skill, failed to ask the neighbour on the other side for her spare key and broke the door down instead thus removing any chance the lads in forensics might have had to check if the lock had been tampered with.'

'Sweet. They weed them in at interview. And so?'

'And so the bedroom faces south with a nice big picture window. He'd been lying in the sun for the best part of a week.'

'Good stuff.' This is why I never wanted to do pathology. 'So why was the mortuary decked out in wall-to-wall policemen when I came in this afternoon? The lad had an axe in his head?'

'No. He had synthetic amphetamines – Flatliners – in his stomach contents which was odd because the packet by his bed said they were Migrotol. They look pretty much identical so either someone was selling him a pup or he was starting to go recreational. And he had soda lime dust up his nose. That's where I found the bit we were looking at this evening.'

'The police think that the locals have taken to snorting soda lime? Is that likely?'

'Who knows? I guess if you're a statistician, you'd need something fairly different to make life exciting. Anyway, that's not why the police were here, I called them in before I found that.' She turned over a piece of lamb's lettuce, pushed it to the side of her plate. 'He had mask marks on his face, Kellen. They match exactly, absolutely exactly, with the ones I found on Joey Duncan and even the police can see them.'

'Oh. Hell.' Somewhere, at the back of my brain, is the headache I've been fending off for the past two days. It hasn't really gone since I woke up on Tuesday morning. This is the kind of thing that it feeds on. This and the heat. 'Why, Lee?'

'I'm not sure.' She gave up on the salad. It wasn't a good day for eating. The air pressed in and left no space for anything else – only the mortuary was cool enough to be pleasant. 'He had enough of the amphetamine on board to space him out but there wasn't enough there to kill him, just like the alcohol wasn't quite enough to kill Joey. And there aren't any marks down the back of his throat.'

'Just soda lime up his nose.'

'Right.' She handed her plate to a passing waitress, then tilted her chair back against the balcony and hooked her heels over the edge of the table. 'Do you remember physiology practical classes, way back in first year?'

'Vaguely.'

'Do you remember the one that gave you your first migraine?'

'How could I forget?' Physiology practicals were always something of an unknown quantity. Half of them were random and very boring exercises in bio-statistics. Most of the rest were the kind of things that would have the place fire-bombed if they happened today; decerebrate frogs, one to a pair, proving obscure facts about the nerve-muscle interface; rat hearts in saline being made to beat at different rates by the addition of adrenalin or beta blockers; a thoracotomy in an anaesthetised rabbit as a class demonstration of the vagal reflexes. None of these was significantly different to anything else we had to learn but somehow it was deemed necessary for something to die so that we would understand the mysteries of cardiac function when the equally obscure mysteries of, say, the control of intestinal motility were to be gleaned only from a textbook. Once in a while, though, we paired up and used each other as the models. That's probably been banned by now, too. In our day, the soda-lime experiment was the earliest and easily the most spectacular.

Soda-lime crystals absorb carbon dioxide to produce sodium carbonate, heat and water. If I looked up my notes I could write out the equation but that isn't quite the point. The soda-lime experiment was designed to demonstrate how easy it is to die when there is no carbon dioxide to tell your body that you're suffocating. We were armed, each of us, with a rubber bag connected to a cylinder of soda-lime granules which was, in turn, connected to a rebreathing mask. A mask like Jack Souter's. Or Joey Duncan's. We breathed slowly and gently into the mask. Our breath went out through the cylinder, into the bag and back again at the next breath. The carbon dioxide was removed by the soda lime. Our bodies used up the oxygen. All that was left in the bag was the nitrogen that makes up the other eighty per cent of room air. Breathing pure nitrogen doesn't keep you alive for very long but the trick of it is that without a rise in carbon dioxide to trigger the central reflexes, you don't notice that you're dying. Nobody lasts for long on diminishing oxygen. Most of us passed out within the first three minutes. When I woke up, I had my first ever migraine. It's difficult to forget that kind of thing. It is difficult, also, to forget the colour of Lee's face as her blood oxygen dropped. A deep, dusky purple. Exactly the same as a cardiac arrest. You don't forget that in a hurry either.

I looked over at Lee, found her watching me, waiting for the pieces to fall into place. 'Was our sievable friend blue when they found him?'

'He was black but most of that was decomposition. I haven't got all the lab reports back yet, but I'd say he was completely hypoxic before he died.'

'Shit. You think someone's been practising physiology labs for real?'

'That's what it looks like.'

'But Joey wasn't purple. He was white. I saw him.'

'He didn't have soda-lime grit up his nose, either. I know. I've spent the best part of the afternoon looking. But if I'm right about the mask marks on his face then we have two men dead in the space of seventy-two hours with remarkably

135

similar pathology. Two deaths that almost, but not quite, look accidental. And then there's Eric . . .'

She brought her chair back to the floor. In this light, with the moving shadows of the fan and the swirling smoke from the floor, she looked different. More vibrant than she was before, more like the old Lee. It's the challenge. She lives for the challenge. 'None of these was an accident, Kellen. Martin Coutts wasn't an accident, Joey Duncan wasn't an accident. Eric wasn't an accident. If I can get Colin to give me a second opinion on the mask marks, then I think I can prove the first two. If we can find the missing friend in the rock tomorrow, then we can prove Eric, by circumstance if not pathology. After that, we have to think very carefully about the other things they had in common.' She paused. Bruce stopped by the table on his way past to check that we were happy. He said nothing, asked nothing, offered no sympathy. It's possible he didn't know. We smiled and drank and shared amazement at the weather and he passed on without touching on anything painful.

Lee looked at her watch as he left. 'Will MacDonald be home at this time of night?'

'I doubt it. If he's not at work, the chances are he'll be out with the dog, but we can call in on him on the way back to the farm if you like.'

'If you don't mind.' She raised a finger and called for the bill. 'If nothing else, we have three deaths of three men in three days. Three's a series, in forensics as much as in medicine. I think he needs to know.'

'I thought you'd faxed in a report?'

'I did. One interim pathology report per body. But I can't

put in writing what I haven't got as proof and it's too vague to work with just yet. All I've got now is a hunch and some marks I think I can see on a face. It's not a pathological certainty. The best I can do is spin it to MacDonald and see if he takes it seriously.'

'Fair enough,' I finished my drink and stood up, hunting in my pockets for the keys. 'Shall we go?'

Three is a series. A thesis on death.

Abstract: Three men die in three separate locations within the space of one week. All deaths appear accidental except under very close post-mortem scrutiny when it appears that at least two of the three may have ante-mortem injuries in common. All three subjects work in the same field of medicine. The statistical probability of this being chance is nil. This presentation proposes the apparent and actual cause of death in each case.

Case one. Dr Eric Dalziel, physician and climber.

Apparent cause of death: fall from a height. Multiple fractures. Rupture of internal organs. Precise cause of death: fracture dislocation at C3/C4 leading to complete transection of the spinal chord.

Negation: Eric was a safe climber. You have to believe that. There is no way he would have climbed that rock without a partner. So, we have to ask ourselves what happened to the partner, the one who should have been there to keep him alive?

They got scared when he fell – realised he was dead and ran?

Unlikely. Climbing accidents happen all the time. You don't hold anyone on suspicion of murder if some idiot chooses to fall off a rock. An innocent partner would report an accident as soon as it happened. Only someone with something to hide would remove all of the climbing equipment and leave.

We have no proof of this.

We don't. But if we can find the friend lodged in the rock, we will have enough to ask questions.

You said that last Tuesday. I've already asked the Rescue to take a look.

And?

And they found nothing.

With the greatest respect, they didn't know where to look.

If you say so.

I do.

Case two. Professor Joseph Aloysius Duncan, orthopaedic surgeon, raconteur, husband and father.

Apparent cause of death: drowning secondary to inhalation of vomitus precipitated by an excess intake of alcohol. Subject's plasma alcohol level found to be 173 milligrams per millilitre, adequate to create unconsciousness in the average adult male but not fatal. Fatal level in the adult male is approximately 300 milligrams per millilitre.

Negation: Joey Duncan had a liver that could chew through alcohol like cockroaches through a barrel of biscuits; 173 mg/ml would have rendered him sleepy, but not unconscious. There is evidence, very nebulous evidence I grant you, but I believe it to be real, of ante-mortem bruising in a position that would coincide with the controlled application of a medical mask. A nail mark has been found in his throat that he did not make. Suppose he was made to breathe something that would make him sleep? Not ether or chloroform, neither of those is fast enough, whatever you might have been led to believe. It takes ten minutes of conscious co-operation to mask someone down on ether. But desflurane, or sevoflurane, even possibly isoflurane, any one of the new volatile anaesthetics, would work in seconds. Ten big breaths and you're gone. If he was already sedated with alcohol, you could cut that time in half.

Have you found any traces of these drugs in his blood?

Not yet. It takes time to run the tests. I'll have the results next week.

But these things don't kill, do they?

No. But they'd get him sleepy enough for someone else to stick their finger down his throat to make him sick.

And leave him lying there, drowning?

Yes. It would be very fast. If you kept the mask on his nose, he wouldn't know anything. He certainly wouldn't be in any position to fight.

Christ.

You said it.

Case three. Dr Martin Damien Coutts, statistician.

Apparent cause of death: mistaken ingestion of amphetamine. No evidence of attempted suicide. No note or other common debris of a suicide found at site of death. Empty pack labelled Migrotol found at site. Pack identified as having contained the synthetic amphetamine *4MTA*, known on the street as Flatliners.

Negation: Martin Coutts is the simplest. Perhaps our serial killer is becoming less careful. Or perhaps this was the first and not careful enough. He was sedated with amphetamine. He may have taken it by mistake but he wasn't given it by mistake. Pharmacists don't make that kind of error, or if they do, they don't follow it up with a mask and a cylinder of soda lime. He hadn't taken enough to kill him, but it would have kept him doped up long enough to breathe out his last breath of oxygen into the bag. Martin Coutts was suffocated, it was simply a more sophisticated method of suffocation than the average pillow.

Who, Lee? Who did this?

I don't know. But whoever is doing this, why ever they are doing it, they have to be a medic. No one else could have put all this together.

Why?

I don't know. I have no evidence. Only an idea.

Just tell me. It's up to us to find the evidence. Just now all we need is enough to stop the deaths. Give me something we can use to stop the killing.

The weather is breaking. My head is breaking with it. Outside, the air is caving in under the pressure, folding and twisting in ever tighter knots until the sky weeps. Inside, my brain has long since caved in. I weep and it makes no difference. The pressure in my left eye grows with the pressure in the room until I know that if I move, it will burst. Outside, there is thunder, long and low: the hidden snigger of gods. Inside, my pulse hammers tidal surf through my ears. When I was a child, I held the twisting shell to my ear and heard the waves. Now, as an adult, I have no shell. I lie rigid on the pillow, splinted with pain and the fear of moving. With every heartbeat, I can hear the hissing rush of the sea, louder than any thunder, and I know that if I move, the swelling balloon that is my eye will rupture, that the thin, cracking shell that is my skull will shatter and spill all that is left of me over the pillows.

The rain falls in single, counted drops on the ledge outside the open window. Three is a series. An old medical joke. A way of counting cases for papers because everyone knows that only with papers, properly published, are careers and reputations built. One is unfortunate. Two is a trend. Three is a series. For the police as well as for the medics, three is the key. As in: 'I have created a series of murders so medically perfect that even the pathologist, even *this* pathologist, could not stand up in a court of law and swear that this is murder.'

Four is Lee. Or maybe Hillary Murdoch. Then whichever one of them is left will be five. And then you will have the full grouping. The totality of the team that came together for a single year in the spring of their careers: the physician, the surgeons, the statistician, the pathologist. It was never a marriage made in heaven and the end results were hell but not significantly worse than any of the hell around them and the flames died down in time. Roles changed and people moved. The surgeons stayed friends with the physician and the three of them moved up their ladders together; one progressed to alcohol and professorship, the second moved by force of circumstance from surgery to the dead ranks of pathology, the third made a name in intensive care. These last two shared a passion for climbing and, later, they shared a house. Of the doctors, only the pathologist was never a friend. She walked across the water and made waves and enemies in equal proportions on the other side until the offer of the ultimate promotion lured her back. The number-cruncher faded into statistical insignificance and would never have been remembered if he hadn't been third on the list of the dead. Or maybe first, because these things are difficult to date.

But why would anyone want to kill a handful of junior doctors?

People died. A lot of people died. I can imagine any one of the relatives would have happily seen us all dead.

How long ago? Ten years? Longer? Why now?

I don't know. But until three months ago, they'd have had to go over to Boston to take out Hillary Murdoch. Maybe it's simply convenient that we're all together now.

And you're sure she's next?

I'm sure of nothing. But I'd put money that anyone who cares enough to take out Martin Coutts will be coming back sometime for the woman who made his career.

The rain is faster now. Uncountable. A drumming rhythm of water on slate. It is softer than it was and the thunder is not so constant. If I listen hard, through the pulsing surf in my ears, I can hear other things in the bedroom. I can hear Nina, breathing slow sleep into her pillow. I can hear the soft hush of the duvet as it moves with the breath and feel the twitch of her fingers against mine as the noise of the rain brings her closer to waking. I can hear an old greyed-out cat, purring in his sleep, a steady, sawing ratchet. He lies on the floor, on his blanket, just in reach of my hand. If I dared to move, I could touch him. He would rather be on the pillow but we have limits and we set them for an eighteen-year-old cat of unreliable continence. Ten years ago, two years ago, he would have been out hunting on a night like this, daring the thunder, risking the slamming death of the lightning. (There is lightning. I can see it, even through closed eyes. It does nothing to help move the pain.) Now, he simply sleeps. By day, he sleeps on the Rayburn. By night he sleeps by the bed. In between, he sleeps on whoever will sit still long enough. Lee sat still. And Stewart MacDonald. Both of them sat, first on the fallen log by the river, in the dancing clouds of midges and the dark speckled soot of the thunder flies, her talking and him listening while she spun him her story of a medical series. A series of medics, deprived of life by a medic. Later, they sat still by the fire, and the cat sat on one and then the other as they talked themselves into knots over the how, which was easy, at least for the statistician, and the who which was impossible except that it had to be a doctor, and the why, which was utterly unknowable and always would be without someone there to answer questions.

And then again, all we are going on is mask marks and a hunch. She could still be wrong. There is always that hope. But she sleeps now with the dog on her bed because however loud the storm and however soft the tread, no one will get past Tîr without us knowing. It should let her sleep for tonight, at least. She needs it more than most.

The storm is close now: bright, bright lightning searing through closed lids and the thunder soon after, a hard crack, like breaking wood, nearly overhead. A horse screams in the darkness. The colt. I know his voice. In all his short life there has never been a storm like this. If I could move, I would go to him but if I try to move now, at the very least I will throw up. He's safe where he is. All the horses are safe in the barn and it's stood worse storms than this one. Only once have I been caught on a night like this with them all outside. Now, I feel the storms coming in time to get them into the barn.

The cat sings old cat songs in his sleep, low, like the thunder. He is nearly gone now, and I have a promise, a binding promise, to the living cat, to a dead man, to my lover, to myself, not to let him go on too long. Still, each morning, I reach down for him and feel the stark bones under harsh fur and I am glad that he's there. I reach down now without thinking and feel a rough tongue on the back of my hand. There is some relief in that. I moved and I didn't break. And the cat still lives. The night could be worse.

The storm moves on. More lightning. Less thunder. The pressure is easing. The air is not as heavy as it was. The pain in my head has moved. It runs back now, from my eye to the small point in my head where it started. Claire Hendon has a tumour, a distant metastasis, growing inside her head. Her pain is constant, even morphine doesn't change it. Mine comes from the alcohol and the heaviness of the storm and a period three days overdue and it will go, in time, if I can sleep.

Sleep is not so impossible now. I turn over in the bed and feel Nina turn over beside me, her arm wrapping round my waist, drawing me in to the warmth and the dark, away from the pain. The clock on the bedside table glows white in the dark. Dawn is two hours away. There is time, still, to sleep.

Chapter Seven

❧

The morning dawned dull and damp, dripping with the after-math of the storm. It wasn't raining, exactly, just a steady smirr that filled the air so that it was wet, like a sauna, and cold, like the inside of a fridge. I slept late and then slept again in the car as Lee drove us out towards Knapdale. The traffic was bad and my car hasn't got the best acceleration in the world so when we got caught behind a queue of caravans on the way across from Tarbert, there was nothing to do but sit it out in third gear, all the way through to Inverary. Not the best way to start a morning. I woke once or twice and thought of offering to drive but Lee's a worse passenger than I am and, in any case, I was having serious trouble staying awake. The headaches were beginning to fit a pattern by then: a screaming session with the power drill followed by three or four hours of sedated semi-consciousness that were, in many ways, more debilitating than the pain. I don't think I could have driven even if I'd wanted to.

We were at the turn-off for the headland before I woke up enough to care about what was going on. Lee pulled the car in under the trees and cut the engine. The mist gathered closer – the headlights made curtains of it and drew them shut. If you looked carefully, you could see the ghosted silver of the birch trunks on the edge of the beam, but only if you knew where to look. Lee opened the door and the cold flowed in like melt-water. She stepped out, tested the ground and then stepped back in and shut the door. She tapped a finger on the steering wheel for a moment. 'It might be safer to walk,' she said.

'With the gear?' It's a good mile from the turn-off to the cliff. I am not fond of walking with a full rucksack if I don't have to. 'Your car's wider than this one. You still got it through.'

'My car had solid ground under the tyres. I wasn't driving on an ice rink.'

'Let me look.'

I got out as she had done and walked to the far reach of the headlight beam then a step or two further into the mist and the trees. The track here is not a real track. The Ordnance Survey have it marked as a footpath and even that is stretching the point. A mixed plantation of birch and pine covers most of the headland and if you were to explore it for a while, you would find that other folk had gone ahead and that the worn state of the grass shows the line of least resistance through the trees. That's as far as it goes. It would be tedious, not difficult, to walk. If you wanted speed, you could call it a bridleway, and find a way through with a horse or a bike. Only Lee, in her wilder moments, would seriously contemplate taking a car. But she did, and she made it, and where one can go, another can follow. Except for the ground. The last time we came up here, we drove on bone-dry earth that crumbled to dust under the weight of her wheels. Now, I walked through the mist on a slurry of pine needles and mud, holding on to the trees for support. Not the best terrain for precision driving. Still, it's a good mile out to the headland.

I walked carefully back down the line of the lights. 'We can give it a go.'

'You want to drive?'

'If you like.' In my car, I take the more ludicrous risks. It would work the same the other way around.

The mist thickened as we pushed forward; it changed steadily from a damp, grey veil to the full smoke dense white of a sea-haar. The headlights bounced back off the wall of it, blinding us both. I switched them off and slid on forwards on sidelights, instinct and memory, all of them hazy. I didn't hit anything badly enough to do any damage.

Even in clear daylight with a decent surface to drive on, I don't know the way in well enough to navigate the last quarter-mile. I got out at a turn in the track and Lee took over, weaving slowly through the trees towards the place where we usually park. A patched hulk loomed out of the mist beside us. Her car. It's in this kind of weather that a camouflaged tarpaulin comes into its own. Even if you knew what to look for, I don't think you'd have found it without a hand-drawn map showing every tree in detail. We pulled up and sat for a while in silence, staring out at the tree-shapes and the curved mound of the tarpaulin. I kept the car heating on full. You can't store up heat any more than you can store up sleep. I know this but it never keeps me from trying.

Outside the car, the world was every bit as grim as it looked. The air, without the mutter of the engine, hung very still. Even the wash of the waves on the cliff came up softly, filtered through cotton wool. I blew on my hands and dragged my cuffs down over my fingers to keep warm.

'Eric's bike was in here.' Lee emerged from denser scrub beyond the car. No tracks showed a route in or a pathway out but then, until last night, the ground was like concrete. A biker's convention could have spent the weekend driving across it and they wouldn't have left any tracks. She held back a tangle of bramble and thorn and I looked in at the bed of crushed nettles and flattened grass. A good place, like a nest. You could imagine a dog turning in circles, beating it down for a bed. Several dogs. 'There've been a lot of folk in here.'

'One bike. Half a dozen of MacDonald's minions with size twelve Doc Martens. If there was anyone else, we're not going to see anything now.'

So maybe we should have come up on Sunday morning after all. These things are always easiest in retrospect.

'Any sign of the friend?'

'I can't see it.' She let go of the thorns and the knotwork re-formed in front of us. 'If it's anywhere, it'll be in the rock.'

Which is, of course, why we are here. To climb the top two pitches of an E2 on dripping rock in a world where I can barely see my hands at the end of my arms.

I looked past her, out towards the headland. The fog swirled around us like smoke from a greenwood fire, a cold fire that ate at the lungs and bit sharp on the tongue with the salt from the sea. I walked out towards the edge. A single, well-aged rowan loomed up, a dozen yards out, twisted and bent from the decades of Atlantic weather but solid all the same. I leant on it, hands in pockets, and called back over my shoulder: 'Could we abseil down to the ledge from here?'

'We could.' I heard the smile of it through the mist. She had the ropes out, lying in ordered coils on the rucksacks. Her belt hung from her hand. 'And we could probably check out all the possible placements for the friend. But I didn't come all this way out not to finish the route.' She looked up. 'I need a belay – I'm not going up it without, but I can do both pitches on my own and you can walk out when I get to the top. There's nothing says you have to come up the climb if you don't want to.'

Right.

Challenge. It's all to do with challenge. I am no more immune than she is. 'No. If we're doing it, we'll do it together. As long as you promise me the fourth pitch was the crux.'

'Definitely.'

'Fine.' I skirted half-buried roots and the odd misplaced stone on the way back to the car and lifted my harness and spare over-trousers from the boot. 'We'd better get going, then, while I can still feel my hands.'

There's something completely unique about climbing in fog that's so much more disorienting than the simple blindness of night. In the dark, your mind compensates for the lack of input, your eyes carve faint shapes from the black. In the white-out of fog, like the hiss of white noise, there is so much input, it swamps everything else. At times like this, it's probably safer to close your eyes and go up on the feel in your fingers. But that way, you are more likely to miss the small bit of metal that might be the link to a death. So you don't. You keep your eyes open and climb the way you always climb, only more slowly and with more deliberate care and you pray that you don't lose the feel in your fingers anytime before you reach the top.

Lee took the first pitch. There was no discussion about that. The fourth was mine and so the fifth was hers. Tradition and habit combined. We roped on in the close confines of the fog and muttered the calls, softly, as if the world lay asleep on the other side of the veil. I stood on the ledge, feeling the ropes drag out through my hand and her head was out of sight before her feet passed the level of my eyes. I was standing maybe twenty feet from where I first found Eric. There was no sheep.

The rope tugged in my hand. A whisper, from nowhere: 'I need some slack.'

'You've got it.'

'Clipping in on blue.'

'Fine.' So if she falls now, she will not crack her skull on the ledge. Not unless I let go. The ropes slid on out. The air clung close, a second skin, whispering sea-tales into both ears; truth in the left, the lies in the right. *She loves you. She loves you not. Come on down, the water's lovely. Stand still, it isn't safe. He fell on his own. He fell with a friend. He didn't fall, he was pulled.*

Pulled. If I pulled now, Lee would fall. It wouldn't take that much. If she's balanced on a fine hold, with one hand searching her rack for a hex, maybe, or a sling, then it would take almost no pull at all. It's a sixty-foot drop from there to the ledge. Only fifteen feet less than Eric. Far enough, probably, to die.

'Clipping in on red.'

'Fine.'

The ropes slid on out. I locked them when they needed locking and let them slip when they needed slack. I didn't pull.

She made a hanging belay fifty metres up: three large hexes wedged in a broad horizontal crack with a couple of small runners out at angles above and below. Overkill and then some. You could hang her car off that and it would stay put. I joined her there, clipped on and sat back in my belt, braced on the rock.

'You were right. The fourth was the crux.'

'I know.' She smiled through the mist, a flicker of fire in the damp. 'You OK to go on up?'

'Sure.' I can't see the rock more than five inches above my head but at this stage, all I need to do is to check out gravity and go the other way.

'It's a straight crack all the way to the top.'

'Thanks.' I clipped spare slings into my belt. 'You didn't find the friend?'

'No.'

'I'll keep a lookout.'

'Thanks.'

I climbed up on wet rock. I am not fond of wet rock. I am particularly not fond of wet, white rock with invisible hand-holds – altogether too much like climbing ice. Remind me, if I ever suggest otherwise, that climbing on ice is the end-point of madness. The crack was wide. It took my fist, nicely jammed, and my feet, one over the other, edged in at angles. It took a hex, for protection, that was easily as wide across as my fist. From there, I couldn't see anywhere, I couldn't *feel* anywhere that would take something as small as a 5-mm friend.

'Clipping in on blue.'

'Got you.'

Move on up. This is not so precarious. It would take a serious pull now, for Lee to peel me off this rock. It could be done, but she'd have to pick her moment and from here, unless she cut the rope first, I'd probably drag her off as I fell. Eric's ropes had not been cut.

Another hex, smaller than the last. Still not anywhere near the thumb's width of the friend. 'Blue again.'

'Fine.'

And blue, and blue and once on red and nowhere in reach of my fingers, a friend.

It was a good pitch. I was warm when I reached the last hold. My fingers tingled with the cross currents of fresh circulation. I felt the surging rush of endorphins as I stepped over the top, bright, tingling and alive: the best feeling in the world. It's the challenge: the race fought and won; the exam passed. The enemies, inside and out, defeated. This is still why I do it.

'Safe,' the best word in the climbing vocabulary. I called it down. The mist swallowed my voice and a while later, spat it back, moulded and changed.

'You're off.'

'OK.'

I fixed the belay and called again into the gloom. 'Climb when you're ready.'

'Climbing.'

Take in on blue. Take in on red. There could be anything or anyone on the end of these ropes. If you wanted to kill someone, today would be the day. They'd never see you coming.

But there was no death that day. I took in and I took in and when the ropes ran out, it was something like the old Lee who came over the top with her hair damped down tight to her head, black and sleek, so she looked like a soot-painted otter emerging from water.

'Hey, we did it.'

'Was it good?'

'Not bad.' It was her climb, she would say that. But she was smiling as she made the final step over the edge.

We hugged, because we always hug at the top of a climb, to share of the joy of it, the final release from fear, the sheer, spectacular, mind-numbing thrill of the challenge. It was good. Even on a day like this, on a climb like this, after a month like this, it was good. I held her tight, her head on my shoulder and felt the tone of her under my hands. I would like to say she was back at peace, the way she was when we first started all of this, the way she usually is at the top of a climb, but I'd be lying if I went that far. She was relaxed, she was cheerful, she was alive and the fire was burning. But she was not at peace.

'Have we got a name for it, Adams?'

'I don't know.' She drew back, her hands linking through mine. It was always hers, the naming of this climb. She found it, she mapped it, she planned it. She will have named it, too, in her head, if not on paper. 'I need to think about that.' She dropped her hands and began to untie the knot at her belt. 'Maybe after we've done the E5 variant.'

'I'm sorry?' I didn't hear that. It was the buzz in my ears from the cold.

She was chewing her bottom lip, her eyes focused some-where far off in the fog. 'There's a second route up. The first pitch goes up the overhang and then off to the right. We haven't done it all the way but it's E4 as far as we've done and it gets harder going on up. Eric's pretty sure the crux is E5.'

Wrong tense but I didn't correct it. I was still trying to believe I hadn't heard. In my wildest dreams, I wouldn't do an E5, whatever the weather.

'He wouldn't have . . .?'

Her eyes narrowed. She looked out beyond the edge. 'I don't know. He might have done. They run pretty close together in places. You couldn't tell from the floor which one he'd gone up.'

'Lee, we can't do this now.'

'I know.' She stretched out an arm, away from us both. Her hand disappeared in the fog. 'I'd want to be able to see more than six inches in front of my face before I think about that one.' She pulled in the rope to her feet. 'I thought maybe you could top rope me from the tree. It's not so far off the line and I could go down and have a look, at least as far as the length of the rope.' She bent down and picked up the free end of the rope. 'Trust me. It won't take long.'

It took half an hour and my fingers were white and insensate long before she reached the full length of the rope and turned round to come back up. She found nothing but then I'm not sure she was expecting anything different. I stood up as she came over the edge. 'You're sure you don't want to go down to the ledge and try the bottom bit?' There is, after all, a good eighty feet beyond the end of the rope to the ledge.

'I'm sure.'

'Good. I'd have you committed if you did.' I started coiling the ropes. 'Are we going to get the cars out without a tractor, do you think?'

'Of course.' She grinned, still high from the climb. 'And if we don't, we can always call the Rescue and get another air lift off.'

She was right. Her battery was flat and we had to jump start her car but once it was going, the way out was, in many ways, easier than the way in. I followed her tail-lights down the track and out through the trees on to the road. The mist was clear there and the traffic lighter than when we drove up. I kept her in sight while we were still on the peninsula but she has a bigger car with a bigger engine and she drives it in the same way she drives her motorbike and I lost sight of her tail-lights ten minutes after we reached the open road.

Twenty minutes after that, the mist began to thicken into rain. Thin, weedy drops of it strung ever faster together until soon, even with the wipers on high speed, it was hard to see through the windscreen. An hour later it was as torrential as it had ever been. Container lorries and caravans slowed down on the wet roads and I had no chance at all of passing either. I switched on the radio and settled down for the long, tedious journey home.

I drove into an empty yard. Very few things cancel an afternoon's trekking but unremitting rain is one of them. Sandy's car was there, and Lee's, but none of the usual Saturday tourists and no sign of Kirsty or wee Jon or any of the weekend hang-around kids. A day off for the rain and they're welcome. I left my car in its slot in the shed and kicked my wet shoes off at the back door.

'Hi, people, I'm home.' I called it in from the porch. The dog appeared at the doorway, damp and mud-streaked and happy to see me. The cat looked up from the Rayburn and rasped a greeting. Nobody else said anything. Nina was there, and Sandy, they sat on opposite sides of the fire, oddly silent. I stepped in through the doorway, still high on the buzz of it, not thinking too clearly, not feeling the atmosphere. 'What's up, guys? Where's Lee?'

Nothing.

'I'll make the lass her coffee.' Sandy stood up, cracking the knots in his fingers. His eyes scanned past mine, finding other things to see. This is not like Sandy. The last time he looked this bad, his colt was three days old and dying.

'Sandy . . .?'

He shook his head and made heavy work of fitting the top on the kettle. He has arthritis, but it isn't that bad. 'White, no sugar, aye?'

'Yes. Thank you.' I turned round. Nina stood with her forearms on the mantelpiece, staring at the crumbles of burning peat in the fire. All I could see was the shape of her back and the tangled chestnut of hair. Shadows of past nightmares grew up out of the fire. It's the horses. Something's wrong with the horses. Or Lee. Or Nina . . . Dear God, if it's Nina . . . A familiar, throbbing heat swelled at the back of my left eye. It was gone this morning when I woke up, I swear it was gone.

I stood behind her, both hands on her waist. 'Nina? Are you all right?'

'Yes. I'm fine.' She turned round, hooked her elbows on the mantelpiece. 'It's not me. Will you sit down? Please?'

'No. Just tell me what's happening.'

'Here's your coffee, lass.' Sandy came round the counter with three mugs and a tray of biscuits, the very image of solicitude. He tried to hand me a mug. 'Will you not sit down?'

Jesus Christ, what is this? *'No.'*

I moved, for the sake of moving. They stood together by the fire, each of them waiting for the other to speak. I went over to the sink, to the safe space behind the breakfast bar. We have an old steel kettle with a curving, swan-necked spout. It sits all day at the side of the Rayburn, as much a part of the place as the cat. I angled the spout under the tap and turned on the water. Pointless, but I feel better if I have something to do. I kept my back to them both. 'Will one of you please tell me what the hell is going on?'

'It's Dr Adams. She . . .'

'It's Lee. The police were here. She's under arrest.' It was Nina who finished the sentence.

'What?' Water sprayed fan-wise over the sink as the spout swung under the jet of the tap. I switched off the tap, sat the kettle carefully back on the Rayburn and turned to face the fire. 'What for?'

'The murder of Hillary Murdoch.'

'But she's not—?'

'She died sometime early on Friday morning. Her husband found the body this morning.'

Oh, hell. Bloody, bloody hell. *Three is a series. Four is Lee. Or maybe Murdoch. Then whichever one of them is left will be number five.* Lee. The only one left is Lee.

I slid down the side of the breakfast bar. The curved handle of the cupboard dug into the small of my back. The tiles were cold under the damp seat of my jeans. The stoked heat of the Rayburn warmed the side of my face. The power drill behind my left eye drove forwards in an exploding scatter of pain. *The weather has broken. My head has broken with it.*

I don't believe this is happening.

'Kellen . . . come and sit down.' Nina's arms reach under mine. I am pliable, like the newly dead. She walked me over to the chair by the fire. Her eyes were close to mine, examining. 'Is your head still bad?'

'She's next, Nina. This proves the series. Lee's next.'

'Maybe. She's probably as safe with the police as anywhere.' Her fingers were on my wrist. 'You didn't sleep last night, did you?' She looked less pale, as if, for her, the worst of it was over.

'I slept fine.'

'If you say so.' She knows the measure of my lies. She nodded at someone over my head and I heard Sandy pick up his coat and leave. I heard his footsteps on the yard, heard him pull back the door to the barn. The feed bins rattled. The colt whinnied, a high-pitched child's voice with a breaking dip in the end. Nina left me and went back to the Rayburn. 'Did you have anything to eat on the way down the road?'

'What?' I don't remember. 'No. I didn't stop.'

'Right.' She opened the Rayburn. The smell of cooking hit my head and my stomach in quick succession.

'No . . . Not a good idea.'

'Yes it is.' She brought over a plate balanced on a small round tray, and laid it on the floor by my feet. 'Shepherd's pie. Jon's mum made it for when the weather turned.' The rain ran in clear sheets down the window. 'I'd say this counts as turned.' She crouched, half kneeling, at my knee. 'You're not going to be any use to anybody if you're too sick to move, Kells. You may not be getting any sleep but you need to eat at least. You eat and I'll tell you what I know and then we can sort out if there's anything useful we can do to help.' She smiled and it was all so reasonable: the inexorable logic of the surgeon. I am surrounded by this.

I picked up the fork. The smell of food won over the pain in my head. 'OK,' I said. 'Talk to me.'

Nina settled down with her back to the chair. 'Hillary Murdoch was due to come in and cover for Lee from mid-day on Friday. Sometime before that, she had a visitor.'

'A visitor?'

'She let someone into her flat. There is evidence that there was someone else there. There is no evidence of forced entry.'

'It was hot. All her windows would have been open.'

'She lives on the third floor of a tenement block that faces straight on to Great Western Road. A good climber could have got up there but they would have been seen doing it. May I go on?'

'Yes.'

'Thank you. The visitor arrived some time after Professor Murdoch's husband —'

'She's married? Are you serious?'

'. . . after her husband left for work, but before Professor Murdoch finished her breakfast. From this, knowing her usual routine, they are assuming that the time was around seven-thirty. You don't have an alibi for Lee at seven-thirty on Friday morning, do you?'

'No.'

'Thought not. The assailant was offered a glass of water – water, note, not tea or coffee – which was not touched. Murdoch may have made herself a coffee but if so, she dropped it. Pieces of broken mug have been found wrapped in newspaper in the kitchen bin. There was a small volume of coffee found in her stomach contents.'

'So how did she die?'

'They don't know yet. There's a mark behind her right shoulder that looks as if someone's pushed in an eighteen-gauge needle. It went through the muscle and on into her right lung. Something might have been injected but the temporary pathologist—'

'Who?'

'They've called in Colin Storey-Pugh from Edinburgh. Apparently he was Lee's first choice for cover if it was ever needed?'

'Yes.'

'He's trying to find out what was injected but we're talking needles in haystacks. There's some evidence of trauma as if she fell forwards after the blow and her skeletal muscle looked as if she had gone into spasm before she died. There's bruising under her arms and it looks as if she was lifted back into the sitting position while she was still alive. That's as far as they've got.'

'What about the husband?'

'He came home on the first train this morning. He'd been at a meeting in Edinburgh and stayed overnight. Multiple rock-solid alibis. He turned up home at eight o'clock to find his loving wife dead at the breakfast table. He's under sedation at the Western now. Whoever else it might have been, it wasn't him.'

'So what in heaven's name makes them think it was Lee?'

'The body was found in the kitchen. When they went through to the bedroom, they found a pad by her bed. It had Lee Adams's name on it in Hillary Murdoch's handwriting.'

'A name's not evidence, Nina. They can't have taken her in on the strength of that.'

'It was enough for them to take her in for questioning. They let her call a lawyer. She got hold of Doug before they left and he called in twenty minutes ago to let us known they'd just finished the first round of interviews. He's fairly sure they don't have a case unless they find something that can link her directly to one of the murders.'

'One of . . .?'

'They're taking her serial theory seriously. Storey-Pugh's confirmed that there are mask marks on Joey Duncan's face. He and Martin Coutts are now technically the first two in a series which has Hillary Murdoch as the third. They'll add Eric to the list if anyone can prove it was murder.'

'Why the hell do they think it's Lee? She's far more likely to be next in line.'

'Apparently MacDonald thinks she had reason enough to hate Murdoch and the others could have been incidental. It's a known technique, apparently, to wipe out a few innocent bystanders and then hit the one you're really after.'

You have to be kidding. 'Right. This has gone far enough.'

'Where are you going?'

'To find MacDonald and sort out what the hell is going on.'

'Are you sure that's a good idea?'

'Perfectly. Give Sandy a hand to feed the ponies, will you? I won't be long.'

★　★　★

Stewart MacDonald, when he is not at the farm, not at work and not out in the fields with the dogs, is usually to be found at his brother's forge, dallying with the tools of farriery or helping out with the horses or something equally rural. It's not that he has no home of his own to go to, it's just that he prefers not to spend very much of his time actually in it. His cottage, when I passed it, showed no signs of life: no car in the drive; no lights; no smoke from the chimney; nobody home. I took a right at the church and drove the four miles down the lane to the forge. His car was there in the yard, pulled up by the horse trough with room to spare for at least one more. His brother, quite clearly, was out.

My head throbbed, a steady all-over drumbeat, in time with my heart. Too fast, too tight, too near to break-point. Talking shop with MacDonald is a dodgy business at the best of times, doing it with anything but a clear head is downright stupidity. I did not, just then, have a clear head.

I left the car parked by the fence and walked slowly under the archway and up towards the stable block and the paddocks at the back. The walls of the forge stood to my left, thick with centuries of whitewash. MacDonald's father owned this and his father before him and his father before that, for generations back into Scotland's warped and bloody past. It is his home in the way the farm is mine. He is safe here. Until now, I have always felt safe here too. I don't have to let that go. It is not the place itself that is dangerous. Only him. And me, if I don't calm down.

I walked round the corner to the stables: great, high-walled, slate-roofed horse-mansions with oak cladding as high as my shoulder and brass fittings that were new when Victoria was a child. The flagged stones of the walkways are old now, worn down by the weather and generations of horses passing through. The stone feed-bowls in the boxes have grooves cut by the constant rub of resting chins. The walls are green with lichen, dry, crumbling grey-green fungus spreading in snow-flake patterns across the paler surface of the stone. This is the world as it was before Stewart MacDonald and I were ever born. If his brother plays his cards right, it will still be like this and will still be in the family long after we have gone. This is the kind of thing that settles my sense of perspective. I walked on to the far end of the row then turned left and circled the yard and back through the archway to the front door. Pain fuzzed at the back of my head like the heat from an open fire. Not bad, just constantly there. Better than it had been. The rain cooled it on the ten-yard walk from the stables to the door.

MacDonald's dog lay in wait for me in the porchway, a long-legged hooligan in white and tan, guarding the threshold. I bred this dog. She should know where her loyalties lie. I turned sideways to soften the impact of greeting. 'Away and get your father, dog. Tell him he's in big trouble.' The dog grinned and stayed where she was, following other orders. I kicked off my shoes and pushed my way past a tangle of boots in the porchway, on into the long, high-beamed room that Duncan MacDonald has made the centre of his home.

'Oh, it's yourself.' He was there waiting for me by the waterwheel. I love, have always loved, that wheel. I am not going to turn the feel of it sour today.

'Where's Duncan?'

'He's away off out on a job. Moira Galbraith's had one of her event horses throw a shoe and she wants it for competing tomorrow so he took out the mobile forge and he—'

'Won't be back until you tell him it's safe to come home?'

'I dare say he might call in at the farm on the way past, yes.'

'You're a chancy bastard, MacDonald, you know that?'

'It's good to see you too, Dr Stewart.' He smiled. The wheel turned slowly. Tumbling water-light spun past me, out into the room. I smiled back. 'The coffee's in the pot on the table,' he said.

The coffee was hot, fresh ground, fresh poured. Three mugs stood on the table. Wherever Duncan MacDonald had gone, he hadn't been out for long.

'What's going on?'

'I don't know.' He poured himself a second coffee and moved over to a leather armchair that sat facing the water-wheel. 'How much do you know about serial killers?' he asked.

'Very little.' I sat on the edge of the great oak beam running at waist height across the full width of the room. My shoulders fitted comfortably against the glass arc of the wheel casing. Cascades of water made music behind me. 'I know Lee isn't one of them.'

'Is that so?' He nodded slowly, blowing across the surface of his mug. 'Because she's not capable of killing three folk in a row?'

'Amongst other things, yes. And even if she was, it's not the most likely collection of people. Joey was a friend. She wouldn't wish him any harm. Martin Coutts was a nobody, a number-cruncher. I can't think why anyone would care enough to want him dead. That only leaves Hillary Murdoch and she . . .'

'. . . died quite differently to the others. Which is interesting, don't you think?'

'Not particularly. Should it be?'

'It should if we're thinking of serial murder, yes. There should be a signature, some quirk about the way each one died that tells you that the same person was responsible for all of them. We don't have that here.'

'So maybe they're not linked.'

'Absolutely. Maybe they're not. In fact, if you think about it, the only reason we think they might be is because Lee Adams sat in your kitchen last night and told us we had a serial killer on the loose. And then she told us Hillary Murdoch was going to be next, which was interesting, given that the woman had been dead for at least twelve hours by then.'

He talks this way in an interview room, I can feel it: the rolling, lilting West Highland accent seeding doubt and insecurity in its wake. I sat still for a moment, listening to the chirrup of the water, gathering thoughts that made sense. Few of those and far between. I gave up.

'I don't follow.'

'I'm not sure that I do. I've spent all day trying to fit together four separate deaths and it's only since I've come home that I think maybe I've been heading down the wrong track.' He left his coffee on the table and came to sit on the beam at the far end of the wheel. The glass of the casing is thick and wavy and the light coming through it is green. The sheen of it rolled over his face, easing years off his skin, adding strange tones to his hair. From here and like this, he could be thirty, a youth again, still wet behind the ears. 'You went back up to the rock today, didn't you?' he asked. 'You and Lee?'

'Yes.'

'And you didn't find the friend?'

'We didn't find it. That doesn't mean it isn't there to be found.'

'No. But that's you and the Rescue both. So we're back to square one on that one.' He held up a hand. I let out the breath before I knew that I'd taken it in. 'Let's just leave Eric open, shall we? He's dead and he died in a fall. We don't need to know any more at the moment. Then we have Joey and Martin Coutts both drugged or intoxicated, both dying peacefully in their sleep.'

'Each with mask marks on his face.'

'Which is halfway to a signature. I'm not forgetting that. I have your friend Storey-Pugh going over Professor Murdoch with a magnifying glass as we speak but there were no signs of a mask when I saw her and however she died, I wouldn't have said it was peaceful. We're definitely cranking up the action on this one.' He picked up the coffee pot and refilled my mug. The coffee was tepid and heavy with grounds. I swirled the mug and watched them spin up and settle on the sides. I didn't want, at that moment, to think. The water filled the silence until I realised he was waiting for me to speak.

I looked down at the long, seamless channel of stone below the wheel, smooth and worn with the ages. I didn't try to meet his eye. 'Go on.'

'I'm thinking perhaps we have three separate things. We have Eric killed in an accident. Then we have person or persons unknown who have it in for Joey and Martin Coutts in what looks like two sequential murders. And then we have a young woman, a highly intelligent, highly motivated, somewhat unstable young woman, with a life-long grudge, who sees her moment and takes it.' He leant forward, one arm hooked over the casing, the water playing wilder games with the planes of his face. 'It may not be the answer that either of us wants, but it's the only thing I can come up with that makes sense of the facts.'

'But this is Lee, Stewart. You know her. She wouldn't do that. She may be strange, she may be driven, she may be way out there on the far edges of over-achievement, but she's not mad.'

'Did I say she was? You don't have to be that far off normal to kill someone, Kellen. There are days in this job when I think the ones who kill are a deal more sane than the rest of us who plan it all and don't carry it through. Think about it. Think about the kind of woman she is. You said yourself that her work was her life, that all she wanted to be was a surgeon. Then she lost it overnight, all down to Hillary Murdoch. Smaller minds might have cracked at that. Not Lee. She picked herself up and she changed her focus. In her work, she took up pathology, but that wasn't enough, she needed a new passion, a new meaning, something to do with all that energy. Cutting up the dead was hardly going to hit the spot so she diverted into climbing. And she had Eric, a man who, without doubt, shared her loathing of Hillary Murdoch. For years, for half a lifetime, it was enough. Until one day he wasn't there.' He leant forward further. His fingers whitened on the edge of the oak. 'Eric's dead, Kellen. Suddenly, without warning, he's dead and who knows what promises you make in the dark of your soul while you're cutting up the body of the man you shared your life with? When he was alive, he was an anchor, a stabiliser, a reason to stay out of trouble. But in death, is he not perhaps a trigger? Is she free now to do things she would not, could not have done while he was still alive?'

'No.' It came out hoarsely. I cleared my throat and said it again. 'No. She couldn't do it, Stewart. She wouldn't. She's got more to live for than that.'

'Has she?' He leant back on the casing, his eyes turned to the ceiling, and all of him was lost in the slow-spinning shadow of the wheel. His voice was softer than it had ever been and very thoughtful. 'Were they lovers?' he asked. 'Lee and Eric?'

Of all things, I wasn't expecting that. I stared. 'You'd have to ask her that.'

'I did.'

God. 'So then why ask me?'

He shrugged and turned his face back into the half-light of the water. He smiled, open and friendly and with a sliding hint of apology. 'Corroboration?'

'What did she say?'

' "Not often enough to be relevant." '

'So that's it, then.' He was sitting two feet away, watching me. His whole being was still, as if by stillness he could get what he needed. 'Once. It was once and it was a very long time ago. Like she said, that's not often enough to be relevant.'

'Why just the once?'

'Because they were neither of them the type to make the same mistake twice.'

'But they were still good friends?'

'As close as two people can get.' I stood up and moved back to the table. Away from the softening slur of the water, the brighter light of the room aged us both. 'Friendship's an odd thing, Stewart, and sex can be so very, very complicated. Sometimes the closest friends are the ones you don't sleep with.' I turned round again so I could see him. 'I thought perhaps you might know about that.'

He said nothing. The wheel creaked round. Water and gravity played on the stones. In time he said, 'Aye, maybe I do.'

There was peace, a hiatus of quiet. The silence stretched on as if both of us had run out of things to say. He stood up eventually and stretched, snapping his fingers. His dog appeared in the doorway. She's a pup, really, too young for all this hanging around. He ran his hand through the rough hair on her head. 'I thought I'd take her out lamping tonight,' he said. 'If you've no objections?'

'Fine by me.' It's my land, theoretically, but he knows what I think about folk who claim ownership over the land. 'Come in for a coffee if the lights are still on when you're done.'

'I'll do that.' He walked with me to the door and stood with his hand on the lintel while I laced up my shoes. 'Doug McKinnon's a good lawyer,' he said. 'He's got her well looked after.'

'Pity she needs him, all the same.'

'I don't want her guilty, Kellen. You know that.'

'You'd better find out who really did it then, hadn't you?'

Chapter Eight

She didn't come home that night. I went to bed after two and got up at six and there was still no sign. At seven, I called Doug McKinnon's office and reached a machine that gave me his mobile number. His mobile offered to take a message. I left my name and hung up.

I made breakfast and didn't eat it and drank too much coffee instead. Outside, the yard came slowly to life. Sandy was out first, checking the in-foal mares for signs of imminent parturition. Kirsty hauled back the doors to the barn, turned on the taps along the wall and started filling water buckets. Wee Jon slung a handful of head collars over one shoulder and set off down the field. I met him at the gate on the way back in. He stepped carefully through the gate and handed me a fistful of ropes: Echo and Balder in one hand, Friday and Teal in the other. He said nothing that mattered and if I hadn't seen Sandy talking to him when they first drove in, I would have believed he had nothing to say. He is good like that, Jon, not given to unnecessary conversation and it was, in many ways, easier not to talk. We walked in tandem up to the barn. Kirsty had the right doors open. We looped lead ropes over necks and let the ponies find their own way in to breakfast. Jon reached up to a bracket and handed me another fistful of ropes. 'We'd best make the most of the break in the weather,' he said. 'It'll not last.'

'Right.' I learned a long time ago not to disagree with his views on the weather. 'I'll get the rest of them in and start skipping out the pond field.'

He looked at me sideways. 'If you like.'

It's a long time since I wandered round a field shovelling heaps of dung into a barrow. The school kids do it at weekends, normally for free rides or extra pocket money. Even they get bored of it fairly fast. I scoured both of the fields opposite the house until there wasn't a single ball of horse dung left in either of them. Still she didn't come.

I finished about ten. By then, Sandy had the colt out in the paddock, lunging him in long-reined circles, letting him get the feel of a girth and a bit without feeling tied in by either. Nina and Kirsty were moving the mares and foals, a pair at a time, to a paddock further down the burn. Jon had the ponies tacked up and ready and was chivvying the gaggle of kids and west-end matrons who made up his Sunday morning ride, hassling them as a sheep dog hassles late spring ewes: slow and steady and always heading in the same direction. I went inside to fill the feed bins, I think, or sort out the grooming kits, something similarly undemanding. Either way, I was right at the far end of the barn when the car pulled up in the yard. I heard the car door slam and then the kitchen door open and heard wee Jon suddenly snap his dawdling troupe to attention. He had fifteen of the fair, far and forties up on their horses and champing at the bit before I was past the last box and out into yard. He spun Balder round on his heels to face me. His face was closed, unreadable. He nodded back towards the house. 'You'll be needed inside,' he said, then he wheeled back to the top of the ride and was gone.

She was asleep in the kitchen, curled up on the hard wood of the window seat with her head lolling out towards the glass and her arms falling limp at her sides. Her hair was dull and it clung to the side of her face as if she'd spent too long with her hand on one side of her head. The shadows under her eyes were brown, the colour of old tobacco stains. Her face was white as if they'd drained her of blood and for the first time in years, the old, fine-stitched scars of the knife wounds showed up as two shining hair lines bisecting the length of her jugulars. The dog followed me in and pushed her nose on the back of one dangling hand. It swayed and was still. She never stirred.

A shadow moved at the far side of the room. I looked up. Doug McKinnon stood in the space behind the breakfast bar. His jacket hung over a stool. His tie hung out of a pocket and his shirt sleeves were creased over his elbows. 'She needs sleep,' he said. She was not, clearly, alone.

'She'll get it.' I moved over and switched on the electric kettle. It makes less noise than the one on the Rayburn. 'What happened?'

He took off a pair of blue-framed glasses. A livid red dent showed on either side of his nose, glistening in the light from the window. He rubbed a hand across his eyes. 'They couldn't get her to change her story,' he said. 'A name on a pad isn't enough for a charge. They had to let her go.'

'They've been at her all night?'

He nodded. 'The last one gave up half an hour ago. I think they've nailed down every movement she's made in the last six weeks. She can tell you what bit of rock she climbed at four in the afternoon three weeks ago last Friday and it's still the same when they come back to it eight hours later.' He swept a hand through the thinning strands of his hair. 'I'd like to see any one of them doing that.'

'Was Stewart MacDonald there?'

'He drove her in first thing yesterday then went away and came back about eight last night. He stayed through till this morning.'

Did he indeed? Just at this moment, I can't tell if that's good or the worst possible thing he could have done. 'So is that it? Is she free?'

'That's it for the moment.' He took a coffee and spun in a spare sugar. 'They still think that she did it but they can't charge her without more proof. I think she might find she has a dark blue shadow for a while but that's about as far as they can go.'

'MacDonald said that?'

'No. He didn't have to. You get to know these things.'

Great. He hadn't slept either and it showed as much in the lines of strain on his face as in the state of his clothes. In law, like in medicine, long nights go with the job and the ability to cope doesn't necessarily get any better with practice. He leant back on the Rayburn and drank his coffee as if he hadn't seen any for days. The cat muttered something coarse. He's not fond of strangers leaning on his Rayburn. He stepped down slowly from his safe spot on the warm plate to the top of the window seat and from there, unsteadily, to the curve of Lee's arm. She shifted sideways in her sleep to give him space. The grate of his purr rattled out through the room.

McKinnon finished his coffee, and dumped the dregs in the sink and picked up his jacket. I followed him out to his car. 'She said she wanted to come here and pick up her car and then go straight home.' He threw his jacket on to the passenger seat. 'It's none of my business but I really don't think she should drive for a while.'

'No. I'll see to it that she doesn't.'

'She was fairly clear about not wanting to stay. I think you might need a touch of mechanical interference to stop her.' He looked at her car and raised his brows. 'If you follow?'

I followed. 'We'll sort it out.' I leant on the door while he retied his tie, sorted his mobile and retrieved his clip-on sunglasses from the glove compartment. 'Doug . . .?' *They couldn't get her to change her story.* And if they could? 'Do you think she did it?'

His eyes were hidden behind twin polarised lenses: not gone but difficult to read. 'I'm her lawyer, Kellen. Of course I don't think that she did it.'

'But you were Eric's friend before you were ever her lawyer.' More than a friend. In the space after Andy, he was a lot more than a friend. It wasn't that long ago.

'I know.' He nodded. 'And I was her friend too, I think. I know how they were with each other.' Pausing for a moment, he rested both forearms on the steering wheel and leant his forehead on to his thumbs as if he could find his way through the minefield better that way. 'I'm absolutely certain that she didn't kill Eric,' he said, eventually. 'If I thought for one moment she did, I wouldn't have agreed to take her on. But the others . . .' He lifted his glasses and rubbed his knuckles once again into his eyes. 'There are a limited number of folk in the world who'd have the medical know-how to carry this off. She's one of them. So far there's only a name on a pad and a very well-publicised difference of opinion between her and Murdoch. As long as it stays like that, she's fine. If they find anything at all to link her in to the other deaths then I think we're in a deal of trouble. Of course, as her lawyer, I'm sure they won't find it. As a friend' – he slid the glasses back on to his nose – 'the best I can do is to hope that they don't. If you know any good gods it might be time to start praying. She's holding together now, just about. I don't want to think what would happen if they take her in and hold her for any serious length of time. Some folk can handle staring at the walls for twenty-three hours in a day. Lee Adams isn't one of them.'

He reversed in an arc that left marks in the gravel of the drive. I held the gate open for him as he left and was still there five minutes later, staring at the dust of his tracks in the lane, when Nina and Kirsty came in from the barn.

Lee woke just after he'd gone, not completely but enough for me to move her upstairs to the spare room. I left the dog on the bed and the cat on his blanket beside it, the one for protection, the other for mutual comfort. Downstairs, Sunday morning carried on as every other Sunday morning, perhaps a little more quietly than you'd expect but then we were getting used to shattered Sunday mornings. Two in a row is halfway to a habit. One more and we've reached a series.

Sometime just before the first ride came back, I remembered to find and then to hide the keys to her car.

'Kellen, I couldn't eat lunch if I wanted to. And I don't want to.'

'You have to eat something. You can't drive as you are.'

'Watch me.'

'No.'

We stood squared off across the full length of the kitchen: me by the back door with my boots still on and bits of hay flaking out of my shirt, Lee standing with her back to the far wall, swamped in my jeans and my T-shirt, both of them at least one size too big. She looked every bit as bad as she had when I first came in. Certainly not fit to drive.

'Just go back to bed,' I said. 'I'll call you down when lunch is ready.'

She took a breath and I saw her count slowly to ten. Close enough, anyway. 'Kellen. I want to go home and get washed and go to bed in my own bed. And I need to feed the cat. Unless you've been back to the flat to feed him in the last twenty-four hours?'

'No, I'm sorry. I didn't think about that.'

'So if you'll just give me the keys to the car?' She was spelling each sentence out, slowly, precisely, with hard stops on the consonants. It irritated the hell out of me. God alone knows what it must have done to MacDonald.

Nina came in and looked at us both, then crossed through the firing line to the space behind the breakfast bar. I had all the makings of salad and sandwiches lined up along the counter by the sink. She hacked a slice off the loaf. 'Lunch, anybody?'

'Dr Adams doesn't want to eat.'

'Dr Adams doesn't want to eat *here*.'

'Sounds fair enough to me.' Nina cut neat slices off the side of a tomato. 'She's a grown woman, Kells. She's had a rough day and a rougher night. She wants to go home to her own bed. I'd say you should give the lass her keys and let her go.'

'Whose side are you on?'

'I'm not on anyone's side, I just don't want to see either one of you hurt any more than you already are.' She held out a plate. 'Are *you* having some lunch?'

'Not yet.' I leant back on the edge of the window seat, pushed my hands in the pockets of my jeans, looked up and counted the fine cracks in the plaster on the ceiling. I don't think I was being unreasonable. 'Fine, if you want to go, then go. But for God's sake, come back tonight, will you? You're not safe on your own.'

'Kellen, it's really kind, but I need some space for a while. I need time to sort myself out and I don't need folk feeding me or bathing me or wrapping me up in cotton wool while I do it. I'm sorry, it's nothing personal, I'm just feeling really claustrophobic at the moment.'

Claustrophobic. It might have been that, but she looked desperate to me. Desperately angry. Desperately tired. Desperately hurt. And desperately, desperately vulnerable.

'Lee, listen to me. Space is fine. Very new age. Very self-aware. But we're not in the middle of a minor emotional crisis. It's entirely possible that Hillary Murdoch or Joey

Duncan or Dr Martin Invisible Coutts needed space. They were all, I have no doubt, very emotionally aware, self-contained human beings. They are also all dead.'

'I'm not thinking of—'

'No, you're not. You're not thinking at all. Two nights ago, you sat here and explained in real detail why you and Hillary Murdoch were the two folk left on some maniac's hit list. Now there's only one name left to go and that's yours. Ten green bottles – only now we're down to one. I don't think "feeding the cat" is a good enough reason to let you be next.'

'I'm not going to be—'

'Two out of these four have been slaughtered in their own homes. Has it occurred to you that there could be someone waiting for you at the flat when you get back there?'

'I'm not—'

'Or that they might just let themselves in tonight while you're indulging in all your glorious, unclaustrophobic space?'

'Kellen, will you—'

'You've got three thousand acres of space out there if it comes to that.'

'Will you let me finish the fucking sentence?'

Nina was gone. The cat was gone. The dog was gone. We were alone in the room. Still, all of them heard. You could have heard that on the far side of the ben. She didn't shout – I'm not sure I've ever heard her shout – but it carried clearly all the same.

'Why? Have you got something useful to say?'

'Listen to me, Kellen.' She spoke very softly, very carefully. 'I am going to say this to you once and once only. You are the closest friend I've got. You are, I think, the closest friend I've

ever had. That does not give you rights of ownership. I am
going home. I am going now and I am going alone. I am not
coming back tonight, or any other night in the foreseeable
future, and if you push this now, I may never come back at all.
I am not, whatever you choose to think, in any immediate
danger. The same could not necessarily be said for you.
Believe me, we are better off with a good few miles between
us. So either you give me back the keys to my car or I'll walk
to the village and I'll call a taxi. The choice is yours.' She had
her back to the far wall, her fingers splayed at her sides
holding it and herself together. She was chalk-white, shivering
as if she had fever and her hair was glued to her forehead. She
looked worse than she had when she first got out of the car.

'At least will you take the dog with you? Please.'

'No.'

Nobody came near us as she left.

I went riding that afternoon. I brought Maddie in from her
day off in the hawthorn field, tacked her up and rode out on a
route I've never taken before: way out past the loch to the far
side of the ben and then back round the far edge of the moor
and down the line of the river to the beech wood below the
barn. It's not a good route for trekking: too many dips and
rises, too much unmarked bog. Too long as well. It's a good
two hours longer than the full-day ride up to the loch and
back. Or it would be, at sensible trekking pace. But I wasn't
out for a trek and we didn't keep to a sensible pace. The mare
was fit from a half-season's work and was ready to stretch her
legs. I wasn't fit at all but I needed to be moving. We did the
whole thing, I think, in just under six hours.

It was nearly dark as we came in along the line of the river. Jon's promised rain had been and gone and come back again and settled in fitful drizzles, just enough to keep us wet and cool, not enough to be cold. The wind had been bad up on the ben, blowing hair and mane and tail in tangled circles, blasting us sideways, making the footing worse in places where it was already bad. By the time we reached the beeches, it had blown itself out and the evening lay still around us, waiting for the next front to bring in the rain. You could see it, the front, far out on the western skyline: great, sweeping banks of black cloud knifed through with streaks of vicious, sulphurous yellow. A sunset out of Hades, venting its spleen on the land and the sea. I gave the mare her head, let her set her own pace down the side of the water and spent the last twenty minutes of the ride trying not to feel as if I was becoming a part of the sky.

We reached the end of the wood and the path turned in, away from the beeches, towards the farm. All the ponies know their way home from here. I slid down from the saddle and slackened the girth, knotting the reins up out of the way so that the mare could rest as she followed me in. We slowed the pace then, neither of us desperate to be home too soon. Maddie pushed up against my shoulder, the brown patches of her hide fading out in the shadows so that it seemed as if I walked through the fields with a half-horse walking beside me. The false horizon of the cloud covered the sun sooner than you'd expect for the time of year. One moment we were walking in dusk, watching the tussocks of grass at our feet, the next, it was a starless night and the small things of the dark were coming into their own. Bats flittered overhead, half seen in the faltering light. Tawny owls screamed at their young. A vixen barked to her mate, out beyond the woods. The mare's not fond of fox. She pushed in closer to my shoulder. Later, I stumbled on a tussock and slid my arm up over her withers, as if the two of us, melded together, could see better than one. Not true, but the feel of her, solid and warm at my side, made the darkness seem less unfriendly.

It took us an age to reach the far side of west acre paddock. I unhooked the gate and swung it open and swung it back again and the horse grazed for a moment on the far side as I fiddled to get the chain over the stone of the corner post. A hand took it from me and flipped it back into place. I froze and the world turned over. The horse huffed and went back to her eating. A dark shadow separated from other dark shadows along the hedge. 'She didn't stay then?' he said.

'Stewart MacDonald.' The world came back into focus, hard and fast. 'Get the hell off my land.'

'Kellen, I'm not—' Something pale flashed at knee level. White teeth gleamed over a lolling tongue and then disappeared more suddenly than they had appeared.

'And your dog. Both of you. Now.'

'Kellen . . .'

'Or I'll call the police. Aggravated trespass. Your dog is worrying my in-foal mares.'

'Aye, very funny.' He didn't move.

'If you think so.' I walked to the mare, untied the reins, tightened the girth and remounted. There's an advantage to height. I pulled the mobile from my pocket. I found his work number in the directory. My thumb hovered over the key to send. 'Who do I speak to? Andy Baird?'

'Kellen, you're going to have to accept —'

'I don't have to accept anything of yours, MacDonald. I trusted you.'

'Right. So what's changed? We took her in and we questioned her. You knew that. What would you have me do? Pat her on the head and tell her she's fine while she dreams up another fancy way to kill the next one?'

'She's killed nobody, and you know it.'

'I know nothing except the facts and right at the moment, she's the only suspect I've got.'

'Christ, you really can't see past the end of your own nose, can you? Do you think if she really killed Hillary Murdoch, she'd walk out and leave her own name on a pad by the bed? Do you honestly believe she's that stupid?'

'No, I don't. That's why we let her go.'

'Oh, very good. So maybe, just maybe, she's telling the truth. In which case, she's next.'

'And maybe, just maybe, she's brighter than any of the rest of us. Would you believe that?'

'I'd believe nothing without decent proof, MacDonald. But I'll tell you this. If she's right and she's the next in line and something happens and she dies while you and your uniformed fuckwits are spinning in circles digging holes to push her into, then, so help me, I will put the rest of my life into breaking you. I'll have your job, I'll have your livelihood, I'll have your home. I'll find everything that has ever mattered to you and I will destroy it.'

The mare took the last step forward, upset by the tension. Still he didn't move. He stood at her shoulder and his face looked up into mine. All I could see in the dark were his eyes.

His hand came up to the reins. 'You won't have to do that, Kellen,' he said. 'If I'm wrong and she dies, I'll do it myself.'

'Good.' I spun the mare round on her hocks. 'So get the hell off—'

'I'm going.' His shadow became other shadows. His dog was already gone. 'I'll not be back.'

Good.

The night is cool. The moon is growing, peering in through the bedroom window, a sickle sliced in half by the window frame. The cat lies in his place by the bed. His rasp is louder, his heartbeat, when I feel it, beats harder, bigger through the skeletal cage of his ribs. Today he stopped eating. It was the tension. We can believe it was the tension. We have a promise, both of us, that when he stops eating, we will let him go. But not tonight. We will give him one more night. Because tonight, none of us ate and it might not be that he's dying.

Chapter Nine

❧

'They've brought Colin Storey-Pugh over from Edinburgh. Did you know?'

'Somebody has to run the department.'

'Is Lee still not back?'

'Not as far as I know.'

'Is she OK?'

'All things are relative.'

'Have they got a result yet on Murdoch's post-mortem?'

How should I know? Am I the only link to pathology? 'I don't know.'

'How's the cat?'

'He's alive. He ate again this morning. Thank you.'

'Good.' A hand on my arm, a smile. 'Don't let them get to you.'

They got to me. By ten o'clock on Monday morning, less than two hours into work, they got to me. I used not to hate Monday mornings but then I had never before been exposed to quite so many well-meaning, solicitous idiots. Sadly, they were also my colleagues and thus relatively inescapable. Tuesday was no better. Dee was the only one who had the sense to ask pertinent questions about the cat, which I could cope with, and not about Lee, which I could not. So I talked to Dee, in the quiet moments between patients, and she was one of the few who knew what was really happening, as much as anyone did. Only Mike Bailey had a better idea of the truth. Better, possibly than I did. By Wednesday lunchtime, I had had as much of not knowing as I could stomach. I picked up a sandwich from the canteen and headed down to the pathology block.

'Mike?' The door from the corridor to the mortuary was locked. Never, since Lee took the job as pathology resident, has this door been locked. I knocked for a second time, louder. 'Mike, are you there?'

Nothing. If I were somebody different, I might believe he'd gone out to lunch, but Mike Bailey never goes out to lunch, not in the conventional sense. I got out my keys and hammered them on the glass. 'Mike? It's me, Kellen.'

He came out of one of the darkened offices in the far corridor, screwing up his eyes against the glare of the overhead lights. 'Kellen?' He didn't unlock the door. 'What are you doing here?'

'I came to see you.'

'Right.' He didn't say it like a question. He stood on the far side of the glass and probed a hollow tooth with his tongue. His eyes narrowed again and this time it had nothing to do with the light. He's not a straightforward man, Mike Bailey, but fiercely, fiercely loyal. I would have said, until then, that his loyalty was all for Lee. Perhaps not. 'Mike, what's going on? I'm not . . .'

'I know.' He made whatever decision he needed to make. The key turned in the lock. 'Come in.' The lock clicked shut behind me.

His office was in virtual darkness. Close-fitting blinds blocked the daylight from the windows. The only light came from the microscope on the bench. He switched on a desk lamp and cleared a mass of papers from a stool in the corner.

'Sit down and don't make too much noise. If anyone walks past, we're not here.'

'What the hell's going on, Mike?'

'Politics, what else?' He pulled his chair round and sat astride it, his arms folded along the back. The light was all behind him, sparking yellowed highlights off the nicotine streaks in his hair. He probed another tooth. 'Professor Pugh's getting, shall we say, sensitive about who comes in here.'

'Who's he worried about?'

'Lee, mostly.' He chose not to look at me. 'Or anyone who might be her friend.'

'Fine.' I will assume, until told otherwise, that I still count as that. 'Why?'

'This, for starters.' He spun his chair round and nodded his head for me to pull mine up to the microscope. The focus blurred and then sharpened on a histology slide; long wavering black strands on an orange background sprinkled with tiny semi-circles in a wild, fluorescent green.

'What is it?'

'See these?' A pointer moved into the field of view and skittered round the greens. 'Fluorescent antibody test. Pugh had it flown in from the States. We got it last night.' The pointer found more bright green blots. 'The black is skeletal muscle. The green means the neuromuscular junctions are staining positive for suxamethonium.'

'So? What's this got to do with Lee?'

'The muscle came from Hillary Murdoch. This is the third one I've looked at. Three different muscles, three different sites. They all stain the same.' He dulled the field and his face came away from the lenses. The lines around his eyes turned down more than they used to. He spun round on the chair. 'He's good, Pugh,' he said. 'Not as good as her maybe but not far off. This stuff is broken down in the muscle within three hours of injection. He saw the bruises down her back from the cramps and had the biopsies taken within minutes of getting her in here. If he'd left it another hour there'd have been nothing to find beyond a needle mark at the back of one shoulder and you don't die from that even if it does go straight into the lungs.' He leant sideways and unhooked the blinds from the windows. Daylight, harsh and over-bright, flooded the room and lit up a cramped space made more so by the intrusion of the microscope and the haggard, old-young figure of a man, hunched over his chair. He reached down under his desk, pulled out his gear and slowly, carefully, he rolled himself a cigarette. His eyes were on me. 'It's a hell of a way to die, Kellen.'

It is. I don't particularly want to think about it but in this place, there is no choice. Hillary Murdoch died in total paralysis. Suxamethonium is a muscle relaxant, one of the first to be used in this country. The early anaesthetists wanted something to stop their patients from walking off the table when the ether ran low so they took apart the structure of curare, the arrow-tip poison of the Amazon Indians, and re-created it in the lab. Curare is impressive by anyone's standards. One scratch drops a jaguar in fifty paces. Translated into medicine, a couple of ccs injected into the blood stream can drop a grown man just the same and when it hits, every single muscle in the body goes into total spasm, absolutely rigid, like the worst case of cramp you can imagine. The pain is excruciating and the muscle damage lasts long after the surgery's done. The paralysis comes on a minute or so after the cramps. Total neuromuscular blockade. All movement stops. Feeling is there, thinking is there, the ability to panic is there, but none of it is translated into action. You can't walk, you can't run, you can't scream. And you can't breathe.

'God.' It hit then, hard and ugly, like a fist. 'Oh God, Mike. She died in asphyxia.'

'She did.' He nodded. He didn't smile. He used always to smile. 'Right bang on pattern. She came out of the cramps and she found she couldn't breathe.' He crushed the stub of his roll-up between finger and thumb and dropped it neatly in a small metal can at his feet. 'We have a signature, Kellen. Fatal asphyxia. And she's raising the stakes with each one. Joey drowned but he'd pretty well drunk himself into a coma before anything happened so he won't have known much about it. Coutts breathed air with no oxygen in it but he was out of his skull on Flatliners by the time he did it. Poor bloody Murdoch, God roast her soul, was right there, all her faculties working. One hundred per cent wide awake and functioning. Pugh reckons it would take somewhere round five minutes from the point of injection to clinical death and she'd have been conscious for most of that time.' He reached for his gear a second time. 'You'd have to hate someone an awful lot to do that to them, Kellen.'

I watched him fingering the tobacco; I watched still, without comment, as he took out the resin from a separate compartment and crumbled it first on to the paper. He is losing his edge. Lee at least had him straight until six. I waited while he finished lighting up. The heady smell of it filled the room, flowed out through the window and down into the car park. It did nothing to change the nausea twisting the pit of my guts.

'You don't really believe she did it?'

He shook his head. Long coils of hair fell out round his face. Smoke filtered between us. 'I owe her, Kellen. You know that.'

'But . . .?'

He shrugged. 'Who else is there would know how to do that? Who else would want to? There's no one else hated Murdoch that much. Eric, maybe, but you can't point the finger at a dead man. Especially not if he turns out to be on the list with the rest.' He took a long drag and held it in, offered the joint across to me before he'd breathed out and then took it back again when I shook my head. He exhaled through his teeth. 'Pugh's going to go back over him this afternoon and see if there's anything she might have "missed" on the body.'

'Eric didn't die in asphyxia.'

He was mid-way through another drag. The outbreath came, long and unhurried. His pupils flared oddly in the light. His features began to melt, like candle wax by a fire. He shook his head and shrugged again. 'Not so far as we know.'

A clock on his bench beeped a warning. He reached out, slack-jointed, and silenced it. 'Fuck. Time for work.' His voice was steady if his hands were not. He sighed and pinched out the glow. A dark patch on fingertip and thumb marks a thousand other premature endings. He reached up and wrapped a straggle of hair round one ear. 'I'm not happy about this. You have to believe that. But it makes no sense any other way. We have a signature and we have a motive and we have no one else who fits the frame.'

'Did Stewart MacDonald tell you that?'

'No.' He dropped the joint in an old can of Coke on the counter. It fizzled faintly in the bottom as he swirled it round. He looked at me slant-wise under the arc of his arm. 'You're joining the white coats, Kellen. That's a bad sign. Just because I don't have one doesn't mean I can't think for myself when I need to.'

'Have you told the police what you've found?'

'Hardly.' He smiled at that, hard and flat and fully aware. 'But there's nothing I can do to stop Pugh. It wouldn't surprise me at all if he wasn't spending his lunch hour with your friend MacDonald.' The smile faded to nothing. 'If she's inside again by now, it's not on my account. I'm on her side, still, whatever she's done. I'll stay that way just as long as I'm not next. You want to think about that, maybe.'

I am not, whatever you choose to think, in any immediate danger. The same could not necessarily be said for you.

'If I'm on anyone's hit list, it isn't hers, Mike.'

'Right.' He swilled Coke from another can and then spat the results in the waste-bin. 'Tell that to Eric.'

The alarm beeped again. He stood up. 'It's nearly two, sweetheart. Pugh's what you'd call punctual to the point of obsession. He'll be back from lunch on the hour. I'd be grateful if you'd be gone by then. It is, I promise you, more than my job's worth if he finds you here.'

'And that isn't?' I moved my head. Sweet smoke hung heavy in the air.

The smile this time was crooked, deliberately so. 'He needs me. Some crimes are less equal than others.' He sobered suddenly and opened the door. 'Will you go now? Please? I'll let you know if I hear anything else.'

'Is that a promise?'

'You wouldn't be here if it wasn't.'

The forgotten sandwich lay, flat and unappetising, in the bottom of my bag. I threw it in a waste-bin in the car park and walked back the long way to the Unit. It was a warm day, not over-hot, with thin, high cloud and just enough sun to make shadows. Down at the Unit, the gardener rode his mower along the edge of a flower-bed. He's young, the gardener, but he cares and he doesn't believe that gardens should be set out in straight lines. For that, we can overlook any amount of inexperience.

I sat on one of the garden seats under the sycamores and watched him cutting curves in the grass. A fork stuck out of a newly dug bed. A robin sat on the handle scanning the fresh earth for insects.

'Penny for them?'

It was Dee, standing on the grass somewhere behind me. I didn't turn, but then I didn't need to. I could pick that voice out now in a crowd of twenty. 'I was thinking Jack Souter was wrong,' I said. 'There are birds here. He just couldn't hear them for the cars.'

'He knew that. He was making a point.'

'Maybe.' I stared out across the grass, seeing other faces,

hearing other words. 'It's his funeral this afternoon.'

'Fine. So you can go and tell him you cared for him and let him go.' She moved round and sat on the other end of the bench, leaving clear space between us. 'Funerals go with the territory, Kells. You don't like the heat, you should put down your spade and stop stoking the furnace.'

'Thanks.' This is the old Dee. Compassion is for wimps.

'You're welcome. That's what friends are for.' She stretched her legs out on the grass. 'Now suppose you tell me what's really going on?'

With someone else, I would ignore that, but not here, not now, not with her. I shrugged. 'I don't know. I just had lunch with Mike at the mortuary. Hillary Murdoch got a syringe full of sux between the shoulder blades. Pugh thinks she was conscious while she died.'

'Does he, indeed?' Her eyes tightened at the edges. She rested her chin on her hand and watched the mower start a new row. In time, she shrugged. 'You could say much the same for Jack Souter. I'd put money she went a lot faster than he did.'

'Is that supposed to make me feel better?'

'No. It's supposed to give you a different sense of perspective and drag you out of the bog before you sink in past your neck. Does Pugh think Lee did it?'

'Mike Bailey does. He thinks she's working her way through the staff with ever-increasing venom.'

'Ah.' She rocked sideways on the seat. Her stare was as comfortable as it ever is. 'And this is the real reason you look . . . the way you look.'

I flinched. 'That bad?'

193

The smile was sharp. 'Don't go passing any mirrors if you can help it.'

'Thanks.' I found a crumb of pony cube in the depths of one pocket and threw it out on the grass. We both watched as the robin came down off the fork handle to find it. 'What am I going to do, Dee?'

'Give up and go home?'

'I could do.' It's an option. 'I can't see I'm doing anything useful here.'

'Bullshit.' She turned sideways on the bench. 'Do you think she did it?'

'No.'

'Why not?'

I shrugged. I felt like a child. 'Just because' is not an adult response, so I said nothing and there was silence for a while, as much as there ever is at the Unit. When it had gone beyond mere thinking, she stood up.

'Wait here,' she said.

She was gone nearly five minutes. Long enough for the mower to make two full trips down the garden and once across the front of Jack Souter's old room. When she came back, she held a polystyrene mug in one hand and a can of something bland and carbonated in the other. 'Here.' She held out the coffee. 'The real thing. I brewed up the machine in the office.'

I moulded my hands to the soft polystyrene of the mug. The heat burned my palms. The smell of it cleared the last dregs of Mike Bailey's joint from the pits of my mind. 'Thanks.'

'Don't. It's all self-interest, believe me.' She sat down on the grass with her back to one of the bigger trees and laid her can on a stump at the side. In a while, she looked up. It was like looking at flint. 'I've got people dying there, Kellen, and you're about as useful as a wet Tuesday in Galway. We have to get you out of it somehow. Now, have you thought of a good reason why she didn't do it?'

I don't think that's up to me. I drank the coffee. Black, one sugar. Only on the worst of days do I take it either black or with sugar. She knows me better than I thought she did.

'She didn't kill Eric,' I said, eventually. 'I saw her face when she came up over the edge. She didn't know he was there and she absolutely didn't want to believe that he was dead.'

'She could have been acting, Kellen.' Soft, musical Irish, so very different to the implacable stone of her eyes. 'It's not unknown.'

It isn't. But she wasn't acting. Of that, I am sure, as of nothing else. 'She was on the end of a rope, Dee. It's not a time you can act. The rock doesn't allow it.' And that, perhaps, is the other reason why we climb. 'There aren't any masks when you're climbing. What you see is what you are.'

'That would make a change.' She smiled a dry, acerbic smile. 'Remind me not to go climbing with you.' She twirled a sycamore key in her fingers and spun it out on to the unmown grass beneath the trees. 'OK, we'll go with that. It would hardly stand up in court, but I saw how she was after she got here and if she was faking that, she's a better actor than any of us. So we'll agree she didn't kill Eric. What about the others? You need more than decent acting for them.'

Good question. I stared, unseeing, at the twin-tone bands of the grass. The coffee grew cold in my hands. Far out on the edge of the garden, a gaggle of house sparrows fought over the remains of a sandwich. Bloody good question. Just because. Just because I know it in my guts as much as I've ever known anything. But now, just knowing is not enough. I need to find words. If I could think past the sight of her lying out cold on the bench in my kitchen, past the image of Hillary Murdoch, sitting there alive and not breathing, past the fear that she might be next, I might perhaps find an answer.

'Kellen . . .?'

'Yes?'

'Is there anyone else you can talk to? Anyone else who knows her well enough to give real answers to real questions?'

'There's Mhaire Culloch. The madwoman. If anyone knows her, Mhaire does.'

'Can you go and see her?'

'I can try. She might not see me. We don't get on.'

'Still, I think you need to try her. For your own peace of mind as much as anything.' She stood up, brushing the broken leaves from her knees. 'Will you go? Please? For me and the Unit, if not for you?'

What else is there to do? 'If you like.'

She scooped up her can and ruffled tidying fingers through her hair. I put out an arm to stop her as she walked past me. 'Dee . . .?'

She lifted my hand and pushed her lips to the back of it in a small, old-fashioned gesture. 'Don't mention it,' she said. Her smile was as dry as her kiss. 'I need you here, body and soul, for Claire Hendon. I'd have left you to wallow otherwise.'

Chapter Ten

❧

'Funerals are for the living, Kellen. It'll not matter to me if you come or not. We can say all we need to say before I go.' It was still spring then, when death was a long way off, an abstract thing to be spun on the fingers and viewed from all angles. By autumn, it was different. 'Go and look, Kellen. See the land. See what it's like before they drive their bloody road through by the river and everything green goes down under houses. I'd like you to see the places we've been walking.' And then in winter, a day or two before Christmas, when his voice was a thin wind, blown over reeds: 'Bring the dog, Kellen. That would be good. Mind and get me to tell Joan when she gets here. I want everyone to bring their dogs. They know how to feel things better than we do.'

Maybe. We'll know soon enough. There are thirty-odd cars parked in the car park and in almost all of them there is a dog.

It is a warm day and I am chilled to the core. It's difficult, now, to think of Jack Souter without feeling the frost etch cold on the windows, without seeing the snow fall in great slabs off the roof. It takes effort to stay in the present, to stay with the warm of a July afternoon; with the rattle of a badly tuned engine, driving up the hill to the small, south-side village; with the sharp, ammoniacal smell of nettles, crushed under foot on the other side of the wall where fifty people took their dogs to empty their bladders before bringing them on to the mown grass of the cemetery. It takes effort, if I am honest, simply to be in a cemetery. I am not fond of cemeteries – too many childhood memories of tall grey walls and the claustrophobia of repressed emotion. Jack promised me this one would not feel like a prison and, so far, he is right. It's a small place, inoffensive and understated and it merges with the fields around it in the way of a garden, growing back to the wild. The walls are whitewashed stone, not grey brick, and low enough that you could be over them in a moment if the hare on the hill moved closer and the dogs decided not to wait. There are daisies making snow-in-saffron carpets round the headstones, a new crop since the last time the mower ran through. There are always daisies in cemeteries: a universal statement on the cycles of existence. They live, they flower, they die. Nobody writes their headstones. Jack Souter is dead and the family headstone carries his name, newly cut, at the bottom. I find it difficult, standing here, to know what I feel. I am not sorry he died. He was a good man and I am glad that I knew him, but he died when he was ready to die, which is as good as it gets. If I had the right kind of perspective, I expect I could say the same for Eric, but I don't believe that. If I had the right kind of compassion, I could say it, too, for Hillary Murdoch, but I would have to have liked her enough to care. As it is, I can't find it in me to be sorry that the woman is dead. I am sorry for the manner of it but beyond that, I am only sorry because she was a name on a list, and while she was alive there was a chance that Lee might not be next, and whatever I feel about funerals, I would give everything I've got not to be standing sometime in the next few months beside a grave dug for Lee Adams.

The dogs are stirring. The folk closest to the grave are throwing dirt on to the coffin and there are two dozen terriers present who know for a fact that a hole that big must have something truly spectacular to be hunted down in the bottom. Jack Souter was right. Dogs are better at showing their feelings than people. No one here would dare to complain that they're filling the hole in too soon. He said he didn't want a staid, quiet funeral. They have given him his wish. We line up to speak with Joan and Sally on the way out. His wife shakes my hand. His daughter goes down on one knee and hugs the dog.

'Thank you for coming, Kellen.'

'I said that I would.'

'Are you coming back down to the house?'

'No. I'm sorry. I have to get back to work.'

'You'll come back sometime, won't you? Bring the dog down and we'll go for a walk.'

'I will. In a month or two. When the summer's over.'

'Thank you. Jack would have liked that.'

He would. And perhaps I will go, but we both know that it is the saying of it that matters.

199

I have to get back to work. But first I have to make a house-call to a friend of a friend. Mad Mhaire Culloch is not a friend of mine. I don't like her, I don't trust her. I have no desire to spend time in her company. But this is the woman who chaperoned Lee through her childhood. She is the closest thing the lass has ever had to a mother and if anyone knows what's happening to her now, Mhaire Culloch will be that one. All I have to do is find her and then get her to speak to me. Neither of these is necessarily guaranteed to succeed.

Most folk move closer to town and basic amenities as they age. Mhaire Culloch, because she is mad, chose the occasion of her eighty-fifth birthday to move from a perfectly weatherproof council semi on a nice, douce housing estate not far over the river to a battered, leaking labourer's cottage halfway down the Ayr road with fifteen miles to the nearest conurbation. Her home is not at all easy to find and I have directions only from memory. It took a good half-hour to find the turning off the main road and it was gone five by the time I nursed the car up a pot-holed track that looked as if it might lead to her cottage. It was there, behind a gap in the hedge, a mile or two up the lane, and it looked better than I was expecting: a small, squat dwelling with walls radiant in the way of whitewash newly done and a roof of corrugated iron painted matt black to draw in the sun. I turned in and parked the car in the shade of the hedge and looked at it for a while. Next to the climb, this has been Lee's big project for the year, an inordinate absorber of time. She has not done badly although clearly, beyond the paint and the new wood, there are still things aching to be done. The bindweed choking the hedge needs to come out before it takes over the entirety of the north side of the garden. The front door could do with being stripped and repainted before the winter sets in. The vegetable patch at the side is too small, still, to give any serious yield. The fork and the spade standing up in it are both from the farm and both, no doubt, are waiting for Lee Adams to come back and finish what she began. If I was her, I would work on that next. I left the car, whistled the dog from the back seat and went over to have a closer look.

'You're late.' Mhaire stood in the dark space of her doorway. In that kind of light, all I could see was her hair: absolutely white and standing up round her head like a curve-bristled brush.

Really? 'I had a funeral, Mhaire. You can't time these things.'

'It finished an hour ago. You're still late.'

'I'm sorry. I got lost. May I come in?'

She put her head to one side and considered that one as if it were more than a rhetorical question. 'If you must.' A cat slipped out past her feet. 'You'll leave the dog in the car.'

'If you say so.' The dog, I would say, was happier with that than I was.

I followed her in. There was no hallway. In the way of the very old labourer's cottages, the front door led straight into the single downstairs room. It was lighter inside than I might have imagined; Mhaire, for me, is always shrouded in gloom, but here in her own home she had windows on three sides and a fire that flared, freshly lit, on the fourth. Odd interplays of sunlight and flame curled together up the walls.

'Sit down.'

'Thank you.'

The sofa was clean and did not smell unduly of tom cat. Mhaire Culloch pushed a grey striped queen off the chair opposite and sat down in the space she had left. She doesn't age, this woman. I can vouch for the fact she's looked the same since she was seventy. Lee can tell you she was no different in her sixties. I think if you looked at her hard, you'd find she doesn't stand quite as straight as she did and her hair carries more of the nicotine at the forelock than it used to but otherwise, she is simply a white-haired, fearsome old hag with yellowing eyes and no teeth of her own and a voice like wet chalk dragged down a board. Until I met Dee, this woman was my only direct experience of the Irish. It was not the best introduction.

'They took her in again at lunchtime, did you know?'

'I'm sorry?'

'You should be.'

Oh, God, here we go . . . 'I'm sorry, Mhaire, it's been a long day, I'm not in the groove yet. Can we go through this slowly? Who took who where?'

She lit a fresh cigarette from the fire, took a long, long drag and spelled it out. 'The police. Took your friend. Lee Adams. Into custody. At two o'clock. This afternoon.'

Oh, shit. 'Are you sure?'

'Of course I'm sure. Why else would I have you here?'

I hate to think. 'Is she under arrest? Have they charged her?'

'Not yet.'

'Are they going to?'

'It would be safer for her if they did.'

You rarely get sense out of Mhaire Culloch. Not at the first

202

time of asking, anyway. 'So have they let her go?'

'Not yet. They will. They shouldn't but they will.'

Whose side are you on? 'She didn't do it, Mhaire.'

'I thought you came here to ask me that?'

Impasse. I'd forgotten what it was like to hold conversations in hieroglyphics. Everything symbolic, nothing said straight. I rehearsed this conversation four times driving down the A77 to get here. Now, I can't even remember how it was supposed to start. We stared at each other through the growing haze of cigarette smoke.

'You have a headache.' She said it suddenly, out of the blue, a statement, not a question.

I was doing my best not to think about that. 'It's the smoke,' I said. 'I'll be fine when I get outside.'

'Smoke nothing.' The blue trail of her cigarette wove knots in the air. 'It's the coffee. You're drinking too much coffee. You'll need to stop.'

I don't think so. I live for my morning coffee. 'I'll bear it in mind, Mhaire. You were saying about Lee?'

'It'll wait.' She stood up, dislodging the cats. 'You'll have some tea?'

She's kidding? She's not. 'Yes, thank you, Mhaire.'

'Wait then. I'll get it.'

There were two doors to the living room: the one at the front through which we both came and a second at the back that led out to the privy corridor. In the old days, when they built these cottages, they put an outdoor privy twenty feet from the back step. Later, planning regulations forced everyone to bring their privacy indoors and the usual approach was to build a twenty-foot corridor from the back door to the smallest room thus fulfilling the letter, if not the spirit, of the law. I followed her out through the back door and found that between them she and Lee had turned the long, useless tunnel into a kitchen. Not a bad idea. It has the advantage, at the very least, of keeping all the plumbing more or less in one place. I walked down to the end and back. She had been cooking, apparently, when I arrived. A kettle, bigger than mine, came to a slow boil on a two-ring gas cooker. A basinful of rough chopped vegetables sat to the side. From the look of the vegetable rack, she is living almost entirely on the output of the garden. It's going to be a long, hard winter if she doesn't get Lee back in time.

The kettle boiled. She handed me a mug. It wasn't tea.

'Mhaire . . .?'

'Drink it.'

I don't think so. 'Mhaire, I'm not—'

'You'll drink it if you want to drive back with your head still sat where it ought to be.'

'Right.' I don't fight battles I'm not going to win. I followed her back to the living room. A red-eared white tom cat had my place on the sofa. I sat down a cat's breadth to the left. The tea tasted the way you might expect bindweed to taste: a kind of desperate, delicate floral overlay hiding the choking death-hold underneath. Not healthy but then I'm not the one who's into herbal teas. I could have been drinking hemlock and I wouldn't have known it. No doubt they'd pin that one, too, on Lee.

'I can't reach her while she's all walled up.'

At least we agree on something. 'None of us can, Mhaire. I thought you said they were going to let her out?'

'They are.'

'Can't you talk to her then?'

The fire was bright. Brighter than mine has ever been, even in summer when the peat is bone dry. It crackled. The cat spat. Mad Mhaire has eyes like a weasel, small and bright and hungry for blood. They shone red in the firelight. She took a long, long drag on the cigarette. In the relative bright of the room, the end of it glowed like the point of a laser. Her voice was uncommonly quiet. 'I don't enjoy your company any more than you enjoy mine, *Doctor* Stewart. Would you want me drinking tea in your home? Have you thought of that?'

I can think of few things I would like less. 'I'm sorry.'

'No you're not. You don't know what it is to be sorry. You walk through your life with your eyes shut and think the world owes you a living just for being there.'

Is that right? 'Am I so very different, then, to all the rest?'

'We don't all take our mark from the midden.'

Fine. This, at least, is familiar territory. 'So are we going to sit here and trade insults while your fake tea goes cold or are we going to do something about Lee Adams? Unless she's another one who takes her mark from the midden?'

'Not so far off.' She smiled and it was not an enticing smile. The cigarette moved, a red light weaving like a snake. 'She's not so pearly-white as you'd have her be. She knows that, even if you don't, and she'll take what she thinks she's earned for it if you let her. Remember that when you have to act.'

I don't have quite the right threshold for this any more. I moved sideways, displacing the cat. It was easier, for this, to sit face to face. 'Mhaire, just this once, can you tell me whatever you think I need to know in plain English? If I know what's going on, I can get out of here and do something useful. I'm sure we'd both like that.'

She smirked. Or she snarled. Hard to tell without the teeth. 'If I speak to you plain, you'll sit there and argue till you're blue in the face and the time for acting will be past. You do best when you're not thinking at all.' The cigarette stabbed forwards at eye level. 'You need to learn to trust your elders and betters and don't try to get clever with me.'

'I should trust you?' That's ludicrous.

'You should trust her.'

'Is it not supposed to be mutual?'

'Are you going to let her die if it's not?'

Right. There are games and there are games. Never before has she pushed this far. I swallowed a final mouthful of tea. 'Just tell me what I need to know, Mhaire, and I'll be gone.'

'You don't need to know anything. You're the messenger, nothing more. She'll listen to you when she'll listen to no one else so you go in there and you make it count. Do you understand?'

'I don't think she'll—'

'She will. Tonight she will. The police have got her now. They'll let her out soon. If you call on her when she gets home, she'll see you then. Tell her from me that just because she's at the edge of a cliff, doesn't mean she has to throw herself over. That's all she needs to know. She can work the rest out for herself.'

'You're going to have to be more explicit than that, Mhaire. It doesn't make sense.'

The fire hissed this time, the cat and the woman with it. The room darkened, as if the clouds had covered the sun. Out in the kitchen, the vegetable pan boiled over on the stove.

'Just tell her.' It came spelled out, with effort. All I could see was the red glowing end of her cigarette.

'Then what? Are you going to call her or do you want her to call you?'

'Neither. I want her to come out from the coffin she's building for herself and do something useful while there's still time to make a difference.'

'And if she doesn't?'

There was a pause. She leant forward. Her voice, when she spoke, was stripped of every vestige of humour. It was not pleasant to hear. 'If she doesn't, then you'll be standing at another funeral before the month's out and you'll know the meaning of sorry then. Do you understand me? This isn't a few broken fingers this time. This is a life for a life and a death for a death and there's nothing you or me can do about it while she out's there running hell-bent for oblivion like a lemming that's late for the party. She needs to stop and she needs to think and there's precious little time left to do it. You can tell her that too if you think she'll hear you.' The glowing end of her cigarette ground to nothing on the hearthstone. The front door swung wide. 'Now get out of my home.'

My head cleared slowly on the way down the A77. Cleared of the smoke and the tea and the madwoman's rhetoric and the judgmental stare of her cats. Cleared also of the beginnings of a headache that had been hanging over, pressing in on my eyes, since Mike skinned up in the mortuary. She could be right, it could be the coffee, but it will take more than the say-so of Mhaire Culloch for me to give it up.

★ ★ ★

It was late by the time I got to Lee's flat. The traffic was bad from the moment I hit the main dual carriageway and didn't get better all the way across town to the north side and then out towards the west end. I called the farm and left a message for Nina telling her where I was going and not to expect me home for dinner. Somewhere around seven, I parked the car in the street outside Lee's front door and when she didn't answer the land line, I put a call in to her mobile.

'Yes?'

'It's me. Do you want something to eat?'

'No. Thank you.' She was out of breath, panting like a dog on a hot day. 'I don't want to go out.'

'I'm not inviting you out. I got us a takeaway from Barelli's. I was thinking I could bring it in.' I hadn't planned on eating but I saw the sign on the way in from the motorway and it seemed like a good idea at the time. With Lee, sometimes instinct works better than logic.

'Where are you?' She knows me well enough by now, even with the fuzz of a mobile blurring the words.

'Outside your front door.' There was a pause. I heard her run up the stairs. A curtain twitched in the kitchen. I flicked the headlights on and then off, lighting up a couple of kids heading out of the grove.

'Have you got the dog with you?'

'Yes.'

'Come on in.'

She was dressed for climbing: black leggings, black singlet, black Boreal shoes, white hands with chalk packed in under the fingernails, white streaks of it across her face where she'd rubbed her eyes. Her hair stuck out at odd angles as if gravity had pulled at it and then sweat had gelled it in place. Her armpits and the small of her back were stained a darker black. She smelled, strongly, of the climbing room – of rubber mats and hard-pushed sweat.

'You don't have to stop.'

'Yes I do.' She led the way through to the kitchen. 'If I don't take a break once in a while, it becomes an obsession.'

It's always been an obsession. I've never heard her admit it as such.

'Anything special?'

'I built a new route up the overhang. It's as close as I can get to the E5 on Eric's Cliff.'

And so now we have a name. She has the right. The naming of the route following the first ascent is the leader's prerogative. There was a time when she would have gone for something lighter, a parody of description – Oblivion Wall, perhaps, or Feeding the Sharks. I hadn't imagined it as an epitaph. There was a time, too, when we might have talked about it, but she was already moving on, washing her hands, drying them, pulling out plates for the meal. It was like watching a piece of street theatre: a mime-dance, choreographed for the audience, none of it quite true to the source.

I sat down at the table to wait. If she wants to act for me, let her act. Neither of us needs believe it is real.

'How's Claire Hendon?' The question came out of the blue, out of the whirl of unnecessary activity. Like asking about the weather but slightly less relevant.

'Alive.'

'How long has she got?'

'I don't know. I can't tell these things, Lee. I'll be surprised if she lasts past the end of the week.' And you won't be there to do the post-mortem, so why does it matter?

'How's Dee taking it?'

'Better than I thought she would. She's followed pretty much the same emotional curve as the lass. While there was hope, she was angry. Now they both just want it over.' And the rest of us with them. I haven't felt this sense of urgency with any of the patients before but I feel it for Claire. The Unit will be easier with her gone.

'You're looking after her, aren't you?'

'Claire?'

'Dee.'

At the nadir of an entirely inane conversation, that was the most inane of it all.

'I'm doing my best.'

We lapsed back into silence. Her portable computer lay open in front of me, the modem still plugged into the phone line. Climbing, clearly, isn't her only obsession. I tabbed through a Med-line file of published papers, three pages long, retrieved from the net. Names sprang out from the author list: Murdoch, H.S.; Dalziel, E.; Duncan, R.C.; Adams, E.K. *Adams, Elizabeth Kathryn.* You don't often see her as that these days.

'I don't think so, Kellen.' The screen blanked out in front of me, faster than any machine should shut down. She stood at my shoulder, her toe on the plug, a plate balanced in either hand. She smiled, or something like it, in the dusk. 'It's cooler through in the living room,' she said.

Fine.

★ ★ ★

'Better?'

'Better.'

I lay back on the floor with my head cushioned on the arm of the sofa. The dog lay behind me, stretched out and replete, languishing on Anna Dalziel's Scandinavian cushions. I can't remember the last time we ate in the living room. Anna's house-warming, possibly, an event of loud music and finger food and raucous testing of beds. Food was on the floor that night only by accident and only the most drunk of the party failed to clean it up before the lady of the house could see it. Even then, the dog wasn't allowed to set foot through the door, never mind sleep on the sofa.

Lee had claimed Anna's rug as her space, her island in the unfriendly sea of the room. She sat opposite me, on the far side of the coffee table, one knee hugged up to her chest, her cheek resting sideways on her forearm. Her hands and her face showed stark white against the black of her climbing top and the chalk on her feet marked a trail of footprints across the floor, stepping stones across the void. We floated on our separate islands and said nothing.

'So do you want to talk?' One of us has to say something or why am I here? But I am not sure, at this moment, if this is wise. I feel as if gravity has, without warning, stopped pulling downwards and I am no longer sure of the ground beneath my feet.

'You've been to see Mhaire. You probably know more about what's happening than I do.'

'Is it that obvious?'

'No one else leaves you looking quite so stressed.'

211

'She could have come to see me.' It has to be very bad before I argue semantics.

'No she couldn't. She's stuck out at the cottage. If she had any kind of transport, she'd have been camped out on the doorstep for the past three days making a nuisance of herself.' In the kitchen, she was wired, still high on the electricity of the climb. Now there is more of a distance, as if she has built for herself a wall and then moved behind it.

I can't reach her while she's all walled up.

So then I am not the only one. Perversely, there is some comfort in that.

'She seems to think you'd be safer still locked away.'

'She might be right. Was that the message?'

'She gave me several. I imagine that if you wanted to hear any of them, you would have been to see her by now.'

'I'm glad you noticed that.' Talking is like climbing. We move from one unsafe hold to the next, testing the placements, feeling for safer ground. 'But all the same, we have to give her credit for trying. Did she ask you to fix the windows?'

'I'm sorry?'

'Fine.' She smiled. A bright, scalding smile. 'She's not your greatest fan, Kellen. She wouldn't have had you out at the cottage unless she was desperate. There's only one thing would scare her that much and that's the thought of losing her free building consultant before she's had time to sort out a replacement.' The smile mocked us both, denied the words any weight. 'I take it she thinks I have a fairly limited life span?'

Does it matter what she thinks? I shrugged. 'Maybe she just doesn't want to see you locked up for life for something you didn't do. Has that occurred to you?'

'It comes to the same thing, Kellen. Mhaire knows that if no one else does.'

Jesus Christ. 'You *are* a bloody lemming. What's with the hard-wired attraction to dying, Adams? Has it occurred to you that there might be alternative options?'

'Not recently.' She leant back on the arm of a chair, chewed the inside of her lip and nodded quietly to herself. Her voice was hollow, devoid of feeling. 'Well done, Kellen. It's good to know where your loyalties lie. Herself would be proud of you.'

'I'm sorry. It just came out.'

'I'm sure it did.' Her eyebrows arched black in the white of her face, lazy, laconic, infuriating. 'And the rest? This was Mhaire after all. There must have been more.'

'That was the only thing that mattered.'

'You're a really bad liar, you know that, Kellen Stewart?'

'Really? And of course, I'm alone in that.'

'I haven't lied to you, Kellen.'

'Only because you haven't told me the first thing about what the hell's going on.'

'I *can't*. I thought you understood that.'

'I don't understand anything, Lee. To understand, I have to have facts and they're pretty thin on the ground right now.'

'Well, I'm sorry but that isn't my problem.'

'Is it not? So what is your problem?'

'Nothing that need concern you.'

'Fine.' I stood up, snapping my fingers for the dog. 'Then I think we've taken this just about as far as it can go, haven't we?'

'If you say so.'

213

I came as close, then, as I have ever done to walking out on her. She didn't move, she didn't say anything, she didn't ask, she didn't explain. She just sat there, looking at me, the black of her eyes flaring slowly in the light. The moment hung in the balance.

Trust.

Isn't it supposed to be mutual?

Are you going to let her die if it's not?

'I'll go if you want me to. You only have to ask.'

'I know that.'

'So?'

'So I haven't asked.'

I sat down on the arm of the sofa. The dog whined and pawed at the door then stalked back and dropped down beside me, sighing her complaint at the boredom and the tension. Lee moved – not a smile, just a small twitch of the muscles around her eyes. She leant forward across the table and crooked a finger. The dog thumped her tail on the floor, stretched, yawned and made the three steps across the floor to her side. They met on the rug as if they'd been parted for weeks and it was the most emotion I'd seen since I walked in the door. I stood and watched them for a while: a tan-in-white mess of enthusiasm and a slight, distracted climber who was once a part of the family. It never occurred to me that she might have been missing the dog, or that the dog might have been missing her. I went through to the kitchen and made myself coffee. Her computer lay on the table, dead to the world. I made no move to revive it.

She was sitting on the rug again when I got back to the

living room, not relaxed by any means, but less tense than she had been. The dog had settled in by her side, a pale body wrap, curling close to the black of her leggings. She ran a hand absently through the patched tangles of fur, teasing out the burrs from the farm, from the cemetery, from Mhaire's chaotic mess of a garden. I sat and drank coffee. They lay together in the silence. The daylight waned and the heat with it until we sat in the cool of the dusk; two women, a dog and the unravelling threads of a friendship. I should be better at this by now.

I put the mug on the floor and leant forward on the table to where I could see her face. 'Can we talk, Lee? Really talk?'

She shrugged, keeping her hands on the dog. Her face was still closed. 'Up to a point.'

'OK.' It's honest, at least. 'Thank you.'

It was almost night by then. I reached up and hit the switch on the wall behind me. The muted monochrome of the room flooded suddenly, too suddenly, to colour. She flinched. I ran a thumb across the dimmer pulling it down to a softer, less threatening glow.

I only need to see her face to know how much of what she says is the truth.

She let go of the dog and sat up again; pulling her feet underneath her and both knees to her chest, resting her chin on her arms. Her eyes drifted to mine and stayed there, dark and too full of conflict to be easily read. This isn't a time to be reading eyes.

'Why is this happening, Lee?'

'I don't know.'

'Mhaire seemed to think that you did.'

'Then I suggest that we leave Mhaire out of this. You've spent most of your life telling me she couldn't be trusted. This might be a good time to put that into practice.'

Fine. I let the silence draw out for a while. And then: 'Are the police trying to link Hillary Murdoch to Joey Duncan and Martin Coutts?'

'They're not trying, they're stating the obvious. Whoever killed Hillary killed the other two. There are not too many ways to create a fatal hypoxia. We seem to be working through most of them.'

'And you're next in line?'

'Possibly.'

'You don't frame someone if you're planning to kill them. It doesn't make sense.'

'Very true.' She rolled over to lie on her stomach. The dog grunted and moved to make room. 'So maybe I don't get to die. Maybe I get two decades in prison instead.' That smile again. 'Or life. Whichever is shorter.'

'That's not funny, Lee. We've been round this one before.'

'We have. And perhaps Mhaire's right, perhaps there is a way out, although I have to say it's not obvious at the moment. No doubt, if there's time, I'll work out what it was she had in mind.'

'You could pick up the phone and ask her.'

'No thanks.'

She propped her chin on the heel of her hand and watched me think. An unrewarding process. Too many questions, not enough answers. I got up and went to the window and peered out through the hessian blinds. Outside, the street-lamps were on. My car lay in a semi-circle of artificial light. Three lampposts further down, two figures sat in an unmarked car, watching the light in our window.

'They're watching you,' I said. 'Did you know?'

'They'd be negligent if they weren't.'

'Are they here all the time?'

'Mostly.' Meaning always. 'Don't let it get to you. That pair are harmless. It's the ones you can't see that you need to worry about.'

'Thanks. I'll bear it in mind.'

I turned and leant back on the window-frame and watched her lying on the floor with the dog as if police surveillance was part of her everyday pattern. She's taking this too easily. Something, somewhere has changed in her.

'You're enjoying this, aren't you?'

'No.' A long, languid shrug. 'But it makes a change from fighting Murdoch over research protocols.' She came up behind me and pulled the curtains shut, then took my hand and led me back to a seat. 'Come and sit down, Kells. They don't need to see you to know that you're here.'

I went back to the sofa and turned the dimmer down another notch until we could have been sitting with a single small candle hanging down from the ceiling. My coffee was cold. I drank it anyway because making more would have meant putting on a light in the kitchen and that would have been too easily seen from the road. Suddenly I could understand how anyone living here might want to spend most of their time in the climbing room: no windows and thick padded walls, a safe place to hide.

'Can they hear what we're saying?'

'Possibly. We have to assume so.'

'And the phone?'

'Definitely.'

'But not the modem?'

'I've no idea.'

Christ. 'Where does it end, Lee?'

'It ends when the last one on the list is dead.' She sat now with her elbows on the coffee table, leaning forward to see and be seen in the quiet light from the lamp. She smiled, and it was not a comforting smile. 'Or possibly before that if I can work out the details before they get there. Like the harridan said, there's more than one way at the crossroads.'

And that, then, was the change in her. The fire, hidden down behind whatever brick wall she was building. It's the challenge. She lives for the challenge. Death is the consenting partner and all of life is thrown at the biggest chance. This is, after all, why she climbs. Only, when she's climbing, she has somebody sane there holding the rope.

'Lee, I—'

'Don't. It isn't worth it.' She reached her hand across the table and hooked her fingers over mine in an old gesture, worn with familiarity. It has more feeling to it, sometimes, than an embrace. She smiled again and this time it was real. It felt safe, for a moment, to ask the questions.

'Who is it, Lee? Who's doing this?'

'I don't know.'

'But you think they're planning more after Hillary Murdoch?'

'There's got to be at least one. They've got this far, they're hardly likely to stop now.'

'Do you know who?'

218

'Not yet.'

'Would you take help if it was offered?'

'I can't, Kellen. We're too close to . . .' She shook her head and her fingers tightened, like they would on a climb. 'You're too close to the firing line. If I make my own mistakes, I'm dead. I'm not having you out there making them for me.'

Chapter Eleven

It was long past dark. The streets of the west end were as calm as they ever are this side of midnight, lodged in that lull just before the pubs turn the last batch of customers out into the night. I was heading for the farm but I changed my mind on the way up past the university, turned left instead of right at the lights on Byres Road and drove down to the Unit. The car park was empty. I parked under the trees and went to sit for a while on the bench under the sycamores. The gardener had finished long since. Wet clumps of cut grass packed round the soles of my shoes. The sharp, earthy smell of it hung in the air, warm and close, a smell from childhood that speaks of summer and freedom in the way that garden bonfires speak of rain and autumn and the imminent return to school. The wind tugged at the sycamores, lifting the leaves, spinning dry keys to the ground. I sat on the seat and watched the moon make silhouettes of the topmost branches. It was close to half full by then, an upended bowl, pouring cold porcelain light down on to the city. It was new when the killing started. If Mhaire's informed guesswork is right, then it will all be over before it is new again and Lee Adams could easily be one among the dead. If Mhaire is right. If Lee is right with her. If both of them are not working to some other, unspoken, agenda.

Trust. It all hinges on trust. Such a fragile thing and so easily broken. And then what is there left when it's gone? I stood with my back to the sycamore turning over leaves with my toe and tried not to think of a future in which Lee Adams played no part.

A light glowed suddenly in the Unit, fire in the blank mass of the stone. Three-quarters of the way along the bottom corridor, in a long row of blind, darkened windows, someone drew back their curtains and lit a single candle. It wavered and steadied, a great globe of a thing, spewing harlequin patches of coloured light out across the lawn; scarlet and indigo, saffron and jade, all of them weaving round the amber of the flame. I counted along the windows and came to Jack Souter's room. In the massed ranks of my dead, this one does not weigh heavy on my conscience. I left the shelter of the trees, walked across the grass and let myself in through the back entrance, as Sally Souter had done, to visit the bringer of light.

He was a much younger man than his predecessor. He sat up in the bed, his head on a bank of pillows, his face turned to the window, to the flame and the night beyond.

'Hello.' His head didn't turn. 'I thought you'd come in for the light.' His voice was rich; a full, flowing south-side Glaswegian.

'How did you know I was there?'

'How did you know I lit the candle?' He turned then to look at me. His hair was dark, like his eyes, and it hung in long coils to his shoulder. If he had been on any tumour therapy, it wasn't in the recent past. 'I was watching you,' he said. 'You were looking that sorry for yourself. I couldn't leave you like that.'

This from one who is dying, who must be dying or he wouldn't be here.

I moved in and sat on the chair by his bed, on the far side from the window ledge. The wick burned deep in the core of the candle. The air was soft with sandalwood, warm with amber light. His skin glowed darker than mine, as if he was one of the millions making the most of last week's sun. He smelled of sandalwood and patchouli, of clean cotton and liquid soap. There was no smell yet, of death, no sign of why he might be here.

He put his hand on my arm. 'If I lit another candle, would you stay and talk?'

His smile was warm, like the flame. There are candles enough and in this place, I have never been averse to talking. Life is too short to play games.

'No need for the candle.' I put my hand over his. 'I have a friend. She thinks she may be going to die.'

'Is that so very bad?'

'I think it is. She isn't ready.' Or I am not ready. Or, more properly: 'It's not her time, yet, to go.'

'Ah.' He smiled again and it was like looking into the quiet sea where the water is clear enough to let you through and yet so deep you would never reach the bottom. 'Is that not what everyone says?'

'Not always.' Rarely, in fact. And fewer still who have the understanding to ask it. 'Is that what you say?'

'No.' The smile faded but the humour stayed; deep and darkly ironic. 'But then, I know where I'm going.'

It is not often in here that I find nothing to say. In this room, I am suddenly redundant, an unwanted player in someone else's script. He pushed himself higher up in the bed and let the sheets fall away so that he sat as if in a chair by the fire. 'You're the therapist, aren't you?'

'Is it printed across my forehead?'

'No. We've met before.' He dipped his head with the grace of fresh meeting and stretched out a hand and he was not, after all, unscarred. A short row of dark purple bruises showed over the line of his vein. I/v lines, maybe, or blood samples. He pulled down the cuff of his night shirt to cover the marks. 'Back in May,' he said. 'You were looking after Paul. I was here with him when he died.'

And now, this close, I remember. They were not ready, these two, to part.

'Nicco. I'm sorry. I didn't recognise you. You've grown your hair.'

'There was no point in having it cut.' Said differently, there could have been such pathos in that. Said lightly, it came as a matter of fact.

I found his notes near the foot of his bed. Nicco Gallianno: an Ayrshire lad of Italian extraction. Home address in Edinburgh. Next of kin, Mr and Mrs A. Gallianno of Troon. It is not, I would imagine, one of the best of places to grow up if you're not of the mainstream. He came out remarkably balanced. I turned over the page and found his clinical history: paracetamol poisoning, self-induced. Two days ago, the surgeons offered him a liver transplant, providing they could find a tissue match in time. He told them he didn't want them to look. And so the dusk of his skin is not only his heritage. In the candled twilight of this room, the effects of jaundice and the effects of the sun are not easy to tell apart.

On the third page of his notes, the brief case history gave way to the hard data. I leant back against his bed, angling the paper to catch the best of the light. He sat behind me and read the figures over my shoulder. In the Unit, all the patients have full access to their notes. I think, at times, this stops the hard core of the establishment from sending them here, but the prejudice is less than it was. We read the fourth page together; a complex list of serial liver-function tests, taken twenty-four hours apart. The results showed a steady deterioration. He reached a long arm over my shoulder and laid a finger under the last set of bile acid results. 'What does it mean?'

'Your liver's failing.'

'I know that. I mean, how long have I got?'

'I don't know.' These things are never totally accurate. 'A week I would think, maybe two.'

'Thank you.' His arm stayed where it was. The smell of soap was replaced by the warm smells of male sleep. 'The nurse didn't want to say.'

The nurse was probably waiting for me to say it first. 'I'm sorry. I should have been here to tell you.'

'No problem. It's all much the same in the end.'

It is. I wonder if he has any idea at all how bad the end can be. 'How are you feeling?'

'Pretty good so far. It's slower than I thought, that's all.

225

Maybe I didn't take enough.' His other arm came to rest on my shoulder and I was held in a loose embrace. There was diffidence to it, as if there were other things he needed to say. 'I asked them to send me here. Do you mind?'

'Of course not. It's what we're here for. Why would I mind?'

'I thought perhaps I might be taking you away from someone who needs you more.'

'No. You're here. That means you need us most.'

'Thank you. Will you be here when I go?'

It was not an idle question. I thought of what might happen in the next ten days. He felt the hesitation and qualified his request. 'If your friend doesn't need you?'

'Yes, I'll be here. If she doesn't need me.'

He moved closer and we sat together, his chest against my back, his arms round my neck. I have met this man twice before in my life. In two weeks, maybe less, he will be dead. Comfort comes in the strangest places. He balanced his chin on my head and together we watched a bank of cloud, like a spreading stain, slowly cover the face of the moon. Soon the only light was the background glow of the street-lamps and the flickering amber of the flame. We spoke together, softly, as if otherwise something might wake.

'Do you like my candle?'

'I do. It was a good idea.'

'You looked so cold. I couldn't have you being cold.'

'Thank you. I'm not cold now.'

'But she's still going to die, your friend?'

'She's running very close to the line. I think . . .' and I had not thought this before, 'I think that she has just said goodbye.'

'Is there nothing you can do?'

226

'I can find out who's trying to kill her, perhaps, but I'm not sure what I can do after that.'

'Ah.' His arms squeezed tighter. As if this kind of death can be wrong where others are not. 'I suppose the police are out of the question?'

'They are.'

'You'd better get looking then, hadn't you?'

'I think that may be why I'm here.'

His arms released me; his chin moved from my head. 'You'll come back?'

'Yes.' I can promise him that. 'I'll come back.'

I was in the office, printing out files from Med-line when Dee found me an hour later. I didn't see her but I heard the footsteps along the corridor. She walks, always, as if she's just warming down from a run. Once in a while, it's true.

'Kellen?' She pushed open the door. 'I just called for you at the farm. Nina said you were at Lee's.'

'I was.' I tabbed down through yet another screen of references, saw nothing of value, printed it anyway. 'How's Nina?'

'In bed. Wondering when you'll be home.'

'Soon.' I have no idea of time. I'm in limbo, dislocated from the spinning wheels of the world outside. I have joined the growing ranks of the techno-geeks and I could stay here all night. I sat up and stretched. My eyes felt dry from too long staring at the screen. My shoulders were permanently hunched. I hooked my fingers round the back of my neck and felt the vertebrae grind as I turned my head. Home and bed seemed a very long way away. 'What were you calling the farm for?'

'I need you here.' She came in and sat on the edge of my desk, picked a page off the printer and ran her eye down the columns of print. I wouldn't have said they made any more sense to her than they did to me. When she looked up, her eyes, and the skin around them, were grey. 'It's Claire,' she said.

'What about her?'

'One of the pulmonary mets is blocking her airway.'

'So what are you waiting for?' This, of all possible complications, we can manage. 'Call in the duty surgeon and get them to put in a tracheotomy tube and get the ventilator going. You don't need me for that.'

'No.' Her eyes held mine. 'I've talked to her about it. She doesn't want a tracheotomy. She doesn't want any more intervention. She's asked to be let go, Kellen. I have it in writing.'

Christ. 'Has she any idea what it's going to be like?'

'Yes. I've spent the evening with her. She knows everything there is to know.'

'How do you . . .?'

'Beth went like this. I know it all.' Her eyes were too dry. The anger flamed inward, feeding on pain.

'Does she want me there?'

'*I* want you there.' She slid off the desk. 'Will you come?'

'Let me phone Nina. I'll follow you up.'

There are so many different reasons to die. So many different ways. Sometime, somehow, I have rationalised this. I have grown to believe that there is a right time to die and that my job is to be there, back-to-front midwife, holding, containing, supporting. There are times when I believe this is right. There are other times, like now, when I know beyond all knowing that the whole of life is a travesty, that the only reality is pain and that the only thing that truly matters is dignity and speed in the process of dying.

Claire Hendon's death was not dignified, nor was it swift. The mass of the tumour had not completely blocked her airway and she had a space left – the diameter, maybe, of a straw – through which she could still draw breath. You can't live for long breathing through a straw but the body takes over and fights for each molecule of oxygen however much the heart and soul may want to let go. It is agonising to watch. In a normal ward, we would call in the anaesthetist and place an artificial airway. If necessary, we would pass tubes down into the distal bronchi, hook them up to a ventilator and let technology take over the process of breathing. But in this place, the anaesthetist had a signed statement from her patient, taken in the presence of two other independent medical professionals, to say that she wanted no intervention. In this place, this is the kind of decision that matters. And so we sat for that night at the bedside; me, Dee, Claire's mother and Claire's father and we watched a young woman of twenty-three struggle to let go of her life.

She was still breathing at dawn. Long, ragged, hard-drawn breaths, harder to breathe in than to breathe out but neither way easy. Dee sat on one side of the bed, holding her hand, talking her through each cycle. Her parents sat beside her, silent and white. They had said all they could say in the dark spaces of the night, talked themselves to a standstill and beyond. They were not old, but they were lined, then, as if each hour of the night had added a decade beyond the ones they already carried. Dee was the only one who still talked, the melodic rhythm of rich, rolling Irish flowing over us all, binding us all in place. I sat at the far side of the bed and I listened to the music of it, not the lyrics. I didn't think anyone was really listening, not even Claire, until I looked up and found Dee was looking at me and she said it again, the sentence I hadn't quite heard. 'Set up the morphine, Kellen.'

'But she said she didn't want . . .'

'She's changed her mind.'

'Dee, you can't . . .'

'Yes I can.' Her eyes burned bright and red-rimmed across the white of the sheets. 'It's what she wants, Kellen. You can go or you can help. Just don't argue with me now.' And then the girl on the bed, more awake, more aware than any of us, turned her head to me and pushed a long-fought breath, ragged and faint, into the whisper: 'Do it,' she said, 'just do it. Please.'

And so we did.

You can't pretend that it's efficient, morphine, but it's the best we've got. Potassium is sudden and successful but impossible to defend in court. We might have done it in the past but we couldn't do it now. Morphine is allowed, up to a point, because morphine stops the pain and only when there is no more pain does it stop the breathing. Unless the pain comes from the breathing in which case all things stop together. Eventually. It is not perfect, but it has dignity and almost anything is better than the lingering battle of asphyxiation.

It took five minutes, maybe a little less. Claire held the control to begin with and I removed all the limits on the pump. Soon, when she had no strength left to push, Dee sat on the edge of the bed, folded the fine-boned hand in hers and then two thumbs pressed on the button, holding it down until the last drops were running in. At the end, I leaned over and joined them, a third hand, a second offender, because these things are better shared. It was not legal. I make no pretence that it was legal. But I learned a long time ago that when the law and my own conscience speak differently, there is only one of them that is ever talking sense. This is not the first time. It will not be the last, for me or for anyone else in the Unit.

There are things that you do when it's over. Open the windows to let out the spirit. Bring in flowers from outside to lie on the bed. Leave the family alone with the body so that they can remember her as she was, lying at peace, with the lines of tension and pain gone from her face. I followed Dee down the corridor, walking with no sense of direction. We stopped, eventually, at the door of the office.

'You should go home.'

'Later. I need to run.'

'Could I use your shower?'

'Are you not going back to the farm?'

'There's no point. It's too late. I'll get caught up in the traffic coming back.'

'Go ahead. You know the way. I'll be back in an hour.'

'Take the dog with you, huh? She needs to go out.'

'Fine.'

The water is clear and hot and it strips my skin. Steam clouds the room. I am alone in the fog, insulated from the outside world. I am safe, enclosed, encircled, blind. Time has no structure. Space has no form. I have no past, no present, no future. Life ends in a moment. There is such liberation in this. For the first time since the night of Joey Duncan's death, I have no headache.

'Good shower?'

'Very. Good run?'

'Very. Your dog's in the car.'

'You don't have to come back into work, Dee. We'll live without you for a day.'

'I'll think about it.'

'You should sleep.'

'Am I the only one?'

'Maybe not.' We sit at her kitchen table and drink coffee together, hot, bitter, espresso made in the machine by the window. Slowly, the colours of the morning pull back into focus. The mumbling exhaustion of the night gives way to a hollow, light-headed detachment. I can think now, which is more than I could do an hour ago. The night moves into some kind of perspective. What I remember, what I will always remember, is the soft, singing melody of her voice, moving unbroken right through to the end. I listened to the music. I didn't listen to the words.

'I'm sorry,' I say, eventually.

'What for?'

'We could have done something sooner. She didn't have to go on so long.'

'She went when she was ready to go. We could do nothing without her asking. You know that.' The run has done its job. She is hot and damp and the anger is less than it was. Her hair is dark, pasted down to her head in places where she has pushed her fingers through it. Her skin is flushed and there are wet streaks beneath her eyes that might be more than the sweat. She moves about the room, restless, carrying her mug in both hands. Her voice is different now, showing the strains of the night. I remember her face, grey with fatigue, before the worst of it started. Of all of us, she has been here before.

'Was it like that for Beth?' I ask it with care, treading gently past raw nerves. 'Was there someone there for her at the end?'

'Eventually, yes.' She stops pacing, her mind somewhere else. 'They took longer about it than we did but then she was in a general oncology ward. The place was alive with nurses. They had to be careful.'

'I'm sorry.'

'So am I.' She moves over to the sink and turns her back so that I can't see her face. Her head is framed by the window. Outside, the sun is losing the battle with the cloud. The patches of blue are far less than the blankets of grey. I remember a candle, lit in the dark of a room, and a lover, not letting go.

'Nicco Gallianno's here, did you know?' She asks it suddenly, with no preamble, as if the pattern of my thinking has carried across the room.

'Yes. I saw him last night.'

'He's turned down a liver transplant.'

'I know.' But he's not one of those who will go out on a sea of morphine. His lover didn't want it; he will not want it either. 'He knows what he's doing.'

'He's following Paul.'

'I know. He told me.' There are ghosts, now, in this room,

soft and sibilant. They make their own music. I listen, this time, to the words. 'Nicco hasn't chosen to go into medicine.'

'We didn't fuck up over Paul.'

'True.' With Guillaume-Barré fucking up is not an option. All one can ever do is wait and monitor progress. Recovery happens, or not, at the whim of the gods. Cervical cancer is not like that. Ask Claire Hendon. Ask Beth.

I move over and stand beside her, shoulder to shoulder, touching but not holding. The ghosts crowd close, pushing questions, needing answers.

'Would you have followed Beth if what happened to her had been more . . . straightforward?'

'God, yes.' Her voice is quiet. Only this close can I hear it. 'It would have been so easy. And I wanted to so very badly.'

'So why not?'

'I had a promise to keep.' Her face is still. She stares out past the clouds to the space beyond. 'I thought it mattered.'

'Does it not still matter?'

'I don't know. It used to. A lot. Now . . .' She turns round so I can see her, so she can see me. 'What do you do when the promise is over, Kellen?'

I promised I'd become one of them without ever becoming one of them. That I'd stop it and not be a part of it . . .

'That promise is never over.'

'I think it might be. I can't go on with this much longer.'

No. Now, I can see that. 'Then you let go and get on with living your own life.'

'You may have to remind me of that.'

'Just keep asking.'

'Thank you. I will.'

★ ★ ★

We made breakfast after that, toast and scrambled eggs and ageing tomatoes from the back of the fridge. She treats food, at times, like I do: a tedious necessity, easily forgotten. Sitting at the table, in the flat light of the morning, she looked younger, as if the night had loaned her back some lost years. She leant forward and speared a lone tomato from my plate. 'How's Lee?' she asked. It came quietly, slipped in between one mouthful and the next, as if that way I might not think too hard on the answer.

'She's still alive. I think that's about as far as it goes. I got the impression she's not expecting to stay that way for much longer.'

'Hell.' She reached back to the counter and poured hot water straight from the kettle into her mug. The coffee was still pitch black. 'Has she heard from Sarah?'

'I don't know. I'm not sure she'd tell me at the moment. She wasn't at her most communicative.'

'But she was downloading Med-line files by the yard.'

'How do you know that?'

'Why else would you be sitting in the office at midnight when you could be home in bed?'

'Thanks.' It is not any comfort to be so easily read.

'You're welcome.' She abandoned the coffee, stood up and poured the stuff down the sink and ran herself a mugful of cold water from the tap instead. Then she sat down on the floor, hugging the mug to her chest. She thought for a while. 'Are you sure the two of you are asking the same questions, Kellen? You're trying to find out what she knows that you don't. She may be looking for something else entirely. You could go round in circles like that for eternity.'

'I know. But I've got nothing else to go on.'

'Except memory.' She raised a brow. 'Who else was there, Kellen? Of the people around then, who is there still left who knew all of them, one way or another? Who shared ward round and drinking rounds? Who climbed walls and rocks and electricity pylons and took the piss out of Hillary Murdoch?'

'Apart from me?'

'Not apart from you.'

The morning was very still. Outside, the rain started, rinsing the dust from the pavements. I looked at her. She looked at me, long and steady. 'If Lee knows something then you know it too.' She leant over and knocked a knuckle against my forehead. 'You don't need to waste time searching papers on Med-line. It's in there if it's anywhere.'

'You think I haven't thought of that?'

'I think you haven't let yourself think too deeply about anything. You've been progressively less coherent since you brought Eric back to the mortuary. You need to stop feeling and start thinking while you still remember how.'

'Will it help?'

'It probably won't make a blind bit of difference to Lee but it might make you feel less like you're over your head in the slurry pit and sinking deeper with every breath.'

'Thanks.'

'Any time.' She smiled. 'You don't come here to be cosseted. You can get that at home. If you can remember where that is.'

'Just about.'

'Then I suggest you take the dog and go. They don't need either of us in at work today. We wouldn't be doing anybody any favours. Get some sleep while you can. You'll not make much sense of anything without.'

She stood up and walked me to the door. We parted on the landing and my final memory of the morning is of her leaning against her own door-post, her skin translucent from lack of sleep, her eyes warm with the candour of the night. We hugged briefly, chastely, in the hallway.

'Kells . . .?'

'Yes?'

'Thank you for being there last night.'

'You're welcome. I'm glad I could do it.'

'Get some sleep, huh?'

'I'll do my best.'

Chapter Twelve

The day is heavy, overcast and overwarm, waiting for rain that doesn't come. The bedroom is airless, the windows pegged wide for nothing. I lie awake and unclothed, on top of the duvet, drifting between the worlds. Sleep blends with no-sleep. Past blurs into present. Then into now.

Now, I am home at the farm listening to the world at work. Outside, the Galbraiths are cutting silage on the hill above the village. Three hired tractors run relays from the fields to the silage clamp, three hundred horse power, racing the rain. The noise comes in where the wind does not. *I have nothing else to go on. Except memory.* It is impossible to sleep.

Then, I am at home in another place on another close, airless day. I lie unclothed on another bed after yet another night on duty, too tired to sleep. The ceiling here is higher and has no beams and the walls are new-paint white, the smell of it still hanging in the air. The windows are open on other versions of the world at work: the endless commuter cars on

Great Western Road; the Underground; the self-conscious laughter of students queuing for morning lectures – all of it carried in on a gagging mix of pizza and curry and the dregs of last night's beer. A morning like any other morning, after a night like any other night. I lie awake and know that I should call Bridget and can't be bothered to make the effort and lift the phone.

And then, this morning of all mornings, there is something else, not part of the pattern. Feet run up the stairs at a time when I should not be having company. The front door slams open and then shut on the end of a kick. The footsteps come closer, a knuckle taps on the door and a voice, barely heard, asks if I am asleep before she comes in anyway and sits on the edge of my bed. It is Lee, of course, but not the Lee I have known. This one is white to match the walls, whiter still at the flared edge of her nostrils and the tight line of her lips. Her eyes are black because her eyes are always black but never before with such a depth of anger. She is shaking, a fine, vibrating shudder, the same way she was shaking when she held Eric dead on a cliff-top but this time, the first time, she is shaking with anger and not with grief.

She is shaking too much to hold a full mug of tea and so I get out of bed and make two mugs and then pour half of hers down the sink to make it safe. I come back to the bed and sit on top of the duvet with my mug between my palms and I listen while she spins me a story of the night and the day and the night before spent without sleep on the ward. A story of a patient dying slowly and begging for something faster. A patient who mattered, one for whom it was worth taking risks. A patient who held her hand and said thank you in the brief five minutes when the housemen and the nurses were looking the other way and the woman who had trained for half her life to be a doctor drew up the morphine and spiked it with potassium and injected it all into the drip line for a final release into death.

I sit on the bed in silence then, because it is almost a year since I came to this and I have always known that for Lee, in her world of absolutes, it will be a harder bridge to cross. I lose myself in a world of remembered deaths and their meanings and I don't listen, particularly, to what comes next: to the clinical history of a patient who should not have been a patient, to the clinical trials that should never have been run, to the details of the war to end all wars that she has declared on Randolph Duncan. I don't listen because I've heard often enough before the sordid details of surgical politics which are no different, really, to medical politics and I've had my lifetime's fill of that, by now. So I don't even read, at first, the wording of the letter she holds out to me, typed in haste by his secretary, which tells her of the Professor's belief that, in view of the opinions recently expressed, she is no longer able to fulfil the terms of her contract. It is with great regret, therefore, that he is forced to relieve her of her position, with effect from the morning shift. And so slowly, too slowly, the unreal becomes real.

She is no longer his surgeon.

She is no longer anyone's surgeon.

Lee Adams has just lost her job, her life, her future, her soul.

I sit behind her on the bed and wrap my arms around her and I know that the world has ended.

★　★　★

But now I am here, not there, and so the world did not end and the ancient, long-dead pain is overlaid with the screaming fury of the colt, kicking up hell in the hawthorn field, a delinquent adolescent banished from the family fold because one of the new-foaled mares is in season and he hasn't learned yet to control his hormones. On another day, Sandy would go up and spend time with his child but today Sandy has a new love. The last of the foaling mares bedded down last night and the old man sat up with her, watching.

She knows him and likes him and tolerated him sitting in the box, which is more than most of them do. She broke her waters at dawn and gave him, nice and easy, a compact filly foal, chestnut all through but for the pale pewter line around her eyes that tells the world she'll be grey when the foal coat sheds. In a week or two, as she grows, she'll be just another foal in the herd and the colt will be back in his place as the pride and joy. For now, though, he is second in line and if I listen between the clarion cries of frustration, I can hear an old man whistling an endless reprise of 'Marie's Wedding', which is how he always welcomes his new children into the world.

In another time and another place, I sit on the bed and taste the salt of a lost dream on my lips. The world might not have ended but it has stopped, for now, in its tracks. I have known Lee Adams for nine long years and for every moment of that, she has known, we have known, the world has known, not just that she will be a surgeon, but that she will be the best of surgeons. She may not bear the dynastic flame of a Duncan but she will, none the less, carve a high place for herself in the world of bright names and brighter knives. For all the time I have known her, there has been nothing else in her world that matters. And now it is gone.

I am slow for lack of sleep and I will not believe it. Nine years is too long to throw away in a morning. Whatever you have said, whatever you have done, it cannot cancel out the years of extra ward rounds, the days and nights in the library, the months in theatre taking the shit, the long, late evenings in anatomy working and working to know what it is that makes the human frame move and function and fail the way that it does. He needs you, that man. He respects you. You are the first one, bar none, who has stayed the distance. You can't throw it all away. He won't let you.

But I can. He will. He has. You're not listening. I have thrown it all away and more. Last night, for the first time, I killed a dying patient. I have, knowingly and willingly, taken a life because the death that was coming was worse than anything else I have seen and I could not sit by any longer and watch it happen. It should never have come to that. Never. This case was his case, his patient, his part of his clinical trial. His decision to keep on going with a treatment protocol that he knew was useless and worse than useless. He should have stopped this months ago and the only reason he didn't is because Hillary Murdoch said that she needed more cases in the treatment group so that they could publish the results. He is committing murder in there. Long, slow, serial murder of people who trust him, people who know no better, people who go to their collective graves believing that this man has been doing his best when all he has done is rack up numbers for his tame statistician. It can't go on. I won't let it go on. I have lodged a formal complaint, of malpractice, of negligence, of wilful neglect. This man is a Duncan. This man is *the* Duncan. The men in white coats worship the ground he walks on but they have turned blind eyes his way for too long. Now, I will make them see. Now, I will stop him, whatever it takes. But I will never, not ever again, be a surgeon.

In that, if nothing else, she was right.

The day still holds on to the rain. Six families of house-martins have made their homes beneath the eaves. The parents started hunting at dawn. They are still hunting now; they make long, swooping passes through the clouds of midges and thunder flies that swirl like smoke in the air above the pond. They return, time and again, to the nests, to the incessant screaming of their young. I can hear it now only if I think hard, if I pull each of the sounds from the backdrop of noise and name them. I do it once, as an exercise, to bring me back to the here and now but the effort is more than I want to spend and I let it go. I am empty, drained with lack of sleep. I am here and I am there, caught in the no-man's land where time has no meaning. All I can feel is the shock of then and the ripples of it running through to now. I can feel the blinding heat of our tears, hers and mine on the back of my hand. She doesn't weep. Lee does not weep. In all of my life, Eric or no Eric, the only time I have seen her weep was the morning she came home to the flat that we shared and told me that she had just thrown away all hope of ever fulfilling her dream. Even so it was overspill, a small, silent fraction of what was going on inside. I didn't have the understanding, then, to ask for more. Life would have been different if I had. You can't feel that much and keep holding it in without damage to something. In the days afterwards, when the shock of it grew less and was replaced by the aching void of a life without direction, I can remember the feel of her anger, like slow-boiling lava, and me, waiting for, praying for, an eruption that never came. I remember, beyond that, the long days of going in to work and of people not speaking, of eyes not meeting mine, of words not spoken, as if by siding with the accuser I had become one of the accused. Then I remember the days drawing into weeks and the weeks into months and the slow, dawning realisation that nothing was going to happen, that the wheels had turned, the worm had performed a full 360 degree revolution and escaped the bird. The system closed ranks, reached for its broom and the blood and the guilt and the bodies vanished tidily under the carpet. Records were lost by the drawerful. Not just individual case records but an entire bank of research reports vanished from history as if they had never been. Too late, we realised what was happening and, a long way too late, we tried to do something about it. We talked about going to the papers. We tried, I remember, a tame reporter, but she wanted proof in black and white and we had none and, in any case, the press was more servile in those days, editors still paid homage to the high god of medicine. Careers came and went on the need to uphold the patients' faith in the profession. It would have taken more than a folder of facts to print a story.

And so, slowly, unbelievably, everything returned to where it had been. Except that Lee was different. Nothing you could name or put a finger on but changed in small ways that have blurred with memory until I can barely remember the difference between the bright, glowing flame of who she was and the harder, dryer, filtered version of who she became. When they offered her a job in pathology I thought she'd throw it in their faces but she'd been three months out in the cold by then and Lee lived for the hospital in ways that I never did. She took it and she made the best of it and all that she could once have been for the living, she became for the dead. But I have never seen her so much as nod at Randolph Duncan from that day to this.

Randolph Duncan, whose son is dead.

I gave up on the bed. Sleep was never going to come and the black-on-white lines of the ceiling were making me feel ill. I dressed in whatever was nearest and clean, poured a mug of half-cold coffee from the pot by the Rayburn and went outside to lean on the wall by the hawthorn hedge. The air was so very still, the sky so deeply, densely blue. The pond was poured lead, viscous and flat with only the slowest of ripples flowing out from the ducks at the edge. The martins were silent, hunting flies in the way whales hunt plankton: long, open-mouthed trawls through a swarm of smaller beings. A million flies dead to feed one bird. Someone, somewhere believes this to be a fair swap.

'Kellen?' The gravel crunched, once, behind me. You would think that, in the still of the day, I would have heard the car draw up, but I lost the sound of it in the steady grind of the tractors. I turned towards the gate. Dee stood in the shade of the house, propped sideways against the wall like a leaning broom. She was still in the running shorts and singlet from the morning, still with the blue hollows beneath her eyes, as if she'd spent the past hours pummelling her thumbs around her orbits.

'Hi.' She smiled, weary and self-mocking. 'I'm glad I'm not the only one couldn't sleep.'

'It's the weather.'

'If you say so.' She came over to join me at the wall.

'It has to rain soon.'

'The forecasters say wind but no rain.'

'Idiots.'

We stood together for a while, feeling the heat of the day, tasting the damp of it with every breath, watching the older foals – the duns, the bays, the chestnuts and the one out-standing strawberry roan – as they raced each other from tussock to teasel and back again across the field. The mares gathered in a cluster under the shade of the beech trees on the far side of the field, whisking flies in their sleep. I looked down at my hands, clasped together on the stones. A fine tremor ran through to the white knuckle-ends, like cold, or the beginnings of malaria. Or fear.

I stood on the edge of reality and looked out into the void and knew I couldn't face it alone.

'It's Randolph Duncan,' I said.

'What is?' She was watching the foal, the strawberry roan. It stood part-balanced on three legs and used the fourth to scratch the back of one ear. They can only do that when they're young, foals. Like children and young trees, they stiffen as they grow.

'The next one. There is going to be a next one. Lee told me there was. I just didn't think to ask how she knew . . .'

The words ran dry in my throat. My hands were locked tight, jammed hard on the blunt stone of the wall, crushing skin on to bone to stop the shakes. I looked out over the field and tried to find the roan, a small token of reality to keep me falling out over the edge. Dee moved in behind me, her arms looping in under my elbows, her hands covering mine. The tremor ran through them to her, up to the shoulders and down the span of her ribs. I felt her voice before I heard it, deep and resonant, a life-raft of sound.

'She didn't do it, Kellen. You told me that.' Her hands were warm on mine.

'I know. I was wrong. I wasn't thinking. Or I chose not to think. I had forgotten quite how badly she hated Randolph Duncan. Eric always blamed Murdoch. She was away in the States. I suppose it was easier on all of us to despise someone on the other side of the world than a man you have to work with every day of the week.' I sketched out the briefest details of Lee and her war with her mentor. 'She never mentioned him once it was over. She never even said his name. It was as if he didn't exist.'

Her fingers traced lines on the backs of my hands. 'It was half a lifetime ago, Kellen. What would make her start killing now?'

'I don't know. Hillary Murdoch coming back, maybe. Or losing Eric. MacDonald could be right, she needed him there to keep her grounded. I just didn't think . . . I thought she had more to live for than that . . .'

'Kellen . . . don't.' She moved round then, sliding between me and the wall, blocking out the mares and their foals and the blurring fields. Her hands came up to my face; her palms were dry on the wet of my cheeks. The balls of her thumbs flickered over my eyelids, the skin rough, like a dry-tongued cat. 'Kellen, stop it, you're guessing. You don't know any of this for sure. You need to go back and talk to her and see what she says and then you can decide on more than a maybe if she's telling . . .' She stiffened then, without warning, and her hands dropped to her sides.

I spun on the spot. 'Nina, I . . .' and there he was, dressed up for work and without his dog and he looked no more happy to see us there than she would have done. 'Inspector MacDonald.' I swayed back against the wall. 'How very deeply intrusive. I thought I told you to stay off my land?'

'Where is she?' It came out stark and flat, no pretence at friendship.

'Nina? She's at work. She'll be home this evening.'

'Is that right?' He stood with his feet braced and his arms folded and he didn't move, except to chew, hard, on his bottom lip. 'I've a warrant to make a search,' he said. He bit the words short. 'I thought maybe you'd rather we did it the easy way but it's all the same to me if you'd rather have half a dozen men taking the place apart instead.' Outside the gate, a second car drew up. The fizzing whine of a radio sounded through the open windows. Nobody got out.

'*What?*' It was the weather. And the lack of sleep. Even then, I didn't think. It was Dee who stepped between us, breaking the deadlock. Her face was bland, suddenly, without shadows, flattened out to a strange, puttied white. 'I think,' she said, and her voice broke on the strained end of a laugh, 'I think he's trying to tell us that he can't find Lee.'

Stray ears of barley stood tall and dry at the edge of the field, heads bent over the weight of the grain. I sat with my back to the gate and wove them in pairs, bending over and over, across and across, adding new stalks as the old ones came to an end. It's not hard work but it takes some thought to keep the strand unbroken beyond the first few turns. I had eleven inches of woven grass by the time they finished searching the house. Another three for the barn. The uniformed muscle gathered outside the back door; there were three of them, all of a height, sweating in their shirt sleeves. Sandy and Jon stood to the side and you could feel the promises of action building into something that would take some holding. MacDonald came out last from the house. The tread of his feet on the gravel gathered all of the anger and crumpled it tight.

'Well?' I didn't wait till he stopped. 'I do hope you checked the linen cupboard. There's room for at least three in there if you pack them tight.'

'Where is she?'

'Pass.' I looked up. Dee straddled the wall above the pond. I heard the small whistle of an indrawn breath and then nothing. 'Wherever she goes, MacDonald, it won't be here.'

'You'll forgive me if we differ on that.' A thread of sweat ran down the outside of one cheek, gathering mass on the way. 'I counted the saddles in the tack room,' he said. 'There's some horses out.'

'Really? How odd. Remind me to shut the business the next time you want to come out to play.'

'How many?'

'Ask Jon.'

'He said seven.'

'That'll be seven, then.' I picked another stalk, a long one, dried to a good corn yellow but not too brittle to weave. The tractors and the colt and the martins filled the silence.

'So I'll wait, if you don't mind, till they all come back.'

'Fine.' The stalk bedded in well, a nice, solid join. I looked up at Dee. 'You better give my apologies at the meeting. It looks as if I'll be here for a while.'

She blinked only once. 'You can't do that,' she said. 'They'll call it off if you're not there.'

'So reschedule.'

'We *can't*, Kellen. Folk don't reschedule their dying. You can't drop out now.' She looked over at him, spread her arms wide. 'She doesn't have to stay, surely?'

He shrugged, his eyes on me. 'Not on my account.'

'I think I should.'

'Kellen. I'll drive. You just have to be there. We can't do it without you.'

'I really don't think I should . . .'

'Just *go*.'

The last stalk broke. I pulled out the wasted fragment and dropped it back on the grass. On the edge of vision, I saw Dee lie back, very slowly, along the stones of the wall and turn her face to the sky. 'If you insist.' I stood up and looked over at Dee. 'Your car?' I asked.

She stared up at the clouds. 'If you think you can stand my driving.'

MacDonald stood still in front of me, each elbow gripped with the thumb of the other hand. The tendons stood out pale against the summer brown of his skin. The backs of his hands were damp with sweat. 'I need to find her, Kellen.' His voice had lost all inflection, as if someone had taken the curves of the vowels and pared them all down with a razor.

'I know.'

'If she's not a danger to anyone else then she's in real danger herself.'

'I am all too well aware of that.'

'So then why are you lying to me?'

'It's a habit. I don't cope with authority. I thought you'd have noticed that by now.' I pulled together the two ends of the stalk and tied them into one single, wide-looped ring.

'Kellen . . .'

'I don't know where she is, all right? I will swear that on anything you can find that matters enough that we'll both believe it.' I bit off a free strand of straw. 'Go and talk to Mhaire Culloch out on the Ayr road. If there's anyone knows what's happening now it'll be her. If you draw a blank after that, I can't help you.' I looped the weaving round his neck, felt the heat of him on my hands and, beneath it, the layers on layers of contradiction. 'Good luck.'

'I want you to call me if she comes here.'

'I know you do.' I took him by the shoulders, pressed a dry kiss to his forehead and turned him round to face the house. Five men found things to stare at in the gravel. 'The ride should be back by twelve,' I said. 'You can help yourself to coffee in the kitchen while you're waiting. Just don't ask Sandy or Jon for help, I don't want to come home and find you've had to lock them both up for assault.'

'Thanks.' I sat in the passenger seat of Dee's car and watched her negotiate the potholes of the lane. She had changed clothes from a bag in the boot: loose jeans, a longer-sleeved shirt, a waist-pack for her keys. The lack of sleep was less obvious, as if the exhaustion had gone with the clothes.

'No problem. We did improvisation at college. It's supposed to help the creative flow.'

'You're good.'

'I know.' She twitched a smile, her eyes on the road. 'I'll let you see my raku sometime. Are you going to tell me where we're really going?'

'To see Randolph Duncan – left at the end of the lane – and then maybe back to see Mhaire Culloch. If MacDonald doesn't get there first.'

'Where does he live?'

'Duncan? I've no idea. Somewhere on the south side. Just get on to the motorway and get us over the river. I'll have an address by the time we need it.' I pulled the mobile from my belt and tested a number I thought might work.

'Are you sure Lee isn't going to turn up at the farm?'

'Totally. If she's looking for help, she'll go to someone she trusts and that isn't – Hello, Jessica? It's Kellen. Look, I'm sorry to bother you at work, I need to go and see your father-in-law, it's kind of urgent, d'you think you could let me have his address? . . . What? No . . . I'm sorry, I'm on the mobile, the reception's lousy . . . OK, let me write it down . . . Right. Where's that? . . . Yes, I remember. Got it . . . What? . . . Who? . . . When? . . . Yes. I will. Thanks. No, it's all right, don't bother, we'll be there in twenty minutes.'

'Where is it?'

'Whitecraigs. Go out past the Burrell and head towards Giffnock, I'll talk you through it after that. Just keep your eye out for anyone else heading the same way.'

'Because?'

'Because I think we might be having company. That was

Jessica's second call of the day. Lee phoned in and asked her for the same directions earlier on this morning.'

Whitecraigs is the south side's 'desirable' zone, a discreet suburb with three golf courses and one of Glasgow's bigger parks enfolding a select maze of residential streets. We pulled into a discreet, chestnut-shaded cul-de-sac running up the edge of one fairway and drove carefully past a row of sandstone mansions until the road ran out. Professor Randolph Duncan, widower, moved on his retirement to one of the smaller residences at the very end of the road. It nevertheless fills a half-acre site and has, judging from the outside, at least two reception rooms.

'Eighteen.' I pointed at the number, written longhand on the sign. 'This is us.'

His car was in the drive: a vintage Daimler, rebuilt by hand in a succession of on-duty evenings. Lee came home with the story of it one evening when we were students, in the days when she still found everything he did a potential source of inspiration. Dee pulled in behind it and we sat in the sunlight, beyond the reach of the chestnuts, with the engine and the air conditioning still running. There was no sign, on the street or in his driveway, of her car or her bike. We waited a while, reluctant, for no obvious reason, to leave the cool security of the car. Two houses down, a woman in her late twenties bribed a matched pair of toddlers into the back seat of a Rover. She reversed down her drive and out on to the main road without ever once looking in our direction. No point, then, in asking the neighbours if he'd had company. This is not the kind of road where they divulge the neighbourhood secrets to passing strangers. The rest of the houses stayed quiet: the mid-day, lunchtime quiet of a summer afternoon in a land where the patterns of domesticity have remained unchallenged since the Empire was young. Mothers raise children; wives make dinner – for one or ten or twenty as the need arises; daughters learn to sit with their knees together to take dictation; boys play rugby at fee-paying schools and later, chair meetings wearing the old school tie. The new millennium will never touch them.

I looked up the curved length of the driveway to the fresh paint of the front door. I have been to visit this man once before, in another time and another place. He held a party for Lee after she passed her first set of surgical papers. Even then, I felt out of place, as if I'd moved into someone else's reality. The sensation hasn't altered with age.

'I suppose we should go in.'

'If you say so.'

'You don't have to come.'

'No. But I will.'

The front door stood ajar. Nevertheless, I stood on the grey sandstone of the step and rang the bell. No answer. I counted ten and rang again. And again. I turned my back to the door and looked idly down the long slope of drive. Down at the bottom where it joined the road, the gravel sprayed out leaving the dark, earthy scar of a tyre-mark. A single, narrow tyre. Not a Daimler. Not a car of any sort. *Don't think. Just don't think* . . .

'Dee . . .'

'Mmm?' She had her thumb on the bell for a fourth ring.

'Forget it. He's not going to answer. Come on. We're going in.'

It was a cool house. The tall, cool rooms had well-tended plants hanging from unexpected alcoves. Airy blues and watered greens and mirrors enhanced the space. He wasn't downstairs. He hadn't been downstairs for some time. He cleaned, or someone cleaned, and the same someone watered the jasmine and the trailing ivy but left no imprint on the cushions, no papers, read or unread, on the coffee tables, no water in the kettle. Upstairs he had slept in the bed but had not yet found the time to make it. He was not in the bathroom, nor the guest bedroom, nor . . .

'Kellen.' A whisper. A cracking, whistling whisper forced out through a throat too tight to scream. *'Kellen . . .'*

He was in the study and it was Dee who found him.

Oh God . . . Oh please God not that . . .

He was hanging. Hanging and swaying, his feet bare inches from the floor, his face, his whole head, turgid, his tongue forced forwards between grey-purple lips, his eyes bloodshot and bulging . . . *Oh God . . .* I felt the rush of the vomit hit the back of my mouth and got the window up just in time. Beside me, Dee leant forward against the desk, her weight on her hands, her head hanging down so that her hair brushed the wood. She breathed hard through rigid teeth.

'Why, Kellen?'

'Because he was there at the start. He *was* the start . . .'

'But she can't—'

'She can. If she can stick sux into Hillary Murdoch and watch her die, she can hoist him up there and . . .' And then another wave of nausea. Thin, sour fluid poured out between

256

my fingers. Jets of it ran hot and acid down my nose. I choked and fought to breathe and thought of dying, of suffocating, of strangling, of drowning in my own vomit, of the slow, slow death of hanging. You need a long drop to break the neck if you're going to die fast from hanging. Randolph Duncan had no drop at all. His chair lay overturned beneath him, one leg askew as if the violence of the kick had fractured that as well. *Oh God, Lee. What have you done?*

'Kellen?' Dee was still leaning on the desk, white and glass-eyed, staring at the body as if she expected him to speak. She nodded towards him, her eyes not moving from his face. 'Kellen, look.'

I looked. The air from the window was spinning him slowly round on the end of the rope, presenting his head in profile. A perfect circle the size of an old silver sixpence showed black at his right temple. When he spun back, the exit hole on the other side was wider, more the size of a half-crown with irregular margins and a halo of crusted black. Behind him and to the left, clots of blood and paler tissue marked a broad fan across the sponged eau-de-Nil of his walls.

A gunshot. The final, bloody full stop. As if she got bored of watching him die. Or had a reason to cut it short.

I am so slow, sometimes, in sensing danger. Then, when it comes, it overwhelms everything; that sudden, flooding wash of terror that leaves me with tunnel vision, light-headed and incoherent. I looked at Dee. She looked at me. We both looked at the body. We were standing in a room with a man dead by gunshot. Nowhere, on the desk, on the floor, on the upturned seat of his chair, was there any sign of a gun.

I stepped back, slowly, until I felt the solid, bullet-proof brick of a wall at my back, signalled Dee to do the same. The hanged man, suddenly, was of no consequence at all.

'You think she's still here?' Her voice came, stilted, from the far side of the window.

'I don't know.' I slid down the wall. I think better when I make a smaller target. 'I think we'd know by now if she was.' I eased my mobile from my belt. 'I think it's time we called the cavalry all the same.'

I found a tissue in one pocket, cleaned my fingers, my nose, my mouth, fumbled with the buttons to bring the phone off key-lock and bring up the number for MacDonald. His work number, not his home number. I rehearsed, briefly, the apology, for after it was over. *Stewart, I'm sorry. You were right. I was wrong. I didn't want to believe she could* ... The phone rang loud in the tense, airless silence. A single word flashed up on the display: LEE.

'*Lee?*'

'Kellen?' Her voice was distant – beyond the normal distance of a mobile. As if she was dreaming, or drunk, or drugged.

'Lee ... what are you ...?'

'I've found your friend. He was right. It is an E5. I thought you'd like to know.'

What? 'Lee ... where are you?'

'Don't worry, Kellen. Everything's fine.'

The line went dead.

Chapter Thirteen

'I'm going with you.'

'No.'

'You were planning to walk?'

'No, but . . .'

'Exactly.'

We stood on the drive. The Daimler baked quietly in the sun. The shadow of the chestnuts inched up the gravel and flowed into the imprint of the tyre. A faint smell of vomit clung to my clothes. Dee put a hand in her pocket. 'It's my car we're driving.' She held up the keys. 'I come or you walk. Myself, I think we're wasting time, it's a long enough way up to Knapdale as it is and the day's not getting younger.'

It was long. She drives more like Lee than like me and still it was long. We met the new weather coming in from the coast: a lifting of the heat so we could turn off the air conditioning and still breathe; the beginnings of a breeze bending the grass at the side of the road; a real, sea-blown wind carving white horses on the tops of the waves. I slept intermittently, a broken sleep of twitching shadows – worse, probably, than staying awake. Just before we turned right for Knapdale, I called in to Sandy at the farm and told him where to send MacDonald to find the body of Randolph Duncan. I didn't tell him where we were calling from or where we were going. He had the sense not to ask.

'Stop here.' We were at the turn-off for the headland. The main road pulls hard right, the track carries straight on. In the angle between the two, sheltered from the road by a row of young larch, there is space for a car. 'Tuck it in behind the trees.'

'Are we there?'

'No. But the track's dried out again, we'll make too much noise if we drive any further. We'll leave the car here and walk the rest.' It is, after all, only a mile.

Her car is grey, the colour of clouds after rain. I walked back to the main road and looked in through the trees. Not overly conspicuous but you'd see it if you were looking.

'Dee, if you want to stay with the car . . .'

'Forget it, Kellen. You're not going alone.'

'Fine. Walk where I walk. Watch the noise.'

The track was dried and rutted. The mud cracked and crumbled underfoot. Ageing birch spread greenery across the path; long, soft feathers trailed over fear-jarred skin. A cock blackbird, hand-tame from the caravans along the coast, followed us from branch to branch, clucking insults with every fresh tree so that anyone listening would know exactly where we were. Threats and empty promises of food both failed to buy it off. It took a steady twenty minutes to reach the place where her car had been and then, not long after that, the gap for Eric's bike. Both were empty although I took time, going down on hands and knees, pushing through the underbrush, to search for drips of oil or new-crushed grass or any of the other small signs of her passing. I found nothing but that isn't to say there was nothing to find. She isn't stupid and if I know what to look for, it's because she has taught me. Besides, a place like this could hide half a regiment and you'd never know it. All you have to do to become invisible is to stand still.

The heat pressed more closely. The trees swayed in the wind, cracking branches higher in the canopy as if she walked above our heads. The birch gave way to planted pine, dark ranks that cut the sunlight into thick-filtered bands. The blackbird took umbrage and left. I walked on more slowly, with more care, watching for the dead wood underfoot. Still I missed it, the big one, the branch that cracked like a pistol shot and left me holding a trunk for support and spitting bile at the shadows. Dee, a pace behind, stepped over it as we moved on. I felt her voice in my ear, the sound of it lost in the noise of the trees: 'Do you think she knows you're coming?'

'I hope not.'

'But you're sure she's here?'

'I'm not sure of anything.'

Sooner than I thought, the trees ran out and the shadows with them. I spent long minutes just standing, listening, feeling, sensing nothing before I stepped forward on to the bleak, sun-swept space of the headland. The wind pushed in from the sea, salt-fresh and steady, running long, cool fingers through my hair. Ahead of us, the old rowan shivered, the very top of it nodding inland. I turned round, scanning the tree-line and the edge of the cliff for the bike, for her climbing gear, for a sign of the woman herself. I saw nothing and less than nothing. The whole of the cliff-top, from horizon to curving horizon, was empty.

'She's not here.'

I've found your friend.

'She has to be here.'

'Then where?'

He was right. It is an E5.

'On the ledge. She's on the ledge. Where we found Eric.'

I turned round, put my hand to her arm. 'Let me go down on my own now, will you? Please?'

The way down the cliff was worse than I remembered. Twice I have gone up and down this path, once in total white-out, once at dusk with a body and neither time has it seemed dangerous. Perhaps with her there as a guide, it wasn't. On my own, with her waiting somewhere ahead of me, it became a lethal, winding snake, curling round the contours of the cliff in a series of U-bends in a way planned by nature over centuries to give her all the cover she could need. I kept one shoulder to the vertical wall of the cliff for support and tossed small stone, round the worst of the blind corners and across the mouths of the deeper clefts. Even so, each step forward felt like a wilful decision to die. I stood, once, on the wrong side of a gap I had forgotten existed, on a stretch of ledge where the rock narrowed to less than the width of my outstretched arm and I gave serious thought to turning round and going back. Only the memory of her voice on the mobile, the odd distance, the slurred effort in the words, moved me on. *Don't worry, Kellen, everything's fine.* Another lie on top of many. If nothing else, I want to know why and for how long she has lied. I jumped the gap. I tossed my pebble round the corner. I waited for the crack and echo of a gun. It didn't come. I kept going.

She was there in the end, in the place she should have been and all the more surprising for that. I turned one final corner and found her sitting in the shade of the overhang, not far from where Eric had fallen. She sat with her back pressed to the cliff, one leg pulled up to her chest, a resting place for her forearms, for her chin. Her eyes were closed, the lashes dark against the sun-white skin. Sweat pasted strands of black hair to her forehead and made wide circles under the arms of her singlet. A long, livid graze ran the length of one forearm, fresh blood crusting black at the edges. The beginnings of a bruise shone blue at the elbow. A tiny, half-size friend hung limply from one hand. There was no gun.

'Lee.' No movement. No response.

I said it again, louder. 'Lee.'

She lifted her head and peered at me, narrow-eyed, flicked the sweat from her eyes and peered again. I am a mirage, a product of the light. 'Kellen,' she said and her voice had the same distance as the mobile. 'I thought you might come.'

'Lee, I . . . What's happening?'

'I found the friend.' It rocked in her hand. Dry, idle mockery, loosely done.

I looked at the rock above her head. A blank, overhanging wall, like the rounded face of a blown glass vase, polished to perfection. If there was a space for a friend, it was beyond where I could see it. *He was right. It is an E5.*

I nodded upwards. 'You climbed it?'

'Yes.'

'Alone?'

'Yes.'

'*Why?*'

A shrug. A twist of a grin. 'If he could do it, I can do it.' She laid the friend on her pack, put both hands flat to the rock behind her and pushed herself upright. The movement cost her more than it should have done, as if she was halfway to concussion, or losing blood. I wasn't close enough to check the size of her pupils. There was no fresh blood on the ledge.

I took a step forward; 'Lee, what have you done to your — ?' and I stopped at the sudden change in her eyes, in her face, in the tightened snarl of her smile.

'Who did you bring, Kellen?' Soft, so very soft. And dangerous.

'What?' I turned round. Behind me, the ledge was empty. 'I didn't . . .'

'MacDonald.' A weary distaste. 'Tell me you didn't bring MacDonald.'

'Lee. I wouldn't . . .'

'She brought me.' It was only a step to come round the corner and she must have been listening. It is not a big ledge, after all. Dee turned the corner and stopped there, hands in her pockets, leaning sideways against the rock. In a moment, she sat down on a small shelf of stone, a natural seat. Her shadow stretched forward, almost to my feet. 'We found Prof. Duncan,' she said.

'Really? Spectacular, wasn't it? The good Inspector will

have a field day with that one.' The black eyes flared: darkened coals in white skin, growing whiter in the sun. She focused them on Dee. 'I spoke to Sarah,' she said. 'She sends you . . . her love.' She let out the breath and let go of the rock and slid, with poor control, back to the flat of the ledge, biting hard on her lower lip as she straightened her leg.

'Christ, woman, your ankle . . .'

'Tibial fracture. Comminuted, closed.' The smile was no longer a smile, just a tensing of the lips. 'Two, maybe three fractured ribs and a leaking spleen, I think, so we'll not drag this out any longer than we have to, shall we?'

Her climbing pack lay to one side, the top flap open, her belt and her spare walking boots spilling out on to the rock. She reached inside and pulled out a small rectangular pouch, of the size to hold crampons. Out of that, she drew the gun.

Silence. Complete and perfect silence. The sun and the wind and the sea were as nothing. The pressure of it drove away thought, crushed reason, froze everything in a single, static moment.

All the promise of life and it comes to this.

'Lee, you can't . . .'

Metal spun on metal. A fluid, well-oiled, killing sound. I looked up into black eyes made grey with fatigue, with loss of blood, with whatever insanity drove her this far and still further. 'Professor Duncan's,' she said, loosely. 'The late, great, supremely arrogant Professor Duncan. The rest of the country has a total small arms ban and he, of course, can do what he likes. This,' – she let the tip rise up and back down again, as if on a string – 'is his father's revolver. Regimental issue, cleaned often, never used. Until today.' She spun the chamber a

second time, then flipped the barrel round, reversing the grip
so that the black mouth pointed inwards towards her sternum.
I reached forward on instinct: *'Lee. No!'* and, bending, she slid
the thing across the ledge, deftly, accurately, to finish at my
feet. The harsh scrape of metal on stone echoed down off the
cliff long after it came to rest.

'Sit down, Kellen.' Her voice came calm and stable. Her
eyes held mine, not stable at all. 'One of us has to make the
decisions.'

'Lee, I'm not —'

'You are. Trust me. The safety's on. Just pick the thing up
and try not to use it until you have to.'

Trust me.

'No.' I have never held a handgun in my life and I am not
about to start now. I turned, hooked my toe under the dark
metal of the barrel and flicked it, in one looping motion, off the
ledge. For a second or two, the ugly, lethal shape of it spun up
against the blue of the sky before it dropped out of sight. A
long, long time later, we heard it hit the sea. Then I sat down.

'That was . . . not wise, Stewart.' The words came with
effort, over-careful, like a drunk's. 'You're not safe here
without . . . protection.'

'It's a sight safer than it was with you playing —'

'It's not, you know, Kellen.' The words made their own
silence, careful and clear and decisive where ours were not.
She had come closer, slowly and with an eye to her shadow,
until she stood at my side, an arm's length away. Not quite
close enough to touch.

'Dee?' Even now, this close, I didn't fully understand.

'I'm sorry, Kellen. I didn't mean this for you.' Behind me, I saw the flicker of steel from an uncapped needle, the flash of glass from a vial. 'I think you should go now.' She finished loading the syringe. 'Lee and I have some things we need to discuss.'

'Suxamethonium?' Lee sat quite still, her fingers white on her forearms. Her eyes were fixed on the needle; her voice, no longer slurred, held an edge I've never heard before. I could be invisible now.

'No. I wouldn't do that to you.' The needle sparkled in the sunlight, a row of diamonds on a finger. 'It's morphine. You gave her morphine. I would do the same for you.'

It came as an offer. A gift. And was received as such. She breathed, long and deep. Colour flowed back where it belonged.

'Thank you.' The relief. You can feel the relief. 'Enough for two?'

'Of course.' She turned to me. The smile was open, careless almost, the smile of a child at the promise of a pebble; beneath it lay all the warmth and patience of the parent. 'Go on, Kellen.' Her keys chimed on the rock beside me. 'You can take the car. I won't be needing it after this.'

And Lee, calm now, almost peaceful. She is smiling. Dear God, she is smiling. 'Do as she says, Kells. There is nothing you can do now.'

Oh but I can. Sleep or no sleep, shock or no shock, I am not without resource. I stood, scooping up the keys, and turned to go, kept turning and let the momentum of the spin carry me round full circle. She was there, Dee, standing right behind me, watching Lee, watching the needle. Neither of them was watching me. Bone impacted on yielding flesh as the point of my elbow sank deep in her solar plexus. The balled fist of my other hand, the one with the keys, smashed down on her thumb, her fingers, the smooth cylinder of the syringe. It followed her down and down as she dropped, crushing the bones, the flesh, the brittle plastic on to the punishing rock of the ledge.

She fell, almost without noise, a shocked rush of exhaling air and then the wide-mouthed sobbing of a diaphragm in spasm. The needle made more sound, a rolling clatter of metal and plastic overlaid by the scuff of my foot on the rock and then the long, empty silence of the fall. We never heard it hit the water. I jammed the keys in my pocket and turned back to the figure sitting still against the rock. 'Christ, Lee, what the hell are you trying to — ?'

Her gaze went past me, still as if I wasn't there. 'Dee . . .?'

I spun back to face the sea. She lay where she had fallen on the flat rock of the ledge, fingers crabbed, outstretched, clawing for traction more than air. Her body writhed, straining closer to the edge. Two feet away and closing. Three hundred feet from oblivion.

'Dee. No.'

She didn't hear me. She chose not to hear me. I kicked her then. I have never in my life kicked a living being but I had nothing else I could do. I kicked her once and then again, hammering what was left of the air from her lungs. She would have screamed but she hadn't the air to breathe it. Her eyes made the noise. Wave after wave of pain. I turned my head from that, took my eyes and gave them other things to hear, took hold of her arms and dragged her away from the edge, as far as she could go. I laid her out along the rising wall of rock, neck extended, chin up and I held her like that while she fought the long battle to breathe.

'She won't thank you for that.' Lee, grey-skinned and whispering. Fighting her own battles and not obviously winning. 'She's come to the end, Kellen. She's got nowhere left to go.'

'And you? Have you nowhere left to go?' I am so very scared. It comes out as desperate, vicious anger. 'Have you really no reason to live?'

'No . . . yes . . .' She shook her head, fighting to hold on to thought. Her hands pulled her knee tight to her chest as if holding it there kept the life in. Long, raked fragments of skin peeled off at her wrists where her nails bit deep, clinging on to awareness. Each word cost dear; another nail-mark, another breath, another inch away from life. 'Not the point. She's right . . . How else to make . . . them think?'

'Christ, woman, you can't believe . . .'

'No.' Dee, lifting her head from my knees, pulling breath at last. 'Not to think . . . to stop. That was all . . . Whatever it takes to make them stop . . .' She rolled over and sat up, her head tipped back against the rock, her face turned to the open sky. She put both hands to the bridge of her nose. Her voice, when she found the breath for it, spoke defeat. 'What do you do when the promise is over, Kellen?'

'I told you.' God, I am so scared. 'You let go and you get on with living your own life.'

'At Her Majesty's pleasure?' Her lips twisted, bitter at the taste of it. 'I don't think so.'

'No . . . go back.' Lee, from the uncharted depths of her chasm, far away and moving further. 'Go back to . . . who you were.'

'She's dead.' Flat, toneless denial. 'She died with Beth.'

'No. Only on paper . . . Your choice . . . could . . . bring her back.' And then, dry, sardonic, on the last breath before the darkness closed in, 'One lemming is . . . quite enough.' Her fingers lost their hold on her arms and she slid sideways, without grace, on to the ledge.

Stillness. Perfect stillness. Four hundred feet away, the Atlantic smashed a lifetime's mirrors on to stone. Closer than that, an infant gull screamed hell in the mouth of a feeding parent. Above us, the rising tenor of the wind raked the branches of the rowan, lifted the grasses, drew in the wind from the sea to the land. On the ledge, there was only stillness. Dee Fitzpatrick sat like stone between me and the pale, slumped form. She kept her back to the rock, elbows on knees, her palms still covering her eyes.

'Check her, Kellen, she's losing blood.'

'Dee, if she's dead, so help me I'll—'

'She's not dead. God knows how far she fell but she's not dead.'

I leant forward, laid my fingers to a wrist and felt the pulse as a knotted thread far below the surface. Eyelids fluttered to a touch. With a hand pressed to her ribs, there was movement. I dragged my mobile from my belt and held it out at arm's length, beyond the shelter of the overhang.

'What are you doing?'

'Calling the helicopter. We need to get her off here, get her back to the Western to someone who can do something useful.' I keyed the number on the pad, lost the line and tried again.

'The reception's better up top.' An observation, no longer muffled. When I turned, her eyes were open. She looked ill.

'Fine. I'll just run up to the rowan, spend five minutes on the phone and trot back down again. That gives you, what – twenty minutes clear time to take the two of you over the edge? I don't think so.'

'I'll come up with you if it makes the difference.'

'No.'

'You don't trust me?'

'I don't trust either of you.'

The Rescue answered. The phone whistled and crackled and dropped the line a second time but they got the message. The call-back confirmed a helicopter within the half-hour, complete with paramedics, a ventilator and eight units of O-negative blood. I dropped the phone in Lee's climbing sack and dragged the first-aid pack out from under the rest of the gear. Useless. A whole pharmacopoeia of tablets, way too few bandages. Then, under the tight length of her leggings, I found she had already done what she could: three compact layers of dressing, spiral-wound, ran down from knee to ankle and back again. I rolled the leggings back into place, laid her legs together, folded her spare t-shirts in the space between as padding and then bound them tight, right on to left, as splinting.

Dee came to kneel by my side probing gently at the mass of bruising along the curving rib line. 'She's right about the ribs. She needs a body bandage.'

'Maybe, but if she's ruptured her spleen, I'm not messing with any of it. She'll be fine as long as she doesn't come round while they're moving her.' The pain will be unimaginable if she does. She won't stay conscious for long.

'I've still got some morphine.'

271

'What?' I looked up. She looked serious. The anaesthetist offering the analgesic. Her hand moved to her waist. 'No.' I grabbed the wrist, crashed it down on the rock, felt her wince and draw back. I held the hand in place and twisted hard against the angle of her elbow. 'Give it me. Now.'

'Kellen . . . you can't . . .'

'Now.'

'I can't reach it, you're—'

'Which pocket?'

'The waist pack.' She gestured with her head. I reached inside with my free hand, found the vials, the needles and the spare syringe. *Enough for two.* At the very least. I threw them all, one at a time, over the edge. Her wrist, when I let it go, held the imprint of my fingers.

Dee stood up and walked to the edge to look down at the crashing sea. Four hundred feet to oblivion. If she had stepped off then, I would have let her go. She didn't, she turned, put her hands in her pockets and came back towards the overhang. Her eyes were flat, like the stone.

'Kellen, I'm not . . . I was trying to help, that's all.'

'Well, don't.'

I finished the splint, tied off the knots and slid her back into the shade and laid one hand on her forehead, a sensor, feeling for movement, for a return from the dark.

Peace settled back on the ledge, but it was a bleak, harrowed peace, ghost-filled and begging questions. I don't want to know the answers. The ghosts can beg. There will be answers enough at the trial. If they can keep her alive for the trial. Not my problem. None of these is my problem. Except for the shape sitting quiet at the edges, broad-shouldered, smiling, asking nothing. For that one, alone, I need answers.

'Eric,' I called it out to the back of her head. 'What happened to Eric?'

She was facing out to sea, lost in her own world, communing with her own ghosts. The wind caught the words and carried them back to the rock. 'He fell.'

'You didn't pull him?'

'No. I didn't have to. He was climbing right at his limits. He came off twice lower down and I held him . . . The third time I just . . . let go.' She turned round to face the cliff. Her eyes drifted up the line of the route, past the overhang and on up and up to the rest on a fine-angled crack, set apart from the main line of the route. 'He was a long way up.' She bit her lip and took her eyes back to the sea. 'He wasn't ever going to go all the way to the top, he just wanted to check out the moves so he could tell Lee all about it on Saturday. He was going to meet you both after you'd finished your climb and then see if she wanted to come back to the ledge and try the second route up. An E1 with an E5 finish, both on the same day. It would have been good.'

So it would. 'But you had to stop it?'

She turned back from the sea. 'I didn't plan this one, Kellen. The others, yes – afterwards, once he'd gone – but not this. I couldn't. Eric was special, you know that. But then, he was there, a third time, falling . . .' Her eyes moved back up to the rock. 'All I did was let go.'

'Why?' I didn't want to know this. I didn't want to talk. But he's still there, crowding the space, benign, good-humoured, smiling. And dead. I need, now, to know why he is dead. 'Why did it have to be Eric?'

'He was the first. He was her primary care clinician. He booked her in. He put her forward for the trial. Without him, none of this would have happened.'

'Beth. We're talking about Beth?'

'Yes.'

'She was the one who cost Lee her job?'

'Or Lee was the one who cost Beth her life. I'd prefer if we looked at it that way. Yes.' She spun full round then, eyes wide, the fine edge of control cracking at last. 'It wasn't just her, Kellen. There were twenty-four others with her. Twenty-five women and each one died the way Claire Hendon would have died. Beth was the only one who got the morphine at the end.'

'And you hold Eric responsible?'

'Totally.'

I don't believe this. 'You've spent the last ten years a medic, woman. You know better than that. Claire would have died whatever we did. The surgery didn't help but it didn't make that much of a difference. If she'd never come near us – if she'd gone off to Orkney and lived in a tent – she would still have died. It would still have been every bit as bad at the end. Worse, probably. You can't blame anyone else for that.'

'Claire had grade four pathology, Kellen, she was riddled with mets. Beth had nothing close. Not a single secondary mass. She had a handful of cells changed on the smear, nothing special, nothing out of the ordinary. All she needed, all she would have had, was a routine D&C, but no, they had a clinical trial going and she was the right age group with the right kind of meaningless pathology and so instead they implanted radioactive iridium in her cervix for no better

274

reason than Hillary Murdoch said that it might be the start of
a revolution in cancer management.'

And so now, finally, we can see the anger. The boiling,
seething, volcanic anger, laid bare on the surface, without the
masks. She is so like Lee. Fierce, consuming passion hidden
beneath the faceless masks of irony. But not now. Not any
more. The masks have slipped.

She rounded on me, carried on her own tide of memories.
'Think of it, Kellen. Think of Nina. Think of Lee. Think of
either one of them coming home one day with a note from the
GP saying they need to go in for another smear because the
first one wasn't quite right. You don't panic. Of course you
don't. These things happen. Everyone knows someone who's
had a bit of a dodgy smear. So you trust them and you do it and
when they say you need to go on up and see the consultant at
the hospital, you still trust them and you still do it. And when
the wonderful, kind, funny, friendly doctor says that there are
only a few cells that have changed, nothing to worry about, but
that you've been selected for a new treatment, a pilot study,
you thank him and you feel special and well looked-after and
you do whatever he tells you and you ask no questions.'

She turned away, paced the width of the ledge, out to the
edge and back again, eyes, soul, mind, all in the other world.
She stopped then, feet spaced wide, facing out across the sea.
The wind blew in off the water and ruffled the unbrushed
mess of her hair.

'What did they do? I asked it gently, not to break into the
past.

'They put in a rod, a radioactive rod. More like a wire. Not
too big, nicely shaped to fit. You'd barely know it was there

between one period and the next. She wore it for a month. Just a month. And then the nice man with the big smile said the next smear was clear.'

'And wasn't it?'

'Oh, it probably was. It was nearly six months before things started to go wrong. But then they went so badly wrong. They were two orders of magnitude wrong on the dose range. Can you imagine that? Imagine lying under an X-ray tube and letting someone blast your guts with one hundred times the dose of X-rays every hour of every day for a month. And they knew, Kellen, they knew. Not at first, perhaps, but by the time they picked Beth, they did. She was nineteenth on the list. Eighteen other women before her. The first ones were coming back with massive, massive cervical pathology before they ever picked Beth out for the trial. They knew. And still they went ahead.'

'You can't be sure of that.'

'I'm sure. I have the case records. All of them.'

'Eric wouldn't do that.'

'He didn't. Nor did Lee. They didn't know until a long way down the line. Too late to do anything. But Randolph Duncan knew. And Martin Coutts with his double-blind randomised statistics, desperate to get enough numbers to fit into the sums. And Hillary bloody Murdoch working out her beautiful new grading systems up there in the lab so she could sit at her microscope looking at the cellular pathology and predict to within the nearest twenty-four hours how much longer the woman in bed fourteen hasn't got to live . . .'

The words ran out. For both of us, they ran out. She stood there in front of me, breathless, shuddering, broken. Fifteen years of stored pain flayed open and bare to the world.

However much I wanted to see beneath the surface, I didn't want to see this.

'Dee, I'm sorry. I didn't know.'

'Of course you didn't. How could you?' Her hands moved to cover her face and then dropped away. 'I came so close to telling you so often – after Eric, when Claire came in to the Unit, after each time we talked about her . . . and, God, Kells, she was so like Beth. Fifteen years and nothing has changed. *Nothing.* I spent ten years working the hard way and made not a blind bit of difference. I had a promise to keep. I had to do something to make them stop. There was nothing else left I could do.' She brought her eyes back to mine, wide open and asking questions. 'Do you really think in my place you would have done any different?'

I don't know. Even now I don't know. But then I didn't have to know because her head was up like a hound at the horn and her gaze twisted round to the far side of the ledge and there, coming in along the line where the sea meets the sky, was the bluebottle throb of the helicopter.

'Oh, God . . .'

'Dee, no.' Instinct, unthinking instinct. She moved and I moved before her and suddenly I was there again standing with my back two paces away from the drop and Dee Fitzpatrick, athlete, was leaving the blocks on her final sprint for the line. I spread my hands wide and shouted again, louder this time, so she would hear. 'Dee, *no*. Not now . . .'

She stopped, like a dog run to the end of its chain, head up, eyes wide panting. 'Please, Kellen.' No masks now, no games. A voice stripped bare of everything but a desperate, urgent need. 'You let Claire go. Will you not do the same for me?'

'Claire had nothing to live for.'

'And I do? What? MacDonald? You can't do that, Kellen . . . please . . . they'll not bother with a key. You know that. They'll just weld the door shut and walk away. I won't live like that.'

'And if I let you go now, they'll do the same for Lee.' And she also will not live like that.

'No. Listen. I never meant for her to get the blame. I didn't know her name was on the pad. How could I . . .?' The words tumbled out, running into each other, no gaps between. 'There are letters, I wrote letters. In the top drawer of my desk, in our room, unopened, post-marked. The copies are with Doug, sealed in his safe. All except Joey's have dates from before the body was found. They have the details, things no one else could have known: the colour of the mug that broke at Hillary Murdoch's, the dose of amphetamine in Martin Coutts. But I didn't . . .' Her gaze flicked round to the rock and back, 'There's not one yet for Randolph Duncan. I hadn't the time.'

And now, again, she has no time because the helicopter is here sooner than either of us thought and I am still blocking the way, still with my arms outstretched as the winches whine and the lads with the crew cuts and helmets sail down with their stretcher and they look at us oddly and ask for help and shrug when they don't get it and still I stand in her way while they strap Lee, arms and legs and neck brace, to the rigid aluminium and send her up the long fall into hell.

'*Please . . .*'

'No.'

There is one now beside us, a copper-haired lad, watching, smiling still, wide and friendly and understanding nothing.

'Come on, ladies, we'll get you in the harness, it's not as bad as you think. One more time and we'll get you a badge . . .' He shouts it over the banshee howl of the blades, the wind of it driving all three of us nearer the edge, and I shake my head and fumble in my pocket and pull out the car keys she gave me and press them into her hand and I nod my head at the lad and tell him that there will only be one of us going up. 'She'll take the car.' I scream it at him, losing all of it in the noise and then turn and signal to her to go out along the ledge and up to the cliff-top and I make a mime of driving away and slowly, finally, I see the understanding grow into her eyes. She holds the keys and looks at me, gaping questions like a mackerel, and I put my mouth to her ear even as the lad is doing his best to fit the harness and I scream at her: 'Take the car. Go home. Go away. Just let me know sometime where you are . . .' and then I am gone, floating upwards into hell and she is left there on the ledge, staring up at me and then back out at the blue air beyond the ledge and I have no way of knowing which one she will take.

Chapter Fourteen

The helicopter ride was better than the last one if only because the body on the stretcher wasn't dead. I got them to radio ahead to the hospital with details of the injuries and of who it was and then I sat beside her as they raised the veins for the catheters and ran in the blood and the plasma expanders and watched as the death's mask grey of her skin warmed to simply white and the pulse running under my fingers became something more than a knotted thread. We came down sooner than the last time, talked in by air-traffic controllers with the police breathing heavily down their microphones, and this time it was a different reception, a different welcoming committee, in broad daylight and more of them: white coats and blue uniforms mixed, with blood bags and oxygen and warrants for immediate arrest. MacDonald was there at the back of them, a stranger with predator's eyes.

'Can she talk?'

'In your dreams, maybe.'

'Where's Dee Fitzpatrick?'
'I have no idea.'

She was wrong. It was her liver, not her spleen, that was leaking. I have seen the scans and the X-rays and the blood count before and after and I can tell you, without doubt, that if we hadn't given her blood in the helicopter, she would have been dead before we ever hit the roof. As it was, they moved her straight down to theatre, called the team in from stand-by and, within an hour of us leaving the ledge, a young, anonymous surgeon had finished resecting half of one lobe of her liver. Another followed on and spent three times as long screwing a nine-hole compression plate to her leg. Astonishingly, insanely, Jessica Duncan was the anaesthetist for both. She stopped to speak to me in the corridors as they moved the trolley between the theatres. 'She's not losing any more blood. There's no peritonitis. It's up to her now. If she has the will, we'll have her ready by the time they want her for the trial.'

'She didn't do it, Jessica. She didn't kill Joey.'

'Forget it, Kellen. She's a patient. It doesn't matter what she's done.'

Later. A long while later. It is dark, and very peaceful. Muted electronics keep pace with time: ripples of repeating patterns in amber, in green, in blue, each in their own way marking the slow climb back to the light. She lies on the bed, a silent, pliable doll. Wires and drip lines and feeding tubes hold her in this world where otherwise she might be gone. The room already smells of not-quite-death. Once before, for someone else, I sat in a ward like this, my hand on another hand, fingers on another pulse. I was less angry, then. And there was no guard on the door. Here, they change the guard at four-hourly intervals, another way to mark the time. They stand with eyes fixed on the horizontal, carefully intrusive, watching and noting and knowing nothing. They mark who comes to visit, note it down in the book: the nurses who hover, a steady presence, in the background; Jessica who spent the first half of the night coming in at ten-minute intervals to check the progress of recovery, filled the syringe pump with morphine, set the rate and checked the print-out from the monitors; Nina, whose memories of this hospital are not good but who still came in and sat for an hour or two after work; Sandy who swapped places and stayed longer. Once, later than that, MacDonald. He walked in to the bedside on silent feet and stood for a good five minutes, watching, as if he could read her truth in the smoothed-out planes of her face, in the scrawling lines of the ECG. In a while, when she didn't wake, when she didn't open her eyes and roll over and tell him everything, he left. He said nothing to me. The officer on the door took note of his departure and of the fact that I stayed.

I took more note of the ones who didn't come: Mike Bailey, Colin Storey-Pugh, Dee Fitzpatrick. He thinks I lied to him but in this, if nothing else, I have told the truth. Dee Fitzpatrick has gone and I have absolutely no idea where she is.

I should sleep. The new-shift nurse, busily attentive, has been in twice since midnight to remind me that I should sleep. She is right and there is a bed here, in the corner, of the kind they bring for parents to sleep beside their children, but I have tried it once and I have failed to sleep. I am long beyond the need for sleep. I am floating in free fall. The floor and the walls and the ceiling of the world that I knew have disintegrated and all that is left is the vacuum of hollow space. I could sit like this for ever and not know that time has passed.

They changed the guard at four o'clock. Another bland, faceless, stare. I excused myself, more for the feel of seeing a different line in the notebook than for any real need to leave the room, and visited the ladies. From there, with no malice aforethought, I followed the stairs down five flights to the ground floor. Here, A&E is active, as nowhere else in a hospital is active at this time in the morning. I passed stretchers and cubicles and plastic chairs laden with the throw-outs of the pubs and the aftermaths of domestic violence and the occasional, real accidental emergency.

Outside, the night was warm, the path to the Unit clear and well lit. No lights, no candles shone in any window. I let myself in the side entrance and followed the floor-level night lights to my office, to our office. The sense of her filled the corners: abrasive, volatile, hidden, flashing her wild, discordant smile. I opened the top drawer to her desk and found the stack of letters. The top four were laser printed, formal, addressed to Dr D. Fitzpatrick and marked on the top left hand corner with initials: E.D., J.A.D., M.D.C., H.S.M. There were two others, the envelopes handwritten. The first was addressed to Nicco Gallianno, slim, lightweight, two pages at the most. The second, brown, A4 and bulky, was for me.

I took it back to my desk. The computer sat as I had left it, the screen saver accelerating forever into an infinity of unknown stars. It took a long time, staring at the stars, to find the courage to open the envelope and tip out the contents. It could have been worse. Inside was the clinical record of Elizabeth Gail Morgan, deceased: fourteen pages of handwritten detail, from the days before all the records were kept on disc in the server in the basement. The early pages were in Eric's writing, the later ones by Lee. In between a handful of others, unknown. At the end, after all the others, was a sentence from Randolph Duncan: *Terminal asphyxia: presumptive bronchial mass. Awaiting autopsy results.*

Beneath the notes there was a letter, also handwritten, from Dee to me:

Dear Kellen,

If you are reading this, then by now it is over. Seven people are dead and two of them, maybe three, you loved. For that I am sorry. I am not sorry for them, the dead are beyond sorrow, but I am sorry for you – for Eric first and, more, for Lee. If there was another way, for her, I would have taken it but I am too far gone now to go back. With each one, not to go on would make the deaths of the past all the more pointless. For what difference it makes (and for both of us, I think, it makes all the difference) it will have been quick. She knows. I am almost certain that she knows. Somewhere, somehow, she will have left you word. It shouldn't take you long to find it.

I nearly stopped then. It took a long time, staring through the blinding haze that covered the stars, to go on.

Beyond that, you need to know about Eric; Jessica needs to know about Joey. There will be people who need to know about Martin

285

Coutts and Hillary Murdoch and Prof Duncan, although I wouldn't rush to hand out details of those last two, they were a sight less pretty than the rest. At any rate, I've left a set of letters which have all the details you need. If nothing else, they will clear Lee's name. Do with them what you will.

Not much else, I don't think. We are so close now to the end and I am finding it difficult to think straight. I have left a letter for Nicco Gallianno. It may not make the difference, but it will make him think. Please take it down. I have left you also Beth's case record. You will have found it by now. The others are filed under her name in the bottom drawer of the filing cabinet. Twenty-four of them, more or less the same. Read them and try to understand, if not condone, the reasons why. Then if you care about any of this, do what you can to make sure that it gets to the people who matter, the ones who can make a difference. There may be a chance now for change. Take it. For Lee, for Eric, for me.

She signed it *With love, DF.*

I sat for longer afterwards, staring into space. I closed the drawer on the other letters, slid Beth Morgan's case notes back into their space in the filing cabinet and took the letter back up to the ward. Stewart MacDonald was sitting by the bedside, waiting.

'Is she awake?'

'No.' He shook his head. 'Dr Duncan seems to think it won't be long.'

'She thought that four hours ago.' I sat on the other side of the bed and ran my eye along the monitors. None of them had changed.

'We found her bike,' he said.

'Where?'

'On the cliff-top. They took the search dogs in an hour ago.' His eyes were on the envelope in my hand. 'There's no sign yet of Dr Fitzpatrick.'

'No. There won't be.' I handed him the letter. 'Read this. I've just found it in my room.'

He read it once and then again. 'This is from Dee?

'Yes.'

'She's saying she killed them all?'

'Yes.'

He looked at me and said nothing. The paper tapped lightly on his teeth. 'You expect me to believe this?'

Christ, I am tired of this. 'You can believe what the hell you like. There's a bunch of letters there in the drawer, just like she says. I didn't open them. They could be empty envelopes for all I know but if I were you, I'd have a look before I dismissed it for not fitting my favourite theory.'

'Aye. Maybe you would.' He handed me back my letter. 'Where are they?'

'In my room in the Unit. Second floor, 219. Ask one of the nurses, they'll show you the way. The door's not locked.'

'Right.' He stood up. 'I'll do that. Thanks.'

There is a ripple on the monitors. Nothing special, nothing so marked that the one on the door would notice. An eyelid flickers, opens and shuts. A new pattern comes to the breathing: a series of long, shaken sighs. She has had her morphine. Not enough to kill her but enough to dull the pain in her leg, her liver, her ribs. The button is by the bed and she can press for more if she wants it. A hand reaches out, passes the button and comes on. Fingers fold round mine.

'Kellen?'

'I'm here.'

'Where's Dee?'

'I don't know.'

'Is she dead?'

'Maybe.' Oh God, I am so very angry. I can feel the heat of it, pushing through and the desperate, urgent need to take her by the shoulders and shake her, shake out some answers, some feelings, some sense. She *knows*. *I am almost certain that she knows.*

You should trust her.

And what if she doesn't trust me?

'How long have you known, Lee? How long have you been sitting on this?'

She opened her eyes, struggled to find mine and hold them, shook her head once, very slowly. 'Only today . . . yesterday? Sarah called . . . she's out of hospital. She phoned the flat . . . the day before we climbed . . . spoke to Dee . . . She was there with Eric. Dee never said she was there. Only one reason not to say . . .'

The whisper fell to nothing. Her eyes stayed on mine, holding focus through the mixing planes of pain and morphine.

'And you knew nothing before that? Honestly?'

'Honestly.' A twitch of a grin, cut off when it failed. 'The voice . . . knew I'd heard the voice, somewhere . . . sometime. Didn't remember when . . . till the ledge. Stupid. Should have thought sooner . . .'

The guard stirred at the door. He walked the full length of the corridor and still we heard the radio crackle.

'Calling reinforcements?'

'Calling MacDonald.'

Her eyes dulled, recoiled. A brief, unconscious spasm shook the bed. '*No.*' A breath of a whisper. A denial, a rejection, a withdrawing from consciousness. Her head turned on the pillow, more emphatic than her voice. The rhythmic wave of the arterial pressure line faltered. The nurse, always there on the periphery, moved closer.

Trust.

'Lee, listen.' I laid the page on the exposed skin of her arm. 'This is a letter from Dee. She's written it all down, everything that she did.' There was no change in her eyes. She was frowning, trying to hold on to the sense of what was coming. I tried again, more slowly. 'She's called him off. She wrote a letter for each of them, posted before they ever found the bodies. Doug's got copies. It's proof. Legal proof. It'll stand up in court.'

She said nothing. Felt nothing. No release from the fear.

'Did you hear me?'

'Yes.'

'So let up. She's called him off. He's down there now, reading everything. By the time he comes up, you'll be clear. He's got all the details he needs to prove it wasn't you.'

'Can't have. Not . . . Duncan.'

'What?'

'Not Randolph Duncan . . . no letter for him.' Her eyes were wide; the effort to speak corded the veins at her neck.

I put my hand on her arm. 'It's all right, she told me on the cliff. She didn't have time to write the letter.'

'Not the point . . . Couldn't write it. She . . . didn't do it.'

'She said she did.'

289

'No . . .'

She tried to move on the bed and stopped, biting her lip as the pain flooding over from her ribs, from the hand's length scar beneath her diaphragm, from her leg, left her breathing long, shaking gasps through her teeth.

I picked up the button, held it where she could see. 'Do you need some more morphine?'

'*No.*' It was the first word with a sound to it. Stark and violent. Too much of both. The monitors stabbed jagged lines across the screens. Jessica joined the nurse, both of them standing an arm's reach from the bed. The black eyes closed as she fought for control of her breathing. When they opened, they focused somewhere in the shadows behind me.

Oh, God, he walks so very softly. I turned and felt his hand on my shoulder, turning me back. 'Don't stop now, Dr Adams.' The Judas tone, gently encouraging. 'You said, "She didn't do it." How would you know that?'

'Lee, you don't have to . . .' The hand tightened on my shoulder. I shrugged it off. 'Do you want me to call Doug?'

'No . . . not now. No point . . .'

And then Jessica was there on the other side of the bed, her hand on a pulse, the other changing the drip rate on the fluids flooding down the drip line. The nurse stood behind her, drawing up dopamine, waiting for the order to inject. She has her own priorities. 'Inspector, you can do this later.'

'There might not be a later.' His eyes were hungry, feeding on the sheen of her face, on the tremor of her hands. 'Dr Adams?' His voice was generous. 'Do we stop now?'

'No . . .' Her fingers tightened round my wrist, a handhold over the final fall.

'So tell me how Professor Duncan died.'

'Shot . . . then hanged . . . for the signature.'

'Or hanged and then shot. Far more satisfying to watch, wouldn't you say?'

'No . . . couldn't have . . . He . . .' She coughed. The nurse leant forward and wiped the spittle from her mouth. More red than clear.

MacDonald waved her away. 'One step at a time. There's no rush. Go back to the beginning, Dr Adams.' He took the tissue himself, wiped her dry, smoothed the hair from her forehead, slowed her down until the rattle cleared in her breath. He has done this before: nursed his way to a bedside confession. You'd never know from the way he asks that he wants anything more than an end to the pain. 'Go back to when you left your flat this morning. Six o'clock, was it? Just after?'

'Half past.'

'Close enough. You left by the back door. Why?'

'Needed to see Prof. Duncan. Needed to talk. Didn't want you listening.'

'Really? That's very ungrateful. And why was it so important to see him?'

'The killings . . . knew why . . . obvious why . . . not obvious who. Thought if he would publish the old records . . . Beth, the others . . . it might stop . . .'

'But he didn't have the records, Dee had them.' I stopped. Not my place. She looked at me for a moment, unseeing, then her eyes moved back to his. All that holds her now is his need to know. Her need for him to know.

'I called Jessica on the way . . . to ask the directions . . . he's moved since I . . .'

'Since you last worked together. Dr Duncan, can you confirm this?' He sent his voice across the bed without moving his eyes. 'What time did Dr Adams call you?'

'Just before seven. I was starting the morning pre-meds.'

She has stopped working. Her eyes are on the monitors but she does nothing to change what she sees. The priorities have changed. There is a consensus now, to wait. She could die in front of them and still they would wait.

Lee's head rocked on the bed. She looked over towards Jessica. So she does know who it was that kept her alive on the table.

'You must have called him. Told him I was coming . . .?'

'I did. He asked me to tell him if anyone called.'

'Why didn't you call him yourself?' MacDonald, gently bringing her back on line. He can't afford distractions now.

'Didn't want him to know . . . if he thought . . .' She lost the place, shook her head, frowning and started again. 'You thought it was me. He knew that.'

'You had reason to believe he might think you had killed his son?'

'Yes.'

'So you went to visit him unannounced. Go on.'

'Traffic was bad. Got there late. Eight o'clock . . . five past . . . Parked the bike in the drive. He must have heard it, and . . .'

'And what?' The line between them is breaking, like a rope rubbing on the edge, thin strands of it peeling away under the tension. He is losing her and he knows it. He moved round beside me, his hand on the bed, his face filling the world above hers. 'And you walked in through his front door and up to his

292

office and killed him. Hanged him and shot him. Or the other way round. We'll have the PM report soon enough and then we'll know which it was. But what I need to know, what I can't quite picture, is exactly how you did it, Dr Adams. How did you get a big man like that hanging from the ceiling? Tell me. Did you hold the gun on him and make him set the rope up himself, is that it?'

'No.' She is fighting, as he is fighting, to hold the thread between them. 'Not me. Him. Parked the bike . . . shot came just after . . . Him. Not me.'

'What? He did it himself? Come on, Dr Adams, you can do better than that. We've been through this too often, you and me. You have to give me something I can believe in.' His hand is on her shoulder. He would shake, but he can see Jessica moving in. He is breathing too fast, as much as she is. 'Come on, Lee, it doesn't matter now. Just tell me. I need to know how you did it.'

'No . . . not me . . . not now . . . if I . . .' It was like watching a dying fire, a last flicker of flame from the embers. She drew in the dregs of whatever reserves she had left and just for that moment, the irony flared where he could see it. 'I wouldn't have waited . . . this long . . .'

And he lost her. Dropped from the hook like a foul-caught salmon. Gone.

'*Shit.*' He slammed his fist against the side of the bed, turned away and paced the full length of the ward.

They moved in then: Jessica, her nurse, another orderly. Wild, erratic spasms gripped the monitors. Nothing at all showed in the body on the bed.

I peeled her fingers away from my wrist and stepped back.

Four nail marks stood out purple against the soft underskin of my arm. I said nothing to Jessica or to the nurse or MacDonald. There was nothing, just then, I could say.

Stewart MacDonald came back to the bedside. He chewed on the edge of one thumbnail. He has drained her. He has got all he can get, possibly all he is ever going to get. Still he does not look happy.

'Satisfied?'

'Kellen . . .' He put out a hand, thought again and let it drop to his side. 'All I can do is ask the questions.'

'No. You can do more than that, *Inspector*. You can find the answers. Get your minions out there and find who heard the gunshot and who else saw her park the bike. Either she was in the house before he died or she wasn't. It can't be that difficult to find out which.'

'Maybe . . .' He gave the nod to the guard on the door. The radio crackled over the layered sounds of the resuscitation team. We moved back even further out of the way. MacDonald's eyes never moved from the bed. He chewed again at the edge of the nail. 'It's a funny way to kill yourself, Dr Stewart.'

'He needed to leave the signature, remember? And it was still fast. Faster than Hillary Murdoch.' I remembered the look in her eyes, the dread, beyond terror, when she saw the needle and believed it was suxamethonium. 'You'd go a fair way not to die the way she did.'

'And you wouldn't leave a note, you don't think? Most suicides leave a note.'

'Christ, man, do you need it spelled out? He was seventy-five years old, he thought he was about to die and he believed absolutely that she'd just murdered his son and three of his closest colleagues. What possible reason would he have to leave a note?'

I stayed with her for a day and a night, sleeping on the camp bed and eating sandwiches from the canteen. Mike Bailey did come eventually, smelling of alcohol and with his pupils sparked out in the light. I slept, I think, for most of the time he was there. The day after that, they took her off the ventilator and Jessica stood down the nurses. Later in the afternoon, when the monitors showed numbers I could believe in, I walked down the long way to the Unit and took Nicco Gallianno his letter. He lay propped up in the bed, his dressing gown hanging loose from his shoulders, his skin one stage closer to final hepatic shut-down. He looked up as I walked in, the wide, dark eyes set deeper than they had been.

'You came.' He smiled at that.

'I said I would.'

He looked me up and down and took in the unwashed hair and the over-worn clothes. The smile broadened and moved over on the bed to give me space. 'Your friend,' he asked. 'Is she still alive?'

'More or less. She's in intensive care.'

'I'm sorry. Will she get better?'

'Maybe. It's too early to say.' I lit a candle by the bedside then pulled the letter from a pocket. 'I brought you this.'

There were two pages there, close-printed script. He read them through and then folded both carefully back into the envelope. 'She's dead now? The one who wrote this?'

'Dee? I don't know. She's gone. The police found her car

yesterday at the top of the cliff where Eric died. It wasn't there when they went back to look for it the other evening after we took Lee off.'

'So she'd gone away and come back?'

'The car had gone away and come back. There's nothing to say she was in it.'

'But the water's deep out there.'

'Very.' The police divers have gone down and down again for the gun. They haven't found it. I know of no one who believes that they will.

'So.' He looked out across the lawn and smiled quietly to himself: white teeth in the darkened umber of his face. In time he turned back to me. 'She says it's the last retreat of the coward to die without good reason.'

'I think she was trying to say that joining Paul is not a good enough reason.'

'She didn't know him.'

'We didn't know Beth.' I stood up. The candle flared and gave off sandalwood smoke. 'It's not too late, Nicco. There's still time if they can find a match.' His eyes followed me as I left the room. Great, dark oceans of sanity. 'Will you think about it? Please?'

'Of course.' His smile was warm and rich and he meant it. 'I think about everything these days, Kellen.'

Chapter Fifteen

❧

He died the day before Lee came home and I was with him, as he had asked. We held his funeral three days later: a riot of colour and sound, a celebration of community and a quiet honouring of his parents.

It was the week for funerals. Small private ceremonies were held for Hillary Murdoch and Martin Coutts in the days immediately following Nicco's extravaganza. At the weekend, Nina and I took Lee, at Jessica's request, to join the mass of Scotland's medics in the Cathedral for a display of dignity and gravitas such as only a profession under threat can achieve. Jessica alone found the words to remind us who her husband had really been. She earned few friends amongst the hierarchy and many amongst the rest of us. Towards the end of the month, when Lee could walk the length of a room without support, we held a very small, very simple service for Eric. Anna came, and his parents. We spoke, but nothing of meaning. After that, there was nothing left to do but wait.

★ ★ ★

I woke in the small hours of the morning as I have woken every morning for as long as I can remember. I lay half awake on top of the duvet, drifting into dreams I didn't want. Downstairs, someone placed the receiver back in its cradle and the soft ting of its passing rang in the phone by the bed. A while later, dog claws clattered on the quarry tiles of the kitchen floor. A tap ran for a moment and the kettle grated on the Rayburn. Later still, the back door opened and closed. I pulled on a T-shirt and went down to look. She was outside, sitting on the back step, her hands wrapped round a mug of something hot that wasn't coffee. I sat down on the stone trough beside her. 'Are you all right?'

'Alive.' She blew across the top of the mug. 'I just called Mhaire.'

At half past three in the morning. 'Was she awake?'

'Yes.' She looked up at the sky. It was a mild night and very clear. The ghost light of the moon painted out the lines around her eyes. She looked tired beyond exhaustion but she did not look ill. The night is good for these things. She leant back against the door. 'I gather you've risen somewhat in her estimation.'

Hardly. 'I didn't tell you what she said.'

'No. But I think you did all you were supposed to do.'

I don't want to know. 'And now?'

'Pass.' She lowered the mug to the step. 'She's been tapping her sources. She seems to think we might hear something in the morning.'

'From MacDonald?'

'Yes.'

We sat in silence. Ponies cropped grass. The dog sighted rabbits in the far distance and decided to leave them be. The cold of the stone began to make itself felt through my T-shirt. I stood up. 'Are you going back to bed?'

'No. I thought I'd sit here for a while.' She looked up. 'If you don't mind.'

'I don't mind.' I am desperate for lack of sleep and I am sick with the waiting and the fear of what is to come but I have no reason, now, to mind anything she does. I dropped a hand to her shoulder. 'I'll see you in the morning.'

'You will. Sleep well.'

She was wrong. They were both wrong. We did not hear anything from anyone in the morning. Nor the morning after that, nor the ones beyond until I forgot that the conversation had ever happened. Life went on. It wasn't normal, but there was an unvoiced agreement that we would treat it as if it were. Sandy, Kirsty and Jon ran the treks. Nina went into work. I found things to do that never took me far from the farm. The Unit closed beds and took in fewer patients and that way managed without two of its staff. Lee spent her days with the dog and the cat and her nights watching the moon. If she slept, I didn't see it.

It was a Saturday afternoon in August when he came. We were in the yard, all of us. Sandy was with the colt. Jon and Kirsty were worming the mares and foals for something to do between rides. Maddie was lame with pus in the foot. I held her while Nina dug out her sole with a hoof knife. Lee sat on a bale with the dog and worked saddle soap into a bridle. It was the sound of her stopping, the no-sound where there had been sound, that made me turn round. The riders from the last trek had driven in convoy out of the yard and up the lane and he slipped through in their wake, unheard and unseen. His car sat on the far side of the gate. He didn't get out. Lee put the bridle down on the bale and looked up at me. 'Will you do this? Please? I'd rather it came from you.'

'Of course.'

The yard is an infinity of distance. He gets out and comes forward to lean on the gate. He has no one with him, which is surprising. No one from work. No dog at his heels. He shrugs off his jacket and throws it in the car as I reach him.

'How is she?'

'Getting better. She'll climb again if she's given time.'

'Good.'

'Is it?'

'Kellen, I'm not here to—'

'Just tell me.' I feel dead inside. I can hear it in my voice. A voice without hope. Because there is no hope. Because there is, after all, no real way to prove what she said and we all knew that from the start. The timing was too tight. Too few people in that doucé suburban dead-end had any idea of what they saw or when and none of them could time with any accuracy the arrival of a motorbike to a gunshot they are not even sure that they heard. The only surprise is that she has chosen to wait this long before she follows Nicco Gallianno into the dark. And she will follow him. Not the same way perhaps, but the end result will be the same. We have not discussed this but we both know it to be true. So I stand by the gate and I watch her leave the bridle on the bale and walk inside and suddenly I am too afraid to look at him.

He puts a hand on the gate, begins to lift the latch. I cover it with mine. 'No. Not now.'

'I came to talk to Lee.'

'You can talk to me instead. It only takes one word, MacDonald.'

'All right, then. If that's the way you want it.'

She had gone inside to the office to sit in front of the computer. The cat lay across her knees, his head dangling loosely at the side. The monitor spun stars into a backdrop of Eric's Cliff, a glorious shot, all sun and rock and polarised sky, taken from the boat long before there was any reason to name it for the one who held the camera. In the farm, this is the closest she can get to him. I stood outside on the grass beyond the open French windows. She spun the chair to face me.

'And?'

I moved in and stood behind her, resting my hands on her shoulders, my thumbs on the taut muscles at the sides of her neck. Her skin twitched once under my hands and was still. She watched me in the reflection from the monitor. Her eyes asked the question again. She has more courage than I do. I would wait. I would not want to hear.

I said it quickly, to get it over. 'They've dropped the case, Lee. Randolph Duncan's body has been released. The funeral's set for next Tuesday. You're clear.'

She stared at me blankly, her eyes holding mine, the glass veil of the monitor blurring the sense of it. 'What about the trial?'

'There isn't going to be any trial.' I said it again: 'They've dropped the case.'

It was so far from what she expected, from what either of us
expected. Her hands lay still on the keyboard. The cat sat up,
pushing the top of his head on her forearm for attention. She
toyed, unthinking, with his chin. 'Why?'

'They've found a witness. A groundsman with decent hearing who can tell a Ducati from a Yamaha and knows how to
read the time. He heard you stop. He heard the shot. He can
pick out your bike from among five others revved up behind a
wall and he's prepared to stand up in court and swear that the
gunshot came within seconds of you cutting the engine.
Apparently, as far as he's concerned, you wouldn't have had
time to pull your key from the ignition before the gun went
off. It's as watertight as they're ever going to get. There's no
case left to answer. They'd be wasting public money if they
took you to court. You're clear. It's over.'

The change was sudden when it came. I felt it in my hands
at first: the flooding, almost crippling relief, flowing through in
the way the morphine had flowed through in the ward. She
closed her eyes and leant her full weight back in the chair. Her
head tilted backwards to rest on my ribs. Her neck eased
enough to take the weight of my thumb and not bruise. 'God,
Kellen . . .'

'Don't.'

'But I—'

'Just don't.'

One hand came up to her shoulder. The fingers threaded
through mine, her thumb pushing circles in the dip of my
palm. We stayed like that for a long time, silent. Then
eventually: 'Thank you.'

'You don't have to say that.'

'I know. But I want to.' Her thumb moved and moved on my palm, the only bit of her hand that moved. Then her free hand strayed back to the keyboard, tapped a key and brought it back to life. 'I have a present for you, too,' she said. 'We have an e-mail from Canada.'

'Who do you know in Canada?'

'Who do *we* know in Canada?' The message opened on the screen. 'Read it.'

From: raku@hotmail.com
   Subject: Hello?
   To: eka1@pathlab.gla.ac.uk
   Reply-to: raku@hotmail.com
   priority: urgent

Hi,
Checking to see if you're there. I have use of University e-mail for a week (maybe longer) if you want to mail me back.
Take care
F

'I mailed her while you were talking to Stewart. She's in Toronto. She's applying for a scholarship to study ceramic art at the university.'

'Who is?'

'Frances Doherty.' Her head tilted the last fraction to rest on my collar bone. She smiled. 'You knew her as Deirdre Fitzpatrick.'

Headline hopes you have enjoyed *Stronger Than Death* and invites you to sample the beginning of Manda Scott's compelling new novel, *No Good Deed*, out soon.

Chapter One

Summer

In the long list of early prisoner releases, his was one of the least remarked; ostensibly a gift to both sides, in practice, welcomed by neither. He walked out of the gates at nine o'clock on the morning of the thirteenth of July, twenty one years and three months to the day since they had first locked him up. The world lay in the grip of a heat wave so that the air shimmered above the tarmac and it was cooler by far inside than out. He hung around for a while, as if testing the heat and humidity of the air, an act that did nothing to endear him to those watching. In time, he stooped at the driver's door of the car waiting at the kerb side and then the one inside got out and he took over the wheel. There was a moment when it seemed he might have left his companion standing on the pavement outside the gates but he relented and the younger man, whose face was already on file and who was hardly an easy touch, was invited into the passenger side.

He counted three of them following, in varying rotations, in front or behind, as the car passed east towards the ferry at Larne. Two passengers and a very striking red-headed cabin assistant kept their eyes on him on the crossing to Stranraer. At the terminal, they handed him over to their Scottish counterparts and a different three watched him wave good-bye to his escort, rent a car and then followed him on the road up to Glasgow. He took the tunnel and then the switchback and led them out to the pine forests at the southern tip of Loch Lomond where he let himself into a self-catering cabin on the shores of the loch. The school holidays being over, the remaining six cabins in the group were conveniently empty and the watchers, with some gratitude, took up position in three of them.

An hour after the man's arrival, he had a visitor. One of the city's more expensive whores, well known to the local police, drove up to the door, knocked twice and was granted admission. The watchers, all of whom were young and male, rigged up a microphone and directed it at the bedroom window, recording the results for later posterity. It was thus added to the file that the mark was not fluent in gutter Glaswegian but that his appetites were as diverse as might be expected in any man who has spent his third and fourth decades locked in a cell. The woman left in the early evening and the watchers had no more entertainment than the sound of a man breathing heavily in his sleep.

It was a newer, less seasoned watcher who recognised, around five o'clock the following morning, that she had heard the same pattern of breathing repeated three times in the space of two hours. No-one likes to be woken before dawn for the sake of it and so she took the time to play the tape into a portable computer and compare the exact shape of the wave forms before she rang through to her superiors and asked for a back-up and permission to break in. At six thirty, the combat team found a dead woman lying unclothed on the singles bed beside a tape recorder that played a continuous loop of a man's breathing. The received wisdom from those on the scene was that the dead woman had been strangled. The pathologist's report suggested instead that the ring of purpled bruises on the neck occurred at least twenty four hours ante-mortem and that the cause of death was, in fact, a simple fracture of the vertebral column between the third and fourth cervical vertebrae. Bruising on the lower left chin and the upper right parietal region showed where the heels of two hands had been applied to achieve the twist. Later analysis of the records found this to be the method used in at least one previous assassination by the same target. A watch was put on all known associates but was called off on the grounds of wasted expense after a week with no result. A full case report was lodged with Interpol to the effect that the suspect was loose, whereabouts and intentions unknown. It is a sad feature of the technological age that all those involved felt a computer flag to be a sufficient warning to the local police forces and no one deemed it necessary, or even useful, to pick up the phone and tell the one person who might really have needed to know that that Colm Connaught O'Neil was out and looking for trouble.

Spring

14th March

'Jamie?'

The child opened his eyes. It was dark in the room, darker than it had been, and there was snow feathering down the outside of the window. They had promised it for Christmas and it came instead for Easter, a gift from the god to make the world a cleaner, purer place. Large flakes flared orange in the sodium glare of the street light and piled in drifts against the lower sill, tinged to yellow by the years of filth and tobacco smoke staining the glass.

'Jamie? Can you hear me?' The child was entranced by the snow. He watched the patterns of it grow before his eyes and let the voice wash over him. 'Jamie? Please? I need your help.' The voice was smooth, like the glass, but warmer. It flowed around him, easing the pain. He curled tighter in his chair and turned his face to the dark. The snow had deadened all the other sounds as the evening gave way to night; the noise of cars in the street, the kick-out from the pubs, the smash of a bottle dropping from the top of a neighbouring tenement down on to the street below, the lacerating give and take of a beating taking place somewhere far away but not quite out of earshot. That pain was not his. In these small things, life was kind.

Inside the room the quality of the quiet was different. His mother and her friend had been silent long since but there was no surprise in that. He had seen the needles and the small ritual of injection. He knew the pattern of this and the time it would last and he knew he was safe, from that quarter at least, for most of the darkness. The other sound, the voice, was new and uncomfortable. Usually nobody spoke and if they did, it was simplest often not to listen. He had a lot of practice in not listening. Watch the things that move beyond the window and don't listen. That way is safe.

'Jamie? Jamie, listen. The men will come back soon and when they do, they will hurt you again. You know that. If you help me, I can stop them.' The voice was soft and low, and the accent strange, like the ones on the news, entirely unlike the flat vowels and guttural glottal stops of his world. He couldn't place the voice and that worried him. He hunched his shoulders, pulling himself smaller, blocking out the noise. It came through all the same. 'Jamie? It's me, Sandra. Trust me. I can get us out of here. But you have to help me first.' Sandra. He struggled to fit a face to the name. An image came into focus of flashing amber eyes with black stripes flaring outwards, like a tiger. The thought made him smile. He turned in to the dark of the room. 'Jamie?' She sounded more hopeful. 'Over here. Under the sofa.' Under the sofa? Now that really was strange. With regret, he watched one last layer of snow build on the sill and then he left the safety of his chair and turned into the darkness of the room.

The sulphured glow of the street lights pushed in a semi-circle as far as the television but beyond it the room was as black as the night outside. The stench of stale cigarette smoke, cheap scent and congealing chow mein hung, waiting, in the darkness. By the window, the air was cold and clean. He nearly turned back but the voice drew him on. 'Jamie? Not much further now.' So he went on, feeling his way forward, past the bottles and the needles, the remains of the take-away and the debris of clothing, to the inert bulk of his mother's body. She lay across the sofa, locked in a sleeping embrace with one of the other two women. He couldn't remember which of the pair was called Sandra but he searched among the tangle of limbs and heads for the flash of light from the eyes. 'Underneath,' said the voice. He crouched down on the floor. She was right. There was, indeed, a woman lying underneath the sofa. His eyes were adjusting slowly to the absence of light but even in the gloom he could see the pale skin on the undersides of her arms with the flat white planes of the old scars and the fresh patterns around them of hand-prints and bruises. Her hair was crushed and matted, a scarecrow's nest in bottle blonde with the streaks of scarlet through it that matched the fake suede of her skirt. A glimmer of gold pulsed at her navel, rising and falling with the steady rhythm of her breathing. With difficulty, because the space from the base of the sofa to the floor was not great and the weight of his mother made it less than it might have been, she turned her head to look at him. That wasn't good. Her face was a mess – more of a mess than usual and only partly because of her makeup had gone. He had watched her in the mornings as she sat on the edge of the bath, using the only mirror in the house to help her paint her face and he knew the care she took to hide the things she didn't want the world to see. Now the world could see what it liked, and more. A fresh bruise, bleeding at the centre, ran across one cheekbone and up to the inside corner of her eye. On the other side, the stark white snake-line of an old scar bisected one eyebrow and ran on down the side of her nose to make a notch on the edge of her upper lip. On her temple, a palm's breadth of smooth white burn tissue pulled the skin tight, angling up the edge of one eye, so that it seemed as if she was forever doubting what he said. Then she blinked and the eyes gathered him in and he was lost. He was entranced by her eyes. He knelt down and put his head level with hers and peered into them. She smiled for him then and it was a new smile, crooked and conspiratorial and really very warm. He chewed his lip for a moment, thinking, then he lay flat on his stomach and put his head on one side, looked into her eyes and smiled back. She laughed at that, soft and breathless and sliding into something not quite controlled that lasted longer than either of them expected. She caught herself, eventually, and breathed deep so that the navel stud rolled on the wave of it. 'Jamie, sunshine, you're gorgeous and I love you dearly but this is really, really not the right time. I need to get out of here, kiddo. I'm no good to either of us like this. Do you think you could try to untie me? Just one hand, I can do the rest.' He sat up on his heels for a better look and saw what the dark had hidden before; that each wrist, each ankle, was fixed tight to one leg of the sofa. The hand nearest him twitched, palm out, the fingers waggling like the legs of a dying spider. The voice wove out around it. 'Jamie? Can you see the knots?' He could. He nodded. 'I can't see you any more, sunshine. You'll have to speak to me.' He thought about that for a while and decided safer not. Instead, he put his hand down to touch the palm then moved to the rope. 'All right, good lad.' There was a new warmth to the voice. 'Now, can you untie it. Please?' Another novelty. 'Please' was not part of his everyday vocabulary by any stretch of the imagination. He felt around the square-sharp edges of the wood to the opposite side where the knots gathered. 'You might need to use your teeth to loosen them.' He tried. He tried for the novelty of being asked, for her smile and for the memory of the tiger's eyes. He tried until the rope was wet with his spit and his fingers slid across it as he tugged. All the while he listened to her breathing, slow and even, and the steady words of encouragement. And the promises. He listened most to the promises. 'Jamie, if you can get me out of here before they come back, I promise you, I'll take you away from here. There's a cottage in the country, with a mountain at the back of it and you can see the sea from the front door and there's a bedroom you can have all your own. Would you like that, Jamie? But we need to get free, both of us, or none of it will happen and what happens instead will be . . . don't think about that. Think about the cottage. And the snow. Think about the snow, Jamie. With the weather we've been having, the snow will be six feet thick outside on the mountain. We can take sledges up the mountain and race them down to the back door. We can make snowmen as tall as the house. I can make you an igloo outside the back door and you can sleep in it overnight and still be warm. Would you like that kind of snow, Jamie?' He did like the idea of such snow and although he had no idea what an igloo was he thought he might like that too. But liking it didn't get the rope untied, in fact, if anything, the wet of his spit was swelling the fibre and making it tighter. He sat back on his heels and bit a nail in frustration and without really thinking about it, he said, 'Can't.'

There was a brief silence and then, 'Can't you? Bugger it. Well, never mind, you can talk. That's something.' The voice was still calm. If he'd said 'can't' to his mother, the screaming would have gone on 'till his head rang. 'OK. Don't panic.

They're not finished downstairs yet.' They weren't, although if you stopped to listen to it, the sounds of pain were different. There was a sense of things accelerating towards a close. He shut his ears and turned back to the snow. It was piling deeper on the sill and the swirls of filth on the glass made new and interesting patterns. He moved back towards his chair.

'Jamie, no! Don't crap out on me now. We're still in with a chance. We need a knife. Can you find a knife for me, Jamie?' There was a grating edge in the voice now. Threads of panic wove through it, dangerously seductive. He knew panic well. It was not a place he wanted to be. The snow drew him closer. It was falling faster so that the world outside the window was more white than black and the flakes were smaller, almost like dust. He reached the chair and curled himself into it.

'Jamie. Listen to me. The snow will melt soon. The rain will come back. What will you have then? Do you really want to go on living like this? Jamie? Are you listening to me? Jamie?' He wasn't listening. He curled tighter and shut the voice out.

'Shit.'

And then there was nothing. The snow fell dizzyingly fast. He could have slept, hypnotised by the swirling speed of it but the final word echoed round the inside of his head. *Shit*. Just that. A single sound, more of a breath than a word, full of defeat and fear and the promise of pain and all the things he was used to. But there was a kind of dry, twisting humour with it that he wasn't used to at all. It was a voice to go with the smile and the eyes. He listened to it stir round in his head for a while, feeling the newness of it and then he slid down from the chair and padded out across the hallway to the dark pit of the kitchen. The bread knife was in the washing-up bowl. He found it eventually, fished it out and dried it and took it back to the sofa and knelt down so that she could see it in his hands. He thought she might cry at the sight of him but she didn't. She smiled instead, which was good.

'Jamie, I love you. Can you cut the rope, sweetheart? See if you can slide the knife down behind my hand and the wood . . .' He heard the suck of an indrawn breath, bitten off, and then; 'Yes. Good lad. Now, move it up and down. Good. Push it outwards, it needs to bite on the rope. Like that. More. Good. Don't stop now, kiddo, for God's sake, don't stop now . . . *yes*.' That last, whispered exultation as the final strand parted and then, '*Thank you*.'

She worked her fingers for a moment, gripping and re-gripping the hilt of the knife until the life came back to them. She swore with the heat of that but not for long. When she could trust herself to move, she eased across and freed her other hand on her own. He had to help her with her feet because there wasn't room for her to reach down but they came quicker because he knew what he was doing and he didn't make her bleed. He cut the last piece of rope binding her left ankle and then knelt out of the way as she slithered sideways towards him. 'Jamie, I love you forever.' She hugged him tight, running her fingers in the tangled straw of his hair. The amber eyes flashed for him, pulling in the orange light from the window, spinning it round and throwing it out like a beacon. She kissed him, just lightly, on his forehead and smiled so that, for one long moment, his world filled with colour. And then, because it was magic, and magic never lasts, the colours faded.

The woman was shaking. He realised that when he realised she wasn't smiling any more. It could have been the cold. He would have liked it to be the cold but her skin was grey, the way his mother's went grey when she was up on the smack and the shakes had that extra tremor that said it was more than the perennial problem of too few clothes in an unheated room. He searched her arms for the signs of the needle and found it – a single exploded vein spreading out on the ghosted flesh of her inner arm. She saw him looking and shook her head. 'It wasn't me, kiddo.' But his mother said that often enough and his mother's teeth chattered in much the same way as she said it. He looked into her eyes and the colours were already less bright. The smile was forced as perhaps it had been forced before. The arms that held him, let him go. 'Jamie, trust me. We can talk about it later. Just now we have to get you out of here.' He said nothing. Outside, a man cried out, a desperate, long-drawn sound, rising up the scales to fracture in agony at the top. The silence rang loud in its wake. Her head snapped up at the noise of it. 'Oh, Jesus Christ, *Luke*,' and then, in a voice from which all colour and all tremor had gone, she said, 'Stay here. I won't be long.'

She was taller than his mother and lithe and she moved with a feral, fluid grace and a sense of purpose that his mother lacked. He heard the scuff of her bare feet as she ran up the stairs. The light tread moved across the ceiling above him towards the bedroom and something happened in a cupboard and then she was back, standing beside him, fastening a pack round her waist and staring out of the window with an intensity that all but stopped the shaking. She had changed, he could feel it. Sandra-before was all scarlet plastic and east

Glasgow vowels and a laugh that could cut through glass. If she spoke to him, it was to get him to bed, out of the way, and she did it as if he was invisible, which meant that he was. Sandra-under-the-sofa was a friend in the darkness, wide amber eyes and a smile that broke through the silence. Sandra-now was different and not necessarily pleasant. He was setting off down the road to nowhere but she shook her head and nodded forwards and so he stopped and in time he realised that she was listening, not looking and then, when he let go of the snow and listened with her, he could hear what she could hear, which was nothing. Under all the small, wilderness cries of the night, the sounds of the beating had ended.

In the enclosed space of his world, where all women wear cheap plastic min-skirts and all men mete out violence, the end of it somewhere else means only that it is coming closer. He shrugged deep in the chair and bit his lip and started in earnest back down the track to the other world where he would be invisible in this one.

'No. Not now.' A hand fell light on his shoulder. 'We need to get you out of here while there's still time. Get your shoes and we'll . . . oh, shit, no we won't . . .' Down at street level, a door slammed shut against the wind. Hard boots and harder voices filled the stairwell. '*Fuck.*' The fingers tightened in frustration, digging hard through his T-shirt to the collar bone below. It hurt. He turned round to protest but she had already let go and there was a gun in her hand that had, perhaps, been there all along and a shine in her eyes that was quite the opposite of the magic he had seen before. He might have tried to run from her then but the hand came back to his arm and the voice that went with the eyes said, 'Don't move, Jamie. Just sit here and look out of the window and whatever else happens, don't move a muscle. Stay invisible, kid. You can do it. I won't be far.' And then she was gone, feather-footed, out across the hallway to the dank pit of the kitchen, and there was time enough for a single over-sized flake to spiral down the full length of the window before the front door smashed open and the world caved in.

Three. The redhead with halitosis, the blond with the beard who gave the orders and the obese grunt with the gun and the novel uses for living room furniture. She stood behind the kitchen door with her eye to the crack at the hinge and she had the silencer tight on the barrel as the first of them reached the top of the stairs. The doing of it helped with the shaking but not as much as she needed. Luke, grinning, spoke in her head. *'Keep it still, kiddo. You won't hit a barn door if you wiggle the end of it round like that.'* Luke. I don't need to hit a barn door. I need to hit three men, and I need not to hit a boy. Then I can come and find you. Just stay alive for me now. He shook his head, still grinning and the echo of his last cry looped round and back in her skull.

They crashed in through the front door, all three of them together, loud and drunk with the power of another man's pain. The smell of fresh blood washed past her in giddying waves, a rising tide that pushed ahead of the beer and the sweat and the reek of his fear. She breathed in the mess of it and breathed out his name. In: hell. Out: Luke. *They will pay for this, I promise you.* They first one passed the crack in the hinge and she counted each of them through to the living room opposite; redhead, blondie, fatso. Three . . . two . . . one . . .

Now!

The fat one died first.

Her arms moved with a will of their own and the mouth of her gun hung in the air an inch behind his ear. The round mass of his head was bigger than a barn door. A different voice – Strang's – took over inside her head. *Head shots are best. Hit them once if you have to, twice if you can.* The silencer breathed twice and the man's own momentum carried him two more strides to the far end of the sofa before his knees gave way and he fell face down on the floor.

'Get up you fat bastard.' The redhead was slow; deaf to the sound of a weapon simply because it was not possible for there to be one there. The bearded blond was faster. He was moving even before the second shot; spinning sideways, going for the shadows, thinking on his feet. 'It's the bitch. Get the kid.' And so he had to go next. *If the target is moving or obscured, go for the upper torso.* He was down in the angle between the wall and the floor, rolling fast towards the fat one. Four rounds hit the mass of his body. It bucked, as Ciaran had bucked, as her father had bucked, once for each shot. At the end, it lay still, the arm outstretched, still reaching out for the gun. He sighed like a slashed tyre, the final exhalation from lungs punctured more than once. She stepped over him into the room.

The redhead may not have been overly smart but he was intimately acquainted with death and its precursors. He turned very slowly towards her, keeping his hands well away from his sides. 'Whit're you after?' he asked. He smiled, brokenly and the decay of his breath added to the pollution of the room. She said nothing. Possibly she smiled back. The colour drained from his face. 'It wisnae me. It was Tord. Tord did him.' He whined it, as a child whines for a broken window. 'It wasn't me. It just broke.' Who cares? I do. *Luke*. The shaking was back. The end of the gun wavered in her outstretched hands. Cold, very cold.

The target was moving, easing himself back, a step at a time, towards the window. *At all costs, keep the angle of fire away from the public.* She stepped out sideways, moving to put herself between the standing man and the boy. The man moved opposite her, a well-drilled partner in the dance. The orange glow of the street light marked an arc on the floor that kept them apart. *Take extra care in the dark. Your vision will be compromised. Keep away from the light source.* She was outlined against the window. She felt the light stripping her bare, leaving her naked before hostile eyes. She stepped sideways again so that the boy's chair was behind her. The man was keeping to the shadows, moving with her, still whining. The words had no meaning. 'Tord knows all about yous two. He'll be back in the morning. Better to get out while you can. I'll no' get in your way now. Take the kid and go. He'll be needing someone to take care of him. You go now before he comes back . . .' And then she lost him. He dropped down out of sight somewhere between the bodies and the sofa. The fat one had carried a revolver in his shoulder sling. She heard the slick of metal on leather and then the ratchet of the hammer clicking back before it fell. Her body moved once again of its own volition, spinning her sideways into shadows. White light erupted from the black space near the door. The sound of the shot shattered her hearing. She heard herself scream with the shock of it and then heard an echoing cry from the chair. But she was rolling, still, into the darkness and her arms were outstretched and she was firing and firing and firing into the place where the flash had come from and the spit of the silencer gave way to the solid thud of rounds slamming through flesh and bone and then the louder, more solid sound of metal falling on wood and still she fired until the only sound was the faintest of clicks as she pulled the trigger and there was nothing at all coming out of her gun.

Luke.

The body of the redhead blocked the doorway. She stepped over it into the hall, swapping clips unconsciously, filling up the gun with hands that could barely hold the rounds. The first waves of nausea caught her as she passed the kitchen. She fumbled for the light, gagging against a closed glottis. The kitchen was foul. A bowl of foetid water stood in the sink, a rancid dishcloth hung on the edge, growing life of its own. Unwashed tea towels hung from the door handle. A carton of old milk congealed on top of the fridge because nobody could be bothered to open the door and put it away. In all the hell of the months just gone, she had wanted very badly to set fire to that kitchen. Now it was simply a staging post in purgatory. She threw up into the washing bowl, retching and choking on the stench, on the shock of what she had done and the fear of what she was going to find downstairs. *Luke.* She spat a final time, ran a tap and drank the water straight from the spout then wiped her mouth dry on her sleeve. *Wait for me. Live.*

She was at the front door before she remembered the boy. He was sitting where she had left him, curled tight in the chair, staring out at the whirling white-on-black of the night. She crouched down in front of him, not quite blocking the view to the window. 'Jamie? Are you alright?' He was shaking as much as she was shaking. His lips were blue in the snow-lit white of his face. His teeth made a dented line along his lower lip, holding it in. There was a single tear track running down from the inner corner of each wide-open eye. She saw all of this before she saw the blood. It ran in a wash of sticky black from the lower sleeve of his T-shirt down his arm and on to his thigh. The fingers of his other hand gripped tight to the wound, so that it leaked from between his fingers, and they, too, had gone black in the odd sodium glare of the night. 'Jamie, let me look.' He shook his head, still biting his lip. The tears, such as they were, had stopped. 'Luke,' he said. He whispered it, the way she had whispered it before the shooting started. He barely knew him. He just knew that he mattered to her. It was the second word she had ever heard him say.

'In a minute. When you're safe.' She looked around for something to bind the wound, something not worn by the dead. 'Wait here, I'll be back in a second.' She ran for the kitchen, jumping the body of the redhead as if it wasn't there. A pair of clean tea towels lay in a drawer. She tore one in half as she ran back. 'Here. Let me wrap it up.' His hand was limp and cold to the touch as she moved his fingers away. Fresh blood ran freely from the wound in his upper arm. He was only nine and he was small for his age and he had no spare flesh on him anywhere. A .38 bullet has the power to take off the arm of an adult. God alone knows what it can do to a child. She held his hand in her own. 'Jamie. I have to get help. I'll wrap you up and then we'll call people who can do something to make you better. Is that OK?' He nodded. Fatigue and pain warred with the fear of strangers. She wrapped one of the tea-towels round his arm and made a sling of the other. The simple act of movement dragged a strangled half-cry from his throat. 'You can cry, Jamie, it's alright. There's no one to hear you but me.'

He shook his head and bit deeper so that his lip, too, turned dark. She tied the last knot on the sling. He was wearing nothing but his mother's T-shirt in a room where the last flicker of gas ran out of the meter just after the nine o'clock news. It was as cold inside as out, possibly colder. His feet were as blue as his lips, drawn up underneath him for warmth. His hands were like ice. She tried to smile into his eyes and got nothing back. 'Wait here,' she said again. She took the stairs at a run, slamming on lights until she reached his bedroom. He had no furniture beyond a bed and not much in the way of clothes but there was a sweatshirt and a pair of jeans and thick socks for playing football. Back downstairs, the sweatshirt slid down over the injured arm and he let her manoeuvre him into the jeans. The socks took longest because she wasn't used to putting socks on someone else. The steady voice of Strang inside her head was counting seconds, explaining to her that Luke was dying and the boy would live. When he was wrapped against the cold and not bleeding, she listened to it. 'Right, I'll go and find him. Are you OK to stay here?'

He nodded. He was shaking less. She reached into the belt pouch that had held her gun and pulled out a black box the size of a small cigarette packet with two buttons on one side. 'This will call the people we need. They'll be faster than an ambulance and they'll know what to do with your arm.' They will know, also, what to do with the mess of bodies in the room but this is not his problem. She held out the box in front of him. 'I want you to hold this, do you think you can?'

His uninjured hand reached out to take it. His eyes stayed on hers. 'Good. Take a look. There are two buttons on top here, one red, one green. OK?' He nodded. 'Good lad. You can press the red button any time now. Then count, very slowly, to a hundred and press the green button. The guys aren't far. That's the signal to come as fast as they can and be ready to deal with the wounded. If they get here before I get back, make sure they sort out your arm before they do anything else.'

Fear shadowed his eyes. She laid a hand on his leg. 'Jamie, please trust me. None of them will hurt you. You have to believe that.' He nodded. There was no way to know if he believed her. Seconds passed. She crouched back by the chair. 'OK, listen. There are three of them. Alec Strang's in charge. He's solid, like the blond one, but he's clean shaven and he's got wee round glasses, like this.' She made two circles of her fingers and held them in front of her eyes. 'He's fine, but he'll not know how to talk to you. Andy Bennett's lank, like he's been on smack and not eaten for a week. He's going bald, with his hair pushed out over his head, you know?'

He nodded. Bald men, he knew. 'Good lad. Andy's the doctor. He'll sort out your arm. The third one's Murdo Cameron. He's our kind of guy. He's not so broad as Strang but he's taller, about this height,' she held the flat of her palm a hand's length over the top of her head, 'and his hair's black, like treacle and wild. If we're lucky, he'll have it bunched back, like this,' she swept her hair back and held it. The action changed the planes on her face. When she let it go, it sprung up round her head. 'If we're not lucky, It'll be hanging down round his shoulders getting in the way. Either way, you'll know him when you see him. Tell Murdo Cameron, when he asks, that I've gone to find Luke. OK? Jamie?' She did her best to smile for him the way she had done under the sofa. 'Jamie? I know it's difficult but they'll not be hard on you for speaking. Just tell them that, you don't have to say anything else. Do you think you can do it?'

He was nine years old and he had a bullet wound in his arm. It was three o'clock in the morning and he was about to sit alone in a house with the bodies of three men any one of whom, when alive, would have killed him without a second thought. He had more stamina, more courage, than any man she had ever worked with. A smile lit up his face like a candle in the darkness. He blinked once over eyes the colour of night-time snow. 'Tell Murdo Cameron I've gone to find Luke,' he said. If you taped him saying it, you would think it was her.

She took hold of his head, very gently, and pressed her lips to his forehead. 'Jamie, I love you.' He pushed her away. His eyes moved to the door and back.

'OK. I'm going. I won't be long.'

He heard the sound of her feet on the stairs and the close below. He heard the front door opened and slammed shut against the wind. He waited until he saw the shape of her move round the side of the building and then he put both thumbs on the red button and pushed.

'It's OK, son, you can let go of it now.' The boy sat curled in the chair, his whole body curved around the transmitter, both hands stabbing tight on the buttons. She said to press them.

She didn't say to let go. And so he had held tight for twelve and a half minutes, first to the red button, then to the red and the green together and the transmitter sent out its continuous silent scream to the three men waiting on the other side of the city so that they, believing the woman to be dying, if not already dead, had broken all the limits to get there.

Alec Strang was relieved, more than he could have said, not to find her body in the carnage on the floor, but that didn't mean that she was safe. He sent Murdo Cameron upstairs with his gun out, checking for bodies, alive or dead. 'Use your torch. I don't want any more lights on 'till we know where everyone is.'

'Right.'

Bennett, the medic, was already in the living room, playing his own torch over the two women on the sofa although there was nothing about either of them to suggest that they were within reach of anything short of a miracle. That left Strang with the child. The file said nine but he could as easily have been six; small and lean, with pale skin and paler hair and the dark shadows of sleeplessness hammered in beneath his eyes. He looked blank, in the way of all children who have seen too much of the things they should never see, but there was a sense of stone in the stare that said if he broke, it would not be here or now. Still, as he picked his way forward over the debris and the dead, Strang caught the pungent smell of fresh urine hanging over the chair and he saw, and chose to ignore, the darker stain blending with all the other dark stains on the bare wood beneath the chair. His experience of children stemmed solely from a childhood too far gone to contemplate but he knew enough of basic human pride not to pass comment. He moved round the chair and leant back against the window frame, putting himself between the eyes and their target.

'Jamie? It is Jamie, isn't it? It's OK, you're safe now.' His accent was English and educated. It rang oddly in the cold of the room, an intruder in a foreign land.

Over by the sofa, Bennett gave the thumbs down on the two women and knelt down to examine the hulking body of the man lying on the floor beside them. Strang nodded acknowledgement and then, looking back to the chair, saw that the exchange had been noted and understood. He smiled. 'No problem, son. Your mum'll be fine. We'll get someone here to take care of her.' He lied, always, with fluent ease and was surprised to see that, too, noted and understood. He ran a tongue round teeth still thick with sleep and redefined the problem. Nine going on ninety, or at least a reasonable average between the two. He swept a hand through his hair. A pair of snow-pale eyes stared up into his. 'OK, forget it,' he said. 'You know what the score is.' The eyes gave nothing away but there was a faint inclination of the head which showed, at least, that the kid could hear.

Murdo Cameron returned from the upper rooms. He shook his head once and joined Bennett in his examination of the bodies. Cameron had no medical training but he was very good indeed at assessing the patterns of fire. If you know who fired what and when, you can create a reasonable picture of who was left standing at the end. In the absence of witnesses, these things matter. Except that they did have a witness. Of sorts. The boy sat, transfixed by the snow, the transmitter still gripped in both hands, the buttons locked in their silent alarm.

Strang moved out to take it and changed his mind. He tapped it instead. 'Did Orla give you that?' he asked. The eyes gazed through him to the window beyond. He might have been talking to snow.

'She's in cover. She's not calling herself Orla.' Murdo was standing behind the chair. There was fresh blood on the tips of his fingers and, now, streaks of it down the front of his T-shirt as he wiped them clean. 'If the lad's any sense,' he said, 'he'll have learnt long ago not to talk to strange men who don't know the name of his friends.'

'Very funny.' Strang pushed the heels of both hands into the pits of his eyes. Twenty minutes ago, he was sound asleep. Now, with the first adrenalin rush receding, the pall of unfinished dreams dulled his thinking. Murdo, who had been the one sitting up and was by far the most awake, was still smiling at him when he moved his hands away. Strang sighed and wished for sleep. 'Did you find anything useful?' he asked.

'Maybe.' The tall man folded his arms on the back of the chair. 'The damage in all three came from one gun.'

'Whose?'

'Pass. I don't know. It was a small calibre automatic which would fit with it being McLeod's but there's no saying she was the one firing it. Whoever it was, they started in here with the big one by the sofa,' he nodded back towards the dead man, 'went through the blond one for a short cut and then got into a shooting match with the redhead. The revolver's been fired once. We need to trace the angle of shot and find out if it hit anyone.' He was doing it as he spoke, swivelling round on one heel, his eyes measuring an arc from the fallen gun to the wall, seeking out the point of impact and tracing the route in between. He reached the end of the arc, paused and did it again. 'Oh, shit.' He said it quietly, sliding it into the conversation between one sentence and the next. His eyes narrowed and he slid round into the space between the chair and the wall, taking care to keep out of the way of the window. He was tall, as she had said and he did have his hair tied back. With unusual presence of mind he had removed his holster and left it out of sight in the hallway leaving only his radio hanging from his belt. He signalled to Bennett to join him, found a clean space on the floor then crossed his ankles and sank down in one smooth movement. 'Hey Jamie. I'm Murdo. This is Andy, he's a doctor. Will you let him look at your arm?' The boy shook his head, pushing himself deeper into the chair. Bennett slid up beside him. 'He's hit?'

'I think so. Entry site in the back of the chair. Round's in the wall up here. Looks like it's grazed along his back and maybe clipped the side of his arm.' The tall man nodded upwards, his eyes still on the chair. The medic glanced up and then back to the boy then he, too, crouched at the side of the chair. He slid out a hand and laid his fingers on one narrow wrist. A pulse threaded through beneath his fingers, like feeling along knots in a piece of string. The key to medicine in children, in anyone, is to find a common link with the patient. He tried to remember the name the woman had used. Scots. Glaswegian. The kind of thing half the girls use when you pick them up and they don't want to be known. Suzi? Sally? Sandra? 'Sandra?' he asked. 'Did Sandra give you that box you're holding? A nod. 'Did she tell you we'd come if you pressed the buttons?' Another nod. 'So did she say where she was going?' Nothing. The grey eyes wavered and slid off his face. Murdo

Cameron looked up and found them drawing him in. He leant forward and put his hand on the chair. 'Are you sure? She's a smart lass. I think she would have left us a message. Did she not say where she was going?'

'Gone to find Luke.' The voice was husked and strained from lack of practice but the tone and the intonation were perfect. Like a parrot, trained in a single speech, he said it again. 'Tell Murdo Cameron, when he asks, that I've gone to find Luke.'

'Where? Where has she . . . ?' Strang was back, behind Cameron, pushing for answers. He got a hand across his mouth from Bennett. 'Shut up, man. Don't go hard on him now. Murdo go on.'

'Never mind him, he's got no manners.' The man smiled. The skin round his eyes creased like tanned leather. 'Did she say where she'd gone? Did Sandra tell you where it was she'd gone to find Luke?' Nothing. He tried it again, asking in a different way, in case it was the order of words that triggered the answer. Still nothing. Strang turned round to face the window and pressed his forehead to the glass, cursing. The boy looked as if he'd been struck. He shook his head. His mouth opened and shut again like a fish and then, 'Don't know,' he said. 'She never said.' It came out as a whisper, even less practised than the rest and the effort of it was painful to watch.

'OK, lad. You've done your best.' Bennett moved to sit on the arm of the chair. With great care he slid one hand down and over the black box. 'Maybe you'd like to let go of that now we're here? There's no one else waiting to hear it.' The thumbs came off the buttons. The red light on top of the transmitter blinked off, extinguishing as it did so, the matching light on

Murdo Cameron's receiver. 'Thank you. Now, can we get this sweater up and have a look at what's underneath? Good. That's nice. Did . . . did Sandra put this on for you? Fine. That's very good. She'd make a good nurse, eh? I'll just undo this knot here and have a wee look . . .' It was a long time since Andrew Bennett had practised medicine on anyone who wasn't a colleague and even then it was first aid and nothing more. There were well-defined limitations to what he could do and they stopped far short of gunshot wounds in a child. He got as far as the bandage and made the same assessment as had been made before him. 'This is more than I can handle.' He turned back to Strang. 'He needs a hospital.'

'Then call the ambulance.' Strang stood with his hands on the window frame, staring out into the night. 'Where the fuck are they?' No one answered. He turned back to the room. 'Cameron, how long since the three in here died?'

'Not long. The blood's barely clotted on the head wounds so we're talking minutes, not hours. I'd say she was out of here around the time the red alarm went off.'

'Wherever she's gone, it's not that far.' Andrew Bennett had his mobile to his ear and was halfway through dialling for an ambulance.

Strang didn't bother to turn round. 'Because?' he asked, wearily.

'Because she's left her shoes.' The nodded over in the direction of the door and they all looked round, even the boy. A pair of red plastic stilettos stood side by side just inside the door of the living room. 'She needed to run,' said the medic, simply, 'she didn't need to run far.' His line connected. He spoke three words into the phone and hung up. 'The others went out on OD opiates,' he said. He kept his eyes away from the boy's. 'Fast and quick. It looks self-injected but there's no saying they knew it was lethal when they put it in.'

'How long ago?'

'A while. They're down to ambient. Five hours, maybe six. Depends if it's been this cold all night.'

'Christ. This is getting out of control. If the shit hit the fan six hours ago, anything could have happened. Right,' Strang pushed himself clear of the window, 'Andy, you stay in here and wait for the ambulance. Don't let them go until we're back. They may have more than the boy to deal with. Cameron, you come with me.' He led them out to the hall, stepping neatly over the bodies, avoiding the loose shells on the floor.

'Where are you going?' Bennett, stepping where Strang stepped, followed him out.

'To find McLeod. We're wasting time. You're right, all we need to look for is bare footprints in the snow. She's looking for Tyler. If we find her, we've found him and then we can . . .'

'Don't bother, I've found him.'

She was there in the doorway, soft footed, like a cat and God, she was a mess. Her hair was wild; white-blonde with coloured highlights, back-combed away from her face like a mane. A bottled tan darkened her legs from ankles to groin, hiding the worst of the scars. Her fingernails were scarlet, matching the plastic of the crotch-ventilating skirt and the abandoned shoes. She had a cheap stud in her navel and if you strained hard to see through the thin lycra of her top, there might well have been one in her left nipple as well. Even so, it was her eyes that grabbed the attention. A pair of mirrored gold contact lenses with radial black lines caught the dim light

of the overhead bulb and spun it back, sharper, brighter, more
vicious than before. If you didn't know her well you'd never
look beyond the eyes. Strang, absorbing this, gave her credit
for ingenuity. Murdo Cameron wondered how in the name of
God any sane man could ever have believed she was a whore.
Andrew Bennett, who had no real interest in what she looked
like, was already half way down the length of the hall.

'Where is he?'

'No.' Her arm was there across the doorway, like a ram-rod,
blocking his path. 'Forget it, Andy, you don't want to see him.'

'I have to. He needs help.' For a man with a good brain, he
wasn't using it well.

'No, he doesn't. Trust me. I'd have been up here before now
if he did. He's way beyond help and you really don't want
to . . . I said *no*, damn you. Strang, hold him.' The arm that had
been across the doorway thrust suddenly forward and Alec
Strang found himself catching the taller man and clasping him
in the bear hug necessary to stop him throwing himself once
again at the exit.

'Andy, give it up. If she says it's too late then believe her.'

'Thank you, Alec.' Her smile was very distant.

Strang locked his hands in front of the struggling Bennett
and said, 'So where is he?'

'In the basement. There's no reason for any of you to go
down. Let the crime squad do it, that's what they're paid for.'
She stepped in over the threshold, pushing the door shut
behind her and it was only then, as she stood beneath the
naked bulb, that the real mess of her showed; the circular cuts,
as of wires pulled tight, at wrist and ankle, the bruises on her
legs, on her hands, on her neck, the blue track of the needle on

her inner arm. Melting snow leaked from her feet on to the floorboards by the door. Threads of pink spread out across it from a gash on her ankle. Murdo Cameron stepped forward, one hand out. 'Orla You're . . .'

'I'm fine.' She fitted her shoulders to the door, one hand on the handle. 'The ambulance is downstairs for Jamie. He'll need someone to go with him and clear the way at the hospital.' She nodded to the medic. 'I'll talk to him first. You go with him when I'm done.'

'Fuck that.' Bennett broke free of the restraining grip and moved forward. 'What about you? You're a walking disaster zone. You need a hospital a sight more than he does.'

She opened her eyes wide. The gold mirrors lied brightly. 'I'm fine,' she said again.

'Right. And I'm your granny.' He had a medic's way of laying his hands on her unasked. He ran a finger up her arm to the blasted vein. Another hand lifted her eyelid and he tried to look past the contacts to the reality hidden beneath. 'Heroin?' he asked.

'I think so. Maybe something else too.' She tried for a smile and abandoned it half-done. 'I didn't think to ask for the prescription.'

'Right.' He wasn't listening. He was holding her arm up to the light so he could more properly examine the cord cuts at her wrists. There had been an hour, more or less, between the time the first wash of the drugs wore off and the time she realised the boy was alive and was still in the room. For ten minutes of that hour, she lay in a stupor, listening to what they were doing to Luke and waiting for them to start on her. For the rest of it, she was trying to break free. The result was not pretty although the pain of it was responsible in a large part for keeping her awake. She felt her arm dropped and the other one lifted and thought that perhaps it would be nice to be asked.

Bennett looked past her to Strang. 'This is through to the tendon sheath. It needs looking at or she'll lose the use of her hand. She can go with the kid. They'll do her as an emergency, he'll wait 'till there's a free theatre.'

'No.' She pulled her hand free. 'Not yet. There are things I still have to do here.'

'You're . . .'

'*Jesus Christ, just do it, will you?*' Her voice cracked on the rising note. The shaking was visible even to Murdo standing at the far end of the hall. He moved closer, ready to catch her when she fell because it was clear to them all now that she was right on the edge and going over and that the crash, when it came, would be spectacular. She saw him moving and put up a hand to stop him. 'Not yet, OK?' He stopped and sank down with his back to the wall. She smiled dry thanks. 'I'm sorry. It's been a bad night. I'm trying not to make it any worse. Jamie Buchanan may be the only person left alive who has seen Tord Svensen and might be able to identify him. Svensen may know that. The lad needs someone with him who is still capable of acting if the shit hits the fan. That's not me, obviously. We need someone who can handle the medics and knows the inside of a hospital. Andy, that's you. They'll let you places they wouldn't let any of us. I want you there with him even when he's in surgery. Get a round-the-clock watch and make sure it works. Is that clear?'

'Yes.'

'Thank you.' It became necessary to move. She was losing

her grip on the door handle and, with it, on the vestiges of self control that kept her upright. She pushed between Strang and the medic to the living room doorway. The boy seemed impossibly far away. That she could still walk felt miraculous. That she could also think and feel and remember was very possibly a curse. What she wanted more than anything else was to find a clean way to oblivion, a way out that would switch off the sound of a man stretched beyond endurance and the sight of the things that had taken him there. Because this was not a totally new experience, she had held his hand and promised him she would not give way to the dark. It had never been an easy promise to keep.

She reached the window. The child was still sitting as she had left him. His left side was the one she had bandaged. She sat on the right hand arm of the chair. His body looked warmer than it had. His soul looked bleaker. She put a hand on his hair. He looked up at her, his eyes asking the questions that the rest of him wouldn't voice. She shook her head. 'He's gone, kiddo. He's where they can't hurt him anymore.' He took that in as he took in everything else, silently and with due thought. The night was warming, at least outside. Sleet replaced the snow on the window. They sat together in the quiet and watched the patterns dissolve. She dragged her fingers through the lank straw of his hair. 'You have to go to the hospital, Jamie. They need to have a look at your arm. There are things I need to do here before I can come and you may be asleep before I can join you but Andy will go with you. If that's all right?'

He shrugged for that, as if it didn't matter who went with him. Neither of them believed it. His gaze flickered back towards the bodies on the sofa. There was no question this time, simply an incorporation of facts into the bigger picture. She spoke that for him too, 'Kirsty's gone with him. Your mum's dead too. You did know that, didn't you?'

He nodded. His good hand sought hers, and lay within it. She looped her fingers through his the way she would have done with Luke. 'I haven't forgotten what I promised,' she said. 'The cottage is there. We can go and look at it when they let us both out of hospital.'

Bennett took him to the ambulance. Murdo Cameron went with him, to help and because he knew both of them well, so that Orla could be sure that the medic was with the boy and not wandering the basements trying to see things he shouldn't. It didn't take long. When he came back, she was sitting in the boy's chair, her legs drawn in, her chin on her knees. Strang stood off to one side, talking to someone on his mobile phone in the short, structured phrases he used whenever the recipient was of comparable rank. Murdo found a light switch just inside the door and flicked it on. A pink, fly-specked bulb in the centre of the ceiling lit up, casting harsh, roseate shadows on the stiffening dead, on the junk, on the peeling wallpaper and rising damp, on the stinking, sordid squalor of the room. He flicked the switch back off. There is dignity in darkness. He pulled out his pen torch and picked his way across to the window. Downstairs, the ambulance revved up. For a moment, an electric blue pulse merged with the orange of the street light. The tall man fitted his shoulders to the glass and let the colours wash over him on to the woman in the chair. He pulled the band from his hair and shook it free. Hair like steel wool bounced around his shoulders. 'I take it we need to keep

Andy away from the pathology reports?' he asked.

'If you can.' Her voice was flat. 'I don't think any of you should see it if you don't absolutely have to,' she said. 'Andy . . .' she shrugged, 'I can't see you keeping him away from the paperwork but for God's sake don't let him see Luke before he's a handful of ashes in a pot.' She was shaking less now. Her face had lost the grey mask of earlier. The unnatural eyes glittered in over-flushed skin, as if she was the one who had just sprinted upstairs and not yet caught her breath. Murdo put out his hand to feel the temperature of her forehead and thought better of it at the last moment. 'Are you running a fever?' he asked.

'Possibly.' The question came from a long way away. She was beginning to hallucinate which was not good. Luke grinned at her from the ruin of his face. Further back, her father shouted her name. A step back from him, Ciaran screamed blue murder at a man in a hand-knitted ski mark. All of the ghosts out on one night. Not good. She kept her eyes on the swirling flow as the sleet washed the snow from the window and did her best to ignore the rest. Murdo Cameron was still watching her in the way a bitch would watch pups straying too far from the nest. She would have told him to fuck off but there had been enough injuries for one day without her causing more. So she shrugged again and reached through the phantoms to touch the cool, hard glass of the window. 'It might just be the drugs,' she said.

Strang hung up his call. 'Laidlaw's on his way. The crime squad will seal the area. I don't think you need to be here when they arrive. Cameron can drive you to the Western. If he drives like he did to get here, you could still get there ahead of the ambulance and have time for a coffee before the kid arrives.'

'No . . .' Thinking was becoming impossible, oblivion harder to resist. 'You need to . . . They need to . . .' She took a breath and tried again. She had a promise to keep. 'Svensen was here. He's coming back in the morning. He won't come if . . .'

'If Laidlaw's got two vanloads of goons taking the place apart. Right.' Strang flipped his phone open again. 'I'll hold them back 'till the afternoon.'

'No . . .' She gave up trying to keep her eyes open. It was easier looking into the blackness. 'He may not come. We need forensics. He shot him.'

'Who shot whom?' Only Strang would say 'whom' on a night like this. Public school education will out.

'Svensen shot Luke.'

'How do you know it was Svensen?'

'I didn't hear the shot. I would have heard the revolver.'

'Did you hear anything else?'

She smiled at that. Cameron caught his breath and looked the other way. 'All of it,' she said.

Strang pinched the bridge of his nose. 'Thank you.' He nodded absently. It is not possible to silence a revolver. They all knew that. His eyes drifted to the window. The sleet was melting fast. The wind drove it onto the glass in long, drumming sheets. He found a hole in a back molar and probed it with his tongue. The sharp, electric shock of it ran through him, as if he needed to remember what it was to feel pain.

'How long did they have him?' he asked.

'Long enough. I don't know exactly. I was out of it for most of the time but the shit hit the fan in here before ten and they were still working on him at three.'

'And they shot him at the end of it?'

'Yes.'

'Christ.' Murdo said it quietly, reverentially, profanity transformed to respect. Strang said nothing. He watched as the sleet gave way finally to good, honest rain, his mind cluttered with images he didn't need and didn't want, of other men in other places, trying to hold on to the threads of an unravelling cover. There are the myths of what pain a man can stand and then there is the reality. In neither world do you shoot a man who has anything useful left to tell you. He considered the work, the time, the effort, the basic human misery of three months under-cover and saw it consigned, in that one simple fact, to the scrap heap. He sighed.

The woman heard it and closed her eyes. 'I'm sorry,' she said. He hadn't meant it as blame. He didn't believe in a culture of blame. Nevertheless, watching her, he saw it taken as read, saw it turned inwards and hardened into the promise of action. It was what she did best. Later she would act. For now, she was simply fighting to stay conscious. He nodded to Cameron and saw that the tall man was already watching. If she fell, when she fell, he would be there before she hit the floor.

'Come on,' Strang leant over and tapped her arm, 'Bennett's right. You need the medics as much as the lad does. Let's get you out of here while you can still walk.' She was sitting in the chair with her knees drawn up to her chest and she was wearing no underwear. Somewhere in the past half hour he had become aware of that and managed to look elsewhere. Even now, as he reached out to touch her, his gaze was on the window and so he didn't notice that she stood up too fast for the state she was in, he missed the moment when the ghosts and oblivion both staked their claim. She was pitching forward towards the sheet glass of the window before he realised she wasn't upright and then he was back against the wall, nursing a bruised shoulder and swearing roundly and so, for the rest of her life, Orla McLeod owed the lack of further glass scars on her face to her friend and colleague, Murdo Cameron, who was there to catch her when she fell.